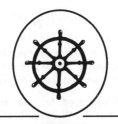

THE
NIGHTHAWK

BY
ALICE JONES

INTRODUCTION BY
GREG MARQUIS

Formac Publishing Company Limited
H

Cover illustration: *Bloomingdale*, painted by Frances Jones Bannerman, Courtesy of the Waegwoltic Club.

Formac Publishing Company Limited acknowledges the support of the cultural affairs section, Nova Scotia Department of Tourism and Culture. We acknowledge the financial support of the Government of Canada through the Book Publishing Industry Development Program (BPIDP) for our publishing activities. We acknowledge the support of the Canada Council for the Arts for our publishing program.

National Library of Canada Cataloguing in Publication Data

Jones, Alice, 1853-1933.
The nighthawk

(Formac fiction treasures)
First published: Toronto : Copp, Clark, 1901.
ISBN 0-88780-538-8

1. United States—History—Civil War, 1861-1865—Fiction.
I. Title. II. Series.

PS8519.O523N53 2001   C813'.52   C2001-902539-4
PR9199.3.J6275N53 2001

First published 1901. Frederick A. Stokes Company, New York.
Series editor: Gwendolyn Davies

Formac Publishing Company Limited
5502 Atlantic Street
Halifax, Nova Scotia B3H 1G4
www.formac.ca

Printed and bound in Canada

Presenting Formac Fiction Treasures
Series Editor: Gwendolyn Davies

A taste for reading popular fiction expanded in the nineteenth century with the mass marketing of books and magazines. People read rousing adventure stories aloud at night around the fireside; they bought entertaining romances to read while travelling on trains and curled up with the latest serial novel in their leisure moments. Novelists were important cultural figures, with devotees who eagerly awaited their next work.

Among the many successful popular English language novelists of the late 19th and early 20th centuries were a group of Maritimers who found in their own education, travel and sense of history events and characters capable of entertaining readers on both sides of the Atlantic. They emerged from well-established communities which valued education and culture, for women as well as for men. Faced with limited publishing opportunities in the Maritimes, successful writers sought magazine and book publishers in the major cultural centres: New York, Boston, Philadelphia, London, and sometimes Montreal and Toronto. They often enjoyed much success with readers 'at home' but the best of these writers found large audiences across Canada and in the United States and Great Britain.

The Formac Fiction Treasures series is aimed at offering contemporary readers access to books that were successful, often huge bestsellers in their time, but which are now little known and often hard to find. The authors and titles selected are chosen first of all as enjoyable to read, and secondly for the light they shine on historical events and on attitudes and views of the culture from which they emerged. These complete original texts reflect values which are sometimes in conflict with those of today: for example, racism is often evident, and bluntly expressed. This collection of novels is offered as a step towards rediscovering a surprisingly diverse and not nearly well enough known popular cultural heritage of the Maritime provinces and of Canada.

Alice Jones

INTRODUCTION

Intrigue, travel, disguise, poisoning, a duel, kidnapping, blackmail, illicit sex, numerous marriage proposals and a plucky heroine who depends on feminine charm, set against the backdrop of civil war—these are some of the ingredients of *The Nighthawk: A Romance of the '60s* which was first published in 1901.

Alice Jones, the author, was the daughter of a prominent Halifax, Nova Scotia family and was well acquainted with the story's main focus: the American Civil War. In Nova Scotia, Jones wrote, "all took a passionate interest in the war." *The Nighthawk* is a skilful blend of fact and fiction, offering a romantic version of history that supports the underdog—the Southern Confederacy—in the "war between the states."

Jones was born in 1853, several years before the Confederates opened fire on Fort Sumter and set off a conflict that would consume more than 600,000 lives and lead to the liberation of more than three million slaves. She was one of seven children of Alfred Gilpin Jones, a wealthy Haligonian who appears to have sympathized with the Confederacy, and Margaret Wiseman Stairs Jones. The Halifax press noted in 1864 that Margaret Jones was part of a ladies committee that raised funds for the relief of Confederate prisoners in

Northern camps. One wonders if ten-year-old Alice assisted her mother in this effort. Her father's mercantile operation specialized in trade with the West Indies. In the late 1860s, A.G. Jones, who was elected member of Parliament, was instrumental in the Nova Scotia Repeal League. The Repealers, who opposed the province's somewhat forced union with Canada and New Brunswick in 1867, often cited the American Civil War in their speeches and writings. He contested a number of other federal elections in the 1870s and 1880s, and later was an advocate of freer trade with the United States. In 1900, he was appointed lieutenant governor of Nova Scotia, at which time Alice Jones moved into Government House and assisted her father in his civic duties.

Raised in a privileged atmosphere, Jones began writing travel sketches and short stories for magazines such as *Dominion Illustrated Monthly* and *The Week.* In the 1880s and 1890s, she spent time travelling at her leisure. From her journals, one learns that in 1894 she was in Egypt in January, Rome in April, Paris in May, England in June and Canada in July. Her writing conveys an outstanding aesthetic appreciation of art and architecture.

The Nighthawk was originally published under a pseudonym—Alix John. Aside from one short story issued under this pen name, Jones reverted to her own name for her second book, *Bubbles We Buy* (1903) and all subsequent novels. *Bubbles We Buy* helped establish her reputation, in the words of one reviewer, as Canada's premier woman novelist. Like other writers of that period, Jones was mindful of a North American readership, but insistent on Canadian settings. When attacked by the *Winnipeg Telegram* for virtually selling out, she explained, "I am a Canadian, but as we Canadians who attempt novel writing must necessarily try to suit the American market, either the hero or the heroine must be of that nationality—better if both are." By 1907, she was living in the south of France, reflecting the cosmopolitan characters and locales of her writing and adding to an English-speaking literary and artistic colony that included the likes of Katherine Mansfield. Jones's other novels were *Gabriel Praed's Castle* (1904), *Marcus Holbeach's Daughter* (1912) and *Flames of Frost* (1914). The stories are often melodramatic and sensational, but the female characters are far from stereotypical, passive Victorian heroines. Instead, they tend to be capable of asserting themselves in spite of society's masculine bias. Jones seemed interested in the contrast between "the superficiality of European life against the vitality of Canadian society and character."

Many of the best-selling books of this early golden age of Canadian fiction were historical in focus. *The Nighthawk* helped to perpetuate the erroneous belief that large numbers of Nova Scotians served on the Confederate side during the Civil War that occurred between 1861 and 1865. Recent research indicates that of the up to 10,000 men from the Maritime region who took part in the war, the overwhelming majority served in the Union army and navy. This was not so much due to political convictions or a desire to fight slavery as it was the result of geography. Most Nova Scotians who moved to or worked in the United

States lived in New England and New York—not Virginia, the Carolinas or the Deep South. The book is a selective reading of Nova Scotia history that downplays the pervasive influence of New England on the province and the importance of trade with the American northeast. It also concludes that true liberty can be found only on "British soil."

Although her stage is international, reflecting her own tastes and travels, Jones made Halifax, the capital of the independent British colony of Nova Scotia, the geographic anchor of the story. And Nova Scotia was not a picturesque "folk society" inhabited by hardy fishermen as authors such as Helen Creighton would later suggest, but rather the crossroads of the transatlantic world. Although officially neutral, the North American colonies increasingly sympathized with the breakaway Confederacy. Nova Scotians traded with both North and South, and were indirectly involved in breaking the United States Navy's blockade of southern ports. Initially supportive of the Lincoln government in its attempts to "preserve the Union," many Nova Scotians turned against the North following the Battle of Bull Run in 1861. Later that year, Haligonians were electrified by news that an American navy vessel had stopped the mail steamer *Trent* on the high seas and forcibly removed two Confederate diplomats who were travelling under the protection of the British flag. A war scare followed, and Britain rushed troops, ships and supplies, partly through Halifax, to reinforce its North American colonies. By the end of the Civil War, the British authorities were ringing in the city's harbour with new redoubts and gun batteries that would make it one of the most strongly protected naval bases in the Empire. The protagonist of *The Nighthawk*, Mrs. Antoinette (LeMoine) Castelle, hails from a Georgia plantation but has been raised in a convent school. Her beauty and poise make her "one of the most admired women in Paris." Although possessed of "a languid southern accent" and able to use her beauty as a weapon, she is no selfish or frivolous Scarlett O'Hara, but rather a woman of principle, Christian charity, intelligence and action. Interestingly, this sympathetic character is not only young and attractive, but also divorced, something of a rarity at that time in both fiction and society. The titillating aspects of the tale revolve around Antoinette's relationship with her spouse, and also reveal how late-Victorian society remembered slavery, America's "peculiar institution." Antoinette's husband, Edward, is a passionate, violent planter who fathers an illegitimate child with a slave mistress. This 'Southern Gothic' subplot, which taps a tradition going back to *Uncle Tom's Cabin* and beyond, drives the heroine to sue for divorce and leave the South for Paris and Halifax.

Although Nova Scotia in 1901, unlike a number of other provinces, did have a divorce court, it was rarely used, and the legal termination of marriage tended to be discouraged as undermining not only the institution of the family, but also the social fabric of itself. In other parts of Canada, divorce was obtainable only through act of Parliament. In the cosmopolitan world of *The Nighthawk*, divorce, although scandalous, is acceptable for a woman wronged; it is also a mark of independence and sophistication. Unlike many books of the era, with plots that revolve around war, *The Nighthawk* was probably written with an eye to the "ladies'" market, with enough history and adventure to appeal to the male reader who preferred detective or spy stories. The main character is female, and the women of the South are portrayed as active supporters of the war. Antoinette, for example, nurses wounded soldiers in field hospitals, safeguards Confederate dispatches and carries a revolver as protection from Yankee agents. Because of her devotion to the Confederacy, she becomes a "hunted-down political fugitive."

Turn-of-the-century readers wanted to read historical novels about extraordinary men and women who influenced real events. Alice Jones, who was acquainted with John Taylor Wood, the Confederate naval officer whose memoirs no doubt influenced the tale, drew on both family and popular recollections of the Halifax elite and its responses to the Civil War. Some of the action is set in Halifax's prestigious Northwest Arm area, with Jones's family home, Bloomingdale— now the Waegwoltic Club—as a key location in the story. Visitors to the club can see a setting very little different today from the scene portrayed in Jones's fiction. A boat trip to Purcells Cove, balls held at Government House and the flagship of the Royal Navy's admiral on the Halifax and West Indies station are all mentioned in the book. Readers learn that "money counted so little" for Antoinette, yet she had "plenty" of her own. The aristocratic Royal Artillery officer who figures so prominently in the plot is a stock character, but he may have been inspired by the British officers who were garrisoned in Halifax until 1904.

Leading Halifax families such as the Almons and Ritchies actually did aid Southern refugees with money, hospitality and legal services during and after the war. Halifax was important in terms of travel and communications because it was a Royal Mail steamer stop, a British naval base and a telegraph terminus with good connections to Canada, New England, the West Indies and Britain. Well-known brewer Alexander Keith and merchant and shipowner Benjamin Wier speculated in blockade goods. Jones's character Alderman Evans is patterned after Wier; he's a pro-Confederate who is not averse to making a profit from smuggling. (Wier was made a senator of the new Dominion of Canada in 1867.) Roman Catholic Archbishop Thomas L. Connolly was another prominent friend of the Confederacy.

Despite official neutrality—and the protests of the United States consul—British officials, including the governor, admiral and officers of the garrison and naval squadron, also welcomed Southerners. Geogiana Gholson Walker, wife of a Confederate officer, appreciated the warm hospitality of Halifax's elite.

The book's depiction of Halifax's role as an entrepot in Confederate supply is based on historical reality; the Northern government proclaimed a blockade of Southern ports in 1861. The task was immense; more than three thousand miles of coastline were under rebel control. Despite the growing strength of the

Union navy, the owners of small sailing vessels from Nova Scotia and other British colonies smuggled in food, clothing, footwear, medicine, weapons and ammunition and brought out cotton, tobacco and naval stores such as turpentine and pitch. Although enterprising and adventurous, small-craft blockade running supplied only a trickle of what the Southern armies required. Far more important were the voyages of roughly three hundred converted or purpose-built steamers operating out of Nassau in the Bahamas, Bermuda and Havana. Most of these fast, shallow-draft steamers, which burned low-smoke coal and had collapsible funnels, muffled paddle-wheels and few masts or deck encumbrances, were British or Southern owned. More than forty of these beautiful craft, including the *Robert E. Lee,* *A.D. Vance* and *Banshee,* visited Halifax. Estimates of the number of direct trips between Halifax and blockaded ports range from a low of twenty-one to a high of eighty-five. Most blockade runners landed at Halifax for coal or repairs, or to trans-ship blockade goods or Southern exports to and from the Caribbean. Local merchant houses such as Benjamin Wier and G.C. Harvey played a significant role in this transatlantic trade. In the fall of 1864, many blockade runners temporarily set up base in Halifax because yellow fever was interfering in turnaround times in West Indies ports. This was an exciting time in the city's history. Early in 1865, with the fall of Confederate Fort Fisher in North Carolina and the capture of Charleston, the seaborne supply effort collapsed and Halifax merchants were left holding surplus goods.

In the novel, Captain Arthur, the "bronzed" blue-eyed skipper of the Confederate blockade runner *Nighthawk*, is described in the original 1901 preface as modelled on a real Royal Navy captain who later served as a mercenary for Turkey. This officer was most likely Augustus Charles Hobart-Hampden, who commanded the smuggling vessels *Don* and *Condor*. Another inspiration was Taylor Wood, who lived in Halifax from 1865 until his death in 1904. A dashing Southerner who had served in the U.S. Army prior to Southern secession, Wood took part in a number of special operations against the North. In 1864, he commanded the converted blockade runner *CSS Tallahassee*, the only Confederate warship ever to reach a British North American port. Steaming north from Cape Fear, the commerce raider destroyed or captured more than thirty Yankee merchant vessels in the summer of 1864. Keeping ahead of a large Union pursuit force, Wood entered Halifax in search of coal. The raiders eluded the U.S. navy by escaping from Halifax harbour through Eastern Passage, where a nearby school still bears the ship's name. Wood and his wife, Lola, came to Halifax as refugees following the war and were embraced by the local elite. The "Confederate agent" in Halifax is an amalgam of several real-life personalities, the most notable being James P. Holcombe, a Virginia professor of law who was appointed diplomatic troubleshooter by the Confederate government in Richmond. Given to dressing in black and carrying a book of poetry, this epitome of a Southern gentleman attempted to intervene in the case of the vessel *SS Chesapeake* when it was impounded by the Nova Scotian authorities. In the novel, he is a "bookworm and historian" who is "transformed into a man of action" in service of the cause of the Confederacy. Holcombe was part of the Confederate mission to Canada in 1865, whose task was to put pressure on Northern domestic politics, destabilize British-American diplomatic relations and assist escaped Confederate prisoners of war. The shipwreck scene described toward the end of the novel is inspired by the colourful and glamorous widow Mrs. Rose O'Neal Greenhow, a Confederate activist who visited Halifax in 1864 en route to the South. She drowned when she attempted to land by small boat on the stormy North Carolina coast.

The plot includes another paragraph taken from the historical record. Antoinette LeMoine learns about a Confederate plot to seize a Northern steamer as it heads north from New York. The hijackers plan to overpower the crew and then rendezvous with a schooner in the Bay of Fundy and run gunpowder past the blockade. This part of the story is culled from a real event: the seizure in late 1863 of the Cromwell line steamer *Chesapeake* by the notorious Confederate guerilla leader John Brain, an Englishman who acted without the authorization of the Southern government. Most of his "pirates" were not Southerners, but New Brunswickers who had been duped with promises of prize money. Pursued by U.S. navy frigates and gunboats, the hijackers crossed the Bay of Fundy and steamed up the southern coast of Nova Scotia. At Sambro, near Halifax, the vessel was seized by an overzealous American gunboat captain, who took his

prize to Halifax. Following a few tense hours, the
Americans handed the vessel over to the Nova Scotian
authorities, who placed the entire matter before vice-
admiralty court. The one pirate captured was freed
from the authorities through the direct interference
of two or three pro-Confederate members of the
Halifax elite.

In keeping with most early-twentieth-century fiction,
the novel's treatment of the topic of race is troublesome to modern readers. The mixed race, or mulatto,
people of the South, for example, are described as infe-
rior to the more humble and sincere slaves with darker
complexions. This repeats the widespread Victorian
fear of racial mingling and degeneration. The only
white Southerners who are mentioned, apart from the
unsavoury plantation owner Edward Castelle, are
refined and sophisticated; worthy peers of the Nova
Scotian elite. Like many romantic short stories and novels of the period—and anticipating Mitchell's *Gone with
the Wind*—*The Nighthawk* dodges ethical debates over
the morality of slavery, portraying the white Southern
rebels as principled strugglers for liberty and helping
to perpetuate the popular misconception that the Civil
War was not fought over the issue of slavery. The
main character longs for "the poor, simple negroes"
of her Georgia plantation, yet she is not above thrash-
ing a small slave boy with a riding crop. Although
Jones was writing nearly four decades after the eradi-
cation of slavery in America, blacks in Canada and the
United States remained victims of poverty, discrimina-
tion and white racism. The message here, as in *Gone
with the Wind*, is chilling: blacks are childlike and

require direction and control by whites; and Southern slaves love their white masters and are better off as slaves than free men and women. In this sense, *The Nighthawk* justifies the racial status quo of its time.

Context is important here; Jones was writing during an era when few white Canadians accepted the social equality of the races and when immigration policy more or less excluded blacks. Volunteer troops from Nova Scotia had just returned from the South African War where they helped extend the British Empire. The book also appeared at a time when American historians, looking back on the failure of Reconstruction in the 1870s and the disenfranchisement of Southern blacks, were justifying racial segregation and blaming the Civil War not on slavery but on radical Northern anti-slavery activists. This message reached its peak in the writings of influential Southern historians and was mimicked in local histories, magazine articles, dime novels and other popular-culture outlets. For example, in his short story "Blind McNair," Thomas Raddall portrays a Nova Scotian who had fought for the Confederacy as morally superior to those who had served in the Union armies. His 1949 historical classic *Halifax, Warden of the North* devoted considerable attention to Civil War issues and underscored Canada's history of ambivalent relations with the United States.

Alice Jones lived at Menton in the French department of Alpes-Maritime near the Italian border. Her sister, the artist and poet Frances Jones Bannerman, resided nearby, and her brother also had a villa in the area. Frances painted the family home, Bloomingdale, as it was when the family lived there. The painting now hangs in the Waegwoltic Club, and appears on the cover of this edition. Alice died in 1933, leaving behind, in addition to her elegant travel stories, four novels and three unpublished works. *The Nighthawk* remains an entertaining read and opens a door to a largely forgotten chapter of Nova Scotian history.

Greg Marquis
University of New Brunswick Saint John
2001

PREFACE

THROUGH this tale of the 1860s there runs a substratum of fact.

The feminine influence wielded by Southern women at the court of the Tuileries would have succeeded in bringing about Napoleon's recognition of the Confederate States, but for England's refusal to cooperate with him, a refusal known to have been due to the personal influence of the Great Queen.

The keen financial and social interests, the elaborate network of plots and spies, that the blockade-running brought to outlying places like Halifax, Nassau and Bermuda, are still remembered by many men and women. The sea adventures of Captain Arthur are founded on those of an English navy officer who for several years ran the blockade successfully under an assumed name, subsequently becoming an Admiral in the Turkish service.

The shipwreck of a Southern hospital nurse while running the blockade from Halifax was a fact, with the great difference that in real life the heroine was weighed down by a belt of gold, and lost her life.

ALICE JONES.

CONTENTS

CHAPTER I

VANITY FAIR

IT was late in the 50's when Paris already shone brilliantly in its new Imperial dress, though with the blood-stains of the *Coup d'Etat* scarcely dried from its streets.

What matter that hundreds of France's noblest hearts were breaking in the Algerian desert of Lambessa, and the fever-rife swamps of Cayenne?

The pleasure-seekers thronged all the same to Paris to behold the splendours and to contribute to the coffers of the mushroom emperor.

The gilded bees and N's on the scutcheons showed no dark red stain on their brightness. The Day of Wrath, when Bismarck's iron hand should crush the shining bubble, was yet in the unguessed future, and Paris was still the capital of the world of pleasure. On a June evening the great, new caravansary of the Hôtel du Louvre glowed with lights and echoed with a babel of foreign tongues.

Men and women of all civilised nations lounged in after-dinner gaiety in the great glass-roofed courtyard, and in the surrounding balconies.

Waiters hurried about with coffee and liqueurs. Many a newly enriched Californian miner or Australian squatter felt, as he sat there that life was beginning to repay him for the lean years of toil.

The new hotel and the whole neighbourhood basked in the light of the adjacent Tuileries, and the days were yet far when the Rue de Rivoli and the Palais Royal were to wither under the trail of the cheap-tripper and the Cook's tourist. Never perhaps had there been such a carnival of millinery as now blossomed in Paris under the sway of the beautiful Spanish woman, and these strangers in their hotel had evidently been drawn into its vortex.

But, amongst all the sumptuously dressed women, perhaps the most striking both in beauty and attire was one who with bare white arms resting on the velvet balustrade, gazed calmly down at the restless crowd from one of the small circular balconies.

Even seated, the slim grace of her young figure showed itself in her pose. She was evidently barely out of her teens, and the virginal gravity of her girl-hood still looked forth from the deep, brown eyes, and rested serene on the low, white forehead, shadowed by its golden-brown hair—hair that Eugenie was already making the ultra chic of fashion.

The full line of the lips alone told of the stormy possibilities of a strong nature. To attempt to describe the details of her costume would only excite the derisive smile, which an earlier portrait by Carolus Duran, or Winterhalter, has power to bring to feminine lips. At that day, however, the ample folds of apple-green silk that billowed around her, set off the first freshness of her beauty to as great perfection in a modiste's as in an artist's eyes.

"The Diana of the Louvre" said to his companion a man who, lounging opposite, enjoyed his post-prandial cigar all the more for the contemplation of that radiant vision. Indeed he was not the first to whom the slim neck and well-poised head had recalled the haughty grace of the great huntress.

"In neck and arms perhaps, but her face has the wistfulness of a Psyche, as though she were still seeking her Eros," his dilettante friend criticised. "But where have her thoughts gone wandering? They are not condescending to any of this motley gathering. They are not even troubling themselves with that dark boy beside her, handsome as he is. French or Italian, I should say."

Boy as he looked, it was her husband of nearly a year who sat smoking beside Mrs. Castelle.

If his dark, almost effeminate, good looks were essentially of the Latin type, his character had been moulded by his boyish upbringing on a Louisiana plantation, in the days, when such were the homes of an indolent luxury and a despotic rule, which created their own hereditary traits.

The later training of foreign education and travel had added an exotic finish to a natural power of attraction. He too had been a silent onlooker, but when he spoke a few words, the critic saw, from the quickly responsive smile, with which she turned her head, that her thoughts had been nearer at hand than he had supposed.

"Yes," she answered. "It does seem rather a novelty to be alone, just we two to ourselves. We have lived in such a mental and physical merry-go-round of late, haven't we? After all, I think that I must have been intended for a quieter life. The whirl of Vanity Fair rather bewilders me, though, all the same, I may miss it when it's over."

"When it's over!" The liquid southern voice had a certain touch of impatience in the repetition.

"Why, what is it going to be over for? To hear you speak one would think that we were bound next week for dreary old Mariposa."

"Well, I suppose that, sooner or later, we are."

She spoke with a certain timidity, as though, in bringing up the subject, she had attained a sought-for aim.

"It is not home, and surely, some time we must go back there, unless you would refer to try my own dear Amity Hall first—Amity Hall"—she lingered over the words—"I love the quaint name. it ought to be a good omen for us."

The gentleness in her voice evidently failed to make any impression on him.

"What an absurdly visionary child you are!" he said. "Getting up romantic sentiments about a place that you haven't seen since you were a child! I tell you what, if you had seen as much of plantation life as I have, you would not be in such a hurry to get back to the troublesome old mammies, and the squalling black brats, the noisy, untidy servants, and the general disorderliness of everything. The very thought of that waving, grey Spanish moss, and the muddy, yellow water sickens me. Here you are one of the most admired women in Paris, made much of at court and invited to Compiègne! You have everything that a woman can possibly wish for, and you begin to talk of giving it all up and going back to plantation life. What

would Worth say, I should like to know, at the idea of
some of his best creations being so wasted? It all shows
what a schoolgirl you still are."

Schoolgirl as she was, or little more, there was a
touch of the indulgent, maternal spirit in the smile
with which she answered him.

"Oh, I know quite well that our lives are all sugar-
plums and roses at present; but then no lives can stay
like that. We must surely have duties and responsibilities, and our own place in our own country.
Remember you are a Castelle of Mariposa, and
remember how people still speak of your mother's
standing and influence for good. If I could only learn
to be like her! Frivolous old people are horrors of
mine, and as we grow older we shall want to do something besides play."

Her tender mention of his mother passed unheeded.

"For goodness' sake, wait until we do grow older
then. That will come soon enough in all conscience.
Thank heaven! Here comes Molly Seton to save me
from my first conjugal lecture. What do you think,
Mollie?" as a thin flaxen-haired woman, evidently
some five years or so older than Mrs. Castelle, and
dressed in black, to a grotesque height of fashion,
joined them.

"Here is Antoinette turned Puritan, and, not only
abjuring cakes and ale on her own account, but wanting me to do so too. She has actually been lecturing
me on the duties and responsibilities of home life.
What course of treatment should you recommend?
Cold water?"

Mrs. Seton sank into a red velvet chair, her black

gauze flounces surging up around her. If not over-sympathetic, her glance at the younger woman was both shrewd and kindly.

"The splendours of Compiègne have been too much for her nerves, and she is following the usual feminine plan and taking it out of you," she said lightly. "I hear that De Morny vows that there never was so fair and 'spirituelle' an 'Americaine' seen at the Tuileries before as Madame Castelle. The women are all gnashing their teeth over it, Nettie."

A little shiver, as at a breath of cold air, ran over Antoinette.

"I cannot bear that man. He makes me feel as though someone were walking over my grave," she said.

"Nonsense," her husband said fretfully. "His word is law in the court society. But you haven't suggested a cure yet, Mollie."

The latter waved her black feather-fan thoughtfully before replying.

"I'll tell you. The Grand Prix is over, and all the life is gone out of the Paris air. Come off with me to the Pyrenees next week. All the naughtiest and most amusing people are bound there, and we can be frivolous in quite a different fashion. It will be such a charming excuse, too, for new clothes. Have you seen the Empress' looped-up skirt, Nettie? Just the thing for the mountains. I will carry her off to Worth's to-morrow morning, and then you won't hear any more about the duties of life, for the present, Edward."

"The very thing," Castelle agreed, with an evident air of relief. "You always do think of the very jolliest thing to do, Mollie. I wonder if Nettie will ever grow as clever at getting the best of things as you are."

"Five years of matrimony can work wonders," Mrs. Seton remarked comfortably with a little pat to the girl's hand—then—"Here comes that Englishman of yours, and I feel it in my bones that you two are going to make a night of it. So we women can have a cozy little chat to ourselves, and I'll give her some lessons in managing husbands. Then we'll get our beauty sleep into the bargain."

Castelle's last trace of discontent cleared, as a stalwart young fellow with bronzed face joined them with a bow of almost chivalrous deference to Mrs. Castelle.

It was she who spoke the first words of greeting in her soft southern tones.

"Ah, Mr. Arthur! Are you prepared to bear the blame of carrying off my husband and leaving me to go to the opera with a scratch match of friends?"

"One word would have made me part of the scratch match, and would have annihilated any other plans. The cruelty lay in not speaking it."

The modulations of his voice showed the high-bred Englishman, though its sonorousness told of its use in the open spaces of the sea.

From Antoinette's smile the newcomer was evidently a favourite.

"I fear that I am too broken in to masculine ways to give much credit to that. However, go with a clear conscience. I have backed out of the opera scheme, and Mrs. Seton and I are going to enjoy an off night and early slumbers. I am really afraid to look in the glass for fear of seeing wrinkles."

"There is no fear of that, even with a microscope," Mr. Arthur dutifully responded, while Castelle, lighting a fresh cigar and rising said;

"Old age again, as a bugbear! Well, *au revoir.* I leave her in your hands, Mollie. Instill some of your worldly wisdom and root out those little sprouts of Puritanism that popped up their ugly heads to-night."

"Don't be afraid," the lady laughed, "the air of Paris soon nips such vegetation in the bud."

As the two men vanished in the crowd, the silence of long intimacy settled upon the women.

At last the elder spoke in a voice from which the forced vivacity was gone.

"Were you really talking in earnest of wanting to go home and settle down?"

Antoinette turned from her contemplation of the crowd and faced her friend, as though relieved to speak unreservedly.

"Yes, I was. Does it seem so unnatural to you that I should want to see my husband's home, and to try to fill my real place in the world?"

Mollie Seton was watching her intently as she said, "I should have thought that there was enough in this kind of life to satisfy any woman."

"So there is, of its kind, and that is just what frightens me. Only think, if it should grow to be the only sort of life that did satisfy me. Of course I know that I am considered a belle—and all that—" she flushed half impatiently—"but then it is only as any stranger with a pretty face, a ready tongue and expensive clothes might be. It gives me no established standing, and"— she lowered her voice.—"I don't want to be

Puritanical, but men like De Morny frighten me," and her looks showed that she spoke in earnest. Mrs. Seton laughed rather harshly: "You little goose—what have you to be afraid of? Edward may be careless, but he is a Castelle and you are safe in his care."

Antoinette looked as though repenting her impulsive words. "Well, at any rate, I want a life of more dignity. I want to be a success as the mistress of Mariposa, a success with dependents and relatives and old family friends. And Edward—he has good abilities. I want him to be some one of importance in his own country, instead of an idler here."

"You want a great deal. But that is the way of young folks." And the other sighed as though having found out the futility of many aspirations.

"Let sleeping dogs lie. What you say all sounds very high-toned, but there is a great virtue in letting well alone. Your husband is amused in his present life, proud of you, and pleased with himself for having married you. When you dispense with your audience, and turn down the light, you dispense with half the charm. When you take him away from amusements that he has not yet tired of, you provide him with his first grievance. Beware that he does not replace them with less harmless ones. However, you are young and you are prosperous, a fatal combination. You are sure to set to work to pull down the structure over your head—"

"Oh, Mollie, don't make yourself out so old and worldly wise. I'm not going to do anything desperate I assure you—"

"If you do, you won't find it out until you've done it,

and it's too late. I speak from experience, my dear. But I won't be unpleasant any more. Do come up to my room and see the magenta walking-dress that Worth has sent me home for Luchon, suppose you get a green one like it, they would go together so well. By the way, which place do you think that you and Edward would rather go to first, Luchon or Bagnères-de Bigorre?"

"What does it matter! I dare say that they are both equally nice," Mrs. Castelle responded somewhat languidly.

The other looked at her sharply, as though guessing at her humour.

"Well, we'll see what your husband says;" then, as though in an afterthought, "And oh, Nettie, I do hate to sponge on you again when you've been so good to me, but that awful Madame Papillion won't wait any longer—and she really has robbed me so! Do you think you *could* let me have five hundred dollars or so, until I can get some money out of that old uncle Robert of mine in New Orleans?"

She had persuasively twisted her arm through that of her cousin, who, as they walked through the corridor, gave a hearty and ready assent to her request. Money counted so little to her, seeming such a matter-of-course background to her brilliant young life.

CHAPTER II

"IN DIXIE LAND"

THE clear, mountain air of the Pyrenees and the out-door life brought back Mrs. Castelle's animation, and banished that languid absentmindedness, that had seemed to be growing upon her.

Amongst the solemn mountain peaks and rushing torrents, she dressed and laughed and danced with the best, but, none the less, did she keep many things and ponder them in her heart. When the August days waxed hottest, they came out from the mountain gorges to the shining sands and wave-fretted rocks of Biarritz.

The Empress had set the stamp of fashion on this remote little corner of France, from whence the shores and peaks of her own Spanish land could be seen, and all the gay world flocked there obediently in her train.

There came the soldiers and the wits and the beauties of a court that, if corrupt, was, at any rate, always brilliant: the Princess Metternich with her audacious tongue and grotesque face; Prosper Mérimée the scoffing cynic in words—the loyal friend at heart. Le Pelletier and MacMahon, the rough soldiers: some of the gay throng destined to outlive the Day of Wrath, some destined like Mérimée to die in it.

And Antoinette Castelle, with her life all before her,

sat in her few solitary hours of early morning strolls, and watched the great, Atlantic billows rolling in with a force started in the western world, and pondered her own little problems.

The intensity of her nature was set on making a man out of that weak, wayward, lovable husband of hers, and she instinctively felt that this was not the scene for such a task. Could even the strongest help deteriorating in such a hot-house atmosphere?

And so, in spite of Mrs. Seton's scoffs and warnings, she held to her purpose of persuading Edward Castelle to return and settle down in their own southern home.

It was not all at once, but still, in the course of the next few months, she did have her own way.

She was undergoing the unpleasant process of doubting the advisability of the achievement, on the rainy October evening when she arrived at her husband's plantation of Mariposa.

After some days of travelling in utter discomfort they had disembarked from a Mississippi steamboat at the dilapidated little wharf that marked their own landing. Even before they had left the steamboat wild shouts and laughter greeted them from an excited mob of negroes, the foremost of whom waved torches which, sending rays of lurid light over the dark forest and water, added to the weirdness of the scene.

Faces and voices brought vague associations of earliest childhood to Antoinette, reawakening the hope which burned dim in her heart.

A handsome carriage awaited them, and they were at once whirled off, at a rapid rate, up a long avenue, edged by thick woods, and overhung by live oak trees, from which waved the gloomy, grey banners of the Spanish moss.

A sudden freak of memory recalled to the young wife's mind the brilliant courtyard of the Hôtel du Louvre, where Castelle had spoken with such distaste of the dismal woods and waters of his home. The sight of the waving moss chilled her, as though it might be the fingers of death or time, reaching after her with her fate.

But the dark avenue was opening out into a cleared space where the twilight was still bright enough to show the stretch of low rambling white house, with its many smaller wooden dependencies. A cheerful radiance streamed from open doors and windows, and in its light could be seen another group of servants, scattered from the lawn to within the wide old hall. Castelle had been quite silent, save for a few necessary words, since their landing. Now as the carriage stopped and the faces of those on the verandah became visible, his wife heard him smother a fierce imprecation, and again the cold shadow of a threatening cloud seemed to chill her.

But an old black butler had rushed to the carriage door with tears and smiles of welcome to "Massa Edward!" on his honest wrinkled face.

This was the signal for a vociferous greeting that broke forth on every side. Brushing, with somewhat brusque acknowledgments, past weeping old women and the stalwart matrons, his own contemporaries, Castelle hurried his wife up the steps.

"Yes, yes, Mammie Liza, and all of you. You shall see the new mistress and me tomorrow morning, and have the presents that she brought you from Paris. But she is tired now, so off with you for to-night."

These dismissed, there remained the house servants beyond, comparatively quieter and more deferential in their greeting.

Tired as she was, Mrs. Castelle's senses were now quickened by the vague alarm caused by her husband's unusual ill-humour, and with one quick glance she took in the welcoming group.

The foremost figure was that of a tall young mulatto woman, with the finely modelled, supple figure of her race. Her skin was of a clear brown, far more beautiful than if there had been enough white blood in her veins to have made her of a sickly yellow.

Clad in a well-fitting dress of a brilliant red, she stood calmly facing her new mistress. As Antoinette, looking at her, met the steady stare of the great velvety brown eyes, she read in their depths the subtle thrill of hate, untouched by the welcoming smile that wreathed the face.

At her side stood a fine-looking young mulatto man, and between them was a child of about four years old, with skin much fairer than either of theirs.

The other men and women were of various stages of colour and smartness, but it seemed to Antoinette's quickened vision that, the darker and humbler, the more sincere was the welcome, and that in proportion as the paleness of skin and smartness of attire increased, an antagonism, scarcely veiled by a pretended delight, could be felt.

With these more privileged retainers Castelle's acknowledgments were less brusque, but even then, his manner was forced and utterly wanting in the charm which no one could assume better than himself.

With everything new and strange around her, Antoinette even felt that she was having revealed to her a new side to her husband's character. Where was the winning grace and suavity, that had made him such a favourite with Continental servants.

"Ah, Rosalie and Maurice," he said carelessly to the couple whom Antoinette had noticed, "you got my letters, and told the others about the new mistress? That's right! Now you must try to teach them how to please her, for Mariposa has not known much of ladies these ten years past."

"Sam remembers the old times though!" turning in a more friendly fashion to the black butler.

"Ah, yes, massa! If only the old missus, God bless her, had lived to see Massa Edward's wife! She would have blessed the day!"

"Well, well! show Mrs. Castelle's maid to her room, and leave us to get dressed and ready for dinner."

The house was handsome in an old-fashioned way, and once in her room, with the soothing attentions of her own maid, the young wife began to experience a homelike sense of comfort.

There was an appealing touch of the family past in the slim, old-time furniture and in the dim crayon portraits of young folks and children on the walls.

Lives spent here in honour and dignity seemed to welcome her to worthily fill their vacant places, and to bear their name.

She idly followed this encouraging train of thought,

as, resting upon a sofa, she watched her maid preparing for her toilette.

The girl had left the room in search of a piece of luggage, when she noticed that the excited chattering of the people outside was dying away in the distance. All at once the receding voices were drowned by the sound of her husband's voice, low and cautious, but still near enough to be distinctly heard.

There was a clear-cut enunciation of each syllable, which she had already learned to recognise as a sign of ill-controlled anger. "I had not expected to find you still living in the house, after my having written that I wished you to move to the West Lodge. Maurice should have seen that you obeyed my orders."

The soft guttural voice that answered with mocking calm was one that Mrs. Castelle instinctively associated with the wearer of the red dress.

"Oh, massa, I know you're angry with me, but don't blame poor Maurice! You know he can't read writing and—well, I only read him bits of your letter. The day after I got it the West Lodge done be burned down, and where was the good of telling Maurice to go there then, some of de boys cooking chickens they stole, the overseer think."

A fierce oath was the answer from Castelle—for a moment the listener almost thought that there had been an accompanying blow.

"You fiend! Is there any mischief that you are not up to! You had better take care not to go too far! What do you want, and what are you scheming for?" A sob, which Antoinette scornfully stamped as false, broke upon the silence.

"Oh, if the massa would only not be cross with me, and would let me stay here in the house near him, and be housekeeper like I always have been! 'Fore the Lawd, I'd do everything to make the young missus comfortable, and never let on how things used to be. Why should such a splendid, lovely lady care to know anything about poor, black Rosalie! I'd do anything if only the massa wouldn't send me away to be just a common nigger, and have all the other folks mock at me!" and again came the vehement sob.

"Well, well," Castelle's voice had lost much of its harshness! "there is no doubt that you are a smarter housekeeper than can easily be found here, and I should miss Maurice in the house too. So if you choose to behave yourself, I don't mind your staying on—only mind, now none of your tricks or you shall be packed off to the Mobile auction-room. I am in earnest this time, remember."

"Ah, massa is always so good to his poor Rosalie!" but under the tender words there was the snaky hiss that bided its time.

With a sound of footsteps the conclave ended. Antoinette sat and stared around the room whose presage of home was turned into the shadow of a prison.

This then was the future that she had hastened to meet with such ready feet, such confident trust.

Although she had left America as a child, yet her life since she came from her convent school, had been spent amongst southern women.

In spite of her youth she could hardly have helped gathering some knowledge of the darker side of plantation life.

And yet the blow was none the less keen when these shadows overspread her own pure young life. She was still young enough to divide the world into the two forces of good and bad. There were as yet no halftones in her mental vision.

But, even with all the intensity of her disillusionment, there was in her enough pride, self-control or common sense, call it what you will, to enable her to face the music, and conceal her new knowledge from everyone.

How she got through that evening, or indeed through the succeeding days, Mrs. Castelle could never afterwards have distinctly told. They were all an equal maze of bewildered pain.

Fortunately for her, these days were full of life and movement.

There were numerous batches of neighbours, if such might be counted by dozens of miles, and cousins, of equally distant degree of relationship, coming to make the acquaintance of the new chatelaine of Mariposa.

Then, as her part, there were long rides or drives, through dreary woods and lonely cotton-fields, to return these visits and partake of stately hospitality; and there was a certain relief in anything that took her away from Mariposa, and the daily sight of that brown face.

But, whether at home or abroad, there was still the vague sensation of moving through some nightmare regions, from which she would awake to recover her own and her husband's identity.

For the shadows of Mariposa seemed to have closed over and hidden the gay and gracious young seigneur, the winning charm of whose manner she had so often watched with fond pride, working its own way in fresh surroundings. In his place she saw standing a nervous youth, with furtive glances and uneasy demeanour in her presence, of irritable captiousness toward his servants, who seemed cowed and alarmed.

It was only in society that glimpses of his former self returned, and Antoinette grew to feel the presence of guests a relief and welcome distraction.

Truly, Mollie Seton's prophecies had fallen far short of the grim reality!

She herself was not without causes of irritation in the gradually increasing insolence of Rosalie the housekeeper, and her slightly veiled sense of triumph, as well as in the impish-like pranks played about the house by her boy Herbert.

Towards this child Antoinette instinctively felt a nervous aversion, which she could scarcely control, and it was these same pranks of his which precipitated the overhanging crisis.

One day, returning tired and depressed from a long ride with her husband, she sought the shelter of her own rooms, only to find the hated child sitting in the middle of her dressing-room floor. He was busily engaged, in his uncannily stealthy fashion, in making a species of mud-pie from the contents of the various cases of perfumes and powders on her table; glass and ivory and silver lying scattered around him in confusion.

This was the last straw laid on her daily burden. With

a sudden outburst of wrath she jerked the child to his feet, giving him two or three smart cuts with the riding switch which she held in her hand. The boy's screams of rage and pain brought his mother flying to the rescue.

Antoinette loosened her grasp, giving him a shove towards Rosalie, who crouched over him, winding him in her arms and glaring like an enraged tigress at her mistress.

The latter's wrath was already stiffening into contempt. Her pride of race and habit brought back her self-control before this woman.

She turned from that hostile figure and rang for her maid, saying coldly,

"Take the child away and keep him out of my sight. Remember that he may fare worse if I find him here again."

Her coolness seemed to recall Rosalie to some sense of consequences, but as she rose, soothing the terrified child, she muttered as she went,

"We'll see what the massa says to his own boy being whipped by any missus."

Uncertainly as she had caught the words, their meaning was able to send a chill to Antoinette's heart.

When Mollie her maid came, she found her standing pallid-faced, the whip still in her hand, gazing down upon the havoc on the floor.

Mollie's consternation found a fluent vent in lamentations to which her mistress paid little heed.

At length she roused herself with a vicious snap to the whip, saying,

"The little wretch is smarting well for it, anyhow."

Mollie dropped the cloth with which she was attacking the mud pie.

"Lord sake, missus! You didn't beat him!"

"I did, though. But not nearly as much as I shall the next time I catch him here."

The gravity on Mollie's face was portentous.

"Mercy me! You'd better be careful, missus. Dat's Mr. Castelle's own child. Rosalie done gone tell him for sure! She's getting round him again. She could get round de debbil himself!" she whispered with careful glances around.

That night a fierce combat raged between husband and wife, and a high-spirited girl, who had never heard any save utterances of homage and affection, learned how cruel words can cut and sting, and how brutal a man who is ashamed of himself can be.

It was small comfort to her that he at last shrunk from her presence like a beaten dog, cowed by the greater strength of her spirit.

Fearlessly as she had faced him down, the strain was too much for her overwrought nerves, and she broke down in an hysterical attack through which the faithful Mollie soothed and tended her, bolting the doors so that no one else might come near them or listen to her heart-broken sobs. And thus the night was spent.

CHAPTER III

"A LIFE AWRY"

WHEN, late the next morning Mrs. Castelle awoke from the heavy sleep of exhaustion, she looked around as on a new heaven and earth. The morning sunshine, the breath of the pine woods wafted through the open window brought her no friendly message. Her eyes did not even soften at sight of the wistful face of her little skye terrier, that, with his keen doggish sense of something having gone wrong, had perched himself on the edge of the bed to watch her slumbers. There was no passion or sorrow in her heart this morning. All that belonged to the past night, and she felt a strange new cold strength coming over her.

The terrier's were not the only faithful eyes to greet her awakening. Poor Mollie's soft dark ones filled with tears as Antoinette languidly tried to smile at her. What little slumber she herself had known had been on a rug by her mistress's bed.

"Any news, Mollie?" Antoinette asked, with a dread of what she might hear.

"Praise de Lord, missus, de massa's gone off this mornin' early, to go hunting with Mr. D'Entremont. Won't be back for a week, old Sam said."

"That gives us plenty of time for what we have to do." Antoinette said, half to herself, and Mollie, looking at her curiously, saw her absorption and said nothing.

There was a great sense of relief in the knowledge that she need not meet her husband, or take any immediate action. She knew that the necessity of the next few hours was rest—rest of body, and if possible of mind.

After that she knew quite well what she was to do. Her one idea was to get away from Mariposa as quickly as possible. She would take Mollie and go to her own plantation in Georgia. If ever she could learn to forgive her husband, it could not be at Mariposa. She had no near relatives or intimate friends to look to in America. Well, all the more reason for being strong and brave.

Presently she asked Mollie another question—"That woman, Rosalie, have you seen her to-day?"

Mollie looked round in evident fear before she answered,

"She's working hard in de kitchen, not often she works like dat. I just saw her through de door. Frightened to go in. Wicked woman dat, missus be careful."

"I am not afraid of her!" was the quick answer; but, all the same, some of Mollie's dread did seem to communicate itself to her, and bid her walk cautiously. When Mollie had dressed her she pulled herself together, and, pale and stately, made her usual tour of inspection.

As she passed through the kitchen she saw the flutter of a bright coloured dress as its wearer bent over a tray of pastry, but gave no sign of recognition to the half ironical curtsy that marked her passage.

She was almost alarmed at the bitter tide of cruelty

that she felt surging up in her heart. The despotism of
a line of autocrats was latent there, ready to be
aroused by the mere sight of this scornful slave-
woman. The possibilities of her own nature were at
that moment her worst fear, as she knew that she
could have stood by and watched this woman suffer.

The morning had worn into noon when, idly pacing
the verandah, she heard the mingled sound of laughing voices and horses' feet approaching up the avenue.
She had grown accustomed by now to such visits *en
masse*, and stood on the steps to greet the party whom
she recognised as coming from the nearest plantation,
that of the DeLatours.

She had rather fancied the girls, of a fragile butterfly style of beauty, and the men of more or less the
type of her husband—handsome courteous, gay; but
now, as she smiled her greeting, she wondered how
near to the surface lay the seamy side in each. But
surely, amongst all these faces of new friends she saw
one from her former life.

The thin man, of the bleached blond head, who
rode by one of the girls, was Humphry Martin whom
she had known in Paris.

A journalist of unknown antecedents, Martin had
made himself a certain place in the American Parisian
circles where she had queened it, by his powers of
entertaining and plausible adaptability.

True, Castelle and some others of his ilk had
affected, in their lofty Southern fashion, to regard
him as merely a court jester to the women folks. But
a certain reckless side to his character, making him
an infatuated gambler, had often included him in

some of their wildest night hours. He knew his Paris so well, and could always provide a newcomer with amusement at the shortest notice.

He lived the easy life that a man may live if he always takes care only to associate with prosperous people.

Antoinette had known as little as girls do know of the real life of such a man, and had graciously accepted the deferential homage which he almost timidly laid at her feet. He was such a convenient person, always knowing who the remarkable people at a function were, and ready with amusing little stories about them.

He was artistic, too, and brought from the studios the opinions that the public must learn later as the correct thing. This has always counted for more in Paris than in any other capital, and Antoinette had a real, if somewhat untrained, pleasure in art. She was thus often glad of Mr. Martin's guidance through galleries and in visits to studios. So, after her marriage, he had succeeded in gaining a certain standing with the Castelles.

When they came to America they found that he had taken passage in the same steamer, and neither of them regretted the fact.

It was natural then for him to attach himself to their party on board.

If he drank Castelle's wine and smoked his cigars, he played picquet with him, and talked the endless gossip of the Paris world they both loved and were both leaving.

Then, when her husband was lazy, or had found some other woman to amuse him, he fetched and carried for the wife, sat by her side talking well of books, ideas, art, anything that a clever man makes use of when he is earnestly set on interesting a woman.

He had even got so far as talking of himself in the strain of melancholy cynicism dear to the feminine heart. And she, as most women of her age and experience would have done, had taken him at his own value, and believing in his sufferings had gently consoled and counselled him.

And so she had learned to look upon him as a trusted friend, and it was with a real sensation of pleasure that she saw his face amongst those of people who, friendly as they now were, she yet felt were of her husband's kith and kin, and would judge him the most leniently of the two in any difference. He at least, was the friend of Antoinette Castelle, not only of the mistress of Mariposa. And so, as Humphry Martin mounted the steps at whose head stood the lovely figure in white, he felt a fierce throb of exultation as he read in her face the glad welcome that he had toiled so hard to win.

Had Diana then really come to life for an ordinary mortal?

Antoinette's silvery voice spoke its greeting.

"Cousin Sallie, and Cousin Louise! Mr. De LaTour, this is indeed an act of Christian charity on your part to come when Edward is off for a week's hunting, and I am all alone! Mr. Martin, what a pleasure to have an old friend drop from the skies in this fashion! But I fear that you will be disappointed in Edward's absence."

"Disappointment could not exist in the sunshine of

your presence," was the answer, as Martin held her
hand in a hungering pressure.

Exaggerated compliments were the fashion of the
time and country, and this did not strike anyone as
excessive.

"But how was it that you came here? I never heard
you speak of knowing anyone in this neighbourhood!" she found a chance of asking him presently.

They had strolled to one end of the verandah to
look at some Cherokee roses which he had admired,
and now she stood holding to her face a long spray of
blossoms which he had picked for her.

"I told you, I think, that I hold a roving commission
from an English paper to report on the feeling in the
South as to these growing political troubles. It was in
my duty to make the acquaintance of some of the
southern leaders in Washington, and the fact of Mr.
De LaTour's being a neighbour to Mariposa gave me
all the more motive to get into his good graces. I have
my reward, you see."

His eyes and voice emphasised his meaning, but at
that moment any homage seemed welcome to
Antoinette as pouring balm on the still bleeding
wounds given the night before to her pride.

A tired smile answered him, but she hesitated a
moment before saying,

"I wish that I felt at liberty to ask you to come to us
when your visit to them is ended, but some family
troubles make it an impossibility."

His face immediately assumed an air of grave concern.

"You do not mean any personal troubles, I trust? I

saw at once that you were looking pale and worn."

The friendly voice was almost too much for Antoinette's composure. Her lips trembled and hot tears burned in her eyes but did not fall. With a proud effort she recovered herself.

"Ah! well! I suppose I must have my turn occasionally like other mortals. I fear that I have been but a spoiled child of fortune so far."

"Ah, if only I could give my life to keep you so!" he protested passionately.

"I am sure that you are a true friend," she answered simply.

"If you would only try me! Promise me at least that if there is the humblest service that you think I could do for you, you will let me know. Are you sure that you can tell me nothing now?"

For a moment Antoinette hesitated, but her good angel leant nearer, and she spoke with the loyal reticence of wifehood.

"There is nothing," she answered firmly; "but I promise you that if I should need help I shall let you know."

"That is goodness indeed," he murmured.

"I shall not leave this neighbourhood while there is any chance of your needing me," and in his heart there was a rapturous conviction that he would soon control the heiress' wealth.

Meanwhile the simple stay-at-home cousins were pluming themselves upon their guest's evident success with the lady of Mariposa, whom they regarded with hearty admiration. Had ever such clothes, such fashion stamped with the approval of the Tuileries been seen before in their neighbourhood? "We were so pleased when we found that Mr. Martin was a friend of yours," babbled one of the ladies as they sat at lunch. "Sallie said, 'Now do let us ride over and surprise Cousin Edward's wife, for I'm sure she must often feel dull from the contrast with the gay Paris life.' You *do* find it dull I'm afraid," putting her head on one side like a meditative canary, "for you really haven't half the colour that you had when you first came. It's too bad if Mariposa makes her look pale, isn't it?" appealing to the company at large.

Antoinette looked round, and then beyond the kindly faces turned upon her, she met through the half-open door the watchful stare of those hated dark eyes.

She would have liked to scream out her hatred to the home that had proved no home to her, and in spite of herself the feeling rasped her voice :—

"I fancy that Mariposa will never suit me. There seems some poison taint in the air I breathe. I think I shall probably go soon to my own plantation in Georgia. I fancy I should find a purer atmosphere there."

There was a pause of consternation at this attack on their local pride by a newcomer.

Then Mr. De La Tour, the older brother, whose acquaintance Martin had made in Washington spoke in as cold a disapproval as he could show to a pretty woman:—"You could hardly expect, dear lady, that Edward Castelle should leave his ancestral home to become a prince consort upon his wife's estates. We are conservative folk here, and we look to the master of Mariposa to take his place amongst us. I think that Edward must have told you that both his parents lived to be over eighty, so that *they* found no poison in Mariposa air."

"What is one man's meat is another man's poison," Antoinette quoted lightly. "I can see plainly that unless I want to make all you dear people my enemies, I shall have to run off to Georgia by myself, and leave you my husband."

She spoke looking straight into that dark face in the doorway, and her tone was strained, and a fixed colour glowed in her cheeks.

Her listeners felt the electricity in the air, and it took all Martin's conversational art to start their liveliness again. When they said adieu, Martin succeeded in lingering a moment behind the others. "You will not forget your promise?" he said softly.

"I will not forget," she answered firmly, and as she spoke she heard a rustle of the curtain in the open window behind her, and caught the flash of a red skirt.

She stood and watched until the last figure had disappeared in the curves of the avenue before she turned back into her desolated home.

CHAPTER IV

"DANGER BENEATH AND O'ERHEAD"

NEVER before had the evening shadows seemed to gather with such menacing gloom, as they did now to Antoinette, sitting out on the verandah where her friends left her.

As it grew chilly, Mollie brought her a shawl and urged her to come in to the fire of pine logs which crackled in her room. Silently she shook her head. The air outside seemed purer than, within.

Then her pride warned her against allowing any appearance of forlornness to be visible. She must stick to her usual routine, and not abate one item of personal state and ceremony.

And so she went to her room and ordered Mollie to dress her in her usual evening attire, and then, pale but lovely in her light blue silk draperies, she went to the dining-room and sat down to the courses of her solitary dinner.

Old Sam waited on her with even more deferential care than ever, but even her painful self-absorption was at length pierced to notice the evident agitation of his manner.

Do his best, his hands were shaky and his speech distraught, and he seemed quite helpless to control with his usual discipline the eccentricities of his numerous under-studies.

At last came a moment when they had charged out of the room to see who could first secure the remains of a scarcely touched chicken.

Seizing the chance, old Sam as he handed her the pudding leant low and whispered in his mistress' ear, in tones of trembling earnestness: "For de Lord's sake, don't eat it, missus. Very unwholesome."

A sudden remembrance of that red-clad figure bending over the pastry board with such unusual energy pointed the few broken words. This then was the danger that she had to face!

Save for a more ghastly pallor Mrs. Castelle gave no sign, beyond a slight bend of the head, of having heard his words.

In that land of open doors and windows she did not know what hostile eyes might be fixed upon her. So she deliberately helped herself, and then slowly scattered the morsels over her plate, even lifting the fork once or twice to her lips, while the old man, standing stiffly at attention, watched her with the agonised eyes of a faithful hound. Presently she spoke, and her voice was only a little strained and hoarse:—

"Give me some fruit. I shall want nothing else."

The grapes that he set before her were grateful to her parched lips, and the eating of them gave her time to muster her mental strength. She dared not yield to the impulse which urged her to rush away like a frightened child to the protection of Mollie's presence. And soon she managed with outward calmness which veiled the deadly terror at her heart, to rise from the table and make good her retreat to the shelter of her own room.

Here, with swift noiselessness, she closed doors and windows, before turning towards Mollie, crouched upon the floor. "Why, Mollie, what is it?" she said in amazement, at sight of an empty dish and an inanimate mass of white fur that lay beside it.

There was an ashy grey shadow over the rich brown of the face that the maid raised to meet her mistress, and her rolling eyeballs showed an expanse of white.

"Sam brought me some puddin on a plate and told me to give it to de kitten, and it's *dead*! For de mercy of Heaven, missus, you didn't eat any?"

"No, Sam told me," she whispered back.

Dead! The word seemed to echo through Mrs. Castelle's brain in endless reverberations. But for the whisper of that poor, faithful old slave, she herself would have been lying cold and stiff.

Where and how? she wondered. Would she have fallen on the dining-room floor, and would there have been some moments of agony and of horrible hideous writhings and groans, before unconsciousness had come? Would that hateful slave-woman have come and gazed in triumph upon the completion of her work, upon the overthrow of her young beauty and strength.

In that sudden moment of peril Antoinette first knew how she loved the fair world around her, and the gracious years that lay ahead of her.

Whatever of hope or happiness this foe had power to despoil her of, she should not deprive her of that future, her heritage, if courage and determination were to avail aught.

Every hereditary instinct that came to her from a

long line of brave men, used to rule, sprang into life at call of "the tocsin of her heart."

Mollie felt a new purpose in the touch of the hand upon her shoulder and looked to draw some comfort from the light in her mistress' eyes.

Like many of the Louisiana slaves, Mollie was a devout Roman Catholic, and as she looked up into that dauntless, lovely face, she remembered the picture of St. Michael in the stained-glass window of the chapel.

She vaguely felt that the powers of darkness must flee away discomfited before so peerless a being, and she took courage.

"Get up, Mollie, there is no time to lose! Think a bit and try to tell me if there is any one besides Old Sam, in this accursed place, whom you are sure that we can trust. Sam is too old and feeble to ride to Bellevue tonight. Remember, Mollie, our lives may depend upon whom we trust now."

The light that dawned upon Molly's face was almost a simper.

"I don't need to tink, missus. Dere's Pete down at de stables; he'd do anyting I asked him to. He's goin' to ask massa to let him marry me, when he's quite sure dat dat cat Rosalie won't have a say. He's waitin' for me now down by de well, and if missus will say what she wants—"

Here then was another loyal heart to count upon. Even now, if Antoinette had taken time to think, she might have chosen the wiser part of holding her ground at Mariposa, but, for the first time in her young life, she had looked in the eyes of death, and nothing could allay her terror save flight from this place of dread.

And so a few words of urgent appeal for Martin's presence and help were hastily written and consigned to the care of Pete, who promised to do his best to return from Bellevue in two hours,

"But de roads be bad, and de night powerful dark," he urged.

When he had cautiously crept away to the stables, the two women bolted and barred themselves in as far as possible.

No sound from friend or foe broke the silence of the house, though often they started at the fancied tread of stealthy footsteps or the whisper of voices.

Gradually the distant noises at the quarters died away, and only the mysterious night sounds of the forest could be heard—the wail of the wind in the trees, the cry of some bird or animal.

A revolver lay ready to Antoinette's hand, and she had it in her heart to use it to deadly purpose if molested.

She blessed now the fashionable fancy which in the past summer had set the fine ladies at Biarritz to practising with the weapon. She had a certain amount to do before leaving her husband's home, as she now felt for ever.

She did not know whether, when she presently went out into the darkness, she would be able to take anything with her.

Thus there were her own jewels to dispose about her person and cherished letters and papers to destroy or lock away.

When all this was done she dressed herself for travelling and sat down to wait. How long the time seemed since her messenger had started! Surely he would not play her false, or Martin fail to answer her summons. At last it came—the signal agreed upon with, Mollie, who started up at the first sound of the whip-poor-will's note to listen for its repetition. It came again, and the verandah door was unbarred to admit Martin.

Splashed with mud, his face haggard and intent, the man had lost his drawing-room air and showed an aspect of greater manliness. As she met his eager eyes, a horrible misgiving laid hold on Antoinette, and her pride of *grande dame* seemed to warn her against setting forth under the care of this man. But had she not burned her boats in summoning him to her aid?

And what other course was open to her if she turned away from his protection?

She thoroughly believed that if she tried to leave Mariposa alone she would not succeed in doing so alive, save by the merest chance of luck. The little bundle of white fur had shown her with what a foe she had to deal. And she so dearly loved her life in that hour of peril. And so, too proud to show any weak shrinking, she let Martin as he stepped forward seize her hand while he whispered ardently,

"Your need had called to me without words! I was ready awaiting your summons when your messenger came! Ah! if it were not for your distress I should feel myself the most honoured of men!"

His enthusiasm jarred strongly on the tenseness of her strung-up mood, but she made an effort to respond.

"I would not have claimed such a service save for the soreness of my strait. My husband is away"—a flush of shame dyed her face—"a jealous mulatto woman has tried to poison me to-night. I must get away at once from this place where I can trust no one save these two poor blacks. If you will help me to get to the nearest town, I will go to my own plantation in Georgia and communicate with my friends from there."

"Whatever you wish," he assured her fervently. "My one object shall be to carry out your plans."

A wave of generous trust swept over her.

"Oh," she cried impulsively, stretching out both hands, "I should not call myself solitary when I have one such friend as you!"

"Indeed you shall never be without a friend while Humphry Martin lives!" he said, bending low to kiss the hand that lay in his own.

When it came to the discussing of details Antoinette met with her first obstacle. She had planned leaving the place in a light, strong, double buggy, which driven by Martin, would have ample room for Mollie as well as for some smaller articles of luggage. But Martin, during their ride, had put some questions to Pete as to ways and means. He had ascertained that while Pete could get easily enough of horses and saddles, the key of the coach-house was in the hands of Maurice, Rosalie's husband, who was acting as overseer during the white official's absence, and any attempt to get at it would be full of risk.

"But you can surely ride," Martin urged. "I can manage your valise easily enough."

"But Mollie!" Mrs. Castelle answered in great distress.

"She can hardly stick on a horse, can you, Mollie?"

"For certain sure, not, missus," was the emphatically tearful answer.

"It would be impossible for her to take such a long ride at night, and how can I go without her!"

Martin tried to hide his vexation under the mask of wounded feeling.

"I see you do not trust me," he said sadly. "It was a pity in that case to have sent for me."

The taunt was well veiled, but it stung none the less.

"Indeed I do trust you! Indeed, I have no fear to go alone with you!" Antoinette steadied her voice to say; But Mollie, how can I leave her to that woman's revenge?" and she laid a caressing hand on the shoulder of the sobbing girl.

Over the tragic brown face there dawned a watery smile.

"Lor' sakes, missus, I'se not afraid of her for myself! Guess I can get round Maurice a good sight quicker dan *she* can. She'd be glad enough to get me out of de house to de quarters, if Pete asked leave to marry me. But I'd go with you, all de same, missus, glad and faithful."

Antoinette sadly shook her bead and took her hand away. So even Mollie was better provided with friends and home than she was.

She gave a little laugh:—"Well, Mr Martin, you see no one disputes your guardianship. And I myself," she added with a proud little tilt to her head, "wish for nothing better."

Martin bowed low in silent deference.

CHAPTER V

A NIGHT RIDE

A LATE moon was just rising in the east, and creating a brightness before its visible presence, when Antoinette sat on her horse and looked down at Mollie's tearful face. "Oh, missus, my dear kind missus!" the girl sobbed, but Antoinette though pale as an ivory carving was very calm.

"God bless you, for a faithful friend!" she said touching softly the brown check, and then she looked away to Martin's eager face and to the dark mysterious forest beyond.

A strange shudder of fear ran over her, and then her face hardened and she gathered the reins in her hand, and turned slowly towards the avenue, Martin following.

She was a good rider and was on a horse that she had grown fond of during the past weeks.

There was a relief that was almost pleasure in the sense of action in the fresh air, after that night watch of suspense and fear. She even breathed more free that she was no longer under the same roof with Rosalie.

Martin had come up to her side, but he had tact enough to respect her evident desire for silence.

And then the hand of Night laid its cool touch upon her sore-heated heart, and spoke of fortitude in the present, of peace and dignity to be attained in the future.

She did not notice that they had ridden for mile after mile through the gloom of whispering woods when, if they had been on the road that she had intended to take, they should have long before passed a settlement of poor whites, and should have been approaching their destination of a riverside town.

Martin had taken good care not to rouse her from her abstraction, although he had once or twice asked tenderly as to her fatigue.

More than an hour had passed thus, before Martin pulled up his horse with a smothered exclamation of wrath.

"My horse is dead lame! What haunting bad luck. Fortunately there is a light ahead there! Perhaps we may find help!" he added more hopefully.

The light glimmered, red and flickering, through the opening trees. As they emerged on the small clearing, they saw that it came from the embers of a sinking fire around which one or two negroes were sleeping.

Antoinette at once recognised the forbidding-look-ing, little wayside inn, as one which she had passed with a distasteful glance, on one of her longest and loneliest expeditions to a plantation. Her voice was a cry of dismay as she said, "Oh, Mr. Martin, I know this place! It is miles away from the river miles from anywhere except the plantation of my husband's uncle."

Martin, standing by her horse's bridle, flashed one keen glance up at her.

"You surely must be mistaken," he said soothingly. "There are dozens of such places all over this country, almost exactly alike. We ought to be nearly at Belleville by now. I will make one of these creatures tell us. Here, wake up!" and he stirred vigorously with his foot one of the men, who with many grunts and yawns, sat up and surveyed them.

"Yes, the missus was right. This was the road to St. Germain. The old massa had lots of gentlemen there. Was the missus going there?"

Antoinette shuddered at the thought of appealing to the blear-eyed, vicious-looking old bachelor, whose, wild surroundings had on her one visit filled her with dismay. Even to her inexperienced eye the meaning had been clear of the bold-eyed, overdressed brown women who had giggled and stared in windows and passages.

"No, I am not going there," she answered haughtily, and then drooped in her saddle in the fatigue of utter desolation. Where was she going, a helpless leaf blown before the winter wind?

But Martin's voice spoke soothingly at her side:—"It will be all right. I will rouse the people inside and find out what we can."

Forthwith he proceeded to thump vigorously at the door, which presently opened to reveal the faces of a man and a woman, of a type low almost to savagery.

Their manner, at first surly, changed to a cringing obsequiousness at sight of Antoinette, whom, however, they gave no sign of recognising.

They corroborated the negroes' information, and Martin looked at his lamed horse in disgust. His scheme of getting Mrs. Castelle away from the beaten tracks had been carried out rather more thoroughly than suited his purpose.

There was evidently nothing for it but to make a halt. The man professed some rude skill as a blacksmith, and promised that he would try to do something for the horse.

Mrs. Castelle, too, was beginning to show the long strain upon her nerves, for as Martin helped her to dismount she reeled and was steadied by his arm.

"You cannot do more without rest and some sort of food," he said decisively, and she did not gainsay him.

The interior of the inn was no more attractive than its outside.

Antoinette shuddered with a sick disgust at the sight of the filthy table and dishes. But now Martin showed to the best advantage in his cheery care for her comfort. A fire, that all-glorifying fire of pitch pine that blesses the Southern States, was soon shedding its beneficent glow over the dreary hovel. A dilapidated, old rocker was dragged forward for her to rest in. Martin himself, with the skill of an old campaigner, superintended the execution and preparation of a chicken for their breakfast. Moved by his energy the woman made some languid efforts at producing a hoe-cake.

Broken down in body and soul as she was, Martin's exertions had even brought a passing smile to Antoinette's lips as she watched him. When, heated but triumphant, he place a jug of dubious coffee before her, she made an effort to swallow some of the queer composition.

While he worked, the grey of dawn had gradually filled the room.

"Here is a new day; let us hope it may bring us better luck," he said as he fetched a log of wood and, turning it upright, sat down on it.

She sighed and set down her cup untasted, for the long red rays of sunshine that poured into the room seemed in their bright promise but to reveal and mock at the barrenness of her new life, even as they did at the sordidness of the room. She started to find Martin's intent eyes fixed on her wistfully.

"If only I could save you: from unhappiness," he murmured passionately.

"What should I do without you," she answered sincerely enough; so that he was encouraged to lay his hand upon hers.

Antoinette sat facing the open door, and staring out into the radiant, crisp winter morning of the south.

All at once there dawned upon her hearing the approaching barking of dogs and trampling of horses' feet.

Bridles jingled, men's voices laughed and shouted. Thinking only of gaining means to get away, she cried joyfully:

"Here are people who will be able to get us a horse."

Turning to Martin she shrank back aghast at his livid face of rage and—was it fear?

"Oh, what is it?" she questioned feebly; but no answer was given or required, for the sound of one laugh that she would have known anywhere struck her ear.

It was her husband's, and the day of settlement between them had come.

Her face blanched and hardened to the semblance of ivory; she sat awaiting the march of fate. The riders had crowded up in front of the inn and dismounted. One man stood in the doorway looking in and darkened all the light from her.

It was Castelle's slim, boyish figure, and the eyes of husband and wife met as across a great gulf.

Martin sprang to his feet with a fierce oath, but still Antoinette sat motionless. On Castelle's face the first blank amazement spread into a tempest of wrath, which hardened into disgust and scorn.

One glance of utter contempt he cast upon Martin and then let his burning gaze rest steadily upon his wife. A sudden silence had fallen upon the noisy group of his friends, who, gradually realising that they were in the presence of tragic elements, gathered around in a little circle.

It was Castelle's voice that broke the silence—a voice that came in a strange, hissing sound from his writhing lips.

"So! This is how my virtuous wife diverts herself in my absence! she found the morals of Mariposa too lax for her purity, and thought that she would apply a counter-irritant. I certainly think that when she was in search of pleasure, she might have chosen more luxurious surroundings, and a more thoroughbred companion. The French court might surely have supplied both without taking the trouble to cross the Atlantic for *this*," and a comprehensive wave of his hand accentuated the meaning of his last word.

The spell of horror that had held her silent under his scorn was broken, and, forgetting her wrongs,

conscious only of the horrible falseness of her position, Antoinette sprang toward him with a wild cry of
appeal.

She thought and cared nothing for the circle of
spectators, or for Martin. Her husband and herself
were the two personalities of her drama.

"Edward! Edward! Listen to me! You will be sorry all
your life if you do not listen to me now! That woman
tried to poison me last night at dinner! My life was not
safe at Mariposa! I could not have remained there
another hour! Mr. Martin was staying with the De La
Tours, and I sent for him to help me to get away.
Before God, that is the whole truth!"

Without deigning any direct answer, Castelle put
her aside with a remorseless arm.

"An abnormal melodramatic development," he
sneered in cutting accents. "Mr. Martin," with a sudden change to sternness, "perhaps if you can tear
yourself away from the protection of a woman, and
will come outdoors, we may settle the question
between us in a more manly fashion."

Her pride all gone, in utter desperation, Antoinette
made one more effort to cling to her husband's arm;
but as he fiercely shook her off, she fell and lay powerless, hearing the cabin door close behind them.

A merciful semi-consciousness dulled her anguish.
She lay there, aware of her surroundings, and yet
could scarcely have made an effort to move if the
house had been on fire over her head. At last the
sound of two shots scattered her stupor, and brought
her to her feet with a cry of despair.

In her frenzy of misery she had some difficulty with

the crazy door-latch, and, as she wrenched it open, she heard the sound of receding hoofs.

There were some of the cavalcade riding away, but now with no sound of voices or laughter—but surely— surely there must be someone, somewhere? Yes, over there in a rough garden-patch two men still stood dismounted. They were looking down at *something*. What was it ?

As, numbed by a deadly sickness, she crept towards them, one of the men turned and mounted. Catching sight of her, he bowed profoundly, and she saw, with a cold horror, that it was Castelle who was thus leaving her.

She attempted no word or gesture to detain him. All that was ended.

That dark heap of clothes on the ground, then, was Martin. Was he dead?

She toiled on over the rough hillocks that seemed to her shaking limbs like obstructing mountains.

At last she stood beside the still, recumbent figure, and the almost equally still, grave, little man who watched it.

"Is he dead?" she asked quietly.

"No," he answered in a pleasantly casual fashion, "not by any means, though he may slip away yet if he's not looked after. It was a clean shot, a beautiful shot— took him right through the shoulder. Castelle meant to kill, though—meant to kill. Can't imagine why he didn't do it."

As he seemed quite absorbed in the reminiscence, Antoinette shook him by the arm:

"Aren't you going to do *something* for him?" she

asked wildly. It seemed horrible to see this life ebbing out unaided.

The dreamy little man flashed one keenly comprehensive glance at her, which apparently satisfied him.

"Oh, yes, I'm going to do something. That's what I stayed behind for. You see," he went on deliberately, "he can't be moved. Naturally enough, the others would do nothing for him. With me, perhaps, it was merely professional instinct. At any rate, I cannot stay here now for more than an hour or so. The question then is, madam, whether you will remain with him or leave him to the care of that female over there. It really"—in a politely conversational tone—"seems as though I might call it a matter of life or death."

Antoinette looked down at Martin's white, drawn face, and then over to where her horse was tethered. The longing was strong upon her to mount and ride away, away from them all; but she checked herself. Here was the man who had given her loyal service, who she knew was ready, at her slightest sign, to give her more, and could she leave him to die like a dog by the roadside? What mattered the consequences to her ruined life? Could anything worse come to her than had already come? It was but a few moments of doubt when she turned to the doctor and said simply:

"I will stay with him of course."

As though he had heard her words, Martin's closed eyelids fluttered and lifted. "Antoinette!" he whispered, with an appealing glance, "you will not leave me?"

Her face was very set and grave, as, bending over him, she answered, "No, I will stay with you." But her

hands were deft and skilful, and her attention fully
fixed, when, presently, she aided the doctor to dress
the wound.

CHAPTER VI

BACK in Paris again, where the "Danse Macabre" of the Empire was reeling on to a measure of ever-increasing recklessness. A group of American women, who had won admission to the charmed circles, were gathered to entertain Mrs. Seton with an account of one of the maddest revels of the time—a fancy-dress ball given by the Duchesse d'Albe, the Empress' sister.

Mrs. Seton, having sprained her ankle, had been debarred from the affair, and had sighed and groaned accordingly.

"If only you could have seen the Princess Mathilde as a Nubian! They say that every inch of her was stained! At any rate, the greater part of her was, for we saw it!" lisped a bride with the face of a young angel.

"And, oh, my dear," joined in her painted mamma, if you could have seen the ballet of the elements! I really doubt if they could have allowed shorter skirts at any theatre! The public aren't trained to swallow things as we are! But it was lovely! The Naiads were rivulets of silver, the Salamanders of gold. I wonder how they ever got the powder to stay on their hair like that."

"Mamie Waters said that a man from the Gymnase did it."

"The Emperor said that she looked the best of them all."

Delightful as was this gossip, there were several there who felt it but the *hors-d'œuvre* before the banquet, even as comedy always takes rank before tragedy.

And so when the bride's mamma, who sat next Mrs. Seton's sofa, asked her, "Have you heard any more particulars about the Castelle divorce?" there was an expectant silence, and faces changed to the proper shade of gravity.

Mrs. Seton sighed and shook her head:—

"I know little more than what you all know. That that miserable adventurer Mr. Martin, who called himself a journalist, and used to hang about her here, followed them out in the same steamer, and that her husband, all unsuspecting, encouraged, the intimacy.

"The man got to know Adrian De La Tour, and managed to get invited by him into the neighbourhood. Edward went off for a week's shooting and that very same day, Mr. Martin got the De La Tours to take him over to Mariposa! It's terrible to think how carefully it must all have been planned ! What happened afterwards is not very clearly known, as there is only the negroes' gossip. At any rate, Martin left the De La Tour's house secretly that night, and the next morning Edward, with the hunting party, walked in on the two of them at breakfast in a filthy little inn between Mariposa and St. Germain. It seems as though they must have lost their way or they would not have gone there.

"There was a duel, and Edward left him all but dead on the ground. She had the face to stay there in the neighbourhood, in that low disreputable inn, a mere drinking place, and nurse the man. Since then she has been at her own plantation in Georgia, but whether she took him there or not I don't know. Such a pity Edward hadn't killed him outright!"

"Yes, indeed," chorused her sympathetic listeners. These American women had still the Puritan leaven at the depths of their cosmopolitanism, and had never really adapted themselves to the lax morals of the atmosphere in which they lived.

Mrs. Seton might perhaps have given a more lenient version of her rich cousin's story, if the uncle in New Orleans had not obligingly departed this life, leaving her enough to pay her dressmaker's bills for herself in the future. The consequence was that Mrs. Seton could afford the luxury of disapproval.

"I hear that she calls herself Mrs. Le Moine," suggested one who had used Mrs. Castelle's carriage and servants as her own.

"Yes, she said so, when she wrote me a wild letter. There was a ridiculous tale of a jealous mulatto woman who tried to poison her, and from whom Mr. Martin was helping her to escape. It made me fear that poor Cousin Antoinette's brain must be a little bit queer, you know."

There was a rustling of silken skirts and a wafted breath of perfumes, as a slim, sallow compatriot joined their numbers.

"Are you talking about Antoinette Castelle?" she asked, with hardly any other greeting. "Well, she arrived yesterday in the mail boat with the Dwyers. They told me so just now."

If she had wished to create a sensation, her success should have rejoiced her.

Each woman sat staring, while she mentally arranged her own course of procedure.

Mrs. Seton gave a faint squeak of dismay, paling visibly beneath her rouge.

"Was *the man* with her, did they say?" she asked.

"No, she was alone. It seems she had an illness in Georgia. She was very quiet and kept altogether to herself. The Dwyers had never met her before, so that it was easy for them to avoid her."

"Yes, but what shall *I* do?" wailed Mrs. Seton. "She is my cousin, and we were brought up as children together. It is very hard on me."

"We are all very sorry for you, my dear. But you must be *firm*," answered one of the older ladies, shaking out her draperies prior to her departure.

They all felt that the séance was broken up by this news, and went off in little groups.

Hardly had they gone their ways, when a stately, plainly-dressed woman passed the concierge and went up the great staircase with a familiar air.

Mrs. Seton had lived in this cosy little flat on the new Boulevard Haussmann for nearly two years.

The maid who opened the door ushered her into the tiny salon with an air of astonished perplexity. She generally had a pretty good idea of her mistress's affairs.

Mrs. Seton had limped to her writing table, but at the sound of footsteps, turned on her chair.

"Good God!" she gasped. "Antoinette Castelle! And you come to *me!*"

Antoinette was dressed with as great care as ever, but in the scrupulous plainness of a black and white travelling dress. Her face showed traces in its thinness and delicacy of tinting, of past illness, though it was evident that the sea-voyage had brought back the health of youth.

Mrs. Seton was fairly startled by the subtle charm which deeper experiences had given to her beauty.

The sight of it awoke the old girlish grudge that her rich cousin should have everything.

As for Antoinette, she stood looking down at the other, her first glad movement towards her arrested as was the tremulous smile on her lips, the light in her eyes.

"Yes, I came to *you*, Mollie. To *you*, the only woman relation of my own that I have. I came, as I would have expected you to come to me in trouble. I was so sure that you would want me to do so, but I see that you don't."

Her voice was infinitely sad and sweet, but it only irritated the other, as weak natures are always irritated in situations too difficult for them.

"How *could I* want you after what you have done? I am a widow with no one to fight my battles, and I must think of myself a little. If you could only have heard them all talking about you just now—the Sauterelles, the Pesquiers!"

A strange slow smile dawned on the face looking down so intently.

"The Sauterelles! The Pesquiers! And so *they* were all pulling me to pieces!" she said thoughtfully, then with more earnestness: "And *you*? Did *you*, too, join in the hue and cry? Do *you* think I am utterly depraved, Mollie?" There was still a yearning in the voice which could hardly have failed to touch a woman of a larger nature, but Mrs. Seton's thoughts were only of herself.

She wriggled under the deep questioning of those hazel eyes.

"What can I think, when your own deeds condemn you? When you yourself have no defence to make?"

"But I wrote and told you the whole story. Perhaps you did not get the letter?" and a new hope came into her face.

"Oh, yes, I got a letter where you told your side of the story. But really, you know, it was all such a queer, improbable tale, and as you don't seem to have any witnesses or anything—" she paused helplessly, and her cousin finished the sentence.

"The long and the short of it is that you don't believe me. You, nor the Sauterelles, nor the Pesquiers. Is that it?"

Still that strange, half-pitying smile as if bent upon some lower order of creation. Mrs. Seton twisted herself about, but still she stuck to her guns.

"Well, you see, how could we, when—"

"Exactly, how could such as you be expected to believe that the girl, whom you had known from a child, whose mother and father you had honoured, had not, at the first temptation, become suddenly one of the unclassed of her sex? How could *you* ave judged her differently than you have done? It was the Christ who said 'Neither do I condemn thee,' not fashionable Paris women, who can look without blinking upon the manner in which the second Empire disports itself.

"Now listen to me a moment, Molly Seton, for I do

not think that you and I shall speak together again before the Judgement Day. May God judge between us then! When the world used me hardly, my one idea was to get to you. I was sure of your affection and sympathy, and that kept one soft spot in my heart ! It is gone now! The women I have lived among cast me out. What I am, what I may do in the future remains to be seen. But, whatever I may do or become, one thing is certain, that I ask no more charity from any of you. I go my own way, fight my own battles, and it may be that some of you may yet repent having helped in the making of what I am. Have you anything to say to me now, before I go?"

Sternly beautiful as the great Artemis in her awakened wrath, Mrs. Seton cowered and shrank before her. She was feebly crying now, and sobbed:

"Oh, Antoinette, how can you make it all so painful for me? Your violence quite upsets my nerves! If you want any money or anything when you go away from here, Uncle George is dead now, and I know that I owe you such a lot, and I'll try to let you have some—"

A cruel laugh interrupted her:—

"Thanks, but I don't need any of Uncle George's money. I have plenty of my own, and I'm *not* going away. I'm going to stay in Paris, and spend it here. I dare say that we may often pass each other in the Bois, but I won't upset your nerves again. Please make my adieu to your dear friends, who were once mine. I must try to make some new ones! Good-bye, Mollie!"

The clear ringing tones ceased, and Mrs. Seton, her face hidden in her handkerchief, heard a rustle of silken skirts and the closing of a door.

The silence that ensued seemed to be an awful accusing thing. For the first time for many a day, Mrs. Seton knew that in her pleasure-weakened nature there still lingered enough heart and conscience to suffer and to feel ashamed.

CHAPTER VII

AT THE TUILERIES

As these early spring days went on and the Paris season was at its height, the American Colony gossiped much over the doings of Mrs. LeMoine, who had settled herself in a smart little apartment in the Champs Elysées, and whose carriages, dresses and entertainments were voted the *dernier chic* by many a Parisian. The society that she moved in was almost altogether French, the modern French of the court circles, and the frequency of her appearance at the Tuileries caused many a compatriot to gnash her teeth with envy.

Towards these compatriots her face was as adamant, and when some member of the former circle trying to "hedge," made some timid advances to her she was met with a sarcasm that left her writhing. But there were men—artists, writers, statesmen, with whom she seemed eager to talk of the increasing political differences at home.

These differences had already caused the American Colony to separate into the two camps of North and South, that glared and scoffed at each other at the Tuileries and other common meeting-grounds.

It was the evening of one of the fortnightly court dances, and the rooms of the Tuileries were ablaze with the creations of Worth's prime, with every variety of French and foreign uniform, and with jewels worth a king's ransom. How many of these jewels were, within the next ten years, to go to aid in staunching some of the life-blood of two nations!

In a dress of primrose-shaded silk gauze, wreathed with deep-tinted vine leaves, Mrs. LeMoine looked a personification of a fair Bacchante, and seemed to radiate gathered sunshine.

"It is marvellous how a few yards of stuff can be made to symbolise to our heart the sunshine and the 'glory that was Greece,'" murmured a keen-faced Italian diplomat beside her.

She laughed gaily, and to one who had once loved her, there would have sounded a certain new recklessness in the echo of that laugh.

"For that, monsieur, you must thank the genius of Worth, rather than me."

"Ah, but it is the personality that endows the artist's creation with life and light," and his ardent eyes told of the power of her charm.

"And we are but poor moths fluttering around the flame, Count," put in a stalwart cavalryman whose Norman fairness was set off by the blue and silver of his uniform.

Surrounded by a brilliant group of men Antoinette, as she gazed ahead through the moving vistas of people, suddenly flushed, while such an eager light rose in her eyes that the keen Italian turned his in the same direction to learn its cause. He could not tell, however, that it was a figure from her past life that aroused her interest. All that he saw was a man of medium height and square build in the dress of a navy officer.

His face was bronzed as though from recent tropic voyages, for Captain Arthur had passed an adventurous year since the days when he and Edward Castelle had tasted their "cakes and ale" together in Paris.

Back in his former command in the Chinese navy, he had been pursuing pirates—pirates whose capture meant death to them, whose defeat of him would have meant death, slow and torturing to him. In such a life, civilisation and its component parts had grown to seem as unreal as a remembered dream.

All the same, amongst the faces that had sometimes risen before him in hours of night watches, had been that of the beautiful southern bride with the weak wayward husband.

Now, sickened by the butchery of the Chinese navy, he had thrown up his command, and come back to look once more on the joys of life, before starting on a fresh career of adventure in other lands.

That well-remembered face was almost the first familiar one to meet his eyes that evening.

As their eyes met, Antoinette moved a step forward from her surrounding court, and held out her hand. His full, hearty, English tones greeted her.

"Mrs. Castelle! This is great luck to meet you again, here in the old place. Where is that truant husband of yours? I trust I shall see him to-night?"

Antoinette felt the silence of the listening group behind her, before it politely melted away, and a deeper colour beamed in her cheek. She looked steadily into the frank blue eyes, and spoke with gentle dignity.

"I fear that you must be content with me this evening. My truant husband has turned truant in good earnest, or rather has given me up as a bad bargain. And please, I am Mrs. Castelle no longer. I use my, own name of LeMoine. You see, my dead father and mother cannot disown me."

They were bitter words, but the attempted lightness of tone grew rather tremulous as she read the pity in the blue eyes.

"I am sorry, indeed, to hear it," was his answer, in which, though brief, she read sincerity.

Her social training made her instinctively skim over the thin ice to an easier standing point.

"Ah, well, mine is not the only shipwreck. But wouldn't you like to stroll about and look at the notabilities?"

He agreed and offered his arm with empressement.

They turned to enter a curtained doorway under which a couple passed them somewhat hastily. With his keen eyes Arthur noted the averted face of the lady, and saw that it was Mrs. Seton. She had been introduced to him by Mrs. Castelle as her cousin, and this little incident made Antoinette's tragedy clear to his man-of-the-world vision.

His life of adventure had brought him so little in contact with women of his own station, that he had never mitigated his youthful strictness in the dividing line which he drew between the sheep and the goats. And so, in these few minutes, Antoinette had been weighed in the balance and found wanting, had been dethroned from her pedestal in his imagination, though none the less was his pity for her keen to pain. The situation between them was a bit awkward, for how, after what she had said, could he talk about their past acquaintanceship?

With ready tact she saved it by drawing him on to tell her of his own wanderings.

"And what do you mean to do next?" she asked, with friendly interest.

"I'm in no hurry for a month or two," he answered, comfortably. "I rather fancy that before I am tired of doing nothing, your compatriots will be preparing my next task for me."

"My compatriots?" she asked, turning a startled face towards him. "You surely don't think that it is going to come to war, then?"

"I do," he answered gravely, "and that it will not be many days in the coming. Yesterday's news was very ominous, and haven't you noticed the gravity of certain little groups of men to-night? Everyone who might have private information is set upon as he comes in. I was watching a little while ago, one of the Rothchilds fleeing before his persecutors. See, there now, there must be news."

They had paused in a corridor, where men with intent faces talked and listened.

There were many amongst them of those who have the making and unmaking of nations in their grasp; for gold, "the old man's sword," is as powerful a weapon to-day as ever Warwick the king-maker wielded in his.

All at once there came over these groups that curious crisis which suggests a kettle when, from simmering, it breaks into full boiling.

On the eddying current of speech the words, "Fort Sumter fired on," "War declared," "Virginia ready," might be heard, crisp and decisive.

A bracing and stiffening in face and shoulders seemed like an involuntary response on Arthur's part.

"The die is already cast," he said in low tones, too absorbed in the scene before him to turn to watch the effect upon his companion. A gasping sigh as she swiftly rose from the seat she had taken, made him turn.

What a transfiguration he saw in the beautiful face! All the hard surface-brightness was replaced by the glow of real enthusiasm.

A wonderful fire blazed in the great, hazel eyes, a red spot burned upon each check.

The haughty Artemis of the Louvre had indeed aroused from her white, stony calm into divine life and purpose.

"What are you going to do?" he asked, bewildered by the change.

"I am going home. What right have we American women to be dancing here, *now*. To-morrow I am going to arrange to go home as quickly as possible. I have money, and youth and strength. There must be some work that even such as I can do for the South. At any rate, I mean to try."

He looked at her with a new admiration and respect. Truly women must be more complex creatures in their good and evil than he had guessed.

All he said however was, "It is marching orders, for me too."

"For you?" she queried.

"Yes, I shall probably cross to London by to-morrow night's mail. That is headquarters for those who, like me, fish in troubled waters."

Impulsively she laid her hand upon his arm. "You won't fight against the South?" she pleaded.

He laughed in a very kindly fashion.

"No. I think that I shall try to fight for it. But I am only a poor mercenary, you know. And must follow my chances."

Presently as they moved towards the entrance he began rather awkwardly:—"If you are going to make such a sudden move you must have a great deal to attend to."

"I suppose so," was the absent answer.

"Perhaps I might be of some use to you, if"—he hesitated—"there is no one else."

She turned a grateful smile on him. "There is no one else, and though I think that I can manage everything for myself, yet it would be a pleasure to me if you could come and see me to-morrow—say déjeûner at twelve?"

He felt so sure that she needed a friend that he agreed, though at some sacrifice of his plans, and then, leaving her, went off to seek some of the young men at the English Embassy.

The next morning Antoinette was astir so early that many of her most important arrangements had been made before some of those who had been at the Tuileries, had aroused from their slumbers.

She had driven from house-agent to banker and steamship office, and then returning home had donned a long, white house-gown and was superintending the packing of her jewels and valuables. The first glow of enthusiasm had settled into the steady light of a fixed purpose.

All the morning as she pursued her busy way there was at her heart the pleasant warmth of knowing that she would have one friend to bid her God-speed on her new course. It seemed like an omen of better things to come. For all her dearly bought experience, there must be honest and brave men in the world.

She was standing in her small salon, at a table covered with various cases of jewellery. These she was dividing into two groups for the handling of her maid.

Neither had noticed that the outer door of the apartment had been left ajar, until Antoinette, hearing the click of the door-handle, turned, to confront Humphry Martin.

The days and months were drawing their incriminating lines around mouth and eyes, and a stranger would have given him a less ready trust than he might have done a year ago. His clothes were showy but not new, and there was altogether an air of bad luck upon him.

As for Antoinette, she might have looked upon a deadly snake with less horror of repulsion.

There was no craven fear in face or figure as she confronted him—merely this cold passion of scornful hatred for a defiling presence.

"*You!*" she said, in what, though so clear, was little more than a whisper. "I hoped that you did not breathe the same air as I did. You promised me when I gave you that last money not to follow me. Though, for the matter of that, why should I believe any promise of yours?"

Martin, with calm insolence, advanced into the room, closing the door behind him.

"Why indeed?" he echoed cynically. "Come now,

none of your heroics, please. You must understand readily enough why I have followed you. You don't suppose that I am going to starve while you are splurging round the Tuileries, do you?"

"But what became of the newspaper that I gave you the money to buy?"

"What a woman of business you are!" he scoffed.

"The newspaper, my dear madam, still exists in other hands than mine. The proceeds of its sale have gone in the cursed luck of the cards. And now I want some more money."

"Why should I give it to you?" she asked quietly.

"I only know that it will be deucedly awkward for you if you do not. I shall put some of these pretty trifles in my pocket, and I do not think that you will call in the police. Besides, you profess to hate my company. If so, you had better choose the quickest way of getting rid of it."

"I do not think that you are likely to follow where I am going."

The words evidently startled him, and he cast a quick glance of alarm at her.

"Not contemplating suicide?" he asked lightly.

"I suppose you have heard that war was declared yesterday?"

"What of that?"

Her face softened in what was almost pleading.

"I can hardly yet believe that there was not some good in you once. Has the knowledge that war was to come to your own home and nation not aroused one spark of manhood in you? Have you no desire to take your place among the others, and to fight for the right? Ah, think, only think, what you might yet be!"

For the first time a cloud of shame darkened his face, but it only brought with it a new sullenness.

"The first thing I was likely to be would be a corpse, I suppose. That would suit *you* very well, no doubt, but would hardly answer *my* purpose. Come, no more of this melodramatic nonsense. I want some money or I shall put some of these pretty things in my pocket."

With the fading of that last hope her weary scorn had returned.

"I would pay dearly to be rid of your presence, but you know how much you have had from me these last six months. I shall need money now to contribute to national funds."

Livid fury blanched his face.

"So it is at my expense that you would play the lady bountiful to the nation?" he snarled. "I suppose you think that you can buy your way back into the good graces of the virtuous ladies who have dropped you. But let me tell you that it will take more money than you have got to whitewash you."

"Softly, my friend, softly," came in a deep voice from the doorway, and they both started to see Arthur standing there. Bowing deferentially to Antoinette be said : "I am afraid you find your visitor too emphatic. May I ask who he is?"

Martin gave a measuring glance to the newcomer and underrated the strength of the sturdy frame.

"He is Mr. Martin, the co-respondent in the Castelle divorce case. I suppose our friend Captain Arthur is the man in possession at present. I might have known that—"

He got no further for an iron grip was on his collar, and he was shaken as a rat is shaken by a terrier. He would never again despise the power of that right arm.

"If you speak one more disrespectful word in this lady's presence I will first shake your teeth down your throat, and then hand you over to the police for a blackmailer. Oh, you may threaten to talk"—as an ugly snarl came from Martin—"I don't think the Paris police will bother much as to what you may say. Shall I put him out, Mrs. LeMoine?"

Antoinette silently nodded. She had had the money ready in her hand to give him, but would not yield to his threats.

In grim silence Arthur led him to the door, and in such fashion the man vanished from out her life for the time.

Arthur went down the stairway and saw him outside the great gates, and then, after giving certain instructions and a coin to the concierge returned. The face of mute, white anguish that Antoinette raised to meet him smote through all his wonderment and touched his heart.

"Do not try to speak of it now," he said kindly. "You are too played out to talk. You leave this afternoon at four for Havre ? Well, I shall come back at three to see you safely away from here. Don't be afraid."

"I am *not afraid*, but, oh, I am *ashamed, ashamed!*" and the wail in her voice seemed to follow him as he went.

That evening as he stood at the carriage window in the St. Lazare station, holding her hand in farewell she said:

"You have been a good Samaritan to me, binding up my wounds and pouring in oil and wine. You have almost made me believe again in human nature."

"Leave out the 'almost,' and take the belief as a good thing in a fresh start."

"A fresh start! Do you think it possible?" she asked wistfully.

"All things are possible to a strong will," was the hearty answer. "And now I must say good-bye. Though it is more likely to be *au revoir*, for we are sure to meet out there in the pandemonium that is coming."

As the train sped out into the country Antoinette sighed to herself, "If only I had known sooner that such men as he existed—strong and brave and faithful."

CHAPTER VIII

THE BLOCKADE RUNNER

"This is about the only spot where we may feel safe from spies and eavesdroppers, and act accordingly."

This one spot was the deck of a vessel, and the speaker was the man whom we have met before in Paris, now Captain Arthur of the Southern blockade-runner The Nighthawk.

Three years had passed since that evening at the Tuileries, when it had become known that the gage of battle had been flung down. They had been years of "storm and stress" to those whose hearts and lives had been drawn into the vortex of the great struggle that raged through them. Into many strange perils by land and sea had they brought Arthur. Now, perils and adventures were far from him in the peace of the evening hour and the sheltered harbour.

He leaned back in his hammock-chair with a comfortable air of possession.

The smoke of his cigar curled up into the still evening air, and the hum and stir of the city came off, subdued by the grey spaces of water and sky that surrounded the Nighthawk, where she lay out in the stream in Halifax harbour.

Northern cruisers might be prowling outside, Northern spies watching from the shore, but for the present she was in peace and safety, and in such careers men live for the day and not for the morrow.

A strange craft this vessel of the 60's would seem to us now, with her spars reduced to a light pair, and her lower masts without yards. Her dull grey hull was only eight feet above the water, and her funnel showed that it was telescopic.

Such vessels had become a familiar sight in the harbour of Halifax where the object of their existence was well-known.

It was that of getting successfully through the blockade barring the Southern ports as many times as possible, before, fate overtaking them, they should be towed as prizes into Northern ports, or else be burned to the water's edge to escape that doom.

The Nighthawk had already made a record number of trips in and out of Wilmington, and now with each fresh venture both captain and crew felt that expectation of a change of luck which comes to the fortunate gambler or to the man with a big score at cricket.

Not that Captain Arthur was the man to allow such a sentiment to be guessed at, or even to take definite shape in his own mind. It only lay there, unnoticed and unheeded, like many another queer little bit of philosophy evolved by his life of adventure. In some of the tightest moments of the last three years, in which tight moments had been by no means scarce, he had worn the same impassive bearing as marked him now in a time of apparent relaxation. His profession had become so ingrained as to be really a part of the man.

Face bronzed by many winds and suns; blue eyes made hawk-like in their keenness by long watching over the great spaces of the sea; true sailor's short thickset figure; sonorous voice with crisp accent that still showed the delicacy of modulation that was his caste mark—all these signs and symbols revealed the navy man used to the command of men in hours of storm and peril.

The woman to whom he had spoken was one who might well have brought a softness into the eyes of a man as strong as Captain Arthur, for it was Antoinette LeMoine who lay back opposite him in a hammock-chair like his own.

Perfect repose was expressed by the long slim limbs which formed another point in her resemblance to the Huntress of the Louvre. In her face, however, there was a tense, almost enforced, calm which seemed to imply suspense.

Her dress would have aroused the envy of any feminine onlooker in its novelty of Parisian fashion. And Parisian fashions were Parisian fashions with a vengeance in those days. Fancy a heroine of romance clad in the eccentricities that marked the zenith of Eugenie's Imperial splendour? What modern lover's heart could retain its fervour if its beloved were suddenly to appear in such a garb?

And yet, if all tales be true, love-making was carried on quite as successfully by those ladies in huge crinoline and towering bonnets as it is now by the "newest" and most up-to-date of women.

If those dames of yester-year did not possess the advantages of bicycling and golfing they made such good use of croquet and archery that it was perhaps just as well that they were not armed with more modern weapons of warfare.

Not that there were now any signs of such warfare in Antoinette's bearing. On the contrary it was marked by a quiet gentleness as, seeming to take Arthur's words as permission to ask a question, she said:

"Can you tell me when you mean to start on your next trip?"

For answer he turned his face towards the western sky, where the silver boat of a young moon sailed above the sunset glow, and the darkening town on its hillside.

"I cannot very well go before that enemy of our peace has condescended to make herself scarce. As you know, it is no joke to await the moon's rising when one is in the midst of a swarm of Yankee cruisers. It will mean a fortnight's waiting yet, I expect."

"I wish that we had been going a little sooner, but that will have to do. I was determined to get here in yesterday's steamer on that account," she said in a matter-of-course way.

"You propose going back with me?" he said, raising his eyebrows with a half-comic air of surprise. "Don't you know that I have refused a good half-dozen lady passengers? I am persuaded that they lessen the chances of coming out of this business alive, which I should prefer to do if possible."

She showed that she was hurt although she tried to answer lightly.

"I do not think that I lessened your chances that night off Nassau."

"How can you tell?" then seeing how he had wounded her, he added heartily:

"No, I must say that you were more plucky than

many men might have been. Ah! that was a night that I shan't forget in a hurry! On the whole, it was one of the riskiest passages that I have made," and he seemed heartily to enjoy the recollection.

The light had come back to her face.

"Then if you know that I shall not be a nuisance you will take me now, won't you?"

"That remains to be seen. There is no such hurry about it. I rather fancy from what the agent said that he has some orders as to your next move. At any rate he is coming off here to have a talk with you when it gets a bit darker. He apparently enjoys playing the conspirator in nocturnal prowls."

There was a blankness of disappointment in her face which reminded Arthur of a child trying to keep back its tears.

Although he did not trouble to make an effort to understand the source of her distress, he yet strove to divert it by saying cheerily:

"I suppose you don't know that I have been piling up riches since we last met. This blockade-running is turning out a regular bonanza to me."

"But I thought you were just paid by the trip, to run it for others?" she said, readily interested in all that concerned him.

"Yes, so I am, but I can always take some compact little venture of my own. A fair compatriot of yours gave me a hint that corsets were at a premium. When I was in Liverpool I invested in a thousand pairs at thirteen pence each, and sold them at twelve shillings ditto! There is a nice little sum for you! Coffin-nails and tooth-brushes were nearly as good a speculation.

As for quinine, I could hardly get enough of it. So if you add to that the purchase of a few private bales of cotton at threepence a pound, which sells in Liverpool at half-a-crown ditto, you can have some idea how I am raking in the shekels. At this rate I shall only need to make one or two more trips, and then I shall be able to go back to the little island, bless her, and settle down as a gentleman at ease."

The graver aspect that underlay his words seemed to have struck his listener. She asked anxiously:

"But if little, every-day things like that are so dear, life must be very hard for the people, the women at home?"

"Life in the South at present can hardly be described as, all beer and skittles for anyone," he answered grimly.

"There has, no doubt been a great change for the worse since you were there last autumn. The women, God bless them, are showing at home the same hero-ism in bearing privations and sorrow as are the men in hospitals and in the battlefield: a different type of women though from those who are flaunting their diamonds at the Tuileries."

He had not meant any personal taunt, for he had known of her being sent abroad on an important mis-sion, but she paled under his words.

With slim fingers, nervously interlaced, she leaned forward and spoke.

"Perhaps, wearing my diamonds at the Tuileries, I was doing more for my country than those good women patching and praying at home could ever have done? What influence could such as they have ever got over De Morny and his like?" she added bitterly.

"All the better for them, perhaps," he said gravely, and she caught up his words.

"The better for them, but what about their country? Was I thinking of what was good or bad for myself, when I went to ask favour from such men? He met his match in me, that chill-hearted spectre, De Morny! What woman with name and fame to lose could have done for the South what I did with him and his Imperial brother? But *I*—what do *I* matter when it is the South that needs me? If I lower myself for that, well—I have done so before. But why should I trouble you with my feelings ? As you say, the *good* women stay at home and weep and pray, and you all honour them. Well, so be it." Then in a softer voice she asked:

"Tell me, when you were at Charleston this last time did you hear anything of Edward Castelle?"

"Yes," and there was no sternness in Arthur's manner now. "I have been waiting for a chance to tell you about him. It is only right that you should know. I took a run up to the front after some hot fighting. By a strange chance, I was there when he was carried in dying. He had a bullet through his lungs, and they could do nothing for him. He lived for two days but never fully recovered consciousness. I stayed by him to the last," he said simply.

Antoinette had turned her eyes downwards to the gentle ripple of the water, and he could not see their expression.

She sat very still while there was a long silence between them, broken only by the distant city noises and by the harsh cries of circling sea-gulls.

There was an added shadow of the grey twilight over her when at last she spoke.

"Thank you. I am glad that there was one friend near him when he died. He has passed through his purgatorial fires, and has cleansed his soul in death. Perhaps I, too, may drink of the cup that he drank of, and, dying for my country, may be made whole."

CHAPTER IX

NEW FRIENDS

MRS. LEMOINE was apparently her usual serene self again by the time that the Confederate agent had come aboard, in the shadowy and noiseless fashion that his soul loved.

A few years before he had been a bookworm and historian, but was now transformed into a man of action in his country's service.

Too old and feeble to fight, he could yet give his brains to scheme plans, and his body to exile in her work.

A withered, sallow little man, his lips seemed pursed up as though from fear of letting out some secret.

No sign flitted through his gravity of any admiration for the beautiful woman before him. There was manifest, though, a certain dry enjoyment of her skill as he told her how much her success at the Tuileries had been appreciated.

"So much so that they pay you the sincere compliment of having more work on hand for you, dear lady."

"I am ready," she answered briefly; "only I trust that it is something open and above-board this time. I want to go back now in the Nighthawk—back to the nursing in the camp hospitals."

Her eyes spoke the entreaty that she could not bring

her lips to voice. She had long since resolved to do any task that should be set her "for the South."

Impervious to her wish, the little man chuckled.

"It would be sheer waste to use so fine a tool for such rough work that any old mammie could do as well. No, we are not going to risk your strength like that. I am sorry to disappoint you, but there is a strongly expressed request from Richmond, that you should remain in Halifax until further notice. Of course they claim no power to *order* you," he added.

"Oh, I fully acknowledge their authority. They know that they may command me."

"It is like your loyalty to say so. Do not be afraid. We shall find plenty for you to do here."

He looked over his shoulder to see if the captain were near, but at the beginning of their conversation, Arthur had strolled off to the other end of the deck.

"I think that a Major Warwick, an artillery officer for this garrison, was one of your fellow-passengers on the Asia," the agent suggested.

Antoinette seemed to gather some significance from his word, and a great sadness came over face and voice.

"Oh, that is it, is it?" she said in a hopeless sort of fashion. "Yes, I can do pretty well what I choose with him already, I fancy, if that is what you want. Only remember, he is an honest man and a gentleman." Then, with a sudden flash, "Oh, I should like some straightforward work!"

There was only the interest of the mechanic, experimenting on intricate clock-work, in the inscrutable face into which she looked.

"As I said before, dear lady, the fine tools to the fine work, and surely I could not pay you a higher compliment than that? Yes, I think that it is desirable for you to cultivate your friendship with this Major Warwick. He is fire-master, and might have it in his power to be troublesome about powder and such little contraband matters. Then you must get intimate in the house of a certain Alderman Evans. He has some sort of an afternoon entertainment to-morrow to which I have arranged that you shall go. He is a strong sympathiser with the South, and is also making very pretty little pickings out of the blockade-running business here. Of course we are in thorough touch with him, but we might need a woman's hand on the reins, if anything very special should be required from him.

"He is an able man, and can do more for us in the powder line than anyone else can. He has a nice quiet place on the shore, with a little wharf that a schooner could run up to, and big store-houses at his adjoining foundry. Altogether a very desirable acquaintance."

"And his family?" she asked.

"Two nice-looking daughters. Some people say that he is a widower—others that there is an invalid or lunatic wife somewhere in the background. If there is, she counts for nothing."

Antoinette bowed her head in silent acquiescence, and he went on:—

"You must take a place in society, too. That is an easy enough matter, for these English army and navy people are ready to lionise any Southerner. The Governor, who is General as well, is a bachelor and a wonderful old beau, so that he will be your humble slave, as a matter of course."

"Anyone else?" she asked with quiet bitterness, to which he responded serenely:—

"Those that I have mentioned are the most important. Many other social matters will be placed in your hands no doubt. We have a certain number of Southern ladies here at present; but those with any brains are old and ugly, and the beauties are all fools. It is unfortunately so common an occurrence," he added regretfully.

With a shade of apprehension in her manner, Antoinette asked the names of these ladies, looking relieved, as the agent ran over the list.

"There is no one whom I have ever known," she said; "but what if any of my former friends should appear, and attempt to ostracise me?"

"You must have established your position so strongly by that time, that the women need not matter. You must surely be above minding any slights of petty, feminine malice?"

" I am long past it," she answered, smiling strangely; but she did not claim to be above it.

The next day was one of the earliest and the loveliest of the brief, sweet, northern summer. Antoinette breathed with delight the soft, pine-scented air, as she stood on the wood-circled lawn at Trafalgar with her host, Mr. Evans.

A heavily-built, burly man, with thick, dark hair and moustache, high colour and shrewd black eyes, good-humoured, and in a certain practical way, powerful, Evans, merging now upon his fiftieth year, was not a bad type of a successful, self-made man.

Numerous were the irons that he had in the fire in the working of various gold mines and the opening up of a new line of railroad. He also threw his usual energy into his duties as Alderman.

As the agent had said, he was sometimes supposed to be a widower; but there were some people who knew that his wife had been for many years in a lunatic asylum in Boston.

His eldest daughter was named Mabel. Her delicate, Madonna type of beauty went excellently well with the ritualistic mania which had recently reached the town from England, in the advent of a sensational garrison chaplain, and which had engulfed her in its fascinating round. Her young fastidiousness of taste, that made her shrink from many things in her father's surroundings, she dignified as the superiority of a poetic nature. Her idle self-absorption she regarded as the mysticism of religious feeling. It was delightful to her to dwell for hours on the interesting sins and virtues of her own nature. It was delightful to be associated in a round of church decoration and services with cultured English clergy, in whom she caught glimpses of a society totally unknown to her.

She had a sweet, weak voice, and was, in a surface fashion, musical, and this threw her more familiarly into the clerical coterie.

Fortunately, for her, the chaplain, while in one way a mystic, had another side of the trained common sense of a man of the world. She was one of a type that he commonly met, and he knew how to put a wholesome curb on the enthusiasms of his female devotees.

Hattie, the younger sister, was of a rounder, muddier,

more mundane and less ethereal aspect. A kindly, frank young nature looked out from her brown eyes, and smiled upon her richly-tinted face.

Frankly devoted to the joys of frivolity as she was, it was she who knew most of her father's affairs, she to whom any of the household came when afflicted in body or mind. Though not of correct beauty like Mabel, she was yet a pretty bright-faced girl.

Both sisters had enough of their father's power of will in them, to use each one her own habits towards the end of making for herself a more assured standing amongst the garrison and other best society of the place.

In this element Evans had never yet succeeded in being thoroughly at home. It was like him to recognise this aim of his daughters, and tacitly to assist them in it, treating it with the respect which he gave to all efforts at worldly success.

Evans looked upon this social standing as a necessary preliminary to the girls making good matches, which he fully intended that they should do.

An indulgent and a generous father, he had a private dreamland tucked away in his mind in which they had no place. In it he saw his girls married and liberally portioned, and himself free to make a fresh start in life in some country where no one knew of the poor lunatic wife.

There the money which the Civil War was helping him to pile up would enable him to live in luxury.

And in that dreamland he saw himself with a beautiful, well-bred woman by his side, a woman upon whom it would be a delight to lavish his riches.

What a surprise it would have been to his daughters and business associates, if the carefully hidden, romantic streak in the nature of this hard-working man could have been revealed to them!

But we all walk with our inmost being inexorably veiled from those around us, even perhaps from those nearest to us.

Not only had the Civil War added largely to Evans' fortunes, but it also seemed to have brought the looked-for social chances.

As the agent had said, Southerners were the fashion, not only with the English garrison folk, but with the Halifax people as well.

In his Southern partisanship Evans was sincere enough, but it was like the man to turn it to good account.

Through many an act of real kindness he had made Trafalgar a great haunt, indeed a sort of headquarters, of some of these poor Southern folk, glad to seize any distraction in their weary waiting on fate.

So one of the curious side-eddies from the vortex of the great struggle had the result of bringing the Evans family into a new social prominence.

On this bright June day, then, fairly numerous notabilities were amongst the groups gathered on the Trafalgar lawn, with the ostensible object of playing or watching the new game of croquet.

Mabel, in pure white, looked, as she received the company, like a St. Cecilia or Elaine, who had strayed into such a position in her visions.

Nothing could seem more high-bred than this dreamy detached attitude!

Hattie, whose white muslin was brightened by rose-coloured ribbons, fluttered about with a fair-haired artillery youth in tow.

Captain Arthur was there, looking, as Antoinette was quick to note, very much at home.

She was surprised, and that not pleasantly, to notice how he seemed almost to be sharing Mabel's preliminary work in getting the games under swing.

Antoinette herself was the object of much notice. In those days fashions did not spread as quickly as now. She was thus a very striking figure in her emerald green "gauze de Chambèry," with the *chic* little round turban which Eugenie had introduced that year at Compiègne.

"A hat, my dear! It really is a hat and not a pie-dish turned upside down! Just let us sit down here and take it all in at our ease," said one dowdy-lively English woman to another.

Mr. Evans deserted his duties as host to devote himself to Mrs. LeMoine, who, for her part, found the new type interesting enough to her keen wits. She was intolerant of nothing, save stupidity.

Presently, on the plea of showing her the landscape, Evans led her down a shady path to where a little wooden jetty ran out into the water.

Standing on it, one looked down the inlet between low, wooded hills, for about two miles to where the harbour broadened to meet the open sea. A trim, little yacht lay moored near the wharf.

While Evans stood feasting his eyes on this fair high-bred woman who excelled his most cherished ideals, Antoinette studied her surroundings. She recalled the agent's words, and marked the advantages of the place for any quiet work.

"Down there the water meets the harbour, doesn't it?" she asked.

Evans seemed to follow her line of thought, for he answered with a smile,

"Yes, it would be a simple thing to slip down from here to join an outward bound vessel. Wasn't that what you were thinking of?"

"Yes," and she laughed lightly, though there was a great yearning in her eyes. "I want so much to go back in the Nighthawk. It was with that expectation that I came here, but the agent tells me that they wish me to stay."

Evans gave one keen glance at the wistful face, and then asked with unaccustomed gentleness,

"Cannot you be content to rest among us for a little while? We will do our best to make the days pleasant for you."

One look up to meet his earnest gaze told her that this man might be as wax in her hands.

"I am sure of that. I have been told of your goodness to our exiles," she said with drooping eyelids that had the effect of a blush.

It was not very long, however, before she had managed to turn their footsteps back up the bank again. Climbing the path towards the lawn, they saw numerous couples scattered through the vistas of pine trees.

With a sudden tightening of heart Antoinette recognised the slim white figure of Mabel Evans, in a shady nook with Captain Arthur. It seemed to her that she had known for a long time that it must be so,

although it was hardly an hour since the first premo-
nition of his devotion to this girl had come to her.

The two were about equal in height, and he was
standing looking earnestly into her face, whilst Mabel
was looking down, with her own seraphic gravity, at
some flowers which she held in her hand.

The father gave vent to a pleased chuckle at the
sight.

"A fine honest fellow, Arthur," he said. "I could
hardly wish for a better husband for my girl, if she
would take a fancy to him; but she is only twenty, and
her head is still in the clouds with parsons and
churches and all that sort of thing. There is no hurry
about it, though I cannot understand any girl liking to
moon about after parsons, when a fine, honest sailor
shows such a fancy for her as Arthur does."

Mrs. LeMoine tried to think of some appreciative
remark, but she could only feel how steep the path
seemed to have become; how slippery the pine nee-
dles under her feet.

"He certainly seems very devoted," she managed to
say at last with dry lips.

"Oh, yes," Evans answered comfortably. "He has
been out here nearly every day on one reason or
other, since he has been here. I think he told us that
you and he had known each other before?" he added
inquiringly.

Secure as she felt in Arthur's honour, a chill seemed
to come into the summer sunshine, but she answered
bravely:

"Oh, yes, I knew him some years ago when he had a
command in the Chinese navy. Since he has had the

Nighthawk, I came out with him from Wilmington to Nassau. It was splendid to see him one night when we lay with Yankee cruisers around us. It was all but dawn, and only a light haze hid us from them; but he got off by sheer daring. He seemed positively to enjoy the danger."

"And I am sure that you gave him cause to admire your courage," Evans said with an admiring glance.

"He said that I was not a nuisance, and that was high praise for him. He is not given to enthusiasm," she said with a careless laugh.

All the time she was haunted by the unguessed-at depth of earnestness that she had just now seen in his face. Ah, why had she with all her beauty and her wit never been able to stir him to such feeling!

And the chill breath of defeat came to her through the summer sunshine.

CHAPTER X

KINSMEN

"ADVENTURES to the adventurous" was a rule that had held good in Captain Arthur's case.

As a midshipman in the English navy, he had been wounded in the storming of the forts at Sebastopol. Barely recovered from this wound, he had arrived on the East Indian station in time to go through some of the worst fighting of the Mutiny in the heroic Peel's Naval Brigade.

Peace had not suited his character as well as action. He had fallen into the hands of an aggravating captain, and, in a fit of insubordination, he put himself so seriously in the wrong, that he had no choice but to give up his commission.

It was then that he had taken his Christian name of Arthur when in bitterness of heart he had deemed himself disgraced for life. But he got his chance in the Chinese navy, and, steadied by the first rebuff of fate, had done manful service there. Through ten years of hard work, he had only taken that one holiday when we met him in Paris.

After that, followed the three years of American blockade-running. Into these last years had been crammed enough perils and excitements to have filled the lives of half-a-dozen men.

The adventurous voyage, that Mrs. LeMoine had

made with him, had been to her filled with a new, strange sweetness. So were the ensuing idle days at Nassau, when they were both detained nearly a fortnight in that languorous, tropic land. It was such a wondrous and novel thing to her to look into a man's face, and read there high purpose and dauntless spirit. In all her twenty-five years he was the first man who recalled to her the traditions of her own race—of men who

> "Did their work, and held their peace
> And did not fear to die."

During those Nassau weeks they were each alone and each idle, and it was natural that they should go about together.

Arthur's kindly, but brusque, consideration for her comfort had warmed her heart, and sometimes brought day dreams of a brighter future. Doubtful of her power, however, for the first time, she never felt sure of his being thoroughly under the influence of her beauty.

It was pathetic,—the way in which she craved this one man's love and respect. If only she could have that, she thought, she might yet forget the bitterness of her earlier years, and know serene, contented days. It seemed so easy to get the homage of other men, while with this one, it was always thus far and no farther.

Kindliness and frank comradeship he had given her, but she was too clever not to know that there was an impregnable, inner citadel that she could not attain to.

In spite, though, of her unacknowledged misgiv-

ings, when she turned her face eastward on her mission to Paris, and Arthur went back into the perils that
encompassed the beleaguered land, she nourished a
warm hope in her heart, and counted the days until
she could see his face again.

Now, this long-looked-for meeting had brought her
nothing but disappointment. Yesterday her quick wits
had forewarned her that he was not as much in touch
with her as when they parted.

To-day, she had seen him, heedless of her presence—seen his face bent in grave, concentrated tenderness on the fresh, young Madonna beauty of
Mabel Evans.

That was the look that she had guessed that his face
could wear, and had craved as life's chiefest gift. Now,
she had seen it given to another.

As soon as she could possibly do so, she had made
an excuse to leave the party, and return to town and
to solitude.

In her dreary little hotel bedroom, she sat for
hours, without even exerting herself to take off her
hat and gloves. But it was not her first solitary watch
with sorrow, and from such hours she had learned to
wrest strength, not weakness.

Meanwhile Captain Arthur, after thoroughly enjoying those golden hours at Mabel's side, had ended up
the day at the Artillery mess.

He had been often enough in and out of Halifax
harbour, with pauses there, to feel quite an old inhab-
itant of the place. There were army men there, who
always looked to hear his latest tale of adventure, and
sighed that such diversions might come in their way.

It was a period of profound peace in England, when the Manchester school held sway, and some of the country's bravest were driven to seek their native atmosphere of danger in service under foreign flags.

Many were fighting in the South, and all took a passionate interest in the war. So it was no new thing to Arthur to be seized upon by some cheery, cheeky, English youth, and carried off to the mess.

Here he was, as usual, overwhelmed with questions as to his latest trip, and what he had seen of the progress of the struggle.

He told them tales of the mingled tragedy and comedy which make up the round of life. Flushed and smiling from the applause that a comic anecdote had elicited, a curious chill came over him, when, on the entrance of a newcomer, he was introduced to Major Warwick, the new fire-master.

Looking into the face of this big, stolid, man of the Viking type of Englishman, it was a strange sensation to know that he bore his own family name, came of the same race as himself.

Warwick was the name that he himself had dropped in the bitterness of his spirit, when he had exchanged the English for the Chinese navy.

This newcomer was his cousin, the son of the man for whom his father had been disinherited.

There was a mingled tumult of feeling in this encounter. There was the subtle race sympathy which outlives so much, and which can revive even through periods of hatred. There was also the pride of the man who had fought his way to his place, face to face with the kinsman whose path had been made easy for him.

Both sentiments were there, and the die between them was cast, by the frank grave eyes that met his inquiring glance.

It was almost to his own surprise that Arthur found himself saying what he had resolved not to say.

"I wonder if you happen to know that I am Arthur Warwick's son?"

The reserve of Major Warwick's manner changed at once to heartiness.

"Arthur Warwick himself! So it is! I see it now through all the changes, with the old touch of the family faces at home!"

"I did not know that you had gone into this blockade-running business! The last that I had heard of you was when I met Tyndal, after the Chinese war, and he told me what a lot of kudos you had got."

"More knocks than kudos," his cousin commented grimly. "But you—I see a ribbon there. That is New Zealand, isn't it?"

"Yes. Nothing much to be proud of, though the Maoris were splendid foes. But I wonder I did not think of you when I heard of Captain Arthur. Strange to say, some men at the club were talking of this blockade-running just before I came out. Tyndal was there, and said, 'Bet you anything that Arthur Warwick is somewhere in the scurry. If there happened to be a little row on, in "the red planet Mars," he would turn up there somehow?' It set me thinking that I might come across you somewhere out here. I'm very glad."

Arthur had flushed with pleasure at hearing that men had not forgotten his name. "Good fellow, Tyndal! Always makes everyone out better than himself. He almost apologised for his V. C."

Both men shared in the pleasure of the novel sensation of meeting a kinsman, and when they parted that evening Major Warwick had promised to dine the next night on board the Nighthawk.

In the summer twilight, the two sat on deck and talked, over their cigars. They had in common some boyish recollections of one or two holidays, when the only son of the family black sheep had been admitted to his grandfather's home for inspection.

They had chummed together without any jars. Neither had been of the kind to be fretted by the inequalities of fortune that gave one cousin, ponies, pocket-money, clothes, such as the other had never dreamed of.

If the paths of the navy cadet and the Woolwich boy had not lain so widely apart, they might have grown up into mutual friendship.

From boyish recollections they passed to their subsequent doings by land and sea.

Presently Arthur asked, "And you only arrived here two days ago in the Asia?"

"Yes, a delightful voyage. Perhaps, as you seem to be in with these Southern folk, you have already met Mrs. LeMoine, who was a passenger. Fine woman!"

"Yes, I have met her about the world at different times." Arthur answered dryly.

He had not noticed any special enthusiasm or meaning in Warwick's tones, but from loyalty to Antoinette, he always spoke of her with caution.

A sudden idea seemed to come to Warwick.

"Why, I believe, it must have been you of whom she

spoke. She said that she had run the blockade out with you, and was going to join you here to go back again."

Arthur did not notice what a highly privileged individual his cousin evidently thought him.

"Yes, it was I," he acknowledged. "But she isn't coming back with me, thank goodness! She finds herself detained here by business, greatly to my relief. As you can guess, it hardly adds to one's ease of mind to have a woman on board when you get into a tight place. One has enough responsibility without that. Besides, I have an absurd idea that she brings me ill-luck."

Warwick laughed, and in self-defence Arthur told the tale of their voyage together.

"But that was not ill-luck when you got off safely."

"It was a close shave, and the shave might be too close next time," he persisted.

With a passing scoff at a sailor's superstition the subject passed. Neither guessed at what might have made such a difference, the one man's infatuation, or the other's knowledge.

"If we are going to the Governor's ball, we had better be off," Arthur said, rising and stretching his arms.

It was a brilliant assembly that night in the old Government House, built by Sir John Wentworth in the last year of the past century. The English fleet had come north to their summer quarters, and a French flag-ship had left the Newfoundland fogs, on a polite tour. These two, with the military, furnished a great variety of uniforms.

As the two men stood together in a doorway, taking in the scene, Arthur heard a low "Jove!" of surprise from Warwick. Looking at him he saw that his eyes were intently fixed on Mrs. LeMoine.

She stood under the chandelier having one aspirant after another for dances introduced to her.

There could be no doubt that, in her rose-coloured draperies and shining diamonds, she was the most brilliantly striking figure of the evening.

The black-haired niece of the American consul held her own defiant court in a primrose-tinted dress; so that men said to each other, "What are your colours, rose or yellow?"

The full charm of the most beautiful women is not evident until they are seen in evening dress. When Major Warwick greeted her, the first glance into his face told Antoinette that the man was bewildered with admiration.

He had claimed an early dance which she had saved for him, and after it they were resting in seats at the end of a series of rooms.

Antoinette had been trying to find out all she could as to the intercourse of the two cousins. She had known, in a vague way, that Arthur had changed his family name, but he had never chosen to tell her what this name was.

The news of their relationship had thus come as a surprise to her, and perhaps not a very pleasant surprise at that. As she pondered over it seriously, she felt that the fact could scarcely fail to have some personal effect upon her.

Nothing of this showed, however, as she said with bright interest:

"And it is evidently a case of love at first sight on

both sides. I'm so pleased about it. I like my friends to like each other."

"It's almost strange that you never heard his real name. It's not as though he had any reason to hide it," Warwick said thoughtfully.

"When you have seen more of Captain Arthur you will learn that he is not given to unnecessary speech or confidences."

It was only a statement of fact, not a complaint, and as such Warwick took it.

"A good trait in an Englishman. I hate those men who are always talking about themselves and their feelings."

" I shall take care not to confide in you then," she laughed.

"I said *men*. Women are different. If you, of all women, should ever choose to honour me with your confidence, I should be raised in my own estimation by the fact."

It was with a quick thrill of shame, that Antoinette marked the deep earnestness of his voice. What right had she, for any cause, to be trifling with such a man as this.

She turned her gaze over the crowd, so as to escape the meaning of his eyes. The vista before her was closed in one end of the ball-room, and she saw Arthur standing there with Hattie Evans on his arm.

But whose was that pale, blond head with the malevolent, light eyes which now met her own, as the man stood directly behind Arthur. She barely started; her fingers only closed sharply over her fan as she recognised her evil genius, Humphry Martin.

For a moment all sense of probability or reason was merged in the panic of deadly fear for Arthur. A vision swept over her of a swift knife thrust into his shoulders. As in some ghastly nightmare, she watched for what was to come, feeling helpless to move or to call out to warn him.

Her dry lips parted without the power to cry out.

It was for such a passing moment, this overmastering panic, that Warwick, who had stooped to pick up her programme, never noticed it.

Her self-control was regained, and, as the music stopped and Arthur and his partner walked away, she drew a deep breath of relief.

Martin had slunk out of sight, and, she had a little time in which to think.

Glancing casually at her programme, she said: "This next is Captain Arthur's dance, and if you will tell him where I am, I shall stay here until he comes."

But Warwick, stretching out his long legs, answered coolly:

"Now, I am afraid that my new friendship hardly runs to such quixotism as that would be. '*J'y suis, j'y reste*,' as MacMahon said. May not I wait here until he is clever enough to find you out for himself?"

Hiding her impatience as best she might, Antoinette yielded; but the minutes seemed endless, before the music began and Arthur appeared.

"Take me somewhere where we can talk," she demanded, when Warwick had turned reluctantly away.

Arthur felt bored by her eagerness. There is nothing that men dislike so much as confidential interviews with women with whom they are not in love. However, he led her to a refreshment room, almost empty at this hour.

"Never talk in dark corners," he remarked parenthetically, as they seated themselves. "By Jove!" he said as her story was told "so he was at my back, was he? Though I doubt his having the pluck to do one any real harm." A sudden idea seemed to come to him. "He must be the new Northern spy whom I was warned would be here to-night!"

"A spy! Can he have sunk to that!"

A flush of intolerable shame burned red in her cheeks, that such a creature should ever have come into her life. Arthur may have understood the feeling, for he said in a kindly way:

"It is unfortunate, but you must not be too worried by it. There are dozens of others about everywhere, and your recognition of him has helped to put us on our guard. It is always in the novelty of the spy that the danger lies. As soon as they are known, they become comparatively harmless."

"You feel sure that he has only come here as one of their usual spies?" she asked, seemingly relieved at the idea.

Seeing this, Arthur stifled his own doubts, and reiterated the assurance.

"Keep to the big rooms and the crowd, to-night. Avoid any confidential conversations, and let me take you back to the hotel at half-past one. By-the-bye," looking down at the starry diamonds that followed the soft curve of the neck, "it's a pity you wore your necklace to-night. It lets him know that you have it with you."

She made no protest against such a view of the man, but answered absently:—

"Yes, I will have them locked up in the hotel safe to-morrow"—then with a troubled pallor in her face—"Do you think that it means any danger to us?"

"Danger?" he said cheerily. "My dear lady, don't we both live and move and have our being in danger, and what does a little more or less matter?"

There was no boast in the words, only a simple statement of fact, and she knew it.

"Will he try to blackmail?" she went on in low tones.

"Just let him, and we'll soon settle him." Arthur spoke bravely, though knowing well what harm the man might do her.

"Besides, he is probably under orders, and remember, this is a civilised country. He can do neither of us any harm, save through our own blunders or cowardice. The first we *may* commit—but not the second, I think, eh?" And he bent one of his infrequent smiles upon her.

As he had expected, she answered to the spur.

"Don't be afraid for me," she said proudly. "As you say, danger is no new thing. I carry a revolver."

CHAPTER XI

"OUT TO MOTHER CAREY"

THE time was drawing near for the Nighthawk to start on her next trip.

Anyone watching carefully Captain Arthur's movements (and that there were several doing so, he knew), might have supposed him to be utterly absorbed in society.

He enjoyed nothing more than to get a spy in tow, and entice him out to Trafalgar.

Here, after basking in Mabel's smiles for as long as possible, he would start out with the girls in their little boat, getting them to land him at some road that led back to the town.

Having thus dropped the spy, he would get some important visit paid before he had been again tracked.

Sometimes, he would go on board of the flag-ship where he was always sure of a hearty welcome. At the end of his visit, he would have himself landed at some out-of-the-way wharf, repeating the same manoeuvre with schoolboy zest. To have seen the hearty enjoyment which the man put into such little daily incidents, no one would have suspected him of having weighty and perilous matters on his mind. The Nighthawk, too, looked as idle and as innocent of serious preparations as her master.

All the same, cautiously and gradually, the work of getting her cargo on board went on.

"Blankets, shoes, chloroform, quinine, hardware," Arthur conned over his lists, with a grim smile bestowed on the last word "hardware." It perhaps resembled charity in its covering powers.

Meanwhile, the summer's feasting and fun and love-making went on heedless of the sorrows of nations. Arthur added his quota by issuing invitations for a big picnic, "down at Purcell's Cove."

The cove was a sheltered, little hollow facing the entrance to the harbour. Its steep hillsides, clothed in a thick growth of low whortleberry bushes, gave it the look of a Scotch loch. Across its entrance lay a fantastically shaped island, an ideal spot on a summer evening, when the great stretch of water lay glassy calm, stirred only by the slow breathing of the sleeping sea outside.

The company arrived in various craft. Major Warwick brought a shipload in a military tug. The flag-ship sent launches and big boats. None of the boats or men of the Nighthawk, however, seemed to be on hand. As the long day faded into evening, a heavy sea fog rolled in over the sunset. It happens so often in those early summer months that no one seemed to heed it. Indeed why should they when they were busy feeding, with the primitive and cheerful greed of civilised folk at a picnic.

Only Arthur took, every now and then, long, keen looks at the closing-in horizon.

"I told you that with this wind we were pretty safe in counting on the fog," he said with a casual air to

Evans, as he poured a soda into his whiskey.

Often as Captain Arthur had manoeuvred his ship in hours of danger, he had never spent more skill on it, than he brought to bear now on getting Mabel Evans into a somewhat isolated corner at this repast. His duties as host were forgotten, or left to Evans and Warwick.

He saw only the sweet, delicately-tinted face, as sweet and as delicately-tinted as the northern Mayflower, and with something of that same sense of austere, northern chill in its beauty.

But if those blue eyes were cold, he was only conscious of their purity. If he longed to disturb the soft serenity of her smile, it was from his desperate sense of the shortness of the hours in which it might still gladden his heart.

"My own society on the high seas will be rather a come-down from the happy days that I have been enjoying," he said, in an effort to interest her in his near future.

"Yes, you must sometimes find it very dull," she responded with polite sympathy.

If it had been anyone else save Mabel, he might have laughed aloud at the girlish inadequacy of the words.

As it was, he said:

"Well, there isn't much *dulness* around when there are 'cruisers to right of one; cruisers to left of one, cruisers behind one,' especially as they very often 'volley and thunder.' One hasn't much time for recollection then. It will be in the days without adventures that I shall long for a sight of Trafalgar and its chatelaine," he added in a lower voice.

Miss Mabel's sainthood did not exalt her altogether above the mundane joys of admiration. She sent a responsive glance and smile towards him, which made his pulses leap, even while she inwardly shrank a bit at the fervour in his voice.

She belonged to the type of woman that has an implanted distaste for scenes, in contradistinction to the hysterical type that lives upon her own emotions, and those which she arouses in others.

"With good luck, I ought to be back in six weeks," Arthur went on, emboldened by her smile—"and then—you won't have forgotten me altogether, will you?"

Under the friendly shade of the grey twilight, his face looked up passionately into hers.

"Oh, I do not forget my friends as soon as that," she responded serenely.

"Ah, but I want so much more. I want to know that I count for something in your life! Mabel, won't you let me have that glove?"

A dainty pearl-coloured pair, lay on her knee, and with determined hand he seized on one.

"Ah, but it spoils the pair!" she protested practically.

"Then I shall take the pair, and bring them back to you. I am your knight now!" he said triumphantly. I shall wear them in the I 'dies irae' of battle, and they will bring me good fortune."

She made a pretty little movement of distaste. "No knight of mine, in that horrid money-making block-ade-running! If it were a work of high motive and aim—!"

Arthur loyally tried not to show how her foolish words had pained him.

"The Queen can do no wrong!" was his motto. "It strikes me that there may be worse deeds than taking quinine and chloroform to the sick and wounded; shoes and blankets to those who are sleeping on the bare ground," he allowed himself to protest.

But he could not be angry with her, and broke out with sudden fervour.

"Say a kinder word than that to me before I go! For I am going now, and it may well be, that I never come back!"

Mabel sat staring, unable to grasp his meaning. She hated any unexpected demand upon her sympathies or understanding. She would have liked to have all the emotions of life marked off beforehand for her, like the church calendar.

She knew the proper sentiment for Christmas and Easter, but she was not equal to impromptu ones.

Arthur had caught and pressed her hand between his own, and with one last, lingering look into her face slipped away down the bank.

In the cold, grey fog-shadows Antoinette sat apart, awaiting her last few words with him, as the famished amidst a shipwrecked crew await the last distribution of food.

Her wistful eyes were fixed on the girl to whom Arthur was giving all those last precious moments, which would have been such treasures to her.

Sitting on the beach, among the big, tide-worn boulders, she was quite remote from the gay groups on the bank. At a little distance from her, Evans was superintending the erection of a bonfire of driftwood, which remained as yet unlighted. The slow plash of the sea against the shore came in from the fog with a sense of mystery. Listening intently, she had, a few moments before, heard the steady beat of a steamer's machinery draw nearer, and then become suddenly silent.

As Arthur approached, she stood up restlessly, and showed a little packet of letters in her hand.

"Here are my letters, all ready for you. They are in cipher, so that you needn't bother about destroying them, if"—her lips seemed dry and stiff—"if necessary. But will you pass on the message to Richmond that the ammunition and the powder will be ready for your next trip? You know where to leave it in Wilmington, and it's just as well not to put it on paper." Here her efforts at a business-like tone broke down into the intensity of low-voiced entreaty, "And promise me that you will get leave for me to go back with you next time."

Her touch on his arm irritated Arthur's highly wrought nerves, so that he had to put a control, upon himself not to shake it off. He tried to make his answer as friendly as possible.

"That is not in my hands, remember, but I will speak of it. We all know that you will not desert your assigned post." Then, with a second thought, he added in a brusquer tone:

"By-the-bye, I have been watching Warwick with you lately. You mustn't make a fool of him, remember."

It was a cruel blow to every instinct. The shadow of utter hopelessness dropped over her face, as her hand fell nerveless from his arm.

"He must take his chance. Is he such superior clay to the rest?" she said with a jarring laugh.

The dry branches and driftwood of the bonfire caught the match, and a flare of orange light shot up, intensifying the outer darkness.

"Jove! It's time to be off!" Arthur said at sight of it. With a perfunctory grasp of Antoinette's hand and "good-bye," he had hurried over to Evans' side.

Leaning her arms on a great boulder, Antoinette bent forward to watch for what was to come.

Almost as a response to that first glare of light the rhythm of heavy oars sounded out of the fog, and all at once the shadows dropped away fully to reveal a heavy ship's boat, which, shooting round the island, ran into the beach close to the bonfire.

It seemed like a momentary vision that Arthur had sprung in and taken his place in the stern, while the boat was backing out again.

As she swept past the shore, the dancing light played full upon them. The gay folk on the bank above had evidently all at once awakened to the inner meaning of the festivity. It seemed to strike their fancy that they had been brought here for the purpose of masking Arthur's departure. There was a sudden babel of voices, then, as he waved his cap to them with a cheery shout of "*Au revoir*," there rang out a sudden hearty cheer. Then Warwick's deep voice started the rousing strains of "Dixie," and, with a universal impulse, young and old took up the song.

But Arthur scarcely heard the cheering or the song. His eyes were strained in one last look at a girl's fair face, and she—she never even troubled to watch him away, but stood with her smile bent down on Warwick, who stood a little beneath her on the bank. Evans had come over to Mrs. LeMoine's boulder and stood beside her.

They two, further out from the shelter of the bank than the others, were the only ones to notice that as the boat vanished into the fog, a green rocket shot up from the hillside across the cove.

It came from a part of the hill that faced out to sea, and could easily be seen from there.

"A signal to the cruiser outside!" wailed Antoinette.

"I told Arthur that it would take more than a picnic to bamboozle those cursed spies. He *will* make a jest of everything," broke angrily from Evans.

Then seeing from the droop of Mrs. LeMoine's figure against the rock how overwrought she was, he tried roughly to reassure her.

"There can be no real risk for him in this fog," he said cheerfully. "Even if there *should* be a cruiser lurking outside, which I very much doubt, he has only to keep within the shore limits until he gets a good chance of slipping past. You need not worry for the fate of your letters. But it is nervous work for women. You would be all the better for a cup of coffee, or a glass of hot wine. Just stay quietly here until I come back."

To her relief he was gone, and she was free to let the sickening tide of desolation sweep over her unrestricted.

Turning her back upon the bright fire and the noisy surrounding groups, she stared out into the blue-grey void, into which the one human being whom she cared for, had vanished.

Ah, if only she might have gone with him and shared his perils!

CHAPTER XII

AT BAY

AFTER the picnic Antoinette spent a troubled night.

When she did sleep, it was only to see fiery serpents darting through the fog to where Captain Arthur stood upon the deck of the Nighthawk.

She had to make an effort in the morning, to rouse herself to go forth to an interview with the Confederate agent.

It was Sunday morning, when the city wharves were abandoned to the sunshine and a few drowsy cats and whirling pigeons. In their solitude they made a good meeting-place, and on one of them, seated on a fragrant pile of fresh lumber, the withered little man and the fashionable woman talked of the affairs they had with equal intensity at heart.

"There can be no doubt that a cipher letter from Benjamin to us has gone astray," the agent said gloomily. "It refers, I fear, to the ammunition for the steamer. If they have been able to decipher it, it will serve to make them doubly keen to get hold of these. The spies would get any price for them. You can hardly be too careful."

"These" were a small package of letters which he proceeded to hand to her.

"You bad better keep them about you always, until you feel that you can destroy them, and then do not delay over it."

"When is the attempt to be made on the steamer?" she asked, but all the answer was:

"That does not concern you or me. We need only see that our share of the work is done. You must show an interest in the scheme to Evans, and keep up his interest in getting the ammunition ready. Make him feel his own self-importance. That is what fetches him."

"Very well," she acquiesced.

Presently, after a few more directions, the agent shuffled away.

In the days that followed Antoinette was very gay, though haunted always by the thought of Arthur's peril and by the memory of that last wistful gaze at Mabel. There was a great restlessness upon her which often drove her out to seek the solitude of the woods and seashore. In such places alone did she seem to find calm. It was thus that she started out one morning, before the dewy freshness was gone from grass and air.

Leaving the town behind her, she took her way along the shore of the woodland park where it stretched toward the sea. That open line of harbour-mouth seemed to bring her nearer to her heart's desire, far away from the weary, futile round of life in this alien land.

She made her way out on to some low shelving rocks, where the soft sea-breeze met her with its prom-ise of future wanderings, and where the great stretch of harbour lay unrolled before her. She recalled the grey Nighthawk where she lay in the stream on that day when she paid her first visit on board, and wondered if she should ever see her there again.

Lost in such thought, she was quite unconscious of her surroundings, until recalled to the grimmest reality by the grasp of a hand upon her shoulder, and by the sound of a hatefully familiar voice, and turned her head to meet the cold grey eyes of Martin.

"Well met by moonlight, at least by sunlight, fair Titania! You are not so well surrounded by your bodyguard as at the ball! And so your valiant Captain Arthur has gone off and left you, has he? Well, he is most likely in a Northern prison by this time. However, you won't mind that, if Major Warwick replaces him. You see, I know all your little affairs. No, don't move! See this little toy! It politely requests you to hand me out your papers, and its requests are generally complied with."

The sun glinted on the steel work of a dainty revolver, that was pointed at her breast.

A passion of helpless rage, at the man's touch, and at her own carelessness which had put her in his power, swept over her. Reckless of consequences, she shook her shoulder free from his grasp.

"Take your hand away from me. Its touch sickens me!" she panted.

"I remember the time when you were not so particular," Martin sneered—then with sudden imperiousness: "Come now, no more nonsense! You must have known that, sooner or later, I should get the better of you. I want the letters that that little rat gave you on that quiet wharf, on Sunday morning. Oh, you needn't start! I should have thought your nautical friend would have taught you the use of glasses!"

His fluent taunts had given her time to recover her second and calmer courage. She knew that the man was a coward and despised him as such.

"Do you suppose that I am a fool enough to carry important papers about me on a country walk?" she asked scornfully.

She was, all the time, keenly conscious of the pressure of the letters inside her corsets. But her bluff was unsuccessful.

"You carried them on you two days ago, so it is natural to infer that you do so now!" was his cool retort.

Her mind, strung up to keen activity, went back at once to a fainting fit which had overcome her in the close hotel dining-room, at the end of that long, hot Sunday after the Nighthawk's departure. She remembered how, on recovering consciousness, she had found herself on the sofa in the ladies' waiting-room alone with a fragile-looking, little woman whom she had never seen before.

Her dress had been unfastened, and her first conscious thought had been to feel for the letters, and find them safe. Even then, she had been relieved at learning from the Irish chambermaid that the stranger had only been alone with her for the brief moment, when the other had gone to fetch the brandy—too short a time apparently in which to do her work.

Now, with quickened memory, it seemed to her that she had been roused to consciousness by groping hands about her dress.

In spite of a sinking at heart, she still showed a brave

face. Her eyes searched desperately the white slopes of road that led townwards for some signs of life. Even a nurse-maid and her charges might help to drive him away.

There was no sign of fear in her answer:—

"It's no use trying to frighten me with that ridiculous thing! I know quite as well as you do that it would be your ruin to shoot me! You would have to clear out of the place as quickly as possible, and your value in your honoured profession would be gone, even if you didn't get hanged for your pains."

Her coolness was having the effect of irritating Martin—a result which she trusted to make for delay, and delay was her only hope.

He was quick enough though, to notice how intently she was watching the road, and sneered viciously:

"You need not look for help. No one is likely to come at this hour. I shall have plenty of time to find what I want. Turn out your pocket first."

There was nothing for it but to obey, if she would postpone a struggle until the crucial moment when he was near success. She did not mean that he should have the papers without a struggle. And then came a sudden thought of the bright, calm water. She could swim, and she would rather trust to it than bear his touch.

And with that thought, her fortitude had come back.

Meanwhile, she emptied her pocket before his greedy eyes. She rejoiced to think that there were one or two cipher memoranda in her card-case of little real value, but which might distract his attention.

He had opened her purse which contained nothing save a few dollar notes. His eyes gleamed as he found the papers in the card-case, and turned them over. "I thought we should find something," he announced triumphantly. "This is a cipher, and you must read it to me."

"Give it to me," she said, stretching out her hand, but he put it aside.

"Softly, if you please. You can read it while I hold it."

She hardly heard his words, for every fear was lost in a glorious heart throb of relief. She had seen on the causeway by Steel's Pond, Major Warwick, in uniform, coming slowly towards her on horseback, evidently on his way to the forts.

Quick as thought, she had struck up the revolver, which going off, acted as an alarm. She seized the papers from Martin's grasp, calling out all the time in her full clear voice: "Major Warwick! Help! help!"

With a snarl of rage, the spy turned to see Warwick dashing forward up the slope—a splendid, warlike figure. He knew at once the game was up, and that he must look to his own safety.

"I might have known that such as you don't walk in the woods without a rendezvous," he panted. "However, another time! Meanwhile to remember you by, I'll take this."

"This" was a locket with a large diamond star, which hung inside her dress but of which his keen eyes had marked the chain showing at her neck. She tried to catch his hand but he was too quick for her. With a mocking laugh, he vanished into the thick spruce woods, just as, with a great clatter of accoutrements,

Major Warwick drew up. She had sunk limply to a
rock, and with dishevelled hair and white face stared
up at him. Her dry lips, through which the quick
breath panted, seemed unable to utter a sound.

Warwick sprang from his horse, crying, "You are
hurt! I am sure you are hurt! Do try to tell me."

He took her cold hands into his, rubbing them with
gentlest touch. Presently the ghost of a smile flickered
on her face and a whispered "Don't be afraid; I shall
soon be all right," reassured him.

That first, faint reaction, after standing at bay, had
been genuine, but in its prolonging there was a
remembrance that she did not want Warwick and
Martin to meet. She could not bear that this man who
honoured her should even see the face that had cast
so dark a shadow on her life. But Warwick was not one
easily delayed from his purpose.

Once sure that she was not injured, he prepared to
turn his attention to the man who had molested her.

"Who was he and what did he want? "he demanded.
"He cannot have got far by this time, and I must go
after him."

But Antoinette, in her eagerness, laid a detaining
hand upon his arm.

"You could never find him in those thick woods. I
know who he is. He is a Northern spy in search of
some papers which he thinks are in my possession. I
blame myself for having been so foolish as to come to
such a lonely place, when I had been warned against
him."

"But this is shameful. Such an outrage cannot be
allowed. I *must* find him," Warwick broke out impetu-

ously, but she answered with gentle decision:

"I do not wish him found. I beg of you to do as I ask and let him go. There are many risks to run in our cause, many mysteries in its service. This is one, and my friends will do me truest service in not tampering with it. You saved me from his ill-treatment, is not that enough?" and her smile was as wine to him.

"Thank God that I did," was his fervent answer. "But it is the idea of danger to you that I cannot stand. He fired the revolver, didn't he?"

"No, I struck it up when I saw you coming, to make you hear. The revolver is only bluff on his part. He could have had no gain by killing me. I knew the worst he could do was to annoy me in his search for the letters." Then, with a laugh, she added, "Come, instead of hunting spies in the woods, you shall see me safely back to the haunts of men, before you go to your work. That is, if you have time."

"Time! As if I should not make time for that, if the General and the whole garrison were waiting!"

And so they turned townwards, Warwick leading his horse beside her.

In spite of all her wiles, she could see that his face was troubled, and knew that he would not easily be put off the scent. As they parted, he urged:

"You will at least promise me that, when the desire to ramble seizes you again, you will call on me as escort? I only give up my search for the man on the condition that you do not go about in that lonely fashion again."

"What a tyrant you are! I promise then," and she smiled up into the grave eyes that looked down so tenderly into hers.

As he rode away she smiled no more, but sighed for what might have been once, for what never could be now, that she could be a fitting wife for a brave and honest gentleman.

CHAPTER XIII

TRAFALGAR

ANTOINETTE had not long left Major Warwick, before her brain was busily sorting out the pieces of the new puzzle.

Of course, it was some weeks since she had first known that Martin was haunting her, but while Arthur was there she had felt that he dared not openly trouble her. Then the man had so completely disappeared that she had felt able to believe Arthur's assurances that he had left the city, afraid of Arthur's knowledge of him.

Now, if ever he had left the town, he had returned, and Arthur was not there to stand by her.

She felt so helpless in her ignorance as to how much the agent knew of her past life. How much should she tell him of what had occurred? And Evans, whom she had been told to trust in, what did he know of her, and how much would be guess?

If only Arthur had been here, she could have got him to tell them about Martin's attack on her, secure in his discretion.

Her life had, however, been one to teach her the lesson that women are longest in learning, that of self-reliance.

She was so thoroughly imbued with the impersonal spirit of her work that all sense of isolation and fear was put aside, and after a systematic rest, she made her confidential report to the agent.

His pained disapprobation of her carelessness struck her as almost ludicrous. But although he had given no sign of it, he must have felt some concern for her safety, for that afternoon brought a visit from Mr. Evans. He had heard the tale from, the agent, and strenuously insisted that Mrs. LeMoine must at once remove to the shelter of Trafalgar.

"I should not be able to sleep at night if I knew that you were alone in the hotel. Why, the villain might get in and murder you."

"Why should he want to murder me?" she asked, striving with all her woman's wit to read in his eyes if he knew of any connecting link between her life and Martin's. But the shrewd business man was a match for her, and his face kept its own secret.

It was thus, with an undefined dread of his power, that she yielded to his demands and had arrangements made for her to move the next day to Trafalgar.

All the same, when she was settled there, the pleasant sights and scents of wood and sea had a cheering and reviving influence upon her.

She was glad to be diverted from graver thoughts by the presence of the two sisters. Hattie Evans' warm, almost affectionate, welcome was like the friendly greeting of some pet animal. A little touch of excitement was added by Mabel's dignified airs of polite indifference.

This frigidity veiled what in a plainer or less saintly young woman might have been more easily recognised as a prolonged fit of sulkiness.

For the last few weeks, Mabel had been so patiently toiling at her pretty web of observances for the undoing of Major Warwick. She received some measure of encouragement from his evident desire to be intimate at Trafalgar. It was some time dawning upon her that this desire was founded on the hope of meeting Mrs. LeMoine there, but at last she knew that, when his divinity was present, he was but barely conscious of any other woman's existence.

And so, as was her wont at times when in any way her supremacy seemed threatened, Mabel absorbed herself in a maze of ecclesiastical doings, wearing costumes that were poems of asceticism, ostentatiously keeping every possible fast day.

The worst was, however, that no one seemed to care much. They did not even make any comments on the smallness of her appetite. Hattie and young Adair, the fair-haired artillery youth, were enjoying themselves immensely at croquet, rowing, and strawberry eating.

Mrs. LeMoine when alone was absorbed in her toil over ciphers and letters. Or else, when not busy, she would sit in absolute stillness listening to the soft murmur of the pine trees, as though their voices held some secret which she might learn.

Major Warwick managed to come frequently, and generally at times when the master of the house was absent. Antoinette had noticed an extra reserve and gravity in him when brought in contact with Evans, which betrayed that he found him uncongenial.

To Warwick, when he came, her manner was always marked by the same gentle almost wistful kindliness.

And the master of the house? Did he too hear a dif-

ferent voice in the pine trees, as he sat on the verandah beside that fair woman, and talked for hours to
her of the cause that lay so near her heart.

Any man who, day by day, would bring her fresh tidings of the great strife, which in these summer months
was slowly but surely inclining to weigh down the balance against the South, must have had the power to
bring the feverish light to her eyes, the pained flush to
her check, and this power held its own danger for the
rash mortal who woke the haughty Diana into life.

Not that Antoinette did not, in her calmer
moments, walk warily with Evans.

She had seen enough of the world to be quick to
recognise the vein of unscrupulousness that lay
behind his bluff good-nature. She knew that if she
should once allow his admiration for her to come to a
crisis, there could be no arousing in him of the chivalrous quixotism that she felt she could count on, even
to his own disadvantage, in Major Warwick.

It was a golden July evening and the girls having
gone out in their little boat, Antoinette sat talking
with Evans in the verandah.

The tidings he had brought engrossed her whole
attention. At length the long schemed attempt was to
be made at seizing an ocean steamer by means of
Southerners disguised as passengers.

"My share of the business is to get the schooner that
is to meet them in the Bay of Fundy loaded with
ammunition here, without their spies finding it out. It
won't be too easy a job," Evans announced.

"What a true friend you have been to the South,"
she murmured. She did admire in the man his enthu-

siasm of partisanship. Although he looked pleased he
answered honestly: "Oh, well! You are a clever enough
business woman to know that it has been to my profit.
I never expected to be as rich a man as these blockade-
running ventures have made me. But money apart,
this war has given me some new beliefs. I had no more
thought possible, as a present-day event, that men and
women would give up home, fortune, life itself for
their country, than that I should meet St. Peter going
round raising dead people. Now I know differently."
Antoinette's spirit flashed responsive.

"You *do* believe then, that we all, good, bad or indifferent as we may be, have that one supreme hallmark
pro patria, don't you?"

"I do. I have been seeing it for months."

"And I am sure that, apart from any business profit,
you do wish to help our cause, don't you?"

"Yes. And above all I wish to help *you*."

She had made a mistake, and given him his chance
to sound the personal note. At the intensity in his
face, Antoinette strained her ears to listen for the
sound of the girls' voices or their returning oars, even
as she answered softly:

"I have good reason to know that you do. Are you
not helping me now in giving me a shelter here in this
quiet haven by the sea. It has been such a rest to a
tired wanderer in alien lands. I wonder," with a sigh,
"if I shall ever see again my home in Georgia, and the
poor, simple negroes who love me. I grow very home-
sick for it all."

Evans hated to hear her speak of anything that
might carry her out of his reach.

"At any rate, you cannot go back there until the war is ended?"

"Why not?" she asked.

"Do you realise what a war-devastated country is? he asked impatiently. "Don't you know that you would only be returning to all sorts of privations and hardships."

"If others must endure them why should I not share them?" she said, and then with a sense of relief: "There are the girls at the landing. Shall we stroll down to meet them." She rose and walked forward, and Evans had no choice but to follow.

The next afternoon there was a group gathered on the shady Trafalgar lawn.

Mabel was in a state of seraphic exaltation over one of the rare visits of the garrison chaplain, her spiritual guide and ideal. That individual, being an honest and shrewd man, found it wisest to keep himself hidden from too much feminine worship. In his society Mabel forgot to feel aggrieved at Major Warwick's presence and absorption in Mrs. LeMoine.

Adair and Hattie formed a cheerful couple in the background of a group, none of the component part of which seemed as though it would have much attention to bestow upon the master of the house, who presently drove up the avenue.

Mrs. LeMoine, though, was always on the alert at his appearance. Now as Evans approached and handed her some notes, she saw in his face that he was the bearer of news and awaited it with that little chill of suspense which was so ready in those days.

Evans gave no sign until he was seated in a deep

chair beside Antoinette. Then he began:

"And who do you suppose has been within a mile or two of you to-day?" he said, addressing Mrs. LeMoine, but still in a tone that all could hear. "Indeed sitting here on the verandah, you might have seen the smoke."

It was from Antoinette's lips, not Mabel's that broke the low startled cry:

"The Nighthawk!"

"You are the only one who remembers absent friends, Mrs. LeMoine," Evans said approvingly. He was vexed to see that Mabel had scarcely turned her eyes from the face of her clerical idol.

"It *was* the Nighthawk, and fallen upon unlucky days, too."

And then he went on to tell how, from the first start, the ship had been delayed by fogs and by pursuit, until her captain had been eventually forced to put into Bermuda for coal.

Overcrowded with the coming and going of the blockade-runners, and in any case badly drained, the little town of St. George's was a hot-bed of yellow, fever. No sooner was the Nighthawk outside the reefs than the disease broke out among the crew.

As the ship would not have been allowed in any Southern port, the only resource was to turn north-wards, and that morning the Nighthawk had appeared at the quarantine station, had landed her convalescents and put to sea again.

Evans paused, and Warwick's even tones were heard saying, "I wish that I had known."

A grey, swirling mist seemed to be wrapping round

one of the listeners, putting their faces and their voices at a great distance from her, but with all her strength Antoinette clung to reality.

She *must* not faint under Evans' keen gaze. There was Mabel's sweetly serious face opposite her, with its usual shell-pink tint undimmed. She was not pale.

Evans went on: "But before they left, I went down in the quarantine boat, and exchanged some shouted remarks with Arthur. I saw with my own eyes that he, at any rate, was anything save yellow, and he said that he felt fit as a fiddle. He sent regretful messages to Mrs. LeMoine and you girls that he could not see you. So I think that I deserve a vote of thanks from his admirers," and his good-natured glance went from Mabel to Mrs. LeMoine.

But the latter heeded it not. All that she was conscious of, was the fact that Arthur was speeding away to sea, carrying the danger with him as he went, that he had been so near without her seeing him.

"Oh, you might have taken me with you!" she murmured reproachfully.

Even as she spoke the words, she awoke to their folly, as she saw all the attention of the others turned to her.

Mabel's grave gaze seemed to have in it an intolerable touch of pity. Warwick was evidently pondering the reason for her distress, while she could see that Evans ascribed it to his usual feminine attribute—nerves.

"I shouldn't have startled you," he said, penitently. Then Mabel's soft voice broke in with its caressing tones:

"What an enthusiastic friend you do make, dear Mrs. LeMoine," she said innocently. But her foe was all her keen self again.

"Perhaps, dear child, if you were cut off from your home, a solitary wanderer, you would be disappointed at losing any channel of communication."

And Mabel was silent before the tone of sad superiority and the hated "dear child"!

Warwick settled the victory by saying, "If I had known, I would have taken you in the engineer boat, Mrs. LeMoine. It would have been nice to have had even a shout from Arthur."

CHAPTER XIV

THE NEW SPY

ALTHOUGH every graceful line of figure, every glint of light on golden hair, every smile in blue eyes or on the curves of Mabel's fresh, young lips acted as a fretting sore to Antoinette's jealous heart, in reminding her of one to whom each charm was so dear, she yet tried her best to maintain friendly relations with the girl. Occasionally she was driven to use her keen tongue to keep her in order, but Mabel was quite aware that she was no match for the older woman, and generally contented herself with a system of defensive warfare.

Finding Mabel one day in difficulties over some church embroidery, which she had undertaken with the zest of inexperience, Antoinette had offered the aid of her skilled fingers and convent training. What Mrs. LeMoine did, Hattie was eager to do too, and so she also was toiling at cutting out patterns of conventional lilies and passion flowers. In the big sunny morning-room at Trafalgar, the three women, different, yet all young and good-looking, presented a very happy family aspect, one morning, when a woman who had applied for dressmaking work was shown in.

As, in a pleasant-enough voice, she explained her wishes to the sisters, Mrs. LeMoine watched her with that careful scrutiny of strangers which had grown habitual to her.

The longer she looked the more strongly she felt an unaccountable aversion to the thin, pale, little woman with the tired aspect, together with the conviction that she had seen her before.

All at once she had caught the loose thread of memory after which she had been groping, and at the first pause said, in a casual fashion:

"I think that it must have been you who was kind enough to help me that day at the hotel when I fainted. I was sorry not to have a chance to thank you."

That her shot had gone home she knew by the hostile glance that flashed furtively upon her from that meek face, flashed and had fallen before the quiet, ready answer came:

"Yes, it was me. I was very glad to do anything for you. I happened to be waiting for an order from the proprietor's wife, when one of the waiters called me to help you. I saw that you were alone."

"I am much obliged to you," Antoinette said with a strong effort at unconcern. Martin's words as to the letters having been on her removed any chance that the woman might be speaking the truth. However, she had better find out all she could, whatever the purpose might be that had brought the woman there.

And so she went on: "You are an American, I think?"

This time she was even more sure of having struck the mark, although the explanation of being a Nova Scotian who had learnt her trade in Boston was perfectly possible. She had no desire to give the woman any excuse to return, and so said that she had no work to be done, and, with a glance and a sign, made Hattie follow suit.

In Mabel's present humour this was quite enough to make her engage the seamstress to come the next week to do some sewing for her. As soon as the woman, who gave her name as Mary Johnson, had left the room, Hattie asked impulsively:

"What was the matter, dear Mrs. LeMoine? I could see that she worried you. Why, you are looking quite pale still! You didn't want her to come here to work, did you?" with an indignant glance at Mabel, who was innocently stitching away at her lilies.

Antoinette was more provoked than she usually allowed herself to be at the girl's tacit opposition. She was annoyed, too, at the feeling of intangible fear which the presence of this quiet little creature had aroused in her. So she showed an unusual touch of bitterness in her answer.

"It is only that I am sure that the woman is a Yankee spy, sent here for some unknown purpose. You heard her acknowledge that she is the woman who helped to revive me at the hotel one evening when I fainted. When I knew what was going on, I found her fumbling at my dress where important papers were hidden. Pah! I seemed to feel the touch of her clammy fingers again, when she looked at me just now!"

"We must send a note at once to tell her not to come, but—oh, only think, she never gave any address! How stupid of us!"

Here Mabel, looking up from her work, with an air of injured mildness, said:

"Don't you think it is a pity to be quite so imaginative? The woman looked such a harmless insignificant little creature. Really, if this spy mania goes on I shall soon expect to have our old Irish washerwoman barred as dangerous. And there will be bombs or hidden letters in the butter and eggs! Housekeeping will not be very easy under such circumstances."

But when Hattie was once aroused, she did not mince matters with her sister.

"Don't be spiteful and talking nonsense, Mab," she said sharply. "You know that father won't stand any of your tricks about that kind of thing, and that you'll be sorry if he finds out."

And as Mabel happened to be very well aware of the fact, she merely retorted:

"It's a pity that you should be so unlady-like when you get excited," and walked off with injured dignity.

This girlish skirmish had passed unheeded by Antoinette. As she leant across the table to draw her work-box towards her, she saw between two reels a folded piece of paper, which had not been there half an hour before.

While seeming to be idly turning over her working implements, she had unfolded the paper and read the few lines traced on it.

They ran thus:

"If the lady desires to open communications for the purpose of securing silence as to her past, and of regaining possession of her diamond locket at the expense of a paper or two, a red ribbon dropped by the right hand gate post at twilight will procure an interview. She must come alone, if she wishes for any result."

With a start Antoinette looked around her, feeling as though Martin's hated touch were on her shoulder, his hateful voice in her ear. She had recognised his writing on the paper.

The sunny morning calm was so undisturbed that she could hardly believe the thing had been possible, but, as soon as she could, she got away to the quiet of her own room.

What was she to do? She could not very well ask the girls to keep this visit a secret from their father. She herself, by foolishly speaking out, had made it of too great importance for that. The question was, if Evans knew part, must he not soon learn all?

Her whole nature of "*grande dame*" shrank from having this self-made man, towards whom she graciously stooped, aware that that contemptible thing, a paid spy, had ever had any place in her life.

There was no one else to whom she could turn for advice in the matter. She felt that the agent would give her no personal consideration, save where her usefulness was concerned, as one of the pawns in the great struggle.

Long she sat and pondered, while the midday heat waxed heavy and then waned towards evening.

At length, as it drew near the hour when Evans might be expected home, she rose and made a careful toilette.

She had decided on playing a bold game. She would show the note to Evans; would tell him that this man was trying to blackmail her so as to get information out of her. She would see what he thought the best line of action to take, trusting to her power to influence him if her opinion did not agree with his. Having thus decided, she took good care that Evans should find her strolling in the grounds, well within sight of the house, however, and keeping in the open, for every bush and tree now seemed a menace to her.

She was dressed in the full white muslin of the day, and, as she stood there under her white parasol, the flickering sun and shade playing about her, her face softened by the lassitude of past excitement, Evans felt his breath taken away by her beauty.

He listened to her story and read the note with silent attention, then, handing it back to her, said gravely: "I cannot bear to think that such creatures should succeed in annoying you while in my house. I thank you for having trusted me in the matter. I shall strain every nerve to crush them." He paused and drew a deep breath, and then spoke in a more business-like voice: "I see that this reptile pretends to have known you before—a regular blackmailing dodge which must be put a stop to."

Antoinette noticed that as he spoke thus his eyes did not meet hers.

After a moment's thought, he went on: "We won't go to the agent about this. I think we might just as well keep it to ourselves. You may depend upon it, although this creature makes a threat of publicity, it would suit him no better than it would you at present. If you have the courage for it, I should be inclined to bluff him. Would you appear at the gate alone and act as a decoy to draw him inside the grounds?"

"Yes," she answered, steadily. "But what comes next?"

"That depends upon him. At any rate I should be behind the bushes with a revolver. I am a pretty sure shot, and if I were to lame him when he was molesting you within my own grounds, it wouldn't be a very serious matter, even if it came to the police court. At any rate, it would prevent his creeping and spying for a time."

"You are methodical, even in assault and battery," Antoinette answered, breaking into an hysterical laugh, then pulling herself together she said firmly, "Yes, I will do whatever you tell me to."

Evans inspected her critically but saw no sign of shrinking. "All right," he agreed, briefly.

"But won't they keep a sharp lookout to see if I am alone?" she asked.

"That's all right. I can go around while they are watching you down the avenue."

The dusk of evening was gathering under the pine trees when Antoinette's white figure passed slowly down the road to the gate.

Evans had taken a path which led from the stables through the shrubbery to meet the larger road at the entrance. Her white dress showed ghost-like through the shadows, and in one hand she clutched a knot of blood-red ribbon.

Feeling that worst of things—the presence of an unseen enemy—she would have given much to look around for some sign of Evans' neighbourhood, but that she must not do. Every group of shadowy trees seemed to her fancy to be endowed with a possibility of venomous life.

Something of the unreasoning terror of a child alone in the dark came over her as she neared the grey granite gate-posts, and it required all her determination to make her take the first step outside their imaginary shelter. It was done, though, and the knot of ribbon lay on the grey dust. "Red as blood—red as blood," she found herself muttering. The charm worked quickly. As, at the sound of a jeering laugh, she involuntarily started back, the bushes opposite parted and Martin stepped out.

Instinctively she obeyed Evans' careful instructions, and, as the spy crossed the road, she slowly retreated back into the avenue.

Following her at a little distance, he began, and at the first sound of his voice she guessed that he had been drinking to encourage his wits.

"Ha, ha, my pretty lady! I thought that I should draw you this time! You don't exactly want all your fine friends to hear the story that I could tell of Mrs. Castelle's little doings, do you? And you *do* want that locket with your mother's hair in it back again, don't you? What a thing old acquaintance is for putting us up to each other's weak points, isn't it?"

It was agony to stand there helpless and to know that Evans would hear whatever this man's fantastic humour chose to utter. She must at least make an effort to stem the tide.

"Say what you want, and make an end of it," she said sternly.

"Patience, patience! You shall hear what I want fast enough. First of all, I want to know if you are prepared to give me the real story of this steamer lot and when and where it materialises? Or are you going to read me one of those cipher letters we go hold of, or how are you going to earn your locket and my silence?"

His voice had risen with harsher and more threatening tones. Antoinette, in the fear of his making a sudden spring upon her, had never taken her eyes off him. But she felt Evans' presence near, and as the spy paused she heard his voice ring out strong and fierce, behind her.

"By this!" he said, as, putting the bushes aside, he covered the other with a revolver. A fierce oath was snarled out as a sign of defeat, preceding an angry torrent of words.

"Sold again! Bad luck twice, but look out for the third time! Truly the lady has a varied and watchful guard! Horse and foot! I wonder if they would be as vigilant, if they knew as much of her many adventures by land and sea as I do. Her notoriety at the Tuileries and her voyages with Captain Arthur are only recent history, and so probably known to them. But I think that they would agree that a lady shows a certain self-reliance, who at the age of twenty or so leaves her husband's home with your humble servant."

Motionless under this tirade as under a storm of blows, Antoinette stood, her whole soul crying out to the armed man beside her to defend her womanhood. But Evans did not speak until the other paused breathless.

"You have done your worst, and said your say. I waited to see what you would dare to do. Now go! and take that, to show how futile your threats are held."

"That" was a revolver shot which woke the evening echoes amongst the pine trees. With sure aim the bullet cut a track along the fleshy part of his leg, so that in pure terror the man stumbled to the ground with a howl of pain.

"Fork out the locket," came the stern order, and grudgingly he obeyed, flinging it on the ground before Antoinette. "Now go! And remember that on the third time you spoke of, you will not get as much mercy as this!"

Still covered by the revolver the cowed creature picked himself up and limped groaning away.

Still Antoinette never stirred or spoke. Evans stooped and picking up the locket laid it gently in her hand. Then she slowly raised her eyes and looking into his face shrank back before a certain new sense of power that she saw there.

"Why, I have known it all from the first. He has made no real difference," he said in a low voice, drawing her hand through his arm to lead her back to the house. She walked beside him with the captive weight upon her spirit. Is there any prison so dire as that which we build for ourselves, out of our past?

CHAPTER XV

TRAPPED

IT was only a few days after this that Evans had to leave home on one of his many enterprises—this time, as Antoinette knew, to personally superintend the loading of the ammunition on the schooner that he had spoken of.

An intense longing for the freedom of solitude had been growing upon Antoinette. She saw that it would only entail a struggle of wills if she should let Evans know her purpose. But the day after his departure she made an excuse of necessary frequent interviews with the agent to return to the hotel. She had learned her lesson and went abroad warily and in her own room kept her door carefully locked. She did not intend to fall into Martin's power if she could help it.

Again he seemed to have completely vanished, and she could not but hope that he had left the place, though she dared not count upon it as a certainty. Knowing more people, invitations came in increasing quantities. The old general had grown very fond of including her in small informal dinners which usually ended up with ecarté or nap.

Warwick was sometimes, but not often, at these entertainments, for he was somewhat fretted at the lively old Irishman's free-and-easy devotion to Mrs. LeMoine, and at her cheerful reception of the same.

However, he was often tempted by the mere chance of being in her presence. This had been the case one dark night when a wild, southerly storm was coming up from the sea.

He had secured the privilege of taking her to her carriage, and as he did so, he said earnestly: "I hate your driving home alone, like this. I wish that you would let me go with you."

"That wouldn't be proper at all. It would shock the hotel people," she laughed back carelessly, taking her seat.

No sooner had Warwick closed the carriage door than a horror of some close, unseen presence came over her. She knew that there was someone in the carriage with her. The lights were still shining on Warwick's face as she tried to call out to him, but the windows on both sides were closed and the rain beat against them noisily. Then, as the carriage had driven off quickly into the night, she felt a strong arm grasp her, while a handkerchief was pressed to her face loaded with the heavy breath of chloroform, before which her brain reeled in waves of increasing dizziness.

As the void seemed to grasp her spirit she realised with exceeding bitterness that Martin's third time had come.

When her surroundings once more became real to her she found herself still driving on in the darkness. Her arms were stiff from being fastened together at the wrists by what seemed like a tightly knotted handkerchief.

That she was on a solitary country road she guessed by the complete darkness, and by the slow, uneven movement of the carriage as though over bad roads.

There was no room for more tangible fears when that silent, unseen presence was still beside her like a nightmare. The horror of it crushed any effort at pride or courage, and she broke out in a hoarse strained voice:

"For God's mercy, unless you are trying to drive me mad, speak and tell me who is, there! Is it Martin?"

A voice strange to her answered. "You shall see him soon. He will no doubt be flattered by your anxiety."

"Where are you taking me? What do you want to do with me?" she panted unable to keep silence.

"Martin can tell you that when he comes. It is his affair, not mine."

And this was all the satisfaction that she could obtain before the carriage stopped. The man beside her opened the door and got out. She saw by the faint glimmer of light that came from an open door that they had drawn up before the dilapidated-looking porch of a solitary white house.

"Get out," her companion said briefly, and his firm grasp on her arm led her into the bare passage and up a tumble-down flight of stairs.

There were no signs anywhere of previous occupation save the dim lamplight in a garret bedroom into which he hurried her. Her quick, wild glance around showed her a few articles of shabby furniture such as might be found in any poverty-stricken old farmhouse.

Of her captor's face she could see nothing under the shade of his soft, slouching hat save a straggling black beard. With even that dim light her worst panic had passed and she did not feel that horror of him which the mere thought of Martin's presence inspired.

She fully realised in what an evil case she was, but was absorbed in keeping every sense on the alert.

Seeing that he was about to shut the door on her, she made her one appeal, though with little hope in it.

"My hands! Oh, surely you are not going to leave me helpless like this!" and she reached out towards him the bare, white arms whose beauty might have softened any heart.

The pitiful words and action were without effect. "It will be safer to leave them so until the morning. It won't do you any real harm," he answered in a matter-of-fact way. The door was closed; she heard it bolted on the outside, and Antoinette was alone.

The effects of the chloroform still weighed upon her with a dull drowsiness which certainly helped to dull her mental sufferings. However, she made a determined effort not to yield to it until she had looked carefully about the room.

The windows she found had been whitewashed over, and apparently nailed down from the outside. It was a comfort that there were no other doors. Against the one that she had entered by she managed to shove a heavy chair, so that the room should not at least be stealthily entered if she should sleep. There was a chimney with an open hearth but it was evidently not large enough to offer a possible means of escape or concealment. Still she was thankful for it as ventilating the unaired room with its choking smell of damp, decaying wood and mildewed feathers. The bed had a rough, old rug thrown over a feather-bed and pillows, and here in utter weariness of body and soul, she sank down.

A strangely forlorn figure she was in that sordid room huddled there in her costly dinner dress and opera cloak.

She did make an effort to keep awake and on guard, but it was of no use. Sleep came in short, troubled snatches, from each of which she started in fresh alarm. At last the early July dawn aroused her through the uncurtained windows to a full wakefulness and a complete realisation of her position.

She had no hope of rescue, for she could see how cleverly the thing had been planned for Evans' and Captain Arthur's absence. Indeed she had but little hope of escaping with life itself, but a strange indifference numbed her spirit and gave her a certain courage.

A flash of vindictive triumph temporarily aroused her, as she said to herself: "At any rate, my diamond necklace and those letters that they are after, are in Evans' safe, out of their reach. But, oh, if I only had my revolver!"

It seemed to her that many hours had passed since the sunlight first tinted the windows, and yet no one had come near her.

She knew by one or two sounds of movement below that she was not alone in the house. Once she thought that she heard a woman's voice, and the sound encouraged her.

There was some food on the table—a jug of milk

and some cold meat and bread. She knew that she would be safe in eating it, for they would attempt her no harm until they had made use of her. So she resolutely set herself to eat and drink so as to maintain her strength.

As she wondered what would be their next move, she tried to keep at bay that horrible curiosity as to what means of compulsion they would attempt in order to wrest her secrets from her.

Could it be possible that they would dare to torture her? It seemed incredible when she knew that she could only be an hour or two's distance from friends and from the powers of the law.

Ah, but she had the means to defeat that. She had not embarked her womanhood in the dark ways of warfare without having in hand the one supreme refuge.

She rubbed her arm against a hidden inner pocket and felt the hard pressure of a little, silver smelling-bottle that held the means for a swift and painless entrance into the cold "frustration of death"! "They shan't drive me to that if I can help it. I will make a fight for life yet. It would be ridiculous for a body like mine, for brains like mine, to be destroyed by such as they."

As she thus stayed herself with what strength she could, she heard the soft roll of wheels, as upon grass.

With heavy choking heart-throbs she sat still upon the edge of the bed, listening, listening.

Presently there came slow uneven footsteps upon the stair, and a wicked smile curved her lips as she muttered, "Limping still!" Harshly the bolt cracked as though new; the door dropped open, and she saw the expected figure of Martin.

With smiles like those of two lost souls meeting in the nether world, jailer and captive, betrayer and betrayed, looked upon each other, but the malice of the one almost cowered before the dauntless defiance of the other.

Antoinette had risen to her feet, and her cloak of amber brocade hung open showing the beauty of her bare shoulders. For all her dishevelled hair and haggard face she was a stately figure in her silent scorn.

Striding into the room Martin shut the door behind him. An added greyness in the pallor of his prisoner was all that told what that closed door meant to her.

"Well Mrs. Castelle!" he began in a voice of mocking triumph. "You see what I told you was right about luck in odd numbers. You got the best of me twice; the third time is mine. This, our third merry meeting, is not likely to be disturbed by any of your knights errant. And you are all arrayed in your best to do honour to the occasion!"

His eyes rested with cruel delight on the shining folds of silks that trailed on the bare, dusty floor.

"So Major Warwick did not like you to go home alone. What a pity that you had not let him go with you! I dare say it would not have been the first time."

The lurid fire in the large eyes that met his was the only answer to his taunt.

"And Mr. Evans—" he was beginning again, when with an impatient movement of her head she stopped him.

"What is the use of all this?" she asked in a weary

fashion. "Wouldn't it be better to tell me what your object was in bringing me here. I don't suppose you want to kill me for mere spite and revenge. It would not do you much good."

Seeing that she was not to be aroused to anger, Martin answered lightly:

"It might not do us any good, though that remains an open question. But if you should be foolish enough to force us to strong measures, it would do us no harm. You can make up your mind to one thing, and that is, that you certainly have no chance of leaving here until you have done what we mean you to do."

Antoinette noticed how he used a vague "we" instead of a straightforward "I."

"And what may that be?" she asked quietly.

The mere fact of her asking the question seemed to raise Martin's hopes, for he answered eagerly:

"You have only to decipher for me two letters which are in my possession. I fancy you have known for some time that we intercepted them. Hand over to me that package of letters which the agent gave you—yes, and I really think that I must have your diamond necklace this time to make up for all the trouble you have given me. After that, take a solemn oath of secrecy as to your little picnic, and you shall be back in the midst of your adorers two hours after dark this evening."

"And where do faith and honour come in, in such a large 'only'?" came in sweet, mocking tones, while the dark eyes studied him with meditative scorn.

"You may, as others have done before you, find that they are rather too expensive luxuries to keep in hand. My 'only' is a very necessary one, I assure you."

A wild flash of triumph lit the beautiful, haggard face.

"My diamond necklace and the letters upon which you set such a fictitious value are locked up in Mr. Evans' safe! Do you care to go and ask him for them?"

Such a passion of rage convulsed the man's face that, as he took a hasty step forward, Antoinette instinctively closed her eyes to await the final blow. He seemed however to put a curb upon himself in time, though his voice was hoarse with anger as he spoke.

"You had better be careful how far you defy me. Major Warwick and Mr. Evans are not likely to come to your rescue to-day. We shall see presently if it is true that you haven't the letters or the diamonds about you. Meantime you shall read my cipher letter to me."

"I shall not," was her ready retort. "I know no cipher, and if I did I would *die* rather than betray it to you."

As she grew vehement Martin recovered his sneering composure.

"Your favourite tall talk! The first statement I know to be a lie, the second remains to be proved. I have seen you in your hotel room rereading and correcting a cipher letter. An overlooking room and a blind left up made that a very simple matter. It is strange how many small precautions astute ladies like yourself neglect. For your second statement, a few days of solitude and prison fare may bring a change of opinion. You will soon realise how small the chance of rescue is. The time of Mr. Evans' return is quite uncertain. It may not be for a fortnight. Major Warwick and your precious agent are just as likely to think that your mysterious absence is due to your having joined him."

"How dare you!" his victim flashed. A cold dew of anguish was thick on her forehead. She saw the horrible possibility, but she could not believe that Warwick would think that of her. No, she *must* not die. She must live to tell the tale of these days.

"Why shouldn't they?" Martin retorted insolently. "Now, if you won't give up those letters, I must search you for them, that's all."

"You shall not touch me. Bring that woman you sent to me. I know she is here. I heard her voice." She spoke bravely, but with a sick dread at her heart.

"I shall not! How particular you are nowadays!"

"If you touch me I shall manage to kill either you or myself, it doesn't matter which," she panted.

There was a compelling force of will in her words which made him yield, saying, with a savage laugh:

"All right. I'll send her. It doesn't really matter. You'll find her quite as hard to take in as you would me. You mustn't grumble if your hands are left tied until we have made certain that the letters are not where you can get at them to destroy them."

He left the room and she fell forward on the bed helpless after the long strain of defiance.

CHAPTER XVI

THE SIGHING OF THE CAPTIVE

FOR an hour or more after Martin's departure Antoinette was left undisturbed. She knew that the delay was for the purpose of wearing out her patience.

The midsummer sun burned on the white windows creating a close, unaired heat which stifled her.

Her hands being bound together made every movement constrained, and a moan of misery broke from her lip when a spider dropped from the roof upon her shoulders, and she could not raise her hand to brush it, away. At length she heard an approaching footstep. It was with the sensation with which she might have watched a noiseless brown snake curving towards her, that she saw the bedroom door gently opened, and the woman who had called herself Mary Johnson glide in.

She had somehow been quite sure of her presence in the house. Yet an irrepressible shudder crept over her as she caught sight of those long, bony fingers, and remembered their touch.

It seemed to her that the woman looked still more worn and haggard, and that behind the defiance of her stare there lurked the furtiveness of fear.

Unfortunately for her own peace her quick wit told her that what frightened the woman was the prospect of Antoinette's dark fate.

Did this creature already see the shadow of death over her? Forcing such thought aside she faced her.

As the cold, grey eyes travelled over her she felt more keenly conscious than ever of the wretched travesty of her incongruous attire.

The quiet, derisive smile with which she was studied maddened her before the woman had so much as spoken, but she tried hard for the self-control to cow her as she began:—

"You have come to make sure that I have not the letters or the diamonds hidden about me? Well, let us be quick about it, and get it over."

"There is no such hurry. You're not likely to be leaving," the woman answered with leisurely insolence. "Here, I suppose that I must unfasten your hands to get your finery off. Now, remember," she went on as she did so, "that Martin is close at hand and will make short work of any of your revolver tricks. You are not going to get the chance of laming him again in a hurry."

As the woman seemed to be trying to work herself up into an hysterical rage, Antoinette set her teeth and endured her touch in silence.

In a vindictive, feline fashion her persecutor pulled and ripped and turned inside out the beautiful Paris gown. Even her corsets came in for the same handling, with the passing jeer "White satin, indeed!"

All in vain was the search, for there was nothing there to be found. With a faint sense of relief Antoinette saw that her last friend, her little silver bottle, was still undiscovered.

Presently, as she crouched inside her cloak,

Antoinette watched her, and saw a spasm of distress distort the worn face, and as she dropped the clothes in a heap upon the ground, the woman burst into a short sob of despair.

"Oh, if I cannot find either the letters or the diamonds what will Martin do to me?" she moaned under her breath.

A sudden, fantastic interest seized Antoinette as she watched this poor little waif of humanity, and she asked in all but a whisper:

"What is Martin to you?"

She repented her rash question as the woman turned upon her savagely.

"He was my husband before you ever knew him, and when you were playing the heroine nursing him in Louisiana, I was half-starving in Paris, where he had left me when he followed you. More fool I, I ran away from my New York boarding-school with him when I was only sixteen, little idiot that I was, but he was handsome and plausible then. When I saw him going off after you in Paris I used to say to myself, that your turn to repent ever having known him would come, and it has done so pretty thoroughly, I guess."

Her voice was rasped by hatred and a momentary hope of some softening in her died away. Sick at heart at having her youthful rashness thus recalled to her, Antoinette dropped her face into her hands to shut out the hatefulness of that face, but she could not shut out the voice that went on—

"I don't wonder you want to forget it all, when you are going about in your fine Paris clothes with generals and admirals running after you. Oh, I've been watching you many a time when you never guessed it and I had to go to you the other day to humbly ask for work, and you were so polite and grand, thanking me. And was I this, and was I that, and all the time you were making signals to those girls to send me away.

"But I dare say that you wouldn't mind being in my place to-day, and putting on my old, black alpaca instead of your fine theatre clothes, and free to walk out of that door. There is a lovely fresh wind blowing to-day, and the air is sweet with the flowers on the old syringa bushes. You don't get much of it in here."

Here she paused for breath, and stung beyond endurance by her taunts, Antoinette raised her head.

"I would sooner die than be in your place, the willing slave of low villainy! All I want is to be free of your presence."

A shrill laugh greeted her words.

"If that's all you want, you're easily satisfied. You may want worse to see me before I come back again! Here, take the clothes that suit your work so well."

Flinging the dress at her enemy's feet she left the room, locking the door behind her. After this, the long hot midday dragged on into evening without any event to mark it save the changing light. No one appeared with any food, but there was some water in a jug, which tepid as it was, Antoinette drank eagerly, taking care however to save a little. It had occurred to her that they might try the power of thirst.

Hour after hour passed, and she grew more fevered and wretched from the heavy air of the room. At length in sheer desperation she muffled her elbow in the heavy folds of her cloak, and drove it against one of the window panes, until she had succeeded in breaking a small hole.

Putting her face to this she could breathe the air and get a sight of the wistful beauty of the summer evening. She saw a stretch of neglected meadow-land, blue-grey in the twilight, sloping uphill to a dark belt of woodlands against the eastern sky. Never had the dewy, scented breath of the summer night brought greater physical relief to her when she was free to walk abroad in the soft gloom—never before had she so realised the calm pitilessness of nature towards her suffering, weary children.

But the fresh air did renew her strength and cool her fever. It was something to watch the evening red fade into dove-colour, and the first evening star shine out above the hill-tops.

The last chirp of a sleepy bird and the chorus of frogs from a swamp were sounds of infinite interest to dwell upon. And so, through the gathering darkness, she crouched there on the floor, her face pressed to the hole which every now and then she ventured to make larger.

There, with her head resting against a chair, she got some snatches of uneasy sleep. Often in the night she started into wide-awake alarm at the sound of fancied footsteps, but the daylight came without her having been molested, and so passed the second night of her imprisonment. The second morning found her with lessened strength but with unlessened determination.

As its early hours passed she knew that she needed food, but tried to keep her mind from dwelling upon the problem as to whether it would be brought to her or not. She knew that to think of hunger or thirst, only brought its misery the sooner. It was with mingled feelings of dread and relief that she recognised Mary Johnson's lighter foot upon the stair. At any rate, she would rather have her come than Martin.

She came in, bringing meat and bread and drink of the same coarse kind as before.

She had evidently schooled herself into greater reserve. Hardly glancing at her prisoner she said stolidly: "Here is some food for you." Then as she saw the broken window she went on in the same fashion: "If you do that again Martin will have the windows boarded up."

"Is he here?" the other asked, hoping to hear that he was not.

"Yes. Do you want to see him? If you choose to say that you will show him the cipher, he will come fast enough. It means a lot to us."

"No, I'm not going to read it," Antoinette answered, as though she were refusing a cup of tea.

She stood watching the woman stuffing up the window pane with an old shawl, and almost involuntarily she broke out into a piteous protest:

"But I must have some air."

"You can have as much as you like when you have read the cipher." And with this brief retort the woman left her. And after that another day and another night of solitude wore away, shortened by heavy stupor that seemed to be creeping over her.

And then again the hours of another morning wore on in suspense—suspense which, as it gathered force cleared her brain and flashed into it the knowledge that they meant to starve her.

With this new lucidity she understood that if she did not yield, her death was the only possible solution of the position for her foes. They could never venture on giving her her liberty.

She tried to concentrate her mind on the probabilities of the case. She did not believe that they had yet gone away and left her helpless.

She felt sure that she would yet be given another chance of yielding. And that to-day's neglect was merely a grim hint as to future possibilities.

If she saw that they were really going to stop the food altogether, she would pretend to temporise, and so gain a little time. Oh, surely, there would be someone to miss and search for her. Surely Major Warwick would not be content to see her vanish into space in that fashion! Why, she had made an appointment to drive with him the very day following the dinner. He would thus have learned of her disappearance hardly twelve hours after she had driven off in the cab.

Even if Martin's vile suggestion should be correct and he were to think her absence a voluntary one, Evans on his return would soon clear that up, and then they would search in earnest.

Oh, there was hope, there must be hope for life if only she could endure a little longer. She was never very clear afterwards as to how many of these days there were—days of sickening suffering and suspense, which at intervals were relieved by the appearance of portions of food, each one of which she expected to be the last. Always the same woman brought it and always with the same question.

She had hitherto invariably returned the same answer, but she knew that she was growing weaker and that if she meant to save her life she must soon seem to yield to their wishes.

CHAPTER XVII

"IS SHE WRONGED? TO THE RESCUE OF HER HONOUR"

THE same morning sunshine that dawned upon the first day of Antoinette's captivity found Major Warwick feeling that the world was a very pleasant place.

As he went over the events of the evening before he felt as though he had got through the veil of gentle reserve which Mrs. LeMoine had hitherto kept between them.

It was but the frugal fare that lovers feed upon. She had for the first time made one or two allusions to her own girlhood which had seemed to give him a more intimate standing. Then too she had yielded to his pleading to be allowed to drive her to a picnic tea, at the musketry range, the soldiers' summer camp.

His little mare seemed to feel his good humour contagious as he drove from the barracks down to the hotel.

There seemed to him something queer in the servant's face and manner when he asked for Mrs. Le Moine.

"Mrs. LeMoine did not come home last night," was the startling answer.

He stood and stared in the man's face, mechanically repeating his words.

"Did not come home last night"—then spoke sharply. "What are you talking about, my man? I saw the lady into the carriage myself, at Government House."

"Sorry, sir, but—perhaps you'd like to see the manager."

"Fetch him then, and be quick."

But the manager had no other tale to tell save that Mrs. LeMoine must certainly have intended to return, as she had asked the maid to put some lemonade in her room.

"Still, I merely supposed that she had changed her mind at the last, and gone out to Trafalgar as she has done before. Her luggage is all in her room. Some of her valuables are in our safe. You don't suppose—"

No. Warwick hastened to assure him, he didn't suppose anything. In fact he himself utterly refused to suppose anything save that she was at Trafalgar. If there was a sickening prescience in his heart that he should not find her there, he stifled it down. Without more words, he turned the mare's head westwards and took her out to Trafalgar at a pace that considerably astonished both mare and groom.

He *would* find her there—he *must* find her there, and she would smile in her pretty scorn at his needless alarm for her. The usual sunny afternoon quiet hung over the house and grounds. There were no signs of agitation there, at any rate.

Mabel was loitering among the flower-beds, all in white, and, with her hands full of white roses, she seemed a fashionable version of St. Elizabeth of Thuringia, as well as the epitome of the summer's peace and beauty.

Inwardly rejoicing at the romantic pose in which her visitor had found her, Mabel smiled him a welcome.

Scarcely glancing at her, Warwick flung down the reins and jumped out of his dog-cart.

"Is Mrs. LeMoine here?" he asked, without other greeting, not even seeming to be aware of her outstretched hand.

Mrs. LeMoine! It was always Mrs. LeMoine with everyone now! A cold vindictiveness roused from its snaky folds in Mabel's heart and hissed in her soft voice.

"Mrs. LeMoine? Oh, no; why should she be here? Father is away, you know, and it is nearly a week since we have seen her. I think that we girls bore her. I had an idea that she had left town, but I always feel that I mustn't seem to notice her mysteries. Poor dear, how tired she must get of them!"

In spite of her gentle voice and smile, the lover's true instinct felt the want of real sympathy.

"When will your father be back?" he asked abruptly. He had not yet taken in the girl's innuendo, which omission she was keen to note.

After this question, Mabel's plaintive embarrassment, shown in her drooping eyelids and fluttering colour was a triumph of art.

"I am sorry that I cannot tell you," she murmured, sadly. "His daughters are generally the last to know of his movements." Then, with an air of heroically suppressing her private grief in the cause of friendship, she looked up at him with a smile of saintly self-abnegation.

"But tell me what made you think that Mrs. LeMoine was here, and why do you look so disappointed to find she is not?"

"I put her into the carriage at the door of Government House, and she never reached the hotel. I cannot help fearing that some harm has come to her from those spies."

It cost him an effort to first put his fears into words, and it was almost a relief to see that Mabel was not startled by them.

Again she seemed to droop sadly, and to hesitate before speaking.

"I don't think it's likely," she murmured helplessly. "I am sorry." Then, as though with an effort, "But you know how she likes us to leave her mysteries alone. My father will probably be aware of her movements when he returns."

Her shaft had at last pierced the man's stout armour of trust. Mabel's apparent guilelessness lent a sharper point to her words than any insinuation could have done. His spirit was wrapped in a turmoil such as might have seized on some devout worshipper of a fair, white marble goddess of old, who, as he knelt before it, saw the beautiful form take on the similitude of a spirit of evil.

If she were foul, then was there no fairness and purity left.

With brief farewell, Warwick drove away, and until mess time he disappeared into the solitude of his own quarters. The strong do not seek for sympathy in such dark hours of life.

That night, at mess, men respected his evidently

solitary humour, until Adair, of whom he had made somewhat of a pet, came up to him.

The young fellow's bright face was brighter than usual, for he had been receiving congratulations on his announced engagement to Hattie Evans.

Of this engagement Warwick had known for some days, so he rather wondered what the boy wanted, as he drew him aside. The request to go down with him now to the theatre seemed an ordinary one enough, and was simply refused, but Adair persisted. "Hattie is going to be there, and wants particularly to speak to you, sir. She told me to ask you to come," he went on, apparently feeling sure that no one could refuse such a mandate.

The only mark which Hattie Evans had so far made on Major Warwick's attention had been that of a bright, pretty girl, like dozens of others. Of late, there had been the difference that she was to marry his favourite, Adair, and that she seemed fond of Mrs. LeMoine. Still, it was with a sense of surprise that the idea suddenly dawned upon him that help might come to him through her. When once this hope came to him, he tarried not upon the order of his going, but hustled Adair off to the theatre in as great a hurry as even the young lover's heart could desire.

With loyal self-abnegation Adair yielded him his seat beside Hattie.

The girl looked as youthfully frivolous as ever, in her pretty fineries; but there were nervous lines about her mouth, and her eyes were anxious.

Under the shelter of the overture's music, she began impetuously:

"I hope you don't mind my asking you to come here, but I couldn't *bear* not to know to-night what you have done about Mrs. LeMoine. I am sure that you feel as I do, that there should be no time lost."

Warwick felt himself in a tight place, with those frank young eyes questioning him so eagerly. He could not even hint to this girl at any suspicion implanted in him by Mabel's artless words.

"I am sorry to say that I did not feel at liberty to take any steps in the matter. I have had the secrecy of their state affairs so often impressed upon me. Your sister too seemed to think that we might not be thanked for putting our fingers into their secrets."

He tried to speak pleasantly, but the girl was quick to read the soreness of tone.

"Oh, Mabel—" she began impatiently and then checked herself. Warwick put in hastily:

"What did you mean when you said that there should be no time lost? You don't surely know of any danger?"

"Only what you do, I think. The spy's two desperate attempts to get at her papers."

"I only know of the time in the Park, when I came along," Warwick interrupted.

"Oh, well, I don't care now if it's a secret or not, I shall tell you the rest." And she quickly narrated the woman's visit to Trafalgar and what followed.

Warwick's face grew very set and stern as he listened. "What makes me so anxious now," Hattie went on, "is that this man is so likely to have chosen the time of my father's absence for a fresh attempt. I cannot bear to think in what danger she may be at this very minute, nor where she has been since last night! I am so sure that she is in the power of those wretches. Oh, Major Warwick, you will try to do something for her, won't you? I know Harold will help you."

"I will do all that man can do, so help me God!" he answered in low, strenuous tones, then, "But tell me, do you know anyone to whom I can go for some clew? I am so altogether in the dark."

Hattie winked away the tears that the excitement of her appeal had brought to her eyes, and was her shrewd practical self again.

"I don't think you have ever met the Confederate agent? He keeps himself rather dark."

"No, but I have heard Arthur speak of him. But I haven't an idea where to find him."

"Well, listen," and she gave a minute description of the cabinet-maker's shop where he was to be inquired for.

"Don't ask him any questions, but tell him just what has happened and why we are uneasy. If she has gone away on any business he is sure to know it; if not, then you must lose no time, and you must make him help you."

With her last words she paled and shuddered.

"Don't fear that I will lose time. I am going now— God bless you for a true-hearted girl. Adair is a lucky fellow," and with these words Warwick had left his place and gone out into the night.

A deep shame at the superior staunchness of Hattie's loyalty, and a fierce dread of the consequences of this lost day would have spurred him on, if any spur were needed save that of the vision of his divinity helpless in the hands of cruel and unscrupulous enemies.

"My God! she would sooner die than yield to them!" he groaned to himself as he hurried through the quiet streets.

There were diverse forms and ceremonies of conspiracy, with which the agent had chosen to surround himself, to be gone through with before Warwick could reach him at all. Even then, his first attempts were met with a maddening amount of formalism and distrust. But he was in no humour to be checked by trifles.

When with dogged determination he had told his tale, he saw two long creases deepen in the parchment-like face of the inscrutable, little man, and from his lips fell the words of fate.

"They've caught her, sure enough this time, and if her friends want to see her again, they've got to *fly* round."

Then Warwick lost his temper in as thorough a fashion as he generally kept it.

Thundering out an oath, he began: "Hadn't the people who put her at such work better look sharp too, or are you going to sit there talking and leave a woman to be hounded to death? I don't think much of your Southern chivalry if you can't, among you all, take better care than that of a woman who is giving her beauty and her brains to do your dirty work for you? Can't you do like Englishmen and send *men* into danger instead of women?"

The shrivelled-up little man looked at this big, irate specimen of Anglo-Saxon manhood with a new respect.

He had weighed many men in the balance in his day, and found many wanting, but here he felt was the ring of the true metal.

"Oh, we'll look after her all right. Don't be afraid. Talking won't do much, and we can't do much tonight. Still, I think that I can find out if Martin is round still. You had better go and see what you can do to discover who drove that cab. But, mind you," shaking a long, claw-like finger with sudden animation, "the police have nothing to do with this job. It stays in my hands. Mrs. LeMoine would wish that."

"Things have got too far for me to respect even Mrs. LeMoine's wishes. I shall use any means that come to hand. If I see that I can trust in you, I may do as you wish, but I promise nothing."

The agent smiled sardonically. He apparently derived much enjoyment from Warwick's bullying.

CHAPTER XVIII

"RUN TO EARTH"

BY the next morning Warwick seeing a grim determination piercing the philosophical calm of the agent, decided to yield to him on the police question, for fear of his otherwise withholding some necessary clew.

Adair and he, together, ought to be enough for any force that the spies were likely to have at command. Then there was the little agent in whom he began to recognise a spirit that might be relied on in a tight place.

When they first met that morning the latter was able to announce positively that Martin and the woman who passed as his wife had left their lodgings in a Water Street hotel the day before the General's dinner ostensibly for the Boston boat.

This news came as a surprise to none of them, for it was what they had feared to hear. Each man's face set more grimly as he realised that here was no false alarm.

Coachmen and cab-drivers are, the world over, gregarious-minded and gossip-loving. It had needed few questions from Warwick's groom, sent on a round of the livery stables, to elicit the fact that the mysterious cab was "one of Smith's, but with a strange driver, muffled up, and keeping to himself."

Acting on this information Warwick set off for Smith's stables where the mere mention of this cab brought a cloud to the proprietor's brow.

"I was sure I'd hear something queer had happened. I let a boy that I thought I could trust take that cab out, sir, to drive a lady, and I'm blessed if he didn't get talking with some stranger. The man gave him a drink and persuaded him that he had some bet about driving the cab home for a lark, and would tip him well to let him do it.

"The boy waited for him an hour, and then when the cab didn't turn up, he got in a funk and came back and owned up. It was two o'clock when the turn-out got back to our gates, and before I had got out the driver was gone. The poor beasts were all in a lather, and the carriage covered with red mud—mud such as you don't get very near the town, sir. I hope"—and the honest man looked from one grave face to the other— "I hope, gentlemen, that no real harm has come out of it."

"I trust not," Warwick mustered heart to say. Meanwhile until we find out what has happened, you had better keep quiet about the whole affair."

While the man was talking the agent's note-book had been busy, and as he snapped its clasp he summed up.

"From midnight to two o'clock—a drive of an hour and back. Too late for the ferry, so that it must have been on this side of the harbour. It should not take three men long to beat the country for a lonely house at that distance from town. I thought when they disappeared before that they had probably secured some quiet country retreat. We have to deal with deep ones, remember."

Warwick and Adair proceeded to get a weeks leave for fishing, and promptly vanished from the social scene.

They two and the agent then went separately to explore each country road and by-way.

For two or three days this search continued without any result. Warwick was haggard, and even the agent once or twice betrayed a nervous, irritability.

At last the latter shook his head and allowed a brooding thought to take words in the suggestion that she may have been driven to some lonely spot on the coast and put on board of an American vessel—"In which case she is now probably an inmate of a northern prison."

"Good Heavens, sir! Can such an act of piracy be possible in a civilised country?" Warwick broke out wrathfully.

"A good many things are possible nowadays," was the oracular response, "and you must remember, sir, that there may be worse fates than a northern prison."

Too well Warwick remembered it, and it was this haunting fear that was making him a gaunt shadow of himself, and bringing the first grey hairs to his temples.

It was a glorious summer morning, when the jubilant west wind seemed to mock at his despondency as he turned his horse's steps down a grassy woodland track that led through thick beech woods, away from the main road, that, skirting the Basin, ran inland.

Warwick knew that it led to a negro settlement,

strange remnant of an English raid on the South
Carolina coast during the 1812 War. Beyond this he
had learned that there lay one or two scattered farms.
He had no definite bourne, however, but was merely
pursuing a course doggedly marked out and stuck to,
of tracing out every road or track marked on his carefully conned county map. As he jogged along his
thought had turned to his cousin Arthur. He wished
intensely for his reappearance just now in the
Nighthawk. Nor only the instinctive bond of kinship
but the trust of one strong man in another made him
wish for his presence now.

All at once these idle thoughts dropped away as his
whole being leaped to the shock of the conviction that
he had at last stumbled on the place they were in
search of.

A turn in the road opened to view a few barren
fields from which the forest fell away, showing in one
corner a group of tumble-down buildings, cottage
and barn.

Their unpainted wood was weather-stained to a soft
grey, and even at this distance the dilapidation of
gates and fences and the weed-grown, unsown garden
told of desertion. But for a faint curl of smoke from
the one chimney and the rough paper blinds at the
lower windows, the place would have seemed utterly
uninhabited.

It was strange, too, that the garret windows should
have the look of being newly-whitewashed, and—yes,
in the shadow of those beeches where the dew still lingered on the grass, there were marks, which must
have been made since last evening, of carriage wheels

turning in at the gate that led up to the house.

Warwick's courage being of that matter-of-course kind that never feels any need of assertion, his first thought was of caution.

Where Mrs. LeMoine's safety was concerned he would risk nothing by rashness.

Drawing his horse back into the shadow of the trees he sat long, watching the dreary little den, and pondering the chances.

Should he storm the fortress single-handed, or should he hasten back for further help to surprise the place that evening?

Delay was, in his present humour, maddening, and yet failure in a rash attempt might mean increased danger to her of whom he thought with such heart-sickness. Long as he watched, there was no sign of life or movement about the place. At last he bethought himself of a darkey shanty which he had passed about ten minutes before. With the idea of making inquiries there, he retraced his steps. Miniature, imp-like black forms fled wildly before he could bribe them back with cents, but at length a woman peered out and came in answer to his call.

At his first question as to the lonely house, a furtive, frightened look came into her face, and she peered anxiously round.

"No, sir! No one live dere. No one want to eder. Dat house haunted!"

"But I am sure that I saw smoke from the chimney just now," Warwick objected.

That peculiar ashy-blue shade which in an African answers for pallor overspread her face.

"And dere lights dere at night all dis week," she said in a hoarse whisper. "And my man coming home late one night from fishing, saw a carriage, a big town carriage, driving dere like mad. And we're awful frightened dat it's a robbers' den, sir. Tell you what, massa, we're dat powerful scared, dat it's hard to get the children to get de sticks and de water," and her face fully corroborated her words.

With a new idea she looked up at him. "You mightn't happen to be de police, sir?" she asked hopefully.

Warwick gave a short chuckle. He could scarcely style himself an amateur to this sable lady.

"Well, not exactly that, though I hope I may help you to get rid of your robbers all the same. Do you think you could tell me how many days it is since your husband saw the carriage?"

He tried not to show the eagerness with which he put the question and to veil his disappointment as she answered in a bewildered fashion:—

"Might be a week, perhaps—no, dere wasn't any Sunday since Pete went a-fishin'—guess about t'ree or four days, Massa. But you won't say anyding 'bout my tellin' you of de robbers, sir?"

Warwick soothed her with promises and some loose change, and then rode smartly away.

Those few words about the carriage had roused the dull, northern fury in him, that fury of the old *Berserkers*, and nothing would have stayed his hand. Swiftly he made his way back to town, and finding out the agent, he told what he had seen and heard.

"There is no doubt left in the matter. She either is there, or has been there. I shall force a way in as soon as it begins to get dark tonight. I only wait for that so as to take them more by surprise and decrease her risks when they find themselves caught."

"But they may have taken her away, from there," the agent objected.

"I think if they had the black family would have seen something of it," Warwick said. "At any rate, I shall keep guard there in the woods all day. I shall tell Adair about joining me there at sunset. You can come with him if you like. I leave you the choice," he ended, "as to whether we go there to-night with the police or by ourselves; but you can have no other choice in the matter. Nothing can delay or change my purpose now."

"I ask no delay," the other responded promptly. "Indeed, if *you* did not go to-night, I should do so myself. We southern gentlemen are not cowards, sir. Three sensible men with revolvers ought to be a match for any rascals unhung, without bothering with police." Then with an echo of genuine human feeling in his voice:—"You must take into account Mrs. LeMoine's own pluck and shrewdness in this affair. She wouldn't throw away a chance, but would humour them and work for delay. She must know that we would be on the scent. Cheer up! We'll save her yet!"

"God grant it," Warwick groaned.

Then the two men, outwardly so dissimilar, inwardly alike in staunchness of spirit, clasped hands in token of alliance, and went their ways.

CHAPTER XIX

THE HAUNTED HOUSE

"O'er all there hung the shadow of a fear;
A sense of mystery the spirit daunted,
And said as plain as whisper in the ear,
The place is haunted."

WARWICK gave Adair careful directions for joining him
that evening in the turn just past the darkey hut.

He also arranged for him to let Hattie know that if
they succeeded in finding Mrs. LeMoine they should
take her to Trafalgar. Naturally Adair took this message there in person and delivered it in full length.

She was warned to have all preparations made in
case she should arrive ill or in an exhausted condition.

"The poor old chap all but broke down when he
told me to say that. Somehow, I am almost afraid that
he hardly expects to find her alive."

Adair rather choked as he ended his tale thus. Then
Hattie's long suspense found vent in tears of genuine
feeling.

Adair then had to turn comforter, so that between
them they got a certain amount of melancholy enjoyment out of their anxieties, admiring severally each
other's courage and warm-heartedness.

Hattie predicted that Adair would be the one to

capture Martin, and Adair was sure that Hattie would nurse and comfort Mrs. LeMoine when they had rescued her, and so together they wiled away some hours of the anxious day.

These hours were spent by Warwick in the shelter of the thick bushes that edged the rising slope of meadow behind the old farmhouse.

He tried to keep as quiet as possible, though there were no visible signs of life or movement. It seemed as though his yearning eyes must pierce the secret which those flimsy wooden walls hid from him.

Ah, if he could have guessed that there, behind that window with the stuffed-up hole, the woman he loved was lying in a stupor of wretchedness!

How welcome was the sight of the lengthening shadows, and the reddening light. The sun was almost gone—there, it was quite gone, and the earth lay in a tender, golden haze.

The time for action was at hand, and skirting the woodland he made his way to the appointed meeting place.

An hour before sunset Adair and the agent had set off in a light, strong double-seated trap and followed the road that Warwick had explored.

By the time that they had reached the forest-shaded cross-road the twilight was already gathering. At the darkey's hut Warwick emerged from the shadow of the trees to meet them.

"Anything fresh?" the agent asked in cautious tones.

"Nothing. Not one sign of life since I saw that smoke this morning. There has been none since."

"You couldn't see it now if there were."

"One could smell it."

"I trust in Heaven that—" the agent was beginning, but checked himself. It was of no use putting into words the fear that Warwick had been observed. He guessed what tortures he must be enduring, and prepared to set out without more words. In spite of his remonstrances that the old horse would stand until the Day of Judgment, Adair was left in charge of the vehicle.

A whistle would summon him if need were. Then the two men quietly climbed the grassy road that led towards the barn. It was dark enough by now for them not to fear observation, but they instinctively drew back, when, just as they neared it, the stable door opened, and a man carrying a lantern came out, followed by the small figure of a woman.

The lantern light shone upon her pale scared face.

Warwick took a shorter grasp of the heavy-headed oak cudgel that he carried, and he drew a deep breath.

The woman was speaking rapidly and in a voice in which the agitation broke every now and then through its lowered caution.

"Why did I ever tell him that I had seen that man, that Major Warwick spying round here to-day," she wailed. "There was something in his face makes me afraid that he means to give up trying to get anything out of her and will finish her to-night."

"What else can he do, after making such a mess of things? He *must* now. There is no other way out of it. What's the matter with you? I thought that you were more down upon her than he was?"

He had halted and turned on her, staring into the white face, wild with horror.

"So I was, and God knows I had cause to be. I thought I shouldn't care, but—my God, I *cannot* stand it," she broke out, wringing her hands. "Let me go! I'll walk all the way to town. Only let me get away from this place of horror before I hear her scream, and go mad."

"*She* won't scream. He'll take good care of that. Martin's no fool. You'd better not cross him to-night. If you don't want there to be *two* murders done, keep quiet."

Before he had finished speaking, he had set the lantern on the ground, and catching her deftly around the arms, he lifted her with ease inside the stable door, which he pulled to, and locked on the outside.

"Phew! women are kittle cattle;" he gasped, putting up his hand to wipe his face.

Even as he did so, Warwick, with one long stride forward, brought down his heavy stick upon the man's head, felling him to the ground as a butcher would an ox. The suspense, the smothered wrath of many long hours all went into that blow, and he needed no second one.

All that day Antoinette had been alone without food, and what was worse without water. The day before she had finished what had been in the room, though she had eked it out into the smallest possible portions.

Neither Martin nor the woman had been near her since the evening of two days before. As hour after hour passed she felt sure that the end was near—that they were not going to give her another chance of yielding.

She was so stupefied by weakness that there was no bitterness over the life so nearly slipped from her grasp. All she hoped was that she might die without seeing their hateful faces again.

As it grew dusk Martin's limping step on the stair roused her. In her weakness she momentarily knew for the first time the coward's thrill of deadly fear, but her hand grasped the little silver bottle. It would soon put her beyond his reach.

When, however, he stood before her, a cold, concentrated rage supplied a brief vitality. The sight of him aroused a strangely impersonal anger that such as he should have power to put an end to the surging life within her.

With sneering leisure he scrutinised her drawn, white face, and shrunken figure.

"Well, have you had about enough of this?" he asked.

She had, on his appearance pulled herself upright on the edge of the bed, and sat pressing each hand down to it for support, and staring blankly at him.

"Yes, but it will soon be over now." Her voice was weak and low, but she was pleased to hear that it sounded composed.

"How will it be over?" he asked shortly, evidently perplexed by her bearing.

"There are several people who will connect you with my disappearance, and when once the search was begun, it could not take men like the Confederate agent long to run you down."

Even at this pass, her powers of observation were still quick, and she somehow knew that her random shot had struck home. With the knowledge a faint spark of hope rekindled in her breast. Perhaps Martin knew that her rescue was more imminent than she had even dreamt.

"I'm not such a fool as not to be able to cover up my tracks as I go," he retorted. "If you let the hope of rescue make you obstinate, you may be past rescue when it comes. You had better believe what I say when I tell you that I don't intend to waste any more time in this forsaken rat-hole. You have the choice still to-day of leaving it, or of staying here forever. But to-morrow there will be no more choice left."

He was evidently working himself up into brutality, and the physical shrinking from violence was once more threatening her heart's high stronghold.

Driving it back by a tighter clasp on her silver bottle she asked in the same dull voice:—"Do you mean to starve me?"

He seemed glad to have aroused that much apprehension in her.

"That depends upon yourself. As you know it is the simplest process and leaves no tell-tale marks. It is a very easy matter for us to tie you up here, and go away and leave you alone. At any rate, you must decide at once, for I am not going to wait on your shillyshallying any longer. Will you read me the cipher and tell me what you know of it ? Be careful, before you refuse again."

Antoinette saw that if she were to have one more

chance of life she must seem to yield, and gain time—
time at any price. She could not for many more hours
keep her brain clear under this torment of thirst.

Her dry lips could scarcely form the words as she
said with apparent sullenness: "Show it to me, then."

The evident relief in his face and voice told her that
time was also of no small moment to him, and this
strengthened her hopes of speedy help.

"I thought you would soon be singing a different
tune," he taunted her, as he laid a paper upon the
table. Keeping a careful hand upon it, he signed to
her to take the chair which he had pulled up.

"This is not the same as the ciphers that have been
used with me," she said, slowly conning it, although
the first quick glance had made its meaning clear to
her.

It was what she had expected it to be, the missing
letter from Benjamin to the agent. It announced that
the steamer that was to be seized by Southerners was
on the point of departure from New York, and warning him to have the schooner with the ammunition
ready at the trysting-place off the New Brunswick
coast.

As she sat, passing her fingers along the lines in a
puzzled fashion, Antoinette was trying to force her
dulled brains into deciding whether the news were
old enough for her to safely read it to him. She did
not mean to give up her life for a valueless thing.
There would be great risk in altering dates and places,
for he might have enough information to detect her
deceit.

That Evans had left town a week ago on this very

business, she knew, but all dates were confused to her now, and she had no tidings of the daring deed having been carried out.

There may, at the last, have turned up a dozen causes for delay, and if she were to read Martin the letter correctly he might still have time to ruin the enterprise and put in jeopardy many lives. No, there lay no safety for her with honour, and the momentary hope died a sudden death.

"Can't you read it, or won't you?" Martin asked threateningly.

"I am too weak and dizzy. I can hardly see the signs," she answered faintly, laying her head down upon the table.

"Do you want food?" he asked with baffled impatience.

"Drink. I am suffering tortures of thirst."

"The reward of obstinacy," but he left the room, returning with a plate of bread and meat, and a cup of milk. Pulling a flask from his pocket he poured a liberal quantity of whiskey into the milk. He was evidently afraid that she might give him the slip too soon.

She turned with sick loathing from the food, but drank eagerly, and the strong spirits brought back a momentary strength. "Try the letter now," he said peremptorily, and she obeyed in silence.

"I see the words for 'powder,' and 'ammunition,' also 'blockade' and 'steamer' repeated frequently. But I cannot put the sentences together all at once, from memory, without my key. I would have to work it out with pencil and paper, and it will take time. Will you leave it with me?"

"To destroy it?"

"What good would that do me, I know very well that if your need of me is gone, my last hope is gone too. But you can fasten my arms so that I cannot reach it. I should probably decipher it by looking at it often. The other way is the quickest. But it is as you please."

"It certainly is, in this case."

A faint stir of movement outdoors caused Antoinette to hold her breath, though she saw that Martin had noticed nothing unusual.

Yes, a window below was softly tried, then another.

Martin heard and as he turned, startled, there came a great crash against the front door, which fell away inward from its rotten hinges.

Antoinette was on her feet before Martin could get to the door, crying out with all her remaining strength:

"Help, help! I am here! Come, oh come quickly!"

"You fiend!" Martin's hand on her mouth choked her cries, but as he heard a swift rush of feet on the stairs, he flung her heavily from him so that she fell in a corner of the room, and sprang to the door, just as it was flung open from outside and Warwick rushed in.

CHAPTER XX

"THE DEED DONE"

WHEN the man with the lantern lay motionless at Warwick's feet, neither he nor the agent tarried to make out if the blow had dealt death or not.

Both men had heard enough to drive them on over every obstacle without the waste of a word.

"Bring the lantern," Warwick said briefly leading the way up to the house.

As usual in such places, the sill of the lower windows was hardly higher than his knee.

He tried one and immediately found that it was securely fastened down.

"There is a light in the garret," the agent whispered, and they both stepped back to see a faint glimmer through the whitewashed window panes.

"We must hurry! we must hurry!" Warwick muttered uneasily.

He turned to the door and after passing a hand up and down the hinges murmured:

"The wood is rotten. The lock and hinges can have no real hold on it. One good push will send it in. Stand ready with your revolver!"

With a mighty heave of his shoulders he had flung himself against it. The door crashed in, and he went flying after it; but no foe was waiting in the passage or on the stairs. The agent came close after him holding the lantern high above his head.

Good God! whose voice was that breaking the awesome silence of the house with its wild cry for help! She was not past help then! They had come in time!

Hurling himself up the stairs with an answering shout, "I am here! I am here!" Warwick made toward the glimmer of light that came from the cracks of an ill-fitting door.

As he reached it, it was flung open, and Martin, making a dash past him for the stairs, fell into the arms of the agent. The latter wound him in an octopus-like grasp, and the two rolled down the stairs together, in the company of the lantern.

Warwick did not even glance round at the mêlée.

"Never mind *him*," he called back. "Come on. We *must* find her," and he peered anxiously into the dimly lit garret room. A faint moan from one corner made his heart stand still, and then came the ghost of a whisper, "I am here."

Faint as it was, he heard it and was across the room to where, half-huddled against the wall, half-lying on the floor was the dear figure, in the poor pitifully gay dress in which he had last seen her so dainty and gracious.

She lay as Martin had thrown her, too weak to speak or move, the white arms and neck gleaming bare without any wrap, her face upturned so that the light showed the peaked, sharpened features, with no more colour than time-softened ivory.

Even as Warwick bent over her the appealing eyes clouded and then closed, as though the effort to keep them open were too great. He saw, with a great sinking at heart, that she had completely lost consciousness.

Was she really passing from his grasp into death's untrodden realm.

Oblivious to any chances of further warfare, he was absorbed in wetting her lips with the brandy and water that he had brought in a flask, and rubbing her wrists and temples with the same. A fanciful silver smelling-bottle of Hattie Evans' looked strange in those big brown hands, but no woman's touch could have been tenderer than was theirs as they smoothed back the heavy masses of disordered hair that hung loosely around the wan face, as though to veil it in pity.

The flicker of an eyelid, the tremor that stirred the drooping lips, were the first signs to reassure Warwick and banish his worst fears.

Presently he realised that the agent was standing beside him, facing the door, revolver in hand, and had been speaking.

"The slippery brute dodged me and got off in the dark. The man you knocked down, and the woman in the stable are gone too. You didn't hit hard enough. I wish that I had got a good blow at one of them. But, at any rate, the whole nest is cleared out," he began gloomily, as soon as he saw that Warwick was aware of his presence. "The next thing will be to get Mrs. LeMoine away from here," he went on with a troubled glance down at her.

"Can't you see that she is not in a fit state to be moved yet. We must wait until the morning," Warwick growled angrily.

But the hand that had lain so still in his fluttered in his grasp, and there came a whisper, so faint that he had to bend low to hear it.

"No. Take me away from this house. I shall die if I stay here. Take me out under the trees, into God's air."

"We will do whatever you wish. Only take another sip of this brandy now." Warwick soothed her as though she had been a frightened child.

Suddenly the little agent leant over her with a curious new gentleness in his face.

"Try to tell me," he said softly. "Have you been ill or frightened, or what is it that make you so weak?"

A shadow ran over her as she whispered in broken words. "Thirst—hunger—air." Then, as her eyelids drooped again wearily, two grim oaths were smothered as they rose.

"Why wasn't your cudgel loaded with lead?" the agent said reproachfully; but Warwick's eyes and thoughts were again fixed upon her face.

With a strangely vivid smile, Antoinette looked up, as her head lay pillowed on Warwick's arm, into the agent's face, and said clearly :

"But they could not make me read the cipher to them," and then turned her head with the contented movement of a child going to sleep.

Something that was almost a sob broke from Warwick's lips, as he tried to pillow the dear head more easily. The agent immediately became absorbed in practical details.

"She is like ice," he announced after feeling her hands. "We must get her warm before we attempt to move her. I will whistle for Adair and get him to bring the rugs. And he has food in that lunch basket, fortunately. Good child, that Evans girl, to send it! There must be a place in the kitchen to light a fire, and they must have fuel of sorts. I think that she would rest easier on that bed if you lifted her there."

But, again at the suggestion, Antoinette shuddered. "Not that bed. I thought to lie there dead. Oh, please take me downstairs! "

Then Warwick, with infinite care and reverence, lifted the poor light body in his arms and carried it downstairs.

It was a strange sight, if any onlooker had been there to mark Antoinette lying on a heaped-up pile of rugs and cushions in the glow of a great wood-fire which Adair had worked off his unused energy in piling up on the open hearth of the old kitchen.

The agent busily heated soup from the basket which Hattie had packed for any emergency. They might both toil in her service, but it was Warwick who kept close beside her, wrapping her in rugs arranging cushions, persuading her to drink the soup in little sips while she leaned against him.

And so a faint colour flickered in the haggard face, and the drooping head raised itself like a flower refreshed by water.

Once she laid her hand anxiously on Warwick's arm.

"It is *real*, isn't it? I *am* safe with you? All day I have seen so many faces come and go, heard so many voices. But now it is real, isn't it?"

"It is real, and you are safe with me, thank God," Warwick answered from a full heart, and the other men became more busy so that they might not seem to watch his face.

In the meantime Hattie Evans at Trafalgar, in a fever

of anxiety, was awaiting news of their expedition. When Adair had left her that afternoon, she had rushed upstairs to Mabel's room, where that young woman was putting the last touches to hat and veil before the glass. "Oh, Mab, you're not going out?"

"Why not?" Mabel answered with a critical glance at her sister's flushed excited face. "What a state you do get into! What is the fuss about now?"

Hattie hurriedly poured forth the tale that Adair had brought her, but its only effect was to bring the danger signal of a bright red spot to Mabel's checks.

Pulling rather impatiently at the folds of her veil, she answered in her chilliest fashion:

"Mrs. LeMoine again! I might have guessed it! Really, I wonder you haven't more common sense. I don't see why I should break an important engagement, and stay at home, just because Major Warwick takes the liberty of treating our house as though it were an hotel, in father's absence. You seem to have forgotten that I am to read my paper on the Good Samaritan before the Sunday-school teachers' meeting, and had arranged to stay all night at Mrs. Simpson's. I cannot possibly disappoint them all."

Hattie stared at her incredulously.

"But you don't understand! She may have been ill-treated by these people, and be ill, or hurt! Why, they are afraid that those wretches may have tried to *kill* her!"

Mabel whirled round from the glass, her face transformed by one of her infrequent outbursts of temper.

"Well, if they *have*, what difference can we make, and what have we to do with the secret quarrels of those kind of people? I don't believe that she is shut up in *any* lonely farmhouse. She is much too clever for that. I am sure that she is gallivanting round the country with our dear papa, and laughing in her sleeve at them. If *you* are fool enough to be taken in by an adventuress like that, *I'm* not. You'll be sorry when it is too late, and that will be when she has taken possession as our step-mamma, that is, if she can't get Major Warwick. If she could, our dear papa wouldn't have a chance! If I have to go on living among people like that, I'll marry the first decent man that asks me, just to get away from the place."

"Major Warwick doesn't seem likely to ask you in a hurry."

The angry taunt did not act as oil upon the waters. Mabel gasped with rage, but Hattie had the floor, and went on:

"A nice kind of a Christian your dear chaplain will think you the next time you go to confession! Oh, you needn't jump. I know well enough that you go, and nice rigmaroles you must tell him! Perhaps his version of the Good Samaritan maybe a little different from yours. I hope so, for his sake—" but here Hattie's eloquence was interrupted by a most unsaintly shove that sent her flying to the other side of the door, which was promptly locked in her face.

After glaring vengefully at the wooden panels for a moment, Hattie went off for consolation—where she had from childhood been wont to seek it—to the old Scotch cook, who had served her mother before she was born.

Here she was condoled with and comforted as

though she had really been the child that she still seemed to old Janet to be.

"Never you mind her church capers. Let her go! We'll do fine just by our two selves," asserted the old woman, with whom Mabel was no favourite.

And "fine" they did, making all possible preparations, and then sitting one on each side of the kitchen fire, after the maids had been despatched to bed.

Hattie could not have stood those hours of suspense in the solitude of the drawing-room.

Many a false alarm startled them, but at last the sound of slow wheels in the avenue sent them hurrying to the door.

"She's there!" Hattie cried sharply.

The carriage was at the steps, and as Hattie saw Warwick and Adair lift a helpless form from the carriage, she clasped the old woman's hand like a little child again.

"Oh, Harold, is she alive?" she whispered in an awed voice. How cheery sounded the answer.

"Indeed she is! All that she needs is yours and old Janet's good nursing. We will leave her in your hands."

All the same, Warwick did not leave her until he had carried her upstairs and laid her upon the sofa in her bedroom. Even then, he lingered for one last, anxious gaze.

The flickering shadow of a smile and the touch of chill fingers rewarded him before he turned away.

Then the two women tenderly ministered to the poor exhausted wanderer, down whose cheeks the slow tears rolled as they bent over her.

CHAPTER XXI

A BREATHING SPACE

FOR some days Antoinette lay very still and white, smiling her thanks at Hattie and the nurse, taking the food that they pressed on her, answering their questions, but volunteering nothing.

"She must have time to recover from the shock; absolute quiet is necessary," said the Southern doctor, whom the agent had brought.

Then, all at once, a new restlessness showed in her, and she began to ask questions. Had Evans returned, and had he any news for her, and when could she see him, and were there tidings of the Nighthawk? And then the doctor, seeing that she was growing nervous and feverish, allowed an interview with Evans, only urging quiet on the latter, whose first wrath at the news of the abduction was still spluttering fiercely.

Hattie loyally drove her sister's insinuations out of her mind, and made a cheerful little event out of this first visit, taking pains to arrange the invalid's white dressing-gown as prettily as possible, and to enthrone her with a background of shell-pink silk cushions.

Evans was unusually quiet when he entered the room and saw Antoinette propped up on the sofa by the window that looked out through the pine branches down the blue waters of the bay towards the sea. Her chestnut hair was dressed more carelessly than usual, and instead of being twisted into shining plaits and curls, it hung loosely in the net of the day on her shoulders.

Though still much paler and thinner than when he had last seen her, her beauty was merely given the crowning appeal of wistfulness, and in her weakness was the supremacy of her rule. To Evans' surprise, he found himself stumblingly at a loss for words in which to give utterance to his pity for what she had undergone, and wrath with its cause.

"And so none of them had the sense to look after you when I was away! Ah, if I hadn't been away that double-dyed villain, that"—here he choked back a string of too emphatic epithets—"would never have dared to molest you. When you are well, I shall scold you for running away from Trafalgar. But you are safely here again, now."

"Yes, and very humbled and ashamed of myself," she smiled back; "so that you must forgive me. But please let us leave all that horrid time alone. There is so much that I want to know. Hattie and the doctor were perfect dragons and wouldn't tell me a thing for fear of exciting me. Do tell me all about your journey and if the steamer attempt was successful. I have wondered so often, and I do want to know if anything had been heard of the Nighthawk yet. Surely she ought to be due about now. And the war—"

"Softly, softly. One thing at a time, or I shall begin to talk about over-excitement, as well as the doctor," answered Evans, who was more his usual self again.

And then he went on to tell her of the misadventure of the attempt on the steamer Liberty, on the capture of which so much scheming had been lavished, so many perils risked.

He told of the first success when she had sailed from New York to Portland, with the proper complement of Southerners in the guise of ordinary passengers on board. They had succeeded in making themselves masters of the vessel, imprisoning the officers and getting the crew apparently to follow their wishes in heading for the New Brunswick coast. Here they were to have been joined by the ammunition-laden schooner, then lurking in a quiet harbour near by. Once fitted out by her they would have been able to start out as a Confederate cruiser.

But they had failed to reckon on one or two bold New England spirits among the crew. These bided their time to influence the more pliable cosmopolitan element, and watching their chance, got possession of the steamer, released the officers, ran her ashore near the frontier and deserted her—Evans on board the schooner, hovering near, understood the catastrophe. "And so the ammunition and I came back again," he ended with a rueful smile. Antoinette gave a sigh to the eager plans which had ended in nothing.

"All the same, I am glad that they got nothing out of me about it. I might have feared afterwards that I had caused the failure. It was Benjamin's lost letter, the first one about the steamer, you know, that they had got hold of and tried to make me read to them. I would have let them kill me," she added fiercely, "rather than have run the risk of their knowing."

Again Evans felt that strange inability to speak. "Better lose fifty steamers and their crews than that any harm should come to you," he burst out hotly.

She raised her head with its old accustomed pride as she answered:

"That is not the way that we Southern women work for our country."

Then Evans went on to tell her of the search which Warwick and the other two men had made about the deserted farm, and with what useless results.

"They have probably reached Boston by this time," he went on, "and perhaps, so long as they are really gone, it is just as well that they weren't caught.

"But Major Warwick is hot for vengeance and for getting detectives on their tracks. I have kept him quiet up to now by saying that he must not move in the matter without your leave. Perhaps you had better see him as soon as you feel able, and make him understand that you do not wish any more fuss made—at least, I should think it would be better not."

It was a very unusual thing for any change to show in Antoinette's clear creamy skin, but she flushed now, vividly, painfully, under the man's significant glance.

"Oh, yes, far better! I will tell him so," she agreed hastily, and then as if changing the subject, "But you haven't told me if there is any news of the Nighthawk yet."

There was no questioning glance from Evans now. He was bitterly jealous of Major Warwick, jealous with the unreasoning antipathy of a man who felt himself lower-born, older and less attractive, jealous above all that it should have come into his hands to save her from such parlous straits.

On the other hand, Arthur's evident devotion to

Mabel was so firmly established in his mind as a fact, that he had never connected him mentally with Mrs. LeMoine. "No, but he must be due any day now. I trust he has had better luck since he called in here," he answered, never guessing how feverishly her pulses throbbed at his words.

She lay for hours gazing at that blue line of sea that down there to the south met the sky.

Soon she and Arthur would pass away beyond it, away from this summer-tide dallying in a strange land, into the suffering fatherland that called her children to watch the slow draining of her life-blood. Evans had given her evil news of more lost battles, and armies slowly but surely pressed back by sheer force of numbers.

Yes, there was her place, with the defeated, the starving, the wounded and dying. There, she, the divorcée, might be on a level with the good women who, as she had said to Arthur, had prayed and patched at home.

Here what could she be, to anyone, even to those two men who she knew cared for her. Perhaps it was only her physical weakness that made her realise how she shrank from Evans' eager eyes. Perhaps it was the same thing that made her breath come quicker at the thought of meeting Warwick and of trying to thank him for all that he had done for her.

Through the feverish visions that had shrouded her memory of the rescue she could hear so plainly the tender urgence of his voice, could recall the gentle touch of his hands. Could? She had been trying to forget them, as she tried now to put them aside from her mind and think of nothing but her return to the

South, and of what she could do there. What did anything else really matter? she said to herself. And then
she was feverish, and the doctor put it down to Evans'
visit, so that it was a day or two more before she saw
Major Warwick.

She had been promoted to an armchair on the
verandah, where she sat among her cushions bare-
headed under the soft shade of a white lace parasol.

A vague feminine hint of "nervousness" had made
Hattie remain with Adair within sight, and to a raised
voice, within hearing, so that she felt to some extent
under protection from any emotional outbreak.

Two men, however, playing into each other's hands
can do much, and they were practically alone when
Warwick stood beside her looking down at the thin,
white hand that lay in his big palm and from that into
the lovely fragile face.

The wistful pity in the grave face that she looked up
into brought a sudden veil of unaccountable tears
into her eyes.

Perhaps these tears proved her best weapon of
defence, for revealing her weakness to Warwick, they
caused him to draw on his armour of self-control.

Though the passion in his heart was surging high he
would not breathe a hint that would disturb her until
she was strong again. And so it was very nearly in his
ordinary voice that he said:

"Ah, I shall scold Miss Hattie for not having made
you less ethereal yet. I believe that I could pick you up
and carry you as easily as I did the last time I saw you."

Again the rare blush, and Antoinette laughed.

"I'm sure you couldn't, but please don't try. I think

it would be what the doctor calls exciting, and I'm not to be excited, you know. I'm to be humoured and not to do or say anything that I don't want to."

"Quite right. I shall humour you as much as you want. Only, as you are strong be merciful."

As he answered lightly he pulled up a low chair close to her sofa where he could look into her face. What did anything else matter?

She had got the talk on to safe ground now, but then there was the thanking him to be done. Her fingers pulled restlessly at the fringe of her shawl as she began.

"Every day when I have looked out at the sky and the sea and the sun, I have said to myself that I owe it to you that I can still look on them. But for you I might be lying there in that room, dead."

But Warwick laid an arresting hand on hers. "No, I must draw a line, I see. I cannot humour you in talking about that, to-day. Indeed, I doubt if I ever do. Promise me to try to forget it."

She shook her head with a strange mournful smile.

"Please don't make me feel that I ought to go away and leave you. It is so good to sit here beside you again."

She could not resist the pleading in his tone. "No, stay, and I will be very good," she said. "But there is one thing I must say, and that is to ask even another service at your hands. Those people have escaped"— she could not help a shudder—"I want you to let the whole matter drop into secrecy. Believe me, it helps me best so."

She could see that this demand went sorely against

the grain with him, but she knew that she had only to ask and have.

And so it was, and Warwick yielded. One stipulation he made, however. That was that, as the old General had always professed himself a warm friend of hers and of the South, as she had almost been his guest when the affair happened, and as he was civil Governor as well as General, he might go to him and give a confidential account of the whole adventure.

Antoinette acquiesced in his wish, without, however, seeing any advantage to be gained by it.

"It is at any rate some official knowledge of what has happened," he said. However things did not turn out exactly as he had anticipated. The Governor might be an admirer of the charming Mrs. LeMoine. He might even dabble in the enthusiasm for the Southern cause which was with his type of Englishmen a fashionable fad of the day. Yet apart from such passing diversions there lay the permanent fact that as an old friend and comrade of Warwick's father he was growing uneasy at the son's infatuation for this brilliant but mysterious lady. Therefore, after listening with many protestations—of horror and sympathy to Warwick's tale of Mrs. LeMoine's adventures, he hummed and hawed a bit and then said his say with all diplomatic caution.

"My dear fellow, I cannot express my admiration of the coolness and skill with which you conducted the whole matter. Really though, as one man of the world to another, perhaps you would not mind my suggesting that it is hardly advisable for a military man to get too mixed up in these American war matters. It might happen to tell against him, you know. Of course, I'm not saying it officially as General, but merely giving my opinion, as an old family friend, that I'd be cautious if I were you.

"No one could possibly entertain a greater admiration for the lady than I do; but her apparition amongst us was rather comet-like, brilliant and sudden, and her vanishing may be in the same manner.

"Your cousin, Captain Arthur, has known her, you say? Well, to my mind, Captain Arthur must have known some pretty queer folk in his day, and he's not one to tell tales on a woman.

"You see, it's rather significant that she doesn't care to make the violence used against her public. State secrets? Oh, yes, they are like charity sometimes, and cover a multitude of sins.

"Now suppose you were to apply for six weeks' leave and take a run up the Gulf. I'll wire some of the Montreal big-wigs and get you some salmon fishing. It would make such a good break for you. You're just back from long leave? Oh, I'll make that all right. You won't? Well, wilful man must have his way, and I've done my best. You're angry with me now, but some day you'll see that the old man knew what he was talking about. Go off and get into mischief."

Warwick had fumed in silence through this exhortation. He could not speak out his angry protest, but the keen old man had guessed his feelings, remembering the days when he, too, had been ready to do battle with the world for a woman's sake. Warwick's ire was all the greater in that he had brought this upon his own head by his proffered confidence.

CHAPTER XXII

"A WAIF OF STORMY SEAS"

DURING the summer days that had been so eventful to his friends ashore, Captain Arthur had been "dreeing his weird" at sea. There almost seemed to be something in his idea that Mrs. LeMoine had broken his run of good luck, for on the second start fate had still been against the Nighthawk.

True, she had made a run of unexampled speed, and had got safely into Wilmington and out again. Then she had run across to Nassau to get rid of some of her burden of cotton, and was hardly outside that harbour again before the old enemy, the yellow fever, had shown itself, and this time in even more deadly form.

There were fresh grey hairs on Arthur's temples, and some more fine lines around his eyes. These owed their origin to a certain night when, with two of the crew lying dead, no glimmer of light could be shown by which to read the burial service. A watchful foe was lying to right, another to left of them, and must be distanced and out of sight before the short summer night was done.

"They are brave Englishmen and shan't go overboard like dogs," Arthur vowed with that spirit which made his men ready to go through anything with him. And so, through the hours of dark, the Nighthawk alternately dodged and sprang forward with contagion in her breast. At dawn, when, the foe lost sight of, they buried their dead, one of those who carried them on deck fell lifeless as he walked.

Then sharks gathered in numbers around the vessel, which, speed as she might, never seemed able to shake off her ominous escort. All attempts to keep the crew occupied seemed useless—there was always someone with leisure to lean on the bulwarks and watch the black fins, and each man as he watched them shuddered and grew grim and silent.

Brave hearts were chilled and cowed, and courage was conquered by superstition. The captain and his officers did their best in the struggle with their impalpable foe. Arthur's voice rang with a resolute cheerfulness through all those days of gloom, for had not the Nighthawk turned her prow northward toward the haven where he would be?

Doggedly he struggled on in the face of bad weather and fogs. He lost more men from the fever. He was turned out of his course often by wandering northern cruisers, but always back on it again at the earliest possible moment.

"I shall live to see her yet," he muttered to himself, as he looked up at the north star that seemed to beckon him on.

Each day, as it came, found him more gaunt and wolf-like; each day the leaden weight upon his brain seemed heavier. He knew that the hand of illness was upon him, and ran his race with fate.

At last on the day when the Nighthawk rode safely at anchor at the quarantine in Halifax harbour, Arthur lay in his cabin, unconscious of having reached his bourne. The long strain had utterly broken him down and he was in the grasp of malarial fever.

But the pure, life-giving northern breezes wafted fresh strength to him, and the calm of attainment soothed his spirit. Those who know how to rule know how to trust, and he let fall every care of the ship into the hands of his first officer, the silent, solemn Mr. Parke. The second officer, a slim, fair young Englishman, nursed him as men sometimes can nurse with a single-hearted devotion which rivals any woman's.

And so the strong body and soul soon conquered the foe and began to gather fresh force.

The yellow-fever patients were mostly dead or quite convalescent. There were no fresh cases, so that quarantine was not a very lengthy business.

At the earliest possible moment Evans and Warwick were on board with many schemes for the carrying off and nursing of Arthur.

These schemes were ruthlessly tabooed by the doctor, who insisted that nothing could be so beneficial as the sea air where the Nighthawk lay out in the stream.

"The best hospital in the world," he announced.

Arthur looked wistful but acquiesced, feeling a shrinking from being seen by Mabel in his present broken-down condition.

Evans returned with these tidings to Trafalgar. Then Antoinette, who had been very white and restless for the last few days, announced her intention of returning to her hotel quarters from whence she might go daily on board the Nighthawk to look after Arthur. To this scheme Evans made every possible objection. Mabel sneered, and Hattie entreated her not to run any risks, but, regardless of all, she held to her determination.

However, at sight of the sullen frown which had gathered on Evans's face she paused in her purpose long enough to seem to ask his advice.

She dwelt pathetically on her indebtedness to Arthur and on his present forlorn condition; so that to his own surprise Evans found himself applauding her intention, and amiably driving her into town. Whatever her private views, she must not just now risk offending the owner of Trafalgar and its many advantages. But, oh, what a glad sense of familiar comradeship came over her when, standing on the deck of the Nighthawk, she looked down at Arthur's gaunt, wasted form, that, stretched in a hammock-chair, seemed the mere shadow of his old energetic self. Arthur was unfeignedly glad to see her. Good comrades and something more, as he and his officers were, he was near enough to recovery to desire a change from their society. Then, if Antoinette were not the rose, she at least came from the rose's neighbourhood, and could give him news: news for which his soul hungered.

And so his welcome was warm enough to stir in her heart a strange tremulous resurrection of what she had once hoped. Was it possible that that vista was still open to her? But the memory of Mabel's fresh young beauty rose before her and answered no.

Mabel she knew would have no further encouragement for Arthur if Warwick showed any signs of weakness before her smiles. But then Warwick with his usual directness of purpose promptly abandoned Trafalgar and almost daily made a third in the group on the Nighthawk's deck.

So far, the doctor had only allowed these two visitors. But as Antoinette watched Arthur's perfect physique asserting itself against weakness, she day by day counted the restful hours of familiar intercourse that were left to her, before the world absorbed them again.

Hitherto he had mostly listened while she told him recent public events or read to him from the papers.

One day, though, that they were alone, Arthur had roused himself to tell of some of his recent perils.

From that he went on to dwell on the increasing risks that had to be met in the work. The Northerners, he said, had larger and swifter craft and were getting more up to all the tricks of flight and pursuit.

"I have pretty well made up my mind that this trip shall be my last," he said reflectively. "I have got together a comfortable little sum out of the business—enough to give one a fair living at home, and a cosy nook for one's old age. What's the use of tempting fate too far? If I were not pledged to take in this cargo of ammunition, and don't want to fail them, I doubt if I should go back this time."

Antoinette's heart sank with a chill dread of disappointment: but she suppressed the question that rose to her lips, "And what of your pledge to me?"

She remained silent while he went on to ask, "Where *is* the ammunition?"

"In the Trafalgar lofts."

"And the powder?"

"Evans answers for that."

"I hope that there has been no attempt at mixing Warwick up in the business of getting it." And Arthur spoke with something of his old incisiveness.

Seldom had Mrs. LeMoine's voice implied such an indifference, only a shade too languid to be haughty, in speech with Arthur as it did now, when she answered,

"Really, I have never asked. It is Mr. Evans' business, not mine, you know."

Arthur was watching her closely: but in apparent unconsciousness she was lazily following a passing schooner with her eyes.

"Then why have you got him so securely into your toils?"

The sharp sudden question did not seem to startle her.

The flicker of a smile of power momentarily lightened her sombre face.

"Because he chose to put himself there, I suppose."

But Arthur did not smile as he retorted:

"If he should have run any risk, it would be for your sake."

Again the same superb turn of the neck as she answered: "He would not be the first who has risked something for my sake."

Arthur raised himself excitedly in his chair.

"I warn you, once and for all, that I will not have his name tampered with! Heavens, can't you guess what that name means to me when I put it aside from all the wild work that I have been through."

In her set white face the woman's wonderful eyes blazed, the only life, as leaning forward she said with slow, almost cruel emphasis:

"What does *that* matter to me? More things than his

name or yours go to the making of a great nation!"

Arthur checked himself with what was almost pity as he answered gravely:

"There is no great nation amaking. The writing is on the wall even now. My last trip to Wilmington showed me that. Everything is wanting—men, arms, credit, food, and clothing. The resources are failing day by day. It would be mere folly for you to go back into the *dies irae* that is coming. Give up the idea and stay here."

There was something almost gentle in his last words, but they had no effect on her.

"What, would you trust me here with your precious cousin?" she scoffed. Then her white hands clasped each other as she went on in a low strained voice: "Would you break your promise to take me back with you? I claim it as a right."

Arthur ignored the scoff, and answered gravely: "Why not stand clear from the wreck?"

"No, I shall go down with the ship," and in her voice was a great renunciation.

He made a movement of helpless impatience. "I would have saved you from it all, for our old friendship's sake."

"Is that still a spell to charm by?" she flashed out. "Then let me ask you one favour: Promise me that you will not warn Major Warwick against me?"

Again Arthur's hawk-like eyes studied her face and apparently what he read there satisfied him.

"Why should I?" he said, "unless you should drive me to. But why do you ask me that?"

Her voice was a bit shaken now.

"He is different from you and Mr. Evans and the others. He thinks me all that I once might have been and—well, somehow, I'd rather it should be so. I, in my turn," she went on—and now her voice was harder—"promise you to leave his life untouched by mine. I only ask that he should be allowed to remember me kindly."

Arthur was well on his guard.

"You have not let him know of your husband's death, I suppose?" he asked.

A deep stain marked Antoinette's cheek as from a blow. His scorn was very bitter for the woman who had loved him so well.

She laughed harshly.

"Don't be afraid of my marrying him. I shan't 'pour my poison in your Venice glass.' Though remember, I could marry him any day I chose."

"I dare say," he assented gravely. "But in that case I should feel bound to express my opinion to him. Otherwise, and if you will kindly choke him off from this idea of coming in the next trip of the Nighthawk we are still friends."

With a strange smile she answered:

"It's a bargain then. Why should he follow in the footsteps of the stray lambs of many nations? He is not of the type that furnishes 'The Lost Legion.' Now I think that after this very interesting conversation, I should like to go ashore."

And smiling still, though very pale, she waved her hand to him from the boat.

"I doubt if I understand that woman yet," Arthur said to himself before he dismissed the subject from his mind.

CHAPTER XXIII

A MADONNA FACE

'Tis a face to whose oval the gold hair in framing
Lends a halo celestial: the flesh but a veil
For the spirit's perfection—all your carven saints shaming,
In their canopied niche—shows as ivory pale.
                                                    —F. BANNERMAN.

THIS transference of the centre of interest from
Trafalgar to the decks of the Nighthawk, furnished
Mabel Evans with a grievance, the outward manifesta-
tion of which was her favourite trick of meek sulkiness. This sulkiness always took the form of wounded
feeling, sad endurance of injuries, and other such
subtle forms of the feminine complaint.

Her grievances were many:—the supremacy of
Mrs. LeMoine, whom she hated as only those chill
self-centred natures can hate; the knowledge finally
forced home upon her that Major Warwick hardly
realised her existence save as an accessory to
Antoinette; the emphatic disapproval shown by her
father, when on his return he had learnt something
and guessed the rest of her behaviour; the praise and
gratitude awarded to Hattie, as well as the new importance which her approved-of engagement had given
her at home.

All these facts formed, what in her mental language

Mabel styled "the crosses laid upon her." After having passed through the transforming medium of her imagination, they were presented to the notice of her spiritual adviser, the chaplain, with a plea for advice and sympathy.

But that shrewd shepherd of sheep knew his women folk. He was not unfamiliar with this feminine process of mental embroidery, and loved to tear it to rags. Oh, crowning indignity! when he too snubbed the fair devotee, advising her to try to see things in a less self-absorbed point of view, and to strive to be more helpful to others, more considerate of their probable troubles.

After this downfall, only one person remained to whom to turn for reinstatement in her own self-importance, and this was Arthur.

She had been inclined to think rather more respectfully of him since she had heard that he was Major Warwick's cousin, and so belonged to a family that had a baronet for bead.

She had also absorbed several hints, dropped of late by her father, as to the large sums made by Arthur in this blockade-running. Her intuition told her that no amount of Mrs. LeMoine's society could weaken *his* devotion, and in the knowledge she now found her consolation.

Then, with the practical decision which she could display when she chose, she set to work to get her father's aid in bringing Arthur to Trafalgar, which she knew would speedily settle matters.

Nothing was openly said, but Evans was only too pleased to follow her lead. So that on the very day after Antoinette's just narrated interview with Arthur, Mr. Evans brought Mabel on a visit to the invalid. One of his life's ineffaceable mental pictures was stamped upon Arthur's vision when she stepped on deck, the slim girl figure in its summer draperies of naiad-like green and white, swayed around it by the soft breeze as she stood there with a background of sea and sky, one hand holding a basket of glowing roses, her lips parted in a smile gentler and tenderer than he had yet seen there. Was it possible, he wondered, in a mad tumult of feeling, as the soft hand seemed to tremble in his, and her eyes spoke a shy welcome? Had she then learned at last to value his devotion?

"I have brought you some roses from, home," she said softly, and the passionate breath of the flowers seemed to speak her welcome—

Meanwhile, Mabel was saying to herself even as her eyes fell before his: "Yes, anyone can see that he is a gentleman, but it is a pity that he is not as tall as Major Warwick. I'm afraid he's not much taller than I am, and that won't look nearly so well. But anyway, those others shall see that there is *someone* who counts me first."

"Those others," were Mrs. LeMoine and Major Warwick, who seated there in deck chairs were now spectators to this meeting, which brought back to Antoinette the dreary certainty that Arthur was held by no tie of the past. Youth and the future, ever a woman's worst foes, faced her now and marked her defeat.

The cold blue eyes that swept her in passing triumph stung her vitality into self-assertion.

Womanlike she turned to Warwick with a wistful smile and a low-toned remark. While she talked with him she still heard Evans's voice as he insistently urged Arthur to come out to Trafalgar for change of scene and society. Even more distinctly she marked the few gentle words which Mabel put in to strengthen her father's invitation.

"I think that Mrs. LeMoine will give us a good character as nurses," the girl cooed, smiling over at the other woman.

Remembering the many slights and barbed words endured in those days of weakness, the pure audacity of the remark struck Antoinette's sense of humour. Something in the smile with which she answered brought a deeper colour to Mabel's face.

"It would be base ingratitude if I did not," was the sweet-toned answer.

Arthur was longing so keenly to accept the invitation that he felt bound to offer a few objections. These being overruled he half shyly agreed to come the following day.

His heart was throbbing with the knowledge, that the next week held one of the great events of his life, and he was almost awed before this prospect of happiness.

Mabel's grasp on her parasol handle tightened viciously as she heard her father urging Mrs. LeMoine to join the Trafalgar party. Lively fathers will consider their daughters' interests to a certain point, but no further. But she need not have been afraid—Antoinette had no intention of forming a Greek chorus to Arthur's love-making, if she could help it.

She was not yet quite sure in her own mind as to

whether Mabel intended to marry him or not, but at any rate she wished to see as little of the affair as possible. She intended, too, to keep as much out of Evans' way in the future, as she could without offending him.

And so with adroit evasions she slipped through Evans' attempts, and Mabel returned home well content with her day's work. She would show Hattie that she had something else to do but watch her love-making.

Warwick had the instinctive knowledge that his liege lady was in need of comfort, and refusing Arthur's proffers of dinner, he accompanied her when she left the ship.

His dog-cart was in waiting, and he persuaded her to let him drive her in the cool of the late afternoon, through the shadowy pine woods of the Park and by shining stretches of sea.

At first he seemed to devote most of his attention to his little mare, leaving her to her own thoughts. Presently, looking down at her, he spoke with his usual deliberation :

"I am very glad that you did not consent to go out to Trafalgar."

"Why?" she asked, startled by this new idea.

"Oh, well, you know, I have a great admiration for Hattie Evans, and I can see that her father is a reliable and useful man to you. Yet somehow they don't seem to be exactly the kind of people for you to be living among—not what you have been used to, I am sure."

Antoinette laughed out in frank amusement.

"What a *grand seigneur* you are, and how well you hide it!"

"Yes, I'm old-fashioned, I suppose, but one doesn't talk about that kind of thing save to one's equals."

The pride of race swelled in Antoinette's heart as she felt his tacit recognition.

"Then you'll be sorry if your cousin marries Mabel?" she asked. She was in the mood to force her sorrows into definite form.

"Yes, I'll be sorry. She doesn't ring true," he said reflectively, "but he is only my cousin and must go his own way. It seems to come nearer when I see them claiming intimacy with you."

His words were as balm to her wounded pride, and by the time that he had left her at the hotel her jarring nerves were soothed into calm.

When Arthur drove out to Trafalgar the next afternoon, he saw Mabel standing awaiting him on the verandah. From the moment when he met her welcoming smile he was encompassed in sweet observances enough to turn the head of any man.

Given a shady verandah with deep chairs and cushions, through the hot hours of the August day, and the fair young face beside him that had been the vision of many an hour of "storm and stress" what could mortal man want more?

In such times the most self-contained of men is confidential, and now Arthur talked of himself with the fixed purpose of drawing Mabel nearer to him.

He told her of his early life and adventures, of the boyish scrape that had driven him out of the British navy, of the hard times and the good that he had since faced.

"And now I think that I'm making landward at last,"

he went on. "A grim old aunt, who always stood up for me, bless her, has left me her little place on the south coast, and in a modest way I've made my pile at this blockade-running.

"So, one more toss-up with the fates, and then, if the grim sisters only prove propitious, Captain Arthur will retire into the background, and Arthur Warwick will make his reappearance in society."

The significance of his words was plain to her, but Mabel was not of the type that from shyness blunders away from the point, and so misses the right moment. She now leant forward with a pretty show of grave interest.

"Why risk the 'once more,' and perhaps lose all?"

One hand hung temptingly down from the arm of her high-backed chair near where Arthur was sitting on the steps beneath her. He yielded to the desire to take it in his as he asked, looking up into her eyes as though to read her inmost soul :

"Would you care if I were to lose all?"

Heavens, he thought, how pure was the spirit that looked out from those eyes, how candid the tender gravity that lurked in their virginal depths! The man's whole passionate heart humbled itself in worship before what he felt to be a perfect type of pure girl-hood. He watched a lovely colour flicker in her face, the faintest dumpling curve the lines of her mouth, and he listened breathlessly to the low whisper:

"Ah, you know well that I would!"

The hand that he had grasped in his was now pressed with kisses until it was drawn away in pretty distress.

Bereft of that, Arthur then found words to tell her how from their first meeting that spring, he had idolised her as his pearl amongst women.

"And you *did* think of me sometimes when I was away, and *did* care a little what became of me?" he urged. "I seemed to read the first certainly in your dear eyes that blessed day when you came on board. Tell me, do tell me that you did?"

And Mabel, to whom this adoration came as a justly due incense, smiled, and with modestly drooped eyelids murmured a sweet reply.

Straightway Arthur stepped over the magic threshold of that paradise which most of us enter in our day, if only for a few weeks or months.

His only care was how should a rough careless sailor like him be worthy of such a perfect gem of womanhood? How guard such grace and purity with sufficient care through the mazes of life?

It was Mabel who recalled him to some sense of real life by saying gently: "Now you will have to give up this one more voyage."

There was no question in her tone, only a calm certainty, and Arthur looked disturbed.

"I cannot, dearest. Don't you see that I am pledged to get that ammunition in at any risk? Mrs. LeMoine has done her share of the work, you would not have me fail in mine? Then, too, she is counting on me to take her back myself."

"And you consider her fancies more than the anxiety that I shall suffer?" Mabel's calm was ominous.

"Her fancies as a woman are nothing to me. But I must go, and I have told her that she can go with me.

Heaven knows that I don't want to be burdened with her, but I must let her come if she insists," Arthur protested.

"You should value your life for my sake now," Mabel went on with quiet persistence.

"I am ashamed to think how much I *do* value it, how unwilling I am now to run any fresh risks. It almost seems cowardly to think so much of oneself, even for your sake, dearest. But my word is my word, and that ammunition is a matter of not only life and death, but the last hopes of the South. I have benefited by them; I will not desert them now. I am sure that you will understand it, darling," he urged, his voice shaken by anxiety.

But Mabel had no intention of understanding another view than her own. She chose to fancy that Mrs. LeMoine had something to do with this determination of Arthur's, and resented it bitterly.

"Very well," she said drawing her hand away from him with sad decision, "I cannot have any engagement announced until after you have made your last blockade running trip. I will not be placed in a position of such uncertainty. Say that you were detained months in a Northern prison!" .

This was her ultimatum, and neither then nor later could Arthur succeed in moving her from it.

Mabel had been sure that Arthur could never hold out against her wishes, but she did not know him yet. He could not entertain the possibility of not keeping his word, and so stood firm, and affairs were at a standstill.

The downfall of his rosy visions was woeful enough;

but still the delay could hardly be for more than a month or so, and be felt secure of Mabel's affections, and of her father's good-will.

Evans succeeded before long in getting at the root of the matter, and was inclined to be indignant with Mabel. It was Arthur himself who made excuses for her, and admitted the reasonableness of her conduct.

"For all her pretty face and the money that I shall give her, she isn't worth him, though he doesn't know it," the father said to himself.

But Arthur had a present stock of bliss in her smiles and soft speeches.

CHAPTER XXIV

"FIRE AT THE HEART,
'TWIXT HELL AND HEAVEN"

EACH bright day of that passing summer was bringing nearer the end of the great struggle.

The stream of Southern men and women who restlessly came and went seemed rather to increase than diminish. They were ever meeting and parting, watching and praying for those who might never come again, but had gone down

> "In the swirl of the fierce battle flames."

But even now, when the wise were counting the months that lay between their country and the bitter days of defeat, there were "careless daughters who were at ease," who laughed and gossiped and decked themselves in Paris fashion, and, gayly wore the new diamonds, investments of the men against an evil day.

A group of this kind had but lately landed from England, and since their arrival there had been significant little hints and whispers floating about in society, which clustered round Mrs. LeMoine's name.

Warwick had as yet heard nothing of these rumours, nor had the Evanses or Captain Arthur.

But the wily, old General had, on the first hint, quietly followed up the subject. Chuckling sardonically to himself, he reflected:

"'Pon my word, it goes against the grain to be down on a woman as pretty as that; but I must get that foolish fellow Warwick out of her hands, if only for the sake of that day at the Redan, when his father carried me out of fire. I thought that I had done with the folly of meddling with other people's affairs, but there is no fool like an old fool."

Antoinette herself was in complete ignorance that her cousin and quondam friend, Molly Seton, might at any moment meet her face to face.

Her acute power of touch with her surroundings had been dulled of late by a listless indifference.

Since the day when she had talked with Captain Arthur, she had shrunk from all companionship.

Major Warwick's chivalrous tendencies had seemed to pain her as much as the sight of the two pairs of happy lovers at Trafalgar. She seemed to shrink equally from Evans' masterful air of possession. As the tasks that had been given into her hands neared success, she was without the stimulus of work. All that she seemed to care for was to sit brooding in solitude. She did not know how Arthur's love-affairs had turned out; indeed, she seemed rather to avoid knowing.

Then, at the close of a long, hot day, her mood suddenly changed. There was a regimental ball that evening, and although she had, up to now, refused to go, she hurriedly dressed herself in her most gorgeous attire. It was a crimson silk of that barbaric colour of the day, styled "magenta," the crude force of which had, however, no power to dull the purity of her skin.

Warwick was lounging near the ball-room door as she entered, and the listlessness of his bearing changed all at once to glad alacrity, as he came forward to meet her.

"How *could* you be so rash as to come alone?" he urged. "Why did you not let me know this afternoon that you had changed your mind?"

"Because I did not know it myself. About an hour ago the spirit moved me, and I dressed and came. Besides, I really don't always require a body-guard, although I am grateful for it. An accident never happens twice at the same bridge, and no one is likely to try to elope with me in a cab again. I didn't prove a very paying investment, you know."

She had taken Warwick's proffered arm, and looked around as though the brilliant scene were a pleasant change to her.

She did not notice that Warwick, seeing the General approaching as though to greet her, had turned their steps towards him.

At the same time, as she caught sight of the thin and fragile, but still soldierly-looking, old man, resplendent in his scarlet tunic of full-dress, with its shining row of medals, she was aware that the wondrously attired woman on his arm was her cousin, Molly Seton.

Many a French *grande dame* whose past had been far less saintly than that of Madame Elizabeth or the Princesse de Lamballe, may have faced the supreme hour of martyrdom with as serene a grace as they did.

So now there came over Antoinette the mental and physical bearing with which a French Huguenot ancestress had stood before the dread torturers of Nîsmes.

"A martyr by the pang, without the palm."

Her classic head poised itself with a more superb curve on her white neck. Her great hazel eyes rested calmly on the woman before her, while the shadow of a smile curved the repose of her perfect mouth. The gloved hand that rested on Warwick's red sleeve lay motionless in its relaxed repose.

The General's effusive congratulations on her recovered health and looks, had in them a touch of nervousness. He would have been heartily relieved if Mrs. LeMoine had made a move to pass on, but she stood as though awaiting his wishes.

Nothing then seemed to remain to him but to force the situation.

"We are privileged beings, Warwick," he began, "in forming a group where two such Parisian toilettes set forth such charms. Perhaps," turning his courtly smile on the stranger, "the beautiful creations were evolved in concert by the fair compatriots."

An imperceptible pause, while Antoinette's steady gaze never wavered; then the pretty, faded little woman, putting up her eyeglass, said in accents meant to be haughty, but sharpened to tremulousness:

"I had not the honour abroad, *this* year, of meeting Mrs.—er—oh, LeMoine is the *present* name isn't it?"

At the venomous spite of the words, both men turned an apprehensive glance on Antoinette, but neither curiosity nor friendship need have looked to see her flinch.

The soft languor of her voice was a mere shade more incisive as she spoke:

"There *was* a time when Molly Seton had less difficulty in remembering the name of Antoinette LeMoine."

"Heavens! the woman won't even condescend to pretend!" the General said to himself, divided between fear of a scene and admiration of Mrs. LeMoine's courage.

Neither man could understand why the taunt brought a dull red to the other woman's cheek with its memory of the young heiress's never-failing open-handedness to the widowed cousin. The taunt as it pierced home aroused a keener animosity, the keenest of all, that of a consciousness of "benefits forgot."

"That name was then an honoured one."

"And now?"

Quick as two rapiers flash were speech and retort; but now it was a "Warwick to the rescue." General or no general, Mrs. LeMoine should stand there no longer.

"I think that the General will perhaps excuse us, and let me take you to get that cup of tea," he said, bending to her with grave deference.

Then with a smile of acquiescence to him, and a sweeping bow which included both the conscience-smitten old General and her staring adversary, she passed on at his side.

Silently Warwick led her to a seat in the empty refreshment room.

"Sit here quietly for a few moments, and let me get you a glass of wine," he said looking down on her beauty with tragic eyes.

Her silvery laugh, as it rang out in response, seemed to mock at all things in Heaven and earth.

"Dear me!" she said with dainty surprise. "I'm not faint. You seem to think that you are rescuing me a second time."

"I would to God that I were! May I not attempt it?"

"There are some things past even your power. As a man sows so shall he reap! If one sows blind faith and single-minded purpose it is fitting that one should reap scorn and ingratitude. But aren't you going to ask me what it all means?"

It seemed to Warwick that, in contradistinction to the lightness of her words, there was an appeal in her eyes as she raised them to his. It was this appeal that he answered.

"Never! Tell me nothing save what you wish to! If ever you should wish to confide in me, I would be honoured by your doing so. But never feel that I ask to know anything. What you are contents me. I know that, and that is enough."

"You are a *preux chevalier* indeed! Surely, you have guessed how these people talk about me."

"They have never ventured to say it to me. I could guess nothing, listen to nothing against you."

An infinite yearning softened her face as she looked up into his.

"Poor fellow! But it is good to have one such champion against the world," she almost whispered.

"Let me really be your champion!" he murmured passionately.

But she only shook her head, saying, "Ah no, please!" then, with an attempt to return to her ordinary manner, "but you mustn't be too kind just now. Sympathy is always an enervating thing and I want to pull myself together, and go back presently to face the music. A lot of them will be watching for me, and I must turn up smiling. Let us go back and you shall dance the next waltz with me."

"Are you sure that you are able to?" he asked, anxiously noting her feverishly flushed cheeks and bright eyes.

Again she laughed that low mocking laugh that wrung his heart.

"I am able to-night to walk barefoot through purgatorial fires. I think that I am in them now," was her wild answer.

Even while wrestling with herself for strength to return and face her humiliation, she had seen Arthur and Mabel Evans seat themselves in a shadowy corner of the outer corridor.

How virginally fair and fresh she was in her shining folds of white satin,—a halo was all that was needed to complete the picture.

How radiant he looked in renewed strength as he leant over her—nearer, yet nearer—and his hand was on hers as Mrs. LeMoine, rising abruptly, took Warwick's arm, saying:

"Look at those happy lovers out there. *They* don't need to dance. They can sit still and be happy. But there is one dance that we all must tread—they as well as we, the dance Maccabre. Do you remember the old bridge at Lucerne with the pictures? How the blue-green river foams under it in the summer evenings when one strolls there to look at the pictures of Death dancing off with the bride from the altar, and the women singing in the tavern: '*Eh bien! Dansons!*'"

CHAPTER XXV

CAPTAIN ARTHUR'S PARTY

THE day after the ball, great was the stir and gossip over that evening's incident.

The Southern dames began by pluming themselves on having routed the black sheep from out their immaculate fold, and thronged to congratulate Mrs. Seton on the firmness of her moral courage. "And that old General has always made such a fuss over her," they said.

But this feminine self-complacency was not of long duration. Indeed, it did not outlast the reappearance of their men folk, worried and irritated from encounters with the united forces of Mr. Evans and the agent, who were out on the war-path at this insult offered to Mrs. LeMoine.

The agent sneered at the criminal folly of allowing any outburst of feminine spite to publicly discredit one who had been so trusted by the Confederate government, and who had so many times proved herself worthy of the trust.

"Look at how she served us too at the Tuileries! Why, it was she who persuaded the Emperor to consent to the building of those rams at Havre. She had him pledged, too, to the recognition of the South and if the tide had not turned in those reverses in April, he would have done it. And here, this summer, while they have been sneering at her, she has been holding important threads together with a master-hand. And she has suffered as well as worked. Do any of these fine ladies know that she was severely wounded at Gettysburg by going under fire to aid the wounded—wounded, who were perhaps their husbands, sons, lovers? And do they know how she let those spies all but starve her a month ago, rather than betray one of our secrets. And this is the way they repay her they, Southern women, if they are fine ladies. Let them remember this, when the waves of the rising Deluge close over *them* and their virtues."

The fire of this unaccustomed volubility awed those accustomed to the little man's usual chilly reticence.

Mr. Evans' words were still more emphatic and to the point. During the time of the protracted struggle he had acted as a sort of banker to the stormy petrels on the sea of war, often helping those in need with a delicate generosity hardly to be expected in such a man. Thus it came that his dicta, that unless ample amends were made immediately to Mrs. LeMoine, every sum that was owed him by Southerners should be at once called in, carried dismay to many hearts. The irate men blamed the women, and the women blamed Mrs. Seton as the originator of the trouble.

Mrs. Seton, having no man to speak unpleasant truths to her, tried to sniff at her sudden unpopularity in the cause of virtue but found it difficult, and the unpleasant fact remained that both Mr. Evans and the agent demanded a public backing down, and that the men regarded it as inevitable.

Captain Arthur took a more philosophical view of

the difficulty, and did his best to keep out of the fray.

When Major Warwick came to him with an indignant account of the combat, he tried to make excuses for outraged feminine virtue.

His weakness for the saintly type of woman was naturally in the ascendant at present, and he had a lively consciousness that Mabel would have small toleration for any knight-errantry.

He was also not altogether sorry for the chance that might open Warwick's eyes a bit, without his intervention.

However, he had from old comradeship a kindly feeling towards Mrs. LeMoine. First sounding Mabel, who had veiled her secret delight at Mrs. LeMoine's discomfiture in a magnanimously expressed pity, he made a proposal in the interests of peace. He suggested that he should give an afternoon dance on board the Nighthawk, at which Mrs. LeMoine should help him to receive the company.

To this all the local and garrison society should be bidden as well as the southern dames, whose attendance would be a consumption of humble pie.

This proposal was agreed upon, and many and dire were the ensuing domestic combats. One or two men were forced to confess that they had failed to coerce their women folk, but on the whole masculine supremacy asserted itself successfully.

Mrs. Seton, finding no other protection from the agent's pointed remarks, took to her bed, announcing herself very ill.

And so, on a still grey August afternoon, when the harbour water lay oily and motionless, groups of smartly-dressed people gathered on the deck of the Nighthawk, which shone even more trim and spotless than usual.

Antoinette had in her turn fought hard against this entertainment.

"Don't you see, that under the guise of an atonement, you are asking me to go through a far worse ordeal?" she had broken out wildly to the agent.

Bowing with a more chivalrous courtesy than he had yet shown her, he had answered :

"I thought it advisable for both public and private reasons. I know that when I say it is 'for the cause,' I need not urge you twice to any ordeal."

"For the cause! For the cause!" rhymed itself in her mind like a spell, as, pale to the very lips, Antoinette stood beside Captain Arthur to receive the guests. Their very companionship seemed such a cruel mockery.

Her black lace dress and hat, relieved by no touch of colour, seemed to give her the shadowy remoteness of a phantom.

Her faithful body-guard, Mr. Evans and the agent stood near her as the men and women who had once been her friends and family connections bowed to her with a ceremonious courtesy that seemed to strike her like a blow.

Only once she showed any signs of wavering and that was when Hattie Evans, slipping a friendly arm through hers, whispered:—

"*Dear* Mrs. LeMoine! You look more like a queen than ever, to-day! Why wouldn't you let me come and sit with you yesterday?"

"I was better alone," was all she answered, but the swift tears rose to her eyes at the girl's friendly touch and voice. Antoinette was on the alert for the appearance of Warwick, whom she had not seen since the night of the ball.

Not that he had not sought her often, but that she had pleaded the excuses of headache, business, fatigue.

When presently he stood beside her, one glance up into his face told her through what deep waters he had been passing. He had found her, the ordeal of the reception over, resting with Hattie Evans in the quiet retreat behind the wheel-house. That expert young woman was not long in slipping away to fresh pastures, and then they were practically alone.

Antoinette's mood was strung too high for any prudent dallying with commonplaces.

Her eyes studied Warwick's face sadly before she broke out.

"You have been unhappy for my sake, and oh, if you knew how little I am worth it!"

"You are worth all the world to me," came the low strenuous answer—then, going on with the sound of a fresh purpose:

"Tell me, will you answer me one question?"

"I will answer any question that you choose to ask me," was her ready response.

Warwick drew a deep breath before putting that crucial test.

"Have you a husband alive, or are you free?"

It was the question that she had been expecting, and understanding its full significance, a strong temptation seized her. If now she were to break her promise to Arthur and tell his cousin her true story she felt quite sure that nothing the former might urge against it could prevent Warwick from making her his wife.

His wife! Safe in the shelter of an English home, far from the tumult of war and from her own stormy past, safe in such love as she had dreamt of in her girlish days but had never yet known.

She would be amply revenged for Arthur's contempt, bearing his cherished family name as a covering to her own tarnished one.

What did she owe to Arthur that she should abandon all this at his order? What did she owe to the country whose men and women had just shown her how little they valued her self-sacrificing labours?

To be cherished and cared for once more in a safe haven instead of drifting on a solitary derelict of stormy seas! The impulse to fall out of the ranks and rest had swept over her in a slow wave, and Warwick, watching her mood, held his breath for the fall of the dice. Then all at once the languorous weakness that held her cleared away, and she was herself once more.

The cold steel-like pride which the years had forged out of her burning sense of injustice from the world told her that she must not imperil the future of this honest gentleman who trusted her, by joining her life to his. Why should her past overshadow his future? The very man whom she had loved with all the devotion of her womanhood had protested against it, and it was this protest now that stayed her. Arthur would speak bitter words to Warwick—words which he would not heed now, perhaps, but which might be the sowing of a thorny aftermath in their joint lives.

No, Arthur need not fear her coming into contact with his immaculate bride. And so she turned her face away from the land of promise, and looked straight ahead on her solitary path once more. She drew a deep breath, and her hands in their dainty, pearl-coloured gloves closed over each other as she answered slowly:

"He is alive; he is in the South now!" There was no echo of hope left in Warwick's voice, which was sharp with jealous pain, as he asked :

"And you are going to rejoin him?"

"Yes, I am going to rejoin him!" and if possible, she waxed paler than before, and shivered in the August heat.

Warwick rose abruptly. "That is all, then. I need not trouble you any more. Would you like me to take you back to the others?"

Antoinette sat staring up at him in a bewildered fashion.

Then with a sudden childlike sense of desolation at thought of losing the one friend she trusted, she stretched out both hands in appeal, saying:

"Oh no! I was telling you a foolish lie to make you forget me! He and I are parted forever."

The restrained eagerness was awake again in Warwick's eyes, as he caught the slim grey hands in his. "By death?" he asked.

"By life," was her answer. Even now she would not tell him the truth.

"But could you not get your freedom?" he urged. "Surely you must have grounds for a divorce."

"None that would be legal in England."

The excuse sounded weak to her but it did not seem to strike him so.

"What would that matter? The world is wide—" he was beginning passionately; but she stopped him by a gesture.

"Ah, hush! I like you too well to bring such harm to your life, your career."

"What can really harm me save losing you?" Warwick persisted.

The woman who had wiled De Morny and his Master flashed momentarily into sight, as smiling syrenlike into his face, she murmured:

"But you have not lost me yet."

With that smile Warwick was as wax in her hands.

"I am yours," he murmured with a closer clasp of her hands, "yours, to do what you will with, to use or fling aside as you choose. Only remember, I do not give up hope of having my own way yet," he added, more in his usual voice.

"None of us do, I suppose. But then how seldom we do get it," she said lightly. " See, there is Mr. Evans looking for us."

CHAPTER XXVI

LAST DAYS

THE two tonics of happiness and northern breezes had brought back all Captain Arthur's blithe energy. His days of lotus-eating were ended, and he and Evans were ceaselessly coming and going on mysterious business of which Trafalgar seemed to be the centre.

A little while previously Evans had given some reason for parting with his coachman, and while he said that he was looking out for another, a man from the Nighthawk slept in the stables and took care of the horses.

The rumbling of carts was frequently heard in the avenue at nights, as well as the creaking of the great doors of the barns on their hinges.

Arthur was still in possession of a room at Trafalgar, although he did not always pass the night there.

The maids wondered when in doing this room they found old clothes that they had never seen worn, huddled wet and muddy in a corner.

The time was drawing near for the Nighthawk to start with her precious cargo of ammunition and powder, and each one in the secret played his part.

Mr. Evans and Arthur took turns at superintending the arrival of the carts and the patrolling of the grounds at night by the men of the Nighthawk.

Handsome, lazy-looking Jack Hewitt, the second officer, would dance at some festivity half the night, and give the other half to keeping his men in that humour when work seems play, a humour which he could always evolve from them. Then at breakfast-time he would appear spick and span and languid to get a cup of coffee and a gracious smile from Mabel.

He appeared to pass on to her a portion from his unlimited devotion to his captain. Mabel patronised him as "gentlemanly" and "nice," unwitting that his languid smiles covered the most reckless spirit in the Nighthawk's crew, amongst whom recklessness was almost a taken-for-granted quality.

Hattie Evans and the old nurse spent many a night hour in providing food and drink for the watchers and workers, and in afterwards clearing away its traces, without the servants' knowledge.

Mabel alone gave no help or sympathy, elaborately ignoring the mysterious doings around her.

When Arthur, trying to overcome her passive resistance to his work, attempted a joke on the profits of the trip giving them a start in housekeeping, she would look distressed and perhaps murmur something about the curse of war.

And he—well at present he found this feminine sensitiveness altogether charming, and, although it made his high spirits a bit harder to force, still he chose to fancy that it revealed a more exalted nature than did Hattie's frank helpfulness or Antoinette's whole hearted comradeship in the cause. He said to himself that he would like to keep her always thus in saintly calm above

"the town's sordid sinning,"

where he strove and battled for her sake.

Mrs. LeMoine, having no share in this last work, played her part as had been agreed upon. She was to keep away from Trafalgar, and to occupy Major Warwick's attention so that he should know or care little about the doings or plans of his cousin. And so these two found themselves isolated together in a strangely peaceful and pleasant fashion.

The August days were too short for Warwick when they two alone in his little sail-boat sped along before the westerly breezes or drifted in the golden sphere of languorous twilight.

Antoinette was no inexperienced sailor, and often took charge of the tiller while Warwick handled the sheets.

It was thus in after days that he loved most to recall her, when she sat silently staring out towards the horizon with dreamy eyes, or else suddenly roused herself to smile on him in answer to his wistful words.

And there were times when they talked impersonally of the stirring war news that came day by day. Warwick watched patiently for the chances of this news leading her to refer to her own experiences, when he hung on every word which helped to reveal her more personally to him. He loved to see her cheek flush and her eyes deepen in intensity when she spoke of heroism and endurance which he had witnessed.

"But apart from these years of war, you have not been much in the South, I think," he suggested one day.

"No," she answered dreamily as though following her own mental pictures. "My schooldays were in a convent in Paris where my parents mostly lived. But then the old plantation with its childish memories was always 'home' to me. It seemed my natural refuge when a woman with all her hopes shattered, I went back there. The welcome of the old folk, who had known me as a baby, and of the younger ones, who had played with me, softened my bitter heart. They gave so much love, when they had so little. There was so much that I could do for them. It pains me now to think how forlorn and bewildered they must be among all these changes. If there is no work given me to do when I get to Richmond, I shall go back and live among them again. I can be a better woman there than elsewhere."

"Your plantation, Amity Hall, you call it, is not the only place where you can be honoured as you ought to be. Ah, can't you see," and Warwick bent forward towards her, "can't you see, how impossible it is for you to live without the natural human ties? Can't you see that while you are trying to absorb yourself in the fate of nations your heart is crying out for love, and for the womanly care for others that you would give so graciously? Ah, believe me, I am learning to know you better than you know yourself."

Her face softened and quivered under his pleading, but she shook her head.

"I wish that I were what you think me."

All that I think you is in you, only you crush it down and try to harden yourself. Shall I tell you how I see you in my visions?—the mistress of an old Kentish hall, stately and gracious to all, but with the real beauty of our inner self kept for one, for the husband to whom you are the great strength in public life, the one joy of home life. I *will* not give up such a vision as that."

Antoinette had bowed her face in her hands before the ardent stream of his words. As he paused, she raised it, strained and weary.

"Ah, please, you must not!" she said softly. "If you do, I must give up coming out with you, and—you know I like it."

He was alarmed in a moment.

"I will promise anything rather than have you do that," he said hastily.

It never rains but it pours, and Mrs. LeMoine was destined to another emotional scene the following day.

She had been obliged by business to go to Mr. Evans' office, which she did somewhat unwillingly.

She knew that, in spite of the cleverness of her evasions, he had once or twice detected them of late.

"I was sorry not to see you yesterday when I called. They told me that you had gone out sailing for the day with Major Warwick," he began somewhat grimly.

"Yes, those sails are such a relief from the close town streets," she answered propitiatingly.

"I thought that you were fond of the town streets. You seem to prefer them to Trafalgar."

Antoinette stared in innocent surprise.

"But you know the agent said that I had better not be too much at Trafalgar at present. It lessens the significance of everything, he thought," she urged.

"The agent is a fool with his ridiculous mysteries that deceive nobody," Evans grunted. Then in a milder tone: "I suppose I must be thankful for the small favour that brought you here to-day—oh, yes, you wanted those papers, I know. But still, it is pleasant to see you looking even better than ever," and his eyes devoured her beauty, set off by her dainty muslins.

"Yes, I am feeling quite my old self again, thanks to Trafalgar," she smiled. Then, hastily changing the subject:

"But now that I have come to bother you, I might as well talk a little business. I suppose that I had better take all the gold with me that I can put about me?"

Evans' face had hardened as though he felt her evasion, but still he asked in his ordinary tone:

"How would you carry it?"

"In a belt. My diamond necklace I must wear on my neck under my dress."

"The weight of gold in a belt adds to the chance of drowning," Evans said anxiously.

For the first time in his life he knew what it was to be nervous for another's safety.

Antoinette laughed carelessly.

"Oh, if it comes to the water, I should much rather go down quietly, and end it all quickly. There is nothing that I dislike more than the idea of floating about, half dead and alive."

It was a simple matter-of-fact remark, but it proved too much for Evans' equanimity. His big burly frame seemed shaken by unwonted agitation as he began hoarsely :

"How can you speak in that way of such an end. How could it be possible for such as you to die, the life choked out of you by the cruel water, with poor broken-down idiots living on!"

"That is Kismet!" she said calmly.

"We can be stronger than fate if we choose! At least, before you go, promise me to return to me, or to let me join you out there! My girls will soon be married; I am a far richer man than anyone fancies; I have been piling up money out of this blockade-running. You and I could make a fresh start in a new country. You should have everything you fancied that money could buy! Swear to me that you will come back!"

The terrible earnestness of the man increased her habitual shrinking from him. She did her best to veil it, trying to make her answer light:—

"As a ghost?"

"No! As your living beautiful self! Swear!"

"Don't you trust me without that?"

Her wrist was firm in his grasp, and his keen eyes under their shaggy brows searched her face.

Her first feeling was one of exquisite relief when the office-door was suddenly opened, and Arthur walked in.

Then, the good-natured, if slightly contemptuous, amusement in his eyes at sight of the interrupted situation came like a stab to her. Must she have to bear even this? But—what does it matter—a little more or a little less scorn?—was her mental solace, if solace it could be called.

After a momentary awkwardness, Evans was his usual self again.

"The start maybe any day now, I suppose?" he said looking at Arthur for confirmation, which he received in a nod.

Of course you know that the quieter it is kept the
better. So it would be as well not to show any sign of
preparation for departure. We will neither of us come
to tell you when the time is fixed. I shall send Hattie
for you, and then we shall get you on board from
Trafalgar. That's what we settled, isn't it Arthur?"

"That's it," the latter agreed. "That is, if Mrs.
LeMoine still persists in going. There is plenty of time
to take my advice and stay behind."

Antoinette looked down, twirling a heavy ring on
her finger as intently as though it had been a magic
circle to reveal the future. Warwick, Evans, Arthur—
they all formed part of the puzzle. Then she looked
up and said simply: "I will go please," and no man said
her nay.

CHAPTER XXVII

"HANDS THAT MUST PART"

IT was two days later, on a glorious September morning, that Hattie Evans came to Antoinette as the arbiter of fate. Her face was shadowed into gravity by her errand, but that did not obscure the blithe warm-heartedness of her presence.

"I do so hate to be the one to tell you that the time has come to go, when I should so dearly like to persuade you to stay," she said wistfully, holding her friend's hand in hers. "But father sent me to tell you that it is to-day that you are to come out to Trafalgar. And you are to leave your luggage so that it be fetched. You are not to return here at all."

Antoinette drew a deep breath, as does one that turns from the shore to the open sea.

"The time has come then," she repeated dreamily.

"Yes. They say that you go to-morrow:" and Hattie sought in the other's face for any sign of emotion, but found it not.

"How long will it take you to pack?" she asked, again her practical self.

"I could hardly be all ready before late this afternoon—say six o'clock. Would that do?"

"I suppose so. You'll let me stay and help you, won't you?"

Antoinette looked at the girl with kindly eyes but

shook her head with a smile.

"No, child. It's good in you to want to, but I think that I must do it alone. There is work of destroying some papers and leaving others, thinking work, you know, and that has to be done alone. But it will do me good all day to know that I shall have a last evening with you, my kind little nurse," and she touched Hattie's check with one of her rare caresses.

There was plenty of work ahead of her to fill several hours, and Antoinette lost no time about buckling to it. She gave orders that seemed to assure her being undisturbed, and the day passed busily. Soon after lunch she was resting, lying back wearily in a big arm-chair, the table before her littered with odds and ends.

She had all day been keeping at bay the thought of Warwick, and what he would suffer at her departure.

Now, in this moment of lassitude, the temptation to look into his face once more, to say good-bye, and thank him for all that he had been to her, pressed upon her with irresistible force.

At that very moment the door opened, and Warwick walked in unannounced.

Startled in every way, her feminine consciousness went first to her dishevelled white muslin and her loosened hair.

"Oh, I didn't mean to see anyone," she said with a helpless laugh of dismay.

But Warwick stood his ground in unabashed gravity. "I persuaded the maid to let me come up," he said. Then, too full of his subject to hesitate, "Is it true that you are going back this next trip of the Nighthawk?" he demanded.

Antoinette looked up, her fatigue startled away. She had not meant him to know until she was really gone.

"Who told you that?" she asked sharply. "Hattie Evans."

"What made her do that," she exclaimed impatiently.

Warwick's face showed how bitterly he was wounded. "Surely you could have trusted me so far," he said with ominous quietness.

A great compunction came over her, though she tried not to show it, as she answered lightly:

"Of course I trust you. It was only that my professional conspirator's mind was startled at the idea of her talking secrets. And then, you know, I am so dreadfully under the thumb of that grim little agent, that I can never do as I would prefer. Do stop looking so very stern, and sit down and tell me what it is all about."

Warwick condescended to take a seat but was not to be turned from his reproaches. "Were you really going without saying good-bye to me?"

His words cut her to the heart, but she knew that if she allowed herself to be gentle now she could not hold to her purpose.

"Dear me! We shall have lots of time to squabble over that yet. I should never have such bad manners."

"Are you going alone?" Warwick demanded.

"If you call it alone, yes! That's no new thing. Captain Arthur will be there, you know."

"In any difficulty Arthur must count his ship before you. I shall get leave, and go and take care of you."

There was no request in this announcement.

Antoinette seeing that it was not a time to mince matters, sat up in her chair and, leaning forward, said:

"You are not going to do any such thing. To begin with, your paternal General would lock you up in the cupboard rather than give you leave on such an errand."

She laughed lightly, almost maliciously, dangling the while a feather fan from her finger. Warwick looked nettled.

"If he were to refuse me leave I should send in my papers. My father is always urging me to give up the service and settle down. I have often thought that I ought personally to do as lots of other soldiers have done, and go and see something of this war, and"—he paused before adding slowly—"I have even thought of taking a turn in for the South. Would not *that* please you?"

It was as though he were laying his life down into the chances of battle for her sake. A sudden fire of pride leaped into Antoinette's eyes, then, clear as a spoken word there flashed through her brain: "Oh God! Not the stain of this man's blood upon my soul!"

The pause was hardly perceptible before she spoke resolutely.

"That would be madness. The cause is lost."

The bitterness of her rebuff was in his face as he asked:

"Then why should you return there?"

"That is entirely different. It is my own country and I must share its fate. If the good days are over for it, and for me, so much the worse for us both. I am past fear."

She spoke with a calm certainty that chilled Warwick's heart, but, refusing to acknowledge defeat, he fought on. With grim, set face he spoke.

"You shall not go alone to any fate. Whatever it may be, I shall share it."

A wild smile flashed over her wan, white face.

"What will you share? The scorn that the men and women of my own past standing give me? The pay and the treatment of the spy that they call me? Oh, would you add the last drop to the bitterness of my life's cup by making me know that I have harmed your life, left you with a burden of pain?"

Her voice had risen into anguish, and, as she wrung her hands, Warwick, for the first time, saw her break into bitter weeping.

Utterly unmanned by the sight, he knelt beside her, murmuring incoherently tender words, while his hands gently touched the heavy coils of hair on the dear, prostrate head.

Her sobs grew slower, and at last she raised her head and smiled upon him sadly.

"See how weak and foolish you make me. See how we only pain each other when we talk like this. How much better to let me go my 'wanderway', leaving you free from my shadow. Believe me, anything more could only bring harm to your future."

Her voice was sweet and sad as dying music, but Warwick scarcely seemed to heed it as he answered:

"That is my affair, if I choose to risk it. All the same, I warn you that I intend to go with you in the Nighthawk."

Then Antoinette, gathering all her forces to play

her last card, said with an air of wounded reserve:

"I think not. I am sure that you are too true a gentle-man to force your undesired presence on any woman."

He gave a short baffled laugh.

"It's rather too late to try and tie my hands in that fashion. But, even so, I shall hope soon to make you yield. When do you really go? You are not packing now, are you?" And he looked anxiously at the disordered odds and ends that covered the table. Then Antoinette told a heroic lie.

"Captain Arthur makes a mystery of his date, but he has always promised me a week's notice. Now, I am not going to answer any more questions. You must really run away and leave me to finish putting these things in order."

Still he knelt before her, looking with anxious tenderness into her eyes.

"Kiss me once and I will go," he said, under his breath.

Without a protest her lips met his, but in that kiss there was none of love's first gladness, only the prescience of separation. As the door closed behind him, Antoinette bowed her head upon the table and wept the bitter tears of unresisting regret.

That evening the pines at Trafalgar sang their old slumberous song, and the wavelets murmured reposefully on the beach, but all else was well-ordered energy and work.

Instead of the usual elaborate meal, a cold supper at which they waited on themselves in a picknicky fashion, had been got through with a certain amount of suppressed excitement.

"Mabel is such a tender-hearted housekeeper that she has let all the household go to a picnic. You'll have to see to it that she doesn't put you off with cold suppers on every Saint's day, Arthur," Evans said, with a wink at his future son-in-law.

If the supper were cold, champagne was not wanting, in which Evans proposed the toast of "Our next meeting," with a glance at Mrs. LeMoine that gave a serious meaning to the jesting words. The twilight came up grey with a wind in from the sea, before which a trim little schooner stole in and lay up at Trafalgar wharf.

And then some of the Nighthawk's men appeared out of space, Mr. Hewitt at their head; and the night's work began, Arthur and Evans joining in with a will.

The darkness deepened, and the south wind wailed in the pine trees, and the women sat on the verandah, watching the flickering lights and the moving figures. It had grown late before the men had reappeared for coffee and a rest.

"You women had better get to bed," Evans said. "It will be an hour or so more before the schooner is ready for Arthur to take round."

Antoinette's quick eyes saw that Arthur looked pale and worn, as though the coming parting has weighing upon him.

Mabel was perhaps the only one there who was apparently her calm normal self.

"You are to join the Nighthawk at the harbour's mouth, to-morrow evening," Arthur said presently with an encouraging smile to Mrs. LeMoine, "Evans undertakes to hand you over safely."

A sudden impulse seized Antoinette. For Warwick's sake she would put aside her sorely wounded pride.

"Let me speak to you a moment," she said, leading the way into the empty drawing-room.

Arthur looked impatient as he followed. He could think of nothing save the imminent parting with Mabel.

Recognising the fact with an inward scoff at herself, she told him in as brief words as possible how settled was Warwick's determination of joining the Nighthawk.

"This is your doing," he said bitterly. "But I shall see that he does not get the chance of committing any such folly. I won't say good-bye to him, or let him know when we start. You are sure you haven't told him?"

She met his keen gaze steadily.

"What reason could I have for doing so? I have no wish for him to come."

He seemed convinced of her sincerity.

"Very well. It will be all right. *Au revoir* then, till to-morrow," he answered. Turning quickly he hurried out to Mabel, whom he drew away into the shadow of the shrubbery.

With a strange smile Antoinette watched him go.

"He doesn't know that I have but to give a sign to take his cousin off to Southern battlefields, or else let him know that I am free to marry him. Which fate would be the worst for him I wonder! All the same I *know* that I could make him happy for a time. Only for a time, perhaps."

Late that night when the schooner hoisted her sails and made her first tack seawards, Antoinette still sat at her open window listening to the voices of the night. But as Arthur turned with his last lingering look at Trafalgar, Mabel's window was closely curtained. *She* was sleeping peacefully.

CHAPTER XXVIII

"THE OUT TRAIL"

THE hours of the next day passed for Antoinette in a strangely dreamlike fashion.

There was about Trafalgar that blank quiet that tells of the work being done, and only the result to be waited for.

In the morning Evans was in the town, and while Mabel kept apart on the excuse of household duties, Antoinette and Hattie sat together under the trees, as on so many mornings of the past summer. They talked first of Hattie's future. She was to be married to Adair in the course of the next six months, and they would probably go at once to India.

The elder woman dwelt on the roseate hues of that future with a tender interest that would have amazed many of her acquaintances. This warm-hearted girl had seemed to come nearer to her than had any woman for years.

"I want to leave my wedding present with you now, before I go. Here, let me fasten it on," and she clasped a ruby-studded bracelet on the round white arm.

The hand stole up to her neck, and as she kissed and thanked her friend, Hattie's tears fell fast. A girl of her sort can give a very ardent hero-worship to an older woman.

"If only I could hope that you would ever care one

little bit for poor Major Warwick, and then we might be likely to meet each other again," Hattie sighed.

"Then it was on purpose that you told him of my going now?" Antoinette asked, with a new light.

Hattie hung her head. "I wanted so to help him," she said softly.

"Dear child, it only made it the harder for him, though I know you didn't mean that."

The words were a reproof, but the voice was tenderness itself, and her hand closed the tighter over the girl's. Antoinette was looking forward with nervous apprehension to that afternoon's tête-à-tête sail with Evans.

Her fears, however, were allayed at the last moment by the unexpected appearance of the agent, who quietly announced that he was going with them.

By the darkening of Evans' brow she guessed what the prospect of those last hours together had meant to him, and rejoiced correspondingly at their having been reduced to commonplace.

As they must not run any chance of the wind falling at sunset, the autumn day was still bright when Antoinette looked back at Trafalgar, and at Hattie waving her handkerchief at the end of the wharf. An unaccustomed mist of tears dimmed the girl's white figure to her sight.

But soon all gentle regrets were put aside, and her keen wits concentrated on the messages which the agent was entrusting to her, matters of high import, which he could not bear to commit even to cipher.

"I will give you these letters to keep about you," he went on.

"It is better that you should take them than Arthur, for, if anything goes wrong, a woman may be saved where a captain goes down with his ship."

His words sounded rather cold-hearted, but Antoinette was used to his ways by now. Evans, however, muttered an imprecation.

"That's nice kind of stuff with which to keep up a woman's spirits," he growled. " I don't know what has got into everyone lately to set them talking as though running the blockade were the same as starting for one's own funeral! To hear it, one would hardly suppose that it is as much an ordinary every-day business with dozens of crafts as crossing the Atlantic."

The agent maintained his philosophic calm under this tirade. Perhaps he guessed that Evans was scolding down his own uneasiness.

"Ah, but you must remember," he began with dispassionate argumentativeness, "that there can be no doubt that the risks are daily increasing. The Yankees have faster ships, and more of them, and have got up to the various dodges. The percentage of losses has been much larger during the past six months than ever before."

Evans grunted in silent disgust, while Antoinette laughed out in unfeigned amusement at the two men.

"When you have settled whether I am to be drowned or not, I'll take my cloak, please," she said with the high spirits of knowing action begun.

Where the bay joined the sweep of the outer harbour, they landed at a wharf that led to a desolate slate quarry. Here, on the barren shore, among the grey boulders, where they could see up the harbour, they sat and waited through the golden hours of sunset.

The day was growing chilly towards its close, and, seeing Antoinette pull her cloak around her, Evans lighted a small fire of driftwood under the shelter of the bank, by which they sat watching

During a few moments when the agent had wandered up the bank for a wider view, the two others were left alone, and Evans spoke abruptly.

"I met Major Warwick in town this morning, full of the idea of getting leave to go in the Nighthawk. How you have fooled the poor chap!"

His words rasped on high-strung nerves, but she made shift to answer cynically. "It is my *métier*."

"Like you have fooled me?"

The soreness of coming loss was bringing out the rougher nature of the strong man. How Antoinette rejoiced that she was soon to see the last of him.

Heedless of the storm signal in his face, her pride answered his taunt.

"Yes," she said, shoving the logs together with her foot.

"Are you in earnest?"

There was that in his voice which warned her that her nerves were playing her false, and leading her into a useless risk. Even yet, she might not have done with Trafalgar and its master.

The slow smile that met Evans' stern gaze disarmed him even without her murmured, "You know better than that."

"Here comes the Nighthawk," came in a shrill cry from the agent.

With a glad heart-leap Antoinette saw the shapely craft glide out from behind the dark fir-woods of the Point.

The twilight was gathering fast by the time that they stood on the Nighthawk's deck. Antoinette sent a long searching glance around, but saw nowhere the big form of Warwick. Then she looked into the resolute face of the captain and, meeting his smile, knew that it meant that Warwick had been left behind.

"Better so, far better so," she said to herself, trying not to feel a new sense of loneliness.

The agent's farewell was more human than she could have believed possible. Evans' was rough with suppressed emotion, which she scarcely heeded—he had already fallen back into the past.

As Evans was going down the ship's side after the agent, Arthur called out to him:

"Hold on, Evans, I am going back with you. The night is young, and I have two or three hours to spare. I want to put the finishing touch myself."

Evans seemed to recognise a meaning in his words as he answered:

"We will see to *that* all right. Remember that Yankee cruiser reported off Margaret's Bay, and put all the space you can between you and the shore before day-light."

"There is always a Yankee cruiser reported! I am going back if all the Northern fleet were outside York Redoubt." And Arthur emphasised his words by jumping down into the boat.

The darkness closed down around her, but Antoinette made no move to go to her cabin and get settled down. Wrapped in her big cloak she crouched down in a deck chair while a horror of great desolation swept over her.

What had she done in so resolutely cutting herself adrift from the only one who cared unselfishly for her welfare?

If Arthur had given her one word of consideration before hurrying back for one more glimpse of Mabel, she might not have felt so forsaken as she did now. Never in any moment of her stormy life had she realised with a keener pang her isolation from all human ties. The last bitter waves of jealousy, the after-swell of past tempests, rose around her, bringing back a vision of Mabel's fresh young face, with its cold smile. How long she had crouched there Antoinette hardly knew, when she was aroused by a footstep beside her and the quiet English voice of the first officer.

"I am sure that you must be tired and cold here. Mayn't I take you below? The captain would not like it if he thought you were not comfortable."

Antoinette laughed.

"I doubt if he gives much thought to *that* to-night, Mr. Parke. But it is kind in you, all the same. I should really rather stay here, for I have a wretched headache, and the dark and the night air soothes it."

"Of course, if you like it best. I am the officer of the watch, so if you want anything you have just to call me. I shall be quite near."

"Thank you," and in her loneliness she was grateful for the human neighbourhood.

She had nestled her head back against the chair, turning instinctively towards the north, in the direction of Trafalgar, the only place that seemed definite to her thoughts.

All at once she was startled by the fiery flare of an explosion upon the heights to the eastward of Trafalgar. With a sick pang of fear she knew what it meant. The powder magazine! Could that have been Arthur's finishing touch then! Good God! Was he safe? Was Warwick safe? Had *she* had any hand in bringing this thing about? What if either of them were dead, slain for what she had helped to work!

Mr. Parke stood beside her, reassuring her. "I fear it startled you, but it can be nothing to make us anxious. I cannot think what it is," he said uneasily.

"I am not startled, but I know what it is. It must be the powder magazine!"

"Perhaps so," he acknowledged, and moved away to talk in low tones with Mr. Hewitt.

Antoinette paid no heed to them, only crouched there, possessed by fear.

Arthur's boat came without her hearing it, but presently the sound of his voice roused her.

"You are safe then?" she asked in a dulled voice, looking up at him. "I foolishly thought that it was the powder magazine and that—"

"It was," he interrupted briefly.

"Was that necessary?"

"Yes, for the sake of those who remain behind. Exploded powder magazines are like dead men and tell no tales."

"But no lives are lost."

"How *could* there be?" he said impatiently. "You must know how small a quantity of powder could be still there."

"But Major Warwick?"

Again there was the suppressed impatience in Arthur's voice. "Warwick is all right. It is the mess guest-night, and he is there, doing the civil, without an idea that we are on the tramp. He is best *en evidence* to-night, and he is best without any more last scenes."

"You reserve those for yourself! How you mistrust me to the last," she flashed out.

"I have not given you any cause to say that," Arthur said gravely. Then with an effort at cheerfulness which his worn face belied:—

"Come now. We are both tired and rather on the jump to-night, but we must not begin our voyage by quarrelling. To-morrow we shall both feel different people. You had better go down to your cabin and get things ship-shape for the night at once. I shall have the anchor up in half an hour, and I don't want any light shining after we are past Sambro. Remember that bogey Yankee cruiser outside. It might be real, you know."

With a quiet "good-night" Antoinette turned and left him, determined to be at least no burden.

CHAPTER XXIX

THE EXPLOSION

IT was guest-night at the Artillery Mess, and one of a little more importance than the usual weekly function, in the entertaining of the Admiral and his staff.

Dinner was over, and the smoking time had come. Major Warwick formed one of the most silent of a talkative group. A cheerful sub having been bewailing the poverty of the younger son, a navy youth struck in:

"Well, we navy fellows are fools who haven't gone in for making our little haul out of blockade-running. We're not likely to see such another chance in a hurry. I met fellows this winter, down in Nassau and Bermuda, who in two years or so have got enough together to give them a comfortable old age. That's more than Her Majesty's navy is likely to do! Look at Arthur now! In a few months he'll be married and settled down at home in all the odour of sanctity."

"Arthur settled down at home! Not until he is tucked comfortably away in his coffin!" came derisively from another navy man nearer Arthur's age. "By-the-bye," he went on casually, "the Nighthawk has just sailed."

Major Warwick started from his semi-listening attitude into full attention. Turning to the last speaker he said quickly:

"I think you must be mistaken. Arthur does not mean to go before next week."

The other man held firm though.

"I think not. She was in full sight of our ship, you know, and I saw her moving down the harbour as I came ashore this evening. I couldn't be mistaken. They always like to get off on the sly if possible, you know."

Yes. Warwick knew. He felt powerless to speak or move before this horrible certainty.

At that moment a diversion was created by the appearance of Adair, who having just got back from a week's leave, had not been at dinner.

He stood waiting until the navy man had finished speaking, and then with a glance and sign drew Warwick aside.

"What he says is quite true," he said quietly, looking anywhere but into his senior's face. "She was to go down the harbour at twilight, and Mr. Evans took Mrs. LeMoine down in his sail-boat to join her off the Point. I got back from shooting this afternoon, and stopped at Trafalgar on our way into town. They had been gone an hour or more, then. Hattie gave me this note for you, sir."

As he handed the envelope to Warwick he gave no sign of knowing that the address was in Mrs. LeMoine's fine Italian writing.

As he turned away his heart was hot with wrath at the fashion in which the lady had left her knight to learn of her departure from any stranger.

"I wish that we had not taken so much trouble to save her from starving," he thought to himself vengefully.

Meantime Warwick had made for the shelter of his own quarters before opening the envelope. His first glance showed him the writing that had grown so familiar to him.

"I am writing these few farewell words, during my last hours at Trafalgar, where I am waiting to go on board the Nighthawk this evening, to ask your forgiveness for the method of my departure. Believe me, if what I have done seems to you treacherous and deceitful, it was not meant to be so. I only hoped to spare you some pain. Indeed, indeed, I would not willingly hurt you; but I feel so sure that it is best that I should go on my way without any more farewells between us—that I should leave you to stand quite clear from the shadow of my life.

"If in those first days I had fully realised the man you are, *sans peur, et sans reproche,* I would never have allowed our fates to become interwoven! I can hardly be blamed for not believing that such men as you existed. I had never known them. God grant that I may have done you no harm, given you no wound, that a short space of time may not heal.

"You can guess what my life has been; you know what the world thinks of me. It should be easy for a man of your strength to learn to forget me! I try to comfort myself with the thought that, in the past weeks, I may have given you some happiness to atone for any wrong that I may have done you.

"If only your honour stands undimmed by *my* touch, I am content!

"Try, if in a happier future you should sometimes think of me, not to judge me too harshly, remembering that all that I have done, that perhaps seemed cruel and unwomanly, was with the one motive—that of serving my unhappy country in her hour of need.

You, who belong to a great prosperous nation, can hardly realise the passion of pity that moves us less happy ones. If you should ever hear that I have been found worthy of giving my life for her sake, then rejoice that death has washed away the stains of life. Farewell, ah! farewell. Would that I were worthy to bless you as *I* go on my solitary way. You saved me from insult; you saved my life. You saw and believed in the good that was in me still. You laid your life, your name, at my feet, and I—I can give you nothing.

"But in my own sorrowful heart I *do* give you what you can never know, and I go forth alone, the richer for what I give, for what is yours till death."

Warwick read and reread these words before he laid the paper down on the table.

It was his dark hour, and he lived through it, as other men before him have done. How she had smiled at him and lied to him to the last! Evans, Arthur, had been in her confidence, and most likely had scoffed at the fool she had made of him. Would it be possible that Arthur—but no. His own common sense told him that Arthur had no thought for any woman save Mabel Evans.

Outraged in every feeling as he was, he knew that it was not in his power to be really angry with her. If he could have been, it might have come easier to him.

But with the vision of her splendid womanhood rising up before him, with the recognition of the great soul that had once or twice flashed out at him through those hazel eyes, his whole heart cried out "The pity of it, Iago, the pity of it!"

It was the very hour when Antoinette was longing in

her loneliness for his presence, when she would have turned to him as a child runs to its mother. Warwick too was roused from the bitterness that held his spirit, by the flare and sound of the explosion.

He sprang to his feet with a groan. "My God! The Nighthawk!" he cried, with a hurried remembrance of some gossip which he had overheard that day at the club, as to the blockade-runner carrying contraband of war.

Without any definite plan he caught up his hat and hurried to the door. There was a sound of hurried footsteps and voices from the officers' mess, and lights might be seen flashing up in the men's quarters, but without word to anyone, he hurried past out the barrack gates, and downhill towards the wharves.

Everywhere heads were appearing at windows, and people were thronging from the doors into the streets. Everyone was asking bewildered, "What is it? What has happened?"

But Warwick strode on unheeding, like a man in a hypnotic trance. He had left the town behind him and was making his way towards the Point. The only reason that guided his footsteps was the fact that she whom he loved had passed in that direction, and he would go too. How many thousands has that blind impulse driven to the seashore to stand gazing "whither went their lost delight" across the water!

Here he saw merely the grey-black space that brooded over the harbour's mouth, with here and there a light that, rising and falling slowly with the breath of the sea, told of some outward bound schooner waiting for a fair wind.

How little he guessed that one light apart from the others, over under the black shadow of the western hills, showed from the Nighthawk, where she awaited her captain.

But presently on the stillness of night came the measured clink of an anchor being raised, then the gradual crescendo of started machinery. The lights swept out from the bank, and something in sounds and lights told him the truth.

"The Nighthawk!" broke from him in a hoarse cry as he realised that, since receiving Antoinette's letter, he had had ample time, if only he had made swift use of it, to have reached her side. Once on board neither Arthur nor she could have got him ashore again.

Now it was too late, and he helplessly watched those lights until they had passed away beyond the western headland, and in the passing had taken, oh, so much with them.

For all his steadfastness of nature, as Warwick turned away from the shore, he found his mind going in a curiously mechanical fashion to a certain locked drawer where he kept his revolver.

His hand went to find the key of that drawer in his pocket, and he quickened his homeward steps with an instinctive sense that *there* might be alleviation for this intolerably keen sense of bereavement. Once he started to find himself repeating aloud her words, "If only your honour stands undimmed by my touch!" as though he were trying to discover their meaning.

In his room the candle which he had lighted to read her letter was still burning and the General's aide-de-camp was there, fidgeting about with a troubled and harassed aspect.

"I have been here three times in the last hour, and no one had any idea as to what had become of you, sir," he began in an aggrieved fashion. "Did you go out to the place after the explosion?"

"What place? Where was it? I went to the Point but could see nothing."

The youth gave him a quick, questioning glance at these words.

"The Point! Naturally not! Didn't you know that it was the powder magazine?"

Warwick's overwrought senses failed to immediately take in any personal significance in this fact.

"The powder magazine?" he repeated blankly.

"The staff are all at Bellevue with the General, and he sent me to ask you to come there at once, sir."

The stiffness in these words did not strike Warwick's notice, as it passed as officialism. But something less friendly than usual in the other's bearing did begin to pierce his absorption.

As they went out together he asked: "There are no lives lost?"

"No; the sentry was stunned at first, but has come round again. The most curious fact of the thing is the trifling amount of damage done by the explosion. There could hardly have been any powder in the place."

This time the stiffness of the younger man's manner was unmistakable. It did not, however, require that to bring a sudden overwhelming sense of his own position upon Warwick.

"If only your honour stands undimmed by my

touch!" He knew the meaning of the words now.

He could scarcely be blamed for the official care-lessness which had existed before his three months' reign, but he knew that he was responsible for it. He knew, too, that if his thoughts had not been so cen-tred on Mrs. LeMoine he might have been able to show a more vigorous new-broom record during that time. His whole heart had never been in his work. Mr. Evans' reasons for the steadily increasing quantity of powder he obtained had always been plausible.

The new railroad then in course of construction, the gold mines that he was displaying so much energy in opening up—was it possible that a certain amount of those supplies had been diverted into another direction?

He recalled his cousin's vague hints as to mixing himself up in these Southerners' affairs, and the dis-favour with which Arthur had looked upon his grow-ing intimacy with Mrs. LeMoine. He recalled that evening's after-dinner talk of blockade-running, and the money that Arthur had made by it, knowing that men might even now be saying that he had joined in his cousin's good things.

And she, that one peerless woman in the world for him, in spite of all blots on her name—should they be able to say that she had schemed and flattered to use him as her dupe? The first stirring of fighting energy came back to him, and he set his face grimly and thanked God that he had had no time to take the revolver from the drawer, and so once and for all blight his good name. No, he lived still in the light of day to defend his own honour, and still to cherish the hope of leading into serener paths that intrepid spirit of which his own had recognised the innate nobility.

The haggard anxiety that underlay the official gravity in the old General's face, shook his composure, but he hardened his heart against the thought that he had hardly deserved so good a friend.

In the private interview that followed he answered questions and related facts with perfect frankness, but absolutely declined to see any connection between his private friendships and the carelessness which he regretted and acknowledged. The worldly-wise old General had no wish for any embarrassing confidences. He intended to shield Major Warwick to the full extent of his powers, and he did not want to know too much.

More of a diplomat than most men of his class, he had been given his present appointment so that he might help tide the colony through a political crisis, and, as he said, "dine them all into agreement."

His diplomatic powers had to be fully exercised in this task he had set himself of getting Warwick off without any official blame or censure. He did it though, and after a week's anxiety was able to assure him that the affair was settled.

Warwick thanked him with full earnestness and sincerity, but the General now felt himself entitled to indulge in a little crustiness.

"Don't flatter yourself, Sir, that I would have troubled myself about you if it hadn't been for your father's sake, your father's sake, Sir! A man of your age who gets his head turned by the first pretty adventuress who comes along—"

"I am sorry to interrupt you, Sir, but I hope some day to introduce that lady to you as my wife."

"Not to me, Sir, not to me! I shall be out of harness in a month now, then you can make any kind of fool of yourself that you like! I shan't be here to see it."

Warwick's only answer was a bow, but still when the old General stood upon the steamer's deck saying goodbye to his officers, his farewell was warmer to none than to Warwick, who felt a lump in his throat as he grasped the hand of the frail-looking, plucky old soldier. In spite of many differences each had recognized and respected the other's indomitable spirit.

CHAPTER XXX

"THEY THAT GO DOWN TO THE SEA IN SHIPS"

THE next morning, when Antoinette came on deck, it was to find the Nighthawk the centre of a blue globe of sea and sky, radiant in the glow of sunshine.

A soft breeze met her from the south, and seemed to waft her a greeting from the land whose sorrows she was hastening to share.

Merrily the ship sped on, without "rock or tempest, fire, or foe," to check her on her way. Captain Arthur was on the bridge and did not seem to notice her appearance, but Mr. Parke had a chair and rugs placed for her in a sheltered corner and loitered beside her with kindly, if abrupt, questions as to her comfort.

It was the same old story; wherever she went there was always some man to be found ready to wait on her. All faces looked cheerful with fresh energy, save the captain's, which was more set and impassive than usual. For the first day or two Arthur talked but little to Mrs. LeMoine, keeping himself constantly occupied about the ship with his officers, or else going through endless accounts and papers in his own cabin.

With her long knowledge of the man Antoinette could see that he was seeking any occupation that would keep his thoughts from going back to follow the quiet routine of Mabel's life, and to dull his sense of loss.

Gradually, though, this restlessness wore off, and the calm of the sea came over his spirit. Then he tarried for longer intervals at her side, either smoking in contented silence or casually chatting. The old spirit of comradeship seemed at such times to revive between them. Still the same summer seas and skies were with them, and life was easy and pleasant for all on board. "We are south of Bermuda now," Arthur said on the third day, "and getting into more dangerous waters."

"Truly he came of the Blood," the Norsemen's breed, whose fullest life is breathed in the air of strife.

"When I was last in these waters, the Yankee cruisers were as thick as leaves in Vallombrosa," he went on. "You must be prepared to hear an alarm at any time now."

"It will remind me of old times," she answered languidly. Arthur was not the only one glad to have his thoughts diverted from a haunting sense of loss.

If only I had let him come! was a weary refrain to the hours, from which any excitement would be a welcome change.

"Yes, you are not the kind of woman to scream at a mouse," he said, turning a more kindly glance upon her. It had occurred to him of late that he might not have been over-considerate. "You are like the Nighthawk, and its namesake, strong and fearless. One long graceful sweep, and your work is done, and you are off."

"A bird of prey!" she commented bitterly, stung by a

comparison of which she felt the keen shaft.

"In a good cause. War justifies all," he said with careless compunction. He never saw how he had wounded her.

He then went on to ask if she had formed any definite plans of action after her interview with the authorities.

Antoinette leaned forward, watching the black shadow of the steamer's smoke upon the water as she answered thoughtfully.

"What I should like best to do would be to go back to my first ambulance work, but that I fear is impossible. There is an objection to allowing well-known persons against whom some outside charges could be made an excuse for severity to take any share in fieldwork, with the chance of falling into the enemy's hands. They have plenty of things stored up against me, I fancy. I have sometimes heard threats that I should be shot if I fell into their hands again," she said quietly.

"You take it coolly," Arthur said with an unwilling sort of admiration.

"How else would you have me take it? There might be worse kinds of death ahead. But, in the meantime, I suppose that I may go on much as I have been doing. If they should have no work for me, I thought of going to my plantation home in Georgia to see if I were needed there. From all accounts, our people are in sore straits. The agent had an idea that I might be asked to go to New York. It seems that it is a centre for my kind of underhand work, scheming and flattering and lying," and she ended with a weary little sigh.

"But surely that would be the most dangerous place of all?"

"I suppose so," she agreed casually. "But no one knows better than you that there is a certain joy in doing a risky thing. Danger is certainly a stimulant to one's nerves."

"Then I rather think that you have got your stimulant now," Arthur said calmly, as he rose from his seat beside her.

His keen eyes had spied a signal from the man on the lookout in the crow's nest, on the foremast, to the officer on the bridge. He knew that it meant a sail in sight. Before Antoinette had time to make any answer, he had reached the bridge, and was sweeping the horizon with his glass.

Before long Antoinette could see from the deck, with her glass, the significant trail of grey smoke on the sea-line astern. Clearer and higher it rose into sight, telling that the pursuer was gaining, until the decisive words "The stars and stripes!" were called down from the lookout. Then the Nighthawk sprang forward gallantly like a thing of life, under her pressure of steam.

All through the late hours of that cloudless day, Antoinette sat and watched with concentrated tension, while Arthur paced the bridge above her in grim silence, broken only by an occasional short word of command. The opalescent lights of evening were creeping over sea and sky when Arthur came down and spoke to her.

"It's all right now, I think. We are leaving her behind, and ought to be out of sight of her by dark.

We shall have to expect others though, and you must be careful about lights to-night I know that I can trust you for that. By this time to-morrow we shall be all but in sight of the fleet off Wilmington. There is not likely to be any lack of excitement then."

But Arthur's present relief was premature. The masts of the steamer astern were still visible to the naked eye, when again came the word of fate from the mast-head:

"Cruiser crossing our bows, sir." A responsive stir ran over the crew, answering the words.

Mr. Hewitt's languid handsome face was aglow with the joy of battle. Mr. Parke looked first to see how Mrs. LeMoine received the news, then pulled his cap down over his brows, prepared for whatever might come.

Setting his face as a flint the captain of the Nighthawk prepared to do his utmost. He ran off at an angle that might, by good luck, take him away from his two foes, before, discovering each other's neighbourhood, they should attempt to pinch him between them. All his skill must be concentrated on flight. To make any show of resistance or to return the fire of the assailant meant piracy, and, in case of capture, would be dealt with as such.

Once or twice, during those moments of tension, Arthur turned his watchful eyes to a great bank of heavy clouds, that were swiftly rising against the wind, and shrouding the sunset.

"There should be help there. It's the hurricane season," he muttered to Hewitt, the second officer.

"Let me fall into the hands of God and not into the hands of man," scoffed that young sinner.

The sea, which had been rolling in the great oily curves of a ground-swell, was beginning to break into more sharply outlined waves, as though the whispered voice of a coming storm were troubling its heart.

No wind had as yet reached the deck where every sound seemed intensified. The Nighthawk had twisted and wheeled like her own aerial namesake, and every inch of her frame panted under the pressure of her labouring heart. But the angle into which she had been forced had brought her more into view of the first foe astern, who responsively quickened speed.

Arthur could not doubt that not only both cruiser saw the Nighthawk, but that they saw each other too and slowly and remorselessly were closing her in between them.

Every moment things looked darker for the blockade-runner's chance of safety. It was the last-seen foe that first neared her sufficiently to send a shot ploughing the water across her bows as a polite invitation that it would be better to stop.

"The captain says that you must go below," came the message from the bridge. Antoinette compromised her obedience by going into the companion-way where she huddled down between two doors.

Her most definite thought was the hope that she might know the right moment in which to destroy the agent's letters, now in her pocket.

Captain Arthur touched the bell to stop the machinery, and then stood looking round on his men with a grim smile. Beside the engineers, the crew consisted of three officers and twenty-eight men. They were all picked Englishmen, on high wages, who would have followed their captain "through hell and out again." Their perfect discipline prevented a word or sign of remonstrance at this token of surrender, but the fierce glow of excitement in their faces darkened into gloom, and each man drew a deep breath.

In the strange new stillness that had fallen upon the ship, the splash of the waves against her side could be heard. Although not loudly raised their captain's voice, distinct and resolute, rang out sharply.

"Don't look so downcast, men! Even if we *do* let the Yankees come to pay us a visit, they have yet to take us! The dark is coming on, and the ship wasn't named the Nighthawk for nothing! Here comes their quarter-boat! Stand by, every man to his post!"

Tossed up and down on the rising waves, the enemy's boat was drawing nearer.

In utter silence Arthur stood looking down from the low bridge.

Every officer and man, each in his place, seemed inanimate figures save for the glowing, staring eyes fixed on the coming boat as though to check its progress by sheer force of will.

A vivid picture that photographed itself on Antoinette's mind was that of the boy-face of the American lieutenant in uniform seated in the stern of the approaching boat. As the Nighthawk's side dipped with a heavy sea to meet them, he looked up, and started and flushed at such an unexpected vision as that beautiful face gazing down upon him from the dark frame of the companion door. The boat was close under there by now, and at last the captain broke the spell of inaction.

Moving as stealthily as he did quickly, he bent his head above the speaking tube, and said in little more than a whisper:

"Full speed ahead!"

Low as was the voice, it acted as a charm. Like a dog let free from leash the Nighthawk sprang forward on her course. Then what the captain had been counting on, happened.

The coming boat was helpless in the ship's wash. The enemy in the cruiser either thought that their men were on board the blockade-runner, or else hesitated to fire, for fear of injuring their own boat. Then, when they had had time to realise the state of affairs, they evidently were obliged to stop to pick up their boat, on account of the rising sea, and the fast-coming darkness.

By the time that the Nighthawk had succeeded in putting a certain distance between herself and the nearest foe, the long brooding storm had broken.

In the inky blackness, and wild tumult of sea and sky which it brought with it, the blockade-runner was as safe from attack as if she had been at a neutral wharf.

Throughout that last hour of suspense Mr. Parke was the only one who had troubled to speak a word of encouragement to Antoinette.

She had hardly heeded him when, in the midst of his own duties, he had found time to summon the steward to bring her hot soup, and wraps to shelter her.

Her whole thoughts were on the drama which was being played out before her, and her spirit had risen to the level of the fortitude of the men around her.

Though scarcely heeding Mr Parke's kindness she had thanked him graciously enough to send him away with a glow of pleasure in his honest heart.

Presently, stepping under shelter to light a comforting pipe, his oil-skins dripping with wet, the captain almost stumbled over Antoinette, curled up in her rugs in a corner.

"What! Are you up here still?" he said brusquely. Truth to tell, since the firing of that first shot, he had forgotten the fact of Mrs. LeMoine's existence .

"Why, you must go below and get warmed and fed. You must be nearly starved. There is no more danger at hand just now, and you need a go rest to steady you for to-morrow's little games. 'Sufficient unto the day' in our trade, you know."

"And you?" she questioned.

To have his movements inquired into by a woman, on board his ship, was a shock to Captain Arthur's professional feelings.

"Oh, that's all in my day's work," he answered shortly. "But I assure you that there is nothing for you to be nervous about. You had better go below."

Her voice had a touch of pride in it as she answered:

"I did not stay here because I was nervous, but because I liked it better. Roberts brought me soup when yours came up. Let me stay! I won't be in anyone's way! It was worth ten years of life to see you doing that! Somehow, I knew all along that you never meant them to come on board! If to-morrow were to be the last day of my life, I should be glad to have known to-day."

"Oh, it won't be the last by a lot, I hope. You mustn't talk like that. It might bring us ill-luck," Arthur said turning away.

He was annoyed at the return of the superstitious dread of her presence which he had once confessed to Warwick.

CHAPTER XXXI

"FROM THE HANDS OF THE ENEMY!"

THE next day was one of many excitements and alarms on board the Nighthawk. None of these however were quite such touch-and-go affairs as were those of the previous day.

Even these latter risks were won through at last. An hour or two after dusk the blockade-runner was stealing along like a thief in the night, near the low coast at the mouth of the Cape Clear River.

She must be ready to anchor close under the shore, before the late moon should rise, and bring on the scene the added dangers of light.

Antoinette had spent most of the day in her old post in the companion-way.

Even Captain Arthur had not had the heart to suggest that she should remain below alone through such a time of suspense as the next few hours must perforce be.

The Nighthawk had passed in safety through the main body of the Northern fleet that lay, nearly a hundred strong, in a crescent curve, facing the river's mouth.

But that there were still plenty of the foe on the move around them was plain from the sounds that came clearly through the night stillness, and by the occasional flash of a quickly hidden light.

It was this inactivity in the midst of encircling danger which the captain had always found to tell upon even the hardened nerves of his crew.

The training of his discipline had been far too thorough for there to be any outward sign of the strain.

Mrs. LeMoine's face and bearing were as impassive as those of the oldest man on board.

Behind the hills the east had gradually shimmered into a golden glow, which the men watched gloomily, as the forerunner of their enemy, the moon.

Although the Nighthawk was still in deep shadow, the opposite coast and a hostile cruiser, anchored not very far from them, were every moment becoming more distinct in outline.

There could be no possibility of doubt as to the peril of the blockade-runner's situation. Captain Arthur had glanced up once or twice at his masts. He was looking for the fatal moment when the moonlight striking on them would reveal him to the foe.

Just then one of his officers touched his arm and pointed seawards.

"Jove! The luck is with us still!" he muttered.

He had seen the veil of white fog that was creeping inland, low on the face of the water.

It was a race now between light and darkness, the moonbeams and the fog, and the Nighthawk was the stake in the game. Each man stood and held his breath as he watched the contest upon which his fortunes and liberty, perhaps his very life depended.

"The fog has it!" whispered Mr. Hewitt, and a grin on many faces answered him.

A few brief, low-toned orders from the captain

changed the spellbound silence into almost as noise-less an activity.

There was none too much time to spare before day-light when the pin was knocked out of the shackle of the chain on deck, and the cable eased into the water.

In spite, though, of every precaution the fog had carried the sound of their movements to their dan-gerous neighbour. Although the Nighthawk did get a certain start in the race, that start was a far shorter one than Arthur had hoped for.

Gallantly, though, she forged ahead and had all but reached the radius of safety under the guns of Fort Fisher, when at the crucial moment her old friend, the fog, played her false, rolling away like a gathered-in sail before the land wind that heralded the morning.

In the cold grey light of dawn and the dull red glare of the waning moon, the blockade-runner's position was clearly visible to the pursuer. Other hovering cruisers gathered at the sight to share in the chase. Each man on board knew as well as did the captain that the enemy's tactics would be to force them inshore, where, as soon as the Nighthawk grounded, she would become their helpless prey.

It scarcely needed Arthur's order for the crew to be ready if necessary lighten the ship by every possible means.

Their nearest danger evidently lay in a cruiser that lurked ahead close to the shore.

What was to come then, came quickly enough. Although the second officer, who was at the helm, knew every inch of the vicinity as well as any pilot, he was inevitably crowded by the nearest cruiser into the shallow water, and in a few minutes was ashore firm and fast.

At a word each man was working like ten to lighten the ship, but all to no avail. Arthur had many a time won through to safety by refusing to acknowledge defeat. Now it must be faced as sturdily as it had hitherto been escaped from.

The boats had already left the cruiser to come and take possession.

Arthur gave a sweeping glance from them to the shore, where the tide was down, leaving long stretches of brown mud to catch the eastern light.

"We cannot use the big boats. They would only stick in the mud where they might be fired on," he said decisively. "Mr. Parke, keep two men to help you in the dinghy, and get Mrs. LeMoine ashore as quickly as possible. You'll land all right at that ridge of rocks. Let the rest go overboard with their life-belts on and swim for it. The distance isn't much. Mr. Hewitt, come with me." He turned to go below, followed closely by the second officer.

No man dared to ask him of himself, though everyone guessed that he was about to set fire to the ship, thereby adding to the risk for all.

The Northerners seldom fired on a vanquished crew, unless they had destroyed the prize in the moment of attainment.

As the captain disappeared there was a moment's pause and silence, broken by a woman's wail of "Arthur! Arthur!" to which he paid no heed.

At Mr. Parke's order the men had promptly provided themselves with life-belts and jumped overboard to make for the shore. The third officer, the Irish boy Ryan, still lingered to see the others off in the dinghy.

In his simple code of duty an officer might not leave the ship before a woman. Antoinette, her long cloak and hat flung aside, her slim figure in its grey dress outlined against the dark shore, stood watching their preparations with a white intensity of face.

The dinghy had been swung overboard, and Mr. Parke approached her, with exactly his usual grave deference of manner. "We are ready now. Will you come?" he said quietly.

Still she did not move, nor seem to take any heed of his words.

"How will Captain Arthur get ashore?" she abruptly demanded.

Mr. Parke looked at her curiously.

"He must intend to swim for it. He and Hewitt are both crack swimmers. Please come."

"I mean to wait for him."

It was a duel of wills now between the man and the woman.

"You cannot do that. His orders were to get you off as quickly us possible. Mr. Ryan will not leave the ship while you are still on it. You are imperilling his safety."

He was too brave to add "and mine as well," even if he had ever thought of it.

With quick hands Mrs. LeMoine tore open the neck of her dress revealing the flash of diamonds on the whiteness of her skin. "This necklace shall make you both rich if only you will wait for him."

For once Mr. Parke's impassive face showed a deep flush through his tan. "I thought you had understood that we were gentlemen," he said gravely. "We would both go down without a thought at his word, but even in doing it we would obey his orders. I suppose a woman cannot understand that. Captain Arthur told me that when he consented to bring you he had made you swear to obey orders, and this is how you keep your oath. If you will not come, I shall carry you down, that is all."

And he made a step forward, as though about to put his threat into practice.

A strained laugh broke from Mrs. LeMoine.

"Oh, there is no need to do that. I yield to force," she said recklessly.

With one despairing glance back at the companion-way door she let them lower her into the dinghy where the two men awaited her.

"Give way, men!" Mr. Parke cried triumphantly, but they were little more than a boat's length from the ship when Captain Arthur and Hewitt appeared on deck.

When he saw how near the dinghy still was to the ship a fierce exclamation broke from Arthur.

"What has made you so slow in getting off?" The ship will blow up in a few moments and then they will fire on us," he shouted to Mr. Parke.

As the dinghy sped over the water, the two last men leaped from the Nighthawk. When as Arthur dived from the deck the water closed over him an overpowering impulse, such as might have seized on the merest schoolgirl, caused Antoinette to spring to her feet with outstretched arms. The boat had just risen on the long curve of a wave that was about to break in shallow water, and the abrupt movement was enough to overbalance it.

By the time that Arthur and Hewitt had reached the scene of action the men had righted the boat, and Mr. Parke was slowly swimming round in search of Mrs. LeMoine.

"Hasn't she risen at all?" Arthur asked anxiously as he rested himself against the boat. "God! Her belt of gold!" he cried, with sudden remembrance.

"Where did she go down?" he asked of Mr. Parke who was clambering up into the boat. "There!" the latter said, pointing a few yards away. Then joining his hands above his head he sprang, and dived nearly where he had pointed.

There was a breathless pause of suspense. Mr. Ryan had looked back and seeing the dinghy in trouble had returned. At this, the captain swore at him in a low voice. "You all seem hankering after a Yankee prison. Hope you'll like it when you get there. By Heavens! he's got her!" came in a shout from Hewitt as Parke rose to the surface, holding a long wisp of woman's garments with one hand, while he paddled towards them with the other.

Arthur was in the boat by now, and gave his sharp orders. "Get her in, and then you men in the water, hurry ashore, and make for the bushes. Is she alive?" he asked as be stooped over to relieve Parke of his inanimate burden.

"I think so," was the answer, but Arthur looked grave, as the figure that he lifted drooped with all the helplessness of death.

Mr. Parke, spent and breathless, was pulled in too,

and immediately bent over the still form that lay with lovely white face and closed eyes in the bottom of the boat, and, oblivious to all else, worked at reviving her.

At that moment there shot up from the deserted Nighthawk first a column of thick smoke, and then the fierce burst of explosion. As they watched it, no man thought of personal loss or danger, for grief for the ship that had been their pride, their fortress, their home. Each face was set and sombre, and none spoke a word.

But a wrathful shout came over the water from the approaching Yankee boat, and Arthur gave the quick order, "Give way, men. They are certain to fire now." They *did* fire, a vengeful splutter of musketry, and, as the balls fell thick around the dinghy, Arthur, who was standing, reeled and sunk back against the man crouching in the bow.

CHAPTER XXXII

"FACING DEATH"

WHEN Antoinette came slowly back from that shadow-land which is the ante-chamber to "death's untrodden realm," it was to the sound of the boat grating sharply on the shingle.

Her dress had been carefully loosened, and the taste of brandy was upon her lips. This showed that someone had cared to bring her back to life, but there was no one watching for the lifting of her eyelids, or the first movement of her hands.

Was she a prisoner in the hands of the Yankees? she wondered feebly. Wearily, she pushed back the cling-ing masses of wet hair from her forehead, and tried to raise herself. She had a languid desire to see where the low voices with the terrible thrill of earnestness in them were coming from. She was upon her elbow now, and what she saw caused her completely to for-get her own weakness.

At the other end of the boat Hewitt and Parke were bending with set, strained faces over Captain Arthur who lay back in the former's arms, his head drooping backwards with a fearful significance, his eyes closed.

A hoarse cry that lacked the strength to be a scream, rang out:—"Is he dead?"

"Not a bit of it," Mr. Parke answered quickly in a forced tone, without looking round. "But they have got two shots into him, one in the hip and one in the chest. We *must*, at any cost, get him ashore and out of the reach of fire. Keep down, Mrs. LeMoine. There they go again."

And, following the report, the balls could be heard ripping along the water.

That woman's cry seemed in a measure to arouse Arthur from a stupor. A faint frown had shadowed his face, and now his lips tried to form some scarcely audible words.

"Anyone else hurt?"

"No one. They won't try it again," Hewitt answered, lying bravely, for he did not think so. Then the faint whisper came again:

"Lay me down in the bottom of the boat, and get into the bushes, till they are tired of us. You can come back then, though I think I'll be gone. I've as good a chance here as anywhere." Exhausted with the effort, all life seemed again to pass from his face.

"We're, not going to leave you, captain. Don't bother, for I'm in command now," Parke said with gentle decision. Then he looked up at the little circle of men that stood with tragic bearing around the bow of the grounded boat.

"Two men go ahead, and look for the best shelter," he said. "Four form a litter with your arms. Gently, Hewitt! Lift at the same time! You can bear it, sir, can't you?"

A faint smile that seemed to say "I must," was the only answer, and silently they lifted their captain, and laid him on the coats, which had been flung over the brawny crossed arms of the sailors.

A choking sob broke from the "bosun," a big burly Yorkshire man, but no other lament was made.

There could be no delay with the chance of the pursuers landing to attack them in their unarmed condition.

Like a funeral the forlorn little train wound up the long slope of the beach, avoiding obstacles by directions from their scouts.

Behind the rest followed Mr. Parke, half-supporting with his arm Mrs. LeMoine.

With her clinging wet garments and dishevelled hanging hair she was a forlorn spectacle. Nothing but sheer force of will could have taken onwards her faltering limbs.

As if in mockery, the resplendent morning sun beamed down upon the little band, and the soft land wind wafted them a welcome of southern scents.

As they climbed the rough bank, a low moan coming from the prostrate figure caused Antoinette to wince in sympathy.

Mr. Parke feeling the movement said reassuringly:

"We won't try to get him much farther. They would never venture to follow us out of sight of the shore. There ought to be a Confederate camp not far from here, and we are sure to get help from them."

Antoinette made no attempt to respond. She felt sure that Arthur could not live many hours, and a dull despair oppressed her. The sight of his sore stress had awakened her crushed-down feeling, and in that moment she would gladly have given her life to save his.

They were winding up an overgrown cart-track

when word was passed back that a hut of some sort had been found.

Never were the lights of a comfortable inn more welcome to belated travellers than was the sight of the broken outline of that deserted log cabin to that sorrowful little band. The building was of that common southern pattern which may be described as two small square cabins united by a roofed-over passage.

On the floor of this latter they laid Arthur, on every spare garment that the men could shed.

As they carefully lowered him, Antoinette pressed forward, dropping on her knees beside him, and hers were the hands that placed the poor pillow of a rolled coat under his head. Every thought of self, even of her own grief seemed to be driven out by her intense desire to relieve his suffering, and the concentration of her face might have been that of a great surgeon.

It was enough to make a strong man shudder to see that ominous black hole in the front of his coat, with the dark wet stain around it. Worse than this was the trickling red line that ran from the set mouth downwards.

The jolting of the road had done its work. And a hemorrhage had come.

Someone had found an old bucket near a spring and now proffered the water to Antoinette.

With quick fingers she tore a lace-trimmed flounce from the petticoat she wore and made bandages.

There was brandy too handed to her in a small flask with which she wetted his lips and temples.

After this he opened his eyes, which met hers with

the strange compelling force of those hovering on the border-land.

Slightly he shook his head, as though to say, "Where's the use?" But a wistfulness in his eyes seemed to say how fair life looked as it slipped away from his slackening grasp. Then they wearily closed again, though Antoinette thought that he had not again lost consciousness.

Rubbing his clammy hands to try to give them some warmth from her own, sponging his face with water, waving away the flies, trying every little womanly art to save him one added pang or weariness, Antoinette toiled on.

She had heard without heeding Parke's directions to young Ryan to take some men with him and go in search of Confederate troops. He felt sure that there must be some such patrolling the coast.

"And whatever you bring back, see that it's a doctor, if possible," he added.

Other parties had started in search of food, and the heavy noontide stillness of the woods settled down upon the few who remained in the solitary hut.

Mr. Parke and Hewitt sat on the tumble-down steps, keeping from a little distance a tireless watch if their help should be needed while some of the men lay about in the sunshine, sleeping the heavy sleep of exhaustion.

It seemed to Antoinette's concentrated perception that the moments of consciousness were growing more frequent with Arthur: that his eyes remained open for a longer time; and that he was showing some faint intermittent desire to speak.

Knowing that any such attempt would only add to the danger of hemorrhage, she shrank back, and remained motionless, for fear of arousing his attention. But when she saw his eyes wandering in a restless search she bent over him again.

"Do you want me to do anything for you?" she asked, her voice a caress in itself.

"Nothing to be done," he whispered. "Shan't live over another tide; then you will be free to go. Parke will take you to Wilmington all right."

Exhausted with bodily weariness and the long tension of excitement, it would have been strange if she had been able to maintain that overwrought self-control.

As she crouched beside him, a deep sob broke from her.

"Arthur! Arthur!" she breathed in a passion of pitying tenderness. "You *must* live! You *must* not die!"

It seemed as though even this were too much for his weakness. A frown of weariness came upon Arthur's face, and he turned his eyes away from the weeping woman beside him, as though in search of someone else. His eyes wandered, until their wistfulness rested upon Hewitt, who, as if in answer to a spoken summons, rose, and coming forward, knelt by him. The languid calm that was all but superciliousness in Hewitt's usual bearing was changed into an almost womanly tenderness, as he bent over his captain. The sailors had sometimes talked of there being some old tie between the two, and of having sometimes, when they had thought themselves alone, heard them call each other "Arthur" and "Jack."

In this supreme hour there was an unmistakable light of welcome in Arthur's face, and with a pitifully feeble gesture he slightly moved his hand for the other to take in his warm grasp.

"It's going easier, old man?" Hewitt managed to say, though in a somewhat shaky voice.

The answer was that same negative movement of the head as though to put that question aside.

"A last good turn, Jack," that ghost of a voice came. "Mabel—you know"—Hewitt nodded his face set and strained. There were tears in the blue eyes that had not known them for many a day. He would not breathe a word while he saw that Arthur's message was still to speak. The silence of the woods around them seemed to weigh upon the little group, as they held their breath to hear that faint voice.

It came again : "Write or tell her how I died. Not to grieve too long—so young—tell her"—and the voice seemed to gather a strange strength—"tell her, last, only thought of her—tried all day to live for her—must give up now—meet again."

With some remembrance or habit picked up in foreign lands, he managed feebly to raise one hand, and slowly, painfully, to cross himself on his breast.

Either that or the effort of speaking brought back that dreaded stream of red, and as they strove to staunch the hemorrhage they were all three sure that his life had gone out with it.

But a feeble pulse still fluttered in the wrist that Antoinette grasped. She pointed to it, and shook her head, when the two men would have lowered his head, and drawn her away.

All personal suffering seemed to her in that moment to have died. She was calm with that calm that has passed feeling, and nothing seemed able to come near enough to hurt her any more.

She had seen Arthur, in, apparently the very moment of death turn away from her aid, as though Mabel and his love were too holy things for her touch to tarnish. That signed cross had seemed to put her away from him in the outer spaces of both time and eternity.

We die many deaths in our progress through the world, before we are laid to rest in its bosom. In those moments much that had made part of Antoinette's self died, while the maimed rest lived on either to heal into new serener life, or else to perish from the shock of mutilation.

The hours of the long day wore on, and the wounded man lay quite still, without any further effort at speech. Mr. Parke brought some rough food and put it into Antoinette's hand, but the effort to swallow it choked her.

However, she eagerly drank something called by courtesy coffee, and even that gave her some fresh strength. At last, as the vivid southern sky was mellowing into sunset, the trampling of horses' feet was heard, and a little group of unkempt soldiers in grey rode up, guided by Ryan.

The first words spoken were Ryan's quick "Is he alive?"

"Yes. *Alive,*" briefly Parke answered, as if to say that that was all.

Then a lean weather-worn man slipped from his

horse, and came up the steps, announcing himself as the doctor.

Each haggard face was turned to him with a new hope in it, as he bent down beside Arthur in the businesslike fashion of one to whom such scenes had become a part of life's routine.

The silence was breathless while his deft hands hovered about the wounds. Then he turned, and taking Antoinette by the arm, said, gently enough, as he helped her to rise:

"Now, madam, you must give me plenty of room, please. I don't think it's hopeless by any means, and I'm going to do my level best for him." Then in a sudden sharp tone of general warning, "Look out! She's played out, at any rate."

For the tall figure had swayed dizzily, and the arms were reaching out in a helpless blind grasping for support, before Antoinette sank unconscious into Mr. Parke's hastily stretched-out arms. When she revived she found herself lying in one of the unused ends of the cabin, on a rough bed of dry grass, which yet seemed exquisite rest to her exhausted stiffened limbs.

Mr. Parke's long angular frame was perched on a log of wood for a seat. He held in his hand a tin cup from which he proceeded to administer brandy and water to her.

"The doctor has got the balls out," he began at once, "and now he is asleep all right. Hewitt is with him, and you are not to move, not to do anything, but go to sleep. You have gone through enough to kill an ordinary woman."

He paused, seeming to have some difficulty in bringing out his next words.

"The doctor says that his vitality is wonderful, and that he shouldn't wonder if he were to pull through all right. Of course, just now it's still a bit of a toss-up. Now you must rest. Good-night."

He had scarcely left her before Antoinette's eyes were closed in sleep, from which she never woke until the sun was high the next morning.

CHAPTER XXXIII

DIVERSE PATHS

THE golden sunshine was glorifying even that dismal little hovel and a mocking-bird was pouring out his soul in his morning libation as Antoinette awoke to a puzzled sense of her surroundings.

Someone had already thought of her comfort, for a fire of pine faggots, that perfection of fires, was crackling on the old hearth-stone. Near it stood a tin pannikin of water.

It was not much to have done for her, but the sight brought a few hot tears to her eyes. She had come to a pass when the commonest kindness struck her with a pathetic sense of wonder.

A dull, painful red burned in her checks, with the dawning remembrance of how Arthur had turned from her even while she was using her last strength in his service.

Lying there in the morning stillness her mind went back for the first time over those eventful hours since she had stood and watched them making ready the dinghy to take her ashore. She realised with all the acuteness of her keen intellect that Arthur's prognostication had been right. She, if only by her mere presence, had added to his perils.

But it was not only her presence. She had delayed the starting of the boat, and then by that uncontrolled impetuous movement had upset it.

She guessed that but for the delay in saving her they would all have been safely ashore before the Yankee boat was really within range.

Those cruel wounds that she had staunched were really her doing. How Arthur must have loathed her as he felt a life of so much promise ebbing away. No wonder he had turned his head away from the sight of her.

Why, *why* had they not left her to lie in peace under the water? It was at least the shore of her own country, that country that she had never wronged.

She would have rested there well. Warwick would have grieved when he heard of it, but even for Warwick it would have been better so. He would have thus sooner forgotten her, and at the thought of Warwick a sob of new loneliness broke from her.

Held in the bondage of such thoughts, she stood staring out of the little square window, innocent of glass, into the sombre green shade of the pine woods.

She was roused by Mr. Parke's voice outside.

"I heard you move and came to tell you that I am keeping a hoe-cake and some coffee for you at the fire. You, must be famished. The captain is no worse, perhaps even a shade stronger. Everyone is getting dried and rested."

Antoinette looked down at her torn and limp garments, with, even in that hour of intensest self-abasement, a feminine distaste for being so unpleasant an object. She tried with her hands to smooth into some kind of order the dishevelled masses of her hair.

It says much for the perfection of her beauty that

even in such a plight the doctor's glance was one of admiration as she came out to join him and Parke at their campfire.

Mr. Parke's favourite author was Carlyle, and now a vision came to him of the stately uncrowned Marie Antoinette as she came forth in her poor rags to go from her prison to her death.

He felt some intangible change in her from the impetuous highly-wrought woman of the day before. There was a calm as of one aloof from her surroundings in the pale face and the big mournful eyes.

The doctor scrutinised her with professional keenness.

"Ah, you look a little less corpse-like than you did last night," he said. "I was sorry that I could not do more for you, but the captain's case took all my time."

"He is no worse?" she asked.

"Better, decidedly better. Pulse stronger, and very little fever. I am going to try to I take him up to Wilmington in a pilot-boat to-night. There will be very little exertion for him, and he would do so much better in the hospital there."

A look of terror had come into her eyes.

"But the cruisers—the danger of any excitement for him."

"Oh, that will be all right," was the cheerful answer. "Perhaps you don't know that you were all but at the point of safety under Fort Fisher guns, when they drove you ashore, I saw the wreck yesterday as we came along."

"The poor Nighthawk!" she said with a sigh.

Antoinette made a kind of breakfast on the corncake and coffee which Mr. Parke had produced with apologies for the quality. "I tried hard to get you an egg but it seemed an unattainable thing. A gourmet would have a bad time in the South just now," he said.

All the same, she looked better for the food, as she rose from her seat on a log.

"I am ready now to look after Captain Arthur, if you need me," she said gently, to the doctor.

"Oh, Mr. Hewitt and I are doing very well, taking turns about. There's not much to distract our attention about here. And as he is quite conscious now, the sight of a fresh face might excite him. Besides, you yourself need all the rest that you can get, after what you have gone through. I was amazed when they told me about it. Been undressed yet? I thought not. We must find something for you to wrap yourself in while you get your things well dried by the fire."

Antoinette acquiesced without remonstrance and a big army cloak was produced. Mr. Parke heaped up a great fire in her own end of the shanty, and she soon got her clothes into better order.

Arthur had been moved the night before into the other cabin, so that she did not even see him.

It was late in the afternoon when the doctor came to tell her that he would like her to take his place by Arthur.

He and the others were about to busy themselves with preparations for his move to the shore. They wanted to give him a chance of resting before he was taken on board the boat at dark.

For a moment Antoinette almost seemed to shrink back, while a vivid crimson swept over her face. Then, bowing her head, she went silently in, and sat down on the log, placed as seat, a little behind the head of the improvised bed on the floor.

Arthur seemed to be in a quiet sleep, and she sat motionless, careless of time or surroundings, all her being wrapped in the study of that face, familiar to her in so many different aspects, but never until now with the pallor of suffering and weakness over it.

Presently his eyes opened languidly, but she did not move until he said, "Hewitt!" Then she came forward within sight, saying gently, "Did you want anything?"

He shook his head and closed his eyes, and the silence fell again between them while her slow tears dropped one by one.

Towards sunset the improvised litter of blankets on poles was ready, and again they turned their faces shorewards.

Obeying the doctor's directions Antoinette took her place on one side of Arthur while he walked on the other, both ready with careful hand to ease any jar or smooth any uneasiness.

"That's all right!" the doctor said with a long breath of relief, as the precious burden was lowered by the men with infinite care on to the soft sand of the beach.

"Stood it better than I thought—no hemorrhage," he said after a careful inspection.

The getting on board the little craft in the dim twilight haze was not so simple a matter. But it was done at last, and Arthur laid on the deck, while the sails were filled by a soft southerly breeze.

They dodged and drifted alternately for a little while, until, the point of safety reached, they were able to go steadily on their way up the river.

An air of greater cheerfulness was spreading among them. The doctor was evidently satisfied with Arthur's condition. Indeed, they all could see that his strength was greater.

Antoinette had relieved guard so that the men could eat, and sat in the darkness near the radius of light from the ship's lantern that framed Arthur in a luminous circle.

The tinkle of a chain which she wore on her wrist caught his ear with its familiar sound.

"Nearly at Wilmington?" he asked with the wistfulness of helplessness.

"Nearly there," she answered bravely. "I hope you are not very tired."

He let this pass as he did most such words.

"Where will you go?" was what she next heard. She hesitated for an instant, but, sheltered by the friendly night, she took courage to put the question that had been hovering on her lips.

"Do you want me to nurse you?" she asked, past hopes thrilling with life in her heart.

"Thanks, no—plenty nurses at the hospital. Not trouble you," were the words that, though broken, were quite decisive.

He had settled the question. It was parting then. "Very well," was her quiet answer.

"You'll be all right?" he asked, as with an after thought of compunction.

"Oh, yes. I must attend to my business at once, you know. But I think you should not talk any more. The doctor will be scolding me."

And so, in the light of the early morning Antoinette stood on the wharf and saw Arthur carried to the ambulance that soon hid him from her sight.

She had made no effort to say farewell, nor, indeed, to attract his attention in any way since those last words on the deck.

The sense of utter isolation from the last of personal ties or feelings that came over her as she turned townwards almost made her light-hearted.

But a long, striding step sounded behind her, and Mr. Parke was at her side.

"You mustn't slip away like that by yourself," he said. "I am coming with you to take care of you." Her laugh was a very gentle one, with that new gentle aloofness that puzzled him.

"Oh, I am used to taking care of myself, and I thought that you were going to the hospital with the captain."

"Oh, Hewitt has gone. He would rather have him than anyone," and something in his voice made her fancy that he too might feel lonely. Still she protested.

"But you cannot stay with me, for I am on my way to report myself at very high quarters."

"Oh, well, I'll see you there," he compromised, walking along with her.

Before leaving her, he had, with the quiet pertinacity that marked him, got Antoinette to tell him where he would find her later.

It was to a very worn haggard man in whose face might be read the coming doom of the nation, that Mrs. LeMoine presently told her story.

"If everyone had been as staunch and tireless as you,

things might have looked brighter to-day," he said as she ended. "And now what do you do?"

Antoinette had flushed into brightness under his praise.

"Whatever you may want me to. If you have any further tasks for me, I am ready to your hand. If not—well, I will go and plant cabbages," and she smiled gratefully at him.

The statesman seemed to ponder a matter before he spoke again.

"There *is* one affair," he hesitated, "but it is a dangerous one, and I hate to ask you to go. It seems as though you had done your share already. But it is of great importance, in fact it is almost my last hope of lengthening the struggle. You could do it better than anyone else, I know—but—" he paused.

"I will go," she said simply. "Where is it?"

"It is in New York, and you will have to get through the lines."

"That is an easy matter," she answered lightly to hide a certain chill of dismay. She hated to acknowledge even to herself that a Northern prison was the one thing that she most feared. She had heard strange tales whispered of the insults that some women had undergone in them.

A glow of admiration lit the man's tired face.

"If you succeed it will be your crowning service to your country," he said enthusiastically. "Many a general has won a battle without doing more for our freedom, than you have done. Some day your name will be rightly honoured."

"Ah, no, my name is best left to perish where I fall,"

she murmured bitterly.

"It shall never perish while some of us, who know what you have done, still live," he answered warmly.

Antoinette went away from this interview with a new strength and serenity in face and bearing.

Later in the day Mr. Parke sought her out and inquired her plans.

"Secrets of state," she mockingly answered him. He was not to be put off so easily.

"You mean then to remain alone in this unhappy country?" he asked.

"Exactly so. I belong here, you know," she agreed.

"Because," he said, slowly, "I have just had an offer to take out the Spindrift to Nassau. She is a new blockade-runner, with captain and first officer both laid up here with fever."

"But that is splendid, isn't it?" she said heartily.

"Yes, it is one chance in a hundred, but I want to take you with me." Antoinette tried to treat the idea as a joke.

"Really you must be an Irishman to think of such a thing. It would be worth while getting all but drowned coming here, just to turn around and go back again the next day. What put such an idea into your head?"

Mr. Parke hardly seemed to be listening to her words and his usually impassive face was strangely troubled.

His voice was somewhat hoarse as he began:

"Ah, but drop all those secrets and schemes that can only get you into worse dangers yet, and come away with me, and let me marry you, and take care of you.

"I know that it is presumption in a rough sailor like

me to speak of such a thing. But, although I have knocked about in queer places, I do come of gentle folk at home; so that I would know better what you needed, and I would try so hard to please you! I never thought to ask any woman again to share my fate, but when I saw you so brave, so beautiful, so lonely, I—well, I've been able to think of nothing else since—"

He paused, and she laid her hand gently on his, with a soft light in her eyes.

"Mr. Parke, if ever a woman had a kind and honest friend, I have had one in you. Believe me, I have been more grateful than perhaps I seemed. I am so sorry to give you pain, but, ah! it is impossible. I must go on my way alone!"

Mr. Parke's face was drawn into deeper creases than ever as he said hoarsely:

"Well, it can't be helped. I hardly thought that you *would*. But won't you all the same let me take you away from all these troubles?"

She smiled sadly and shook her head.

"There is nowhere I want to be, nowhere that I could be of any use save among my own people," she answered gently. "I must stick to my work. I am best and happiest at that. But—there is one thing I *must* say—" she hesitated, flushing deeply.

"I do not see how you can ever forgive one thing that I did—I mean my insolence, about the diamond necklace, you know."

For a moment Mr. Parke stared bewildered, and then, to her surprise, even in the sepulchral gloom of his disappointment, he laughed out. Then he hastened to reassure her.

"If you had seen as many queer things done in moments of excitement as I have, you would know how little impression it made on me. One needs to have seen a battle or a shipwreck—I've seen both—to know what strange tricks people's nerves can play them. Ah no, you must never worry yourself about that. I only remember how beautiful you looked standing there," and he took her hand into the grasp of one of his, while he patted it gently with his other.

"And now, I'll say good-bye, and not trouble you any more."

Taking, with sombre eyes, one last look into hers, he turned and was gone. And so these two parted.

CHAPTER XXXIV

WARWICK'S QUEST

IN those days all news that came of the blockade-runners, or from the beleaguered land, was uncertain as to date, and often as to accuracy as well. There were, as autumn came, at least two in Halifax who counted the days long until they should have some tidings of the Nighthawk. Mabel Evans went on her seraphic path of church work, with her smile as serene as ever.

Her father, however, was unaccountably morose, and inclined to give but short answers to those who disturbed him.

Major Warwick, too, with each succeeding week of suspense, drew more into his shell, his comrades noticing how thin and gaunt he had grown.

There were different theories to account for this. One laid the change to the worry over the unaccounted for explosion at the powder-magazine. Another theory held that he had never looked the same since his southern charmer had vanished from the scene.

"He couldn't have blown her up in the powder-magazine, and be suffering from remorse," suggested one youngster, who was promptly snubbed for flippancy.

Major Warwick was popular with both old and young of his comrades, and these new moods of his were respected and allowed for.

Nearly two months had gone, and the summer and even the autumn were things of the past, before a blockade-runner brought from Nassau a report of the loss of the Nighthawk.

This rumour was being eagerly discussed in the mess anteroom one evening, when a silence was caused by the appearance of Warwick.

The Colonel seeing that he had heard nothing of the tale presently took occasion to quietly repeat it to him. As he saw the man's face twitch with pain, he turned away and casually stirred the fire.

"And the crew? The—the passengers? What of them?" Warwick asked briefly.

"Nothing seemed to be definitely known about them, as far as I could learn. But they must surely be able to tell you something definite on board the Southern Belle."

Warwick lost no time in interviewing the captain of the blockade-runner, but did not gain much satisfaction thereby.

The captain told how he had been all but safely through the blockading fleet off Wilmington, before he had discovered that Fort Fisher had been taken and held by the Northerners. He had then been obliged to turn and flee for safety through the outside dangers again.

A pilot whom he had picked up had pointed out to him part of the hull of a ship on the sands, which he said had been the Nighthawk, blown up by her own crew. He was not quite sure of the facts, but seemed to think that there could be little doubt of their all being in a Northern prison.

"If they really blew up their ship they wouldn't have too easy a time of it, either," he ended with.

"If there were any ladies on board, they would surely not imprison them, too?" Warwick asked in a curiously dulled tone.

"They would, like a shot, if they were well-known Southerners, or had been at all active in their sympathies. Tell you what, this is no kid-glove war, sir." A sudden afterthought seemed to come to the man who asked: "What's this that I heard them say about Mrs. LeMoine being on board?"

Warwick was startled by some significance in the man's manner.

"She was on board, yes. Why do you ask? Do you know her?" he asked quickly.

"I know of her, and I know how well the Yankees know her. If they've got her now, they may make it pretty nasty for her."

Warwick could say nothing. He was too heartsick. With brief farewell and thanks he left the captain and went his way. A northern prison! He had often heard the wild tales of the day relating to such places. A dull rage possessed him at thought of the woman he loved being alone in such scenes of misery. No wonder that he tramped miles through the sombre autumn twilight before returning to his lonely quarters to one of the night watches that were helping to sprinkle his hair with grey.

By the next morning his resolution was taken. No matter what had been Mrs. LeMoine's commands, or his own promises, he would no longer loiter away his days in this aimless round, while she might be in such peril. He would apply for three months' leave at once. As his old general was gone he did not anticipate any difficulty in getting it. At any rate, if by any chance he should be refused leave, he would give up his commission. What did even his once dearly-loved profession matter compared with Antoinette's safety?

He lost no time in setting the necessary machinery to work. Then he found that even with his leave, he had no means of getting south sooner than by the Bermuda boat, which was to sail in little less than a week's time. And so, with what patience he might, he waited. It was a few days after his decision that he received a dainty note from Mabel Evans.

She tenderly reproached him for not having been to see her of late, when his sympathy would have been such a comfort through "this harrowing time of suspense."

She had always felt, she added, that he had understood her better than most, and she had hoped that he would have come unasked to share her trouble. Now, she begged him to delay no longer but come to her at once, as she had something of great importance which she could say to him—alone.

So absorbed was Warwick in his own one idea that he paid no attention to the tone of this epistle.

Mabel would have been flattered indeed if she could have guessed what a tumult the sight of her writing had aroused in him. For what could it mean but that she had received a communication from Arthur, which would almost certainly include news of Mrs. LeMoine.

And so he hastened out that westerly road, as eagerly

as ever he had done on those past summer days, when
it led him to the sight of what he loved best.

But, scarcely inside the gate, the melancholy aspect
of the place struck him with a sense of chill. The fallen
leaves lay thick under the sombre whispering pines,
and through the bare white birch-trees groomed the
steel-grey, wind-swept water. The last time that he had
been at the house was on the occasion of Adair's marriage to Hattie.

Now they were on their way to India, and love and
hope and sunshine seemed to have gone with them.
But, once inside the door, all was the usual quiet cozy
comfort. If he had thought to notice it he might have
seen what an effective picture Mabel made, as she sat
gazing pensively into a wood fire. That her dress was
all black, he *did* notice with a sudden sinking of heart
at what the fact might foretell. The stiff white collar
and cuffs worn with the plain black dress gave her a
nun-like look, and her smile and bearing carried out
the scheme. It was more pensiveness than sadness that
they suggested. Hattie had often said that she could
tell Mabel's moods by the dresses she wore.

Stretching out a languid white hand in greeting, she
murmured:

"How kind and like yourself to come so soon!"

But Warwick, discarding formalities, asked eagerly:
"Have you had news from Arthur?"

Mabel's pensiveness deepened genuinely. She hated
not to be the first consideration with her audience.
She had expected some comment on her sad and
lonely aspect.

"Nothing directly from him," she had to acknowl-

edge with a sigh, "but of course I have been told all
that the Captain of the Southern Belle said." She
paused. Then with a touching little show of emotion:
"But oh, Major Warwick, I *know* that he is dead!"

"Please tell me what you mean?" Warwick demanded,
with a strong effort at patience. Mabel had sunk back
in her low seat, and he stood by the fire looking down
at her.

The lovely face was turned up to him with more
open signs of distress.

"Please don't think me very foolish! Indeed, I would
not have troubled you if I had not been so utterly
lonely. Hattie is gone, and my father is so changed
and gloomy that I am sometimes quite frightened by
him. I felt that I should go mad if I had not some one
kind to talk to! And you always seemed to understand
so well what I was feeling!"

Warwick gave little heed to the tremulousness of
her voice, or to the brimming over of the soft, blue
eyes.

"Please try to tell me what is troubling you?" he
urged, gently enough, but with something in his insis-
tence which caused Mabel to control her sorrow.

"I suppose it is foolish, but I have been so unhappy
since I had such a strange dream a few nights ago,"
she began, with clasped hands. "I thought that I saw
Captain Arthur struggling in the waves. He had nearly
reached some safety, a boat, I think, when I saw Mrs.
LeMoine's arms around his neck, and I heard him
say—oh, I heard his voice so plainly—'As long as we
go together, what does it matter?' And their faces were
both happy as the water covered them. I could still see

them going down, down together! It seemed as though I had lost him doubly. Death at least would leave one an ideal—" and a sob finished the sentence.

If Warwick had not been strung up to such a state of expectancy, he might have showed some pity for Mabel's fanciful woes. As it was, he found some difficulty in keeping from swearing outright.

"And is this what you had to tell me?" he asked, and his voice told Mabel that her pretty little scheme of winning his heart on the rebound had failed.

"I know how silly you must think me," she sobbed, with genuine tears of vexation. "But if you only knew how unhappy I am! I feel so certain that Arthur must be dead, or that I shall never see him again. He only went on this last voyage to please Mrs. LeMoine. I always thought that she had great influence over him; didn't you?" And she looked up guilelessly into Warren's face.

He, however, cut directly through her innuendoes.

"I must say I hardly see what Mrs. LeMoine's influence has to do with Arthur being dead or not. And what is more, I do not for a moment believe that either of them is dead. Some word of it would have reached us if they were."

Mabel sighed, before she began in a low, reluctant voice, as if it were forced out of her:

"Have you never thought that perhaps they had escaped together to Nassau, or some such place, and that we may never hear of them again?"

The moment's pause seemed very long to her, before Warwick answered her question.

"Thank God! I have never had such thoughts of my

friends as that!" he said, sternly, before going on in a calmer voice:

"However, I intend to do my best to put a stop to this uncertainty, which has evidently upset your nerves. I have got three months' leave, and am starting for Bermuda in a few days. I shall get through somehow from there to Wilmington."

Poor Mabel! Her hands dropped helplessly in her lap, and she sat staring at her toppled-over airy castle. She was, then, never to have the chance of being a baronet's wife, unless Arthur should be really alive, and outlive his cousin.

"I will do my best to send you any tidings that I may gather," Warwick said, more mildly.

He felt as though he had been breaking a butterfly on the wheel, in being wroth with so futile a creature. Now that the first keenness of the disappointment was over, he felt grimly amused at her pathetic attempt at another assault on him. Good Heavens! this was the girl whom his cousin set upon a pinnacle and bowed down to!

But Mabel was not crushed yet. With a guileless upward glance, she asked softly:

"Do you think that my father will join you in your search?"

After all, she had scored last, and his answer, "Not that I am aware of," was of the shortest, as were his adieus.

And so Warwick turned his face southward. It was, however, by devious ways that he reached his destination.

The palmy days of blockade-running were over. The

Northern fleets had increased in quality and quantity, and so had the percentage of captures. English shipowners had become discouraged as to the venture of further capital.

However, from Bermuda Warwick got a passage in a man-of-war to Nassau. From thence he got across to Florida, making his way northwards through the war-ravaged land, still dauntless in its last year of endurance.

The sights that he saw upon that journey were destined to remain long fixed in Warwick's memory.

He was stayed by bad roads or broken-down communications at lonely plantations where solitary women staunchly faced what was next door to starvation for them and their children.

Meals were set before him of which he tried to eat no more than would sustain his strength, it seemed so like taking the food out of the mouths of women and children.

But how willingly it was offered when they learned that he was an Englishman, and had come from Halifax, where he had perhaps seen some relative or friend. He had not gone far before every little trifle from his travelling bag had been scattered as a gift, so small but so valued.

A novel and some old newspapers filled a whole household with rapture. The gift of a paper of pins sent a blue-eyed girl flying off on horseback to distribute some of her treasure-trove amongst her dearest friends. Some envelopes and note-paper brought tears to the eyes of an old lady as she told how the last blank sheet of paper had been taken from the library books, and even the supply of wrapping paper had failed her, so that she had had nothing left on which to write to her sons at the front. In those days Warwick realised the meaning of "the scourge of war" to any country.

At last after many delays he reached Wilmington. Presenting his letters he found that although no one seemed to have a very clear idea as to Mrs. LeMoine's whereabouts, she was certainly alive. Arthur, he learned, was still in the hospital with his wounds.

CHAPTER XXXV

IN THE HOSPITAL

MAJOR WARWICK was ushered into a long bare hospital ward, lit brightly by the winter sun.

Here there was the same atmosphere of the makeshifts of wartime as he had met elsewhere.

The doctors and men attendants wore uniform, and were all either very old or else evidently not long off the sick list themselves.

It was amongst a group of convalescents—also uniformed—and in strange variety of bandages—who sat smoking in a sunny corner that Warwick found his cousin, his leg still stiffly stretched out in splints.

It seemed strange to see the man who had always been the embodiment of energy and resolution so invalided. His clothes hung loosely on him, and his once bronzed face was pale and peaked from confinement.

Over the waxy texture of his skin, there swept a glad tide of colour, at sight of Major Warwick.

"Hugh! This is a sight for sore eyes! Come to hunt me up, have you? Well, it *is* good in you!"

Even as he exchanged a long hearty hand clasp, Warwick had a guilty sensation that such warm thanks were hardly his due. Still, he *did* feel very kindly towards his kinsman, helpless and alone in a strange land.

"I had no idea of your whereabouts, but I somehow never expected to find you in hospital. And you look as though you had been having hard times of it," he said with genuine interest.

"Hard times? Yes, it was pretty bad when they couldn't get the bullet out of my hip and kept prodding at it continually. The wound in my chest, which they thought at first was going to do for me altogether, healed up in no time."

"But how did it all happen?" Warwick asked, anxious to get at the story.

"I'll spin you the yarn presently. Tell me of Mabel first."

"Mabel is well," and Warwick, controlling his impatience, gave as pleasing a sketch as possible of his last interview with her. He had to acknowledge that she fancied that Arthur must be dead.

"Then she has never got any of all the letters that I have written?" Arthur asked wistfully.

"Not one. In fact, all that any of us knew was that the Nighthawk's remains were lying on the shore below Fort Fisher."

"Poor old Nighthawk!" and her captain gave a sigh to her memory.

"And Mrs. LeMoine?" Warwick ventured.

Arthur shot an inquiring glance at him, as he answered moodily:

"*She* came out of it all right. Though her self-will was the cause of my getting potted in this fashion. She delayed us until she gave the Yankee boat a chance of making a target of me. I knew—when she persisted in coming that sooner or later she would get me into a scrape. I hate to have women mixed up in any of my affairs."

"What do you mean? Tell me what really happened," Warwick demanded shortly, not at all fancying Arthur's speech.

Impassively he listened to the tale of the Nighthawk's last hours, though as he heard of the dinghy's upset he could not refrain from a start.

"Mr. Parke?" he queried. "He was that long, lean first officer of yours who hardly ever spoke?"

"Yes, but he is a good fellow in a tight place. Mrs. LeMoine may thank him that she is alive to-day. I rather fancy that she gave him a heart-ache in return as she tries to do to every man she meets."

Arthur's temper was evidently in a convalescent state, and Warwick recognising this fact tried to keep his own in better order.

"But where is she? I suppose she has nursed you?" and he eyed his cousin as though considering him unworthy of that honour.

At that Captain Arthur looked a trifle uncomfortable, as though smitten with a late compunction.

"Well, no. She did offer to when they brought me here, but I told her that I wouldn't trouble her. I knew that they would have plenty of nurses here, and Hewitt, my old chum, was with me. I hate to have ladies messing round me in such places. I'd rather have a comfortable old black mammy whom one can swear at when things go wrong. However, I must give her the credit of having been awfully plucky while I was so bad in the bush. As far as I can remember, she never rested, but was always beside me."

Warwick's heart burned within him.

"But you haven't told me where she is now," he said imperiously.

"I really don't know. She didn't come here at all. Parke told me before he went away that she had gone off on some of their secret missions. He seems to have hung round her as long as he could."

"And you have never taken the trouble to discover her whereabouts?" Warwick asked in the bitterness of his disappointment.

"Where would be the use if she is at some of that conspiracy work again?" Arthur retorted.

"Whatever she is doing, I mean to find her, or to stay in this country until I have made someone tell me where she is," his cousin retorted.

The two men looked at each other very steadily before Arthur spoke again:

"I am sorry to hear it. I had hoped that by now you might be free from her influence."

"That I shall never be as long as we both live," was the firm answer.

"And when you have found her?" suggested the other.

"That is for her to decide. In any case, I am at her service in any need."

The situation was evidently growing strained between the cousins. It was Arthur this time who made a strong effort to restore it to friendliness.

"Look here, my dear fellow, if we were just ordinary friends, I should mind my manners and say nothing more. But blood is thicker than water, and though I haven't used it for a good while, I can't be careless about the dear old name. Surely, what you heard and saw in Halifax this summer showed you that, fascinating as I grant you Mrs. LeMoine is, she is a woman to be pretty careful with. May I ask if you know her past?"

Warwick had leaned a little forward in his chair, a slow fire kindling in his eyes.

"I know enough to tell me that she is a woman into whose soul the iron of suffering has entered, but that it has had no power to sear and corrode one of the noblest natures that ever came out of the hand of the Creator. Tell me," he went on, his voice deepening, "do you believe that any woman could act as she has done, toiling, facing dangers and insults, bearing hardships, all for the most intense love of her country, if there were in her spirit one low or degraded instinct? You will at least allow her patriotism?"

It was Arthur's turn to feel his temper sorely tried. "I allow her the benefit of all her good qualities. No one appreciates her brains and her beauty more than I do," he answered impatiently; "but"—and the pause was impressive—"you know very well that you cannot marry her, and anything else would be a wretched business for you both. Come, remember she is among her own chosen friends and people, and surely can have no need of you. If you want so badly to play the good Samaritan, you can try your hand at carting me out of the country. The doctor seems to think that I am almost ripe for a move now."

It was a strong claim, that of the former leader of men, now asking for help like a woman.

Warwick felt the passing pang of it as he gently shook his head.

His wrath was disarmed by the other's need.

"I should be glad to do what I could for you, my dear fellow, but I am not free. When a man of my age is possessed by the spirit of a woman, it is no joke. Remember, I have tried my hand at giving her up, in the last three months. It wasn't exactly a success. There were times when I began to think of my revolver more than was good for me. *Now*, whether for good or evil, I must follow where she leads—go where she beckons.

"If my profession, my name, my friends stand in the way, they must be brushed aside, that is all. *Nothing*, save her own word, gives me pause."

It was perhaps the first time in his life that Warwick had spoken out his deeper self to any man, and the other was awed as he listened.

It had not been given to Arthur, that gift of counting the world well lost for love. It is not to every one that the fatal inheritance comes. But he was able to recognise the fact that here was a deeper passion than he himself could ever know.

It was a rare thing for Arthur to hesitate over his own actions, but now he pondered the probable result of telling Warwick that Antoinette was free to marry him.

He knew that she had been true to her promise to him, and had left Warwick in ignorance of the fact. He knew too how promptly Warwick would act on the information.

After all, if they were happy together what did old American stories matter in an English home.

He had all but yielded to the impulse when the

remembrance of what Mabel's feelings would be at
the prospect of such a connection changed his ideas.

To see Antoinette the wife of the older cousin, a
probable baronet's wife, the head of the family, might,
he feared, change Mabel's mind as to marrying him.
Of course he put her scruples down to the purity that
could bear no unworthy contact, but all the same they
had settled the question before he spoke again.

"I am sorry, old man, that it must be so, but sometimes the fates are too strong for us poor mortals. I
was only joking about your taking care of me. Hewitt
has been waiting on to cart me out of here, and would
be furious if anyone else attempted the job."

Warwick made a strong effort to follow his lead and
return to more ordinary topics.

"I am glad of that," he said. "I almost, wonder you
haven't tried to go before now. A sea-voyage ought to
be an easy matter for you, and would surely set you up
quicker than this place."

"A sea-voyage is all right enough, but I know rather
too much about blockade-running to ask any man to
burden himself with a helpless passenger. And Hewitt
would never have let me go alone, and I might have
risked his life. He is one of those awkward people who
would insist on saving your life, whether you wanted
him to or not. And so I just stayed on here, with what
patience I might. But I think we'll try it next week in
the Northern Light. A lucky name to take me back to
my northern light, isn't it?" and his face brightened in
anticipation.

Warwick rose. "I wish you all luck," he said as he
held out his hand.

"Thanks. And, look here, you won't mind what I said, will you? I really meant well."

His sincerity seemed evident, and Warwick did his best to reassure him, and to part friends.

This they managed to do in a fashion, but neither man felt any the happier for the interview.

CHAPTER XXXVI

AN UNEXPECTED ALLY

As Warwick had sat talking with Arthur at the end of the long ward, he had noticed with the outer sense that marks such trifles that all the women nurses save one were of shades varying from tawny up to ebony.

This one who proved the exception to the rule, was a neutral-tinted, faded little woman who seemed to be hovering about with an eye to the convalescent corner.

At any rate Warwick caught her watchful gaze more than once in the course of his conversation.

As he walked away through the ward he did not observe her again, but at the first turn of the stairway he came on her standing at an open window. To his surprise she turned round, and put out her hand to detain him.

"You do not know who I am?" she asked, looking him in the face with her pale blue eyes.

As he heard her voice, an unpleasant memory hovered around Warwick, but he could give it no definite place.

"Well, perhaps we never *did* meet, but we certainly came very near it. And I know that you must have heard a good deal about me. I am the woman who was known as Mary Johnson—the one who did jailer's duty over Mrs. LeMoine when she was entrapped."

Unconsciously Warwick drew away from her, shaking

off her grasp upon his arm. Beyond smiling in a queer fashion, she did not seem to resent this however.

"You needn't shrink," she said quietly. "I know that your one thought is of Mrs. LeMoine, and I mean her no harm now. Indeed, I would atone to her if I could."

Something in the woman's manner persuaded Warwick of her sincerity, and yet he hesitated.

"But you are the wife of that man—"

"Martin, you mean? No, thank God, I am his widow now. He died of smallpox in New York, and I was left alone in the world.

"I came of Southern people, and my old father and mother had never guessed that I had been such a thing as a spy. I think it would have killed them if they had. There was a good deal else that they didn't know, either. They still think that Martin was a good man, and that I mourned him when he died. It was better so.

"Well, that's neither here nor there. At any rate the old spirit of 'I will arise and go to my father,' came over me, and I dodged and twisted my way south to them, taking as much trouble to do good, as I ever did to do harm. And when at last I got to the poor old folks, what do you think I found?

"Why that their money was gone, their servants had left them—that they two were alone in the house, old and helpless, nearly starving.

"In fact, they might have starved in good earnest but for Mrs. LeMoine. She happened to have taken rooms in their house, and when my mother fell ill, she waited on her, and spent her own money on food and comforts for them.

I had helped to starve and ill-treat her. *I* might have had a hand in her death if you had not found her that night. *She* fed and nursed my old father and mother, so that when I came and saw what she had done, I fell at her feet and begged her to kill me and put me out of my shame.

"And she—she said, 'There is no shame left for those who would serve their country, and you will serve her all the better for having learned what it was to be false.'

"And then she went to people, and got me this work here in the hospital by which I am able to earn enough to keep the old folks and myself alive. So now you can judge for yourself whether I mean her good or harm."

Such words would have been dear to any lover's ears. How much more were they soothing to Warwick's spirit, harassed and wounded by his cousin's scorn.

"God bless her!" he muttered hoarsely.

"Yes, God bless her!" the woman echoed. "And if I can bring one blessing into her life, my own heart will be the lighter."

"When I saw you," she went on in a more practical tone, "you, who I have good reason to know value her safety so dearly, I said to myself that I should not let you go, without speaking to you of her, and asking if there were nothing that I could do to help you in your undertaking. Believe me I may have more power than you would guess," and in her eagerness, she laid her hand upon his arm.

This time Warwick did not shake it off.

"My undertaking?" he repeated with a puzzled air. "Then you know—"

"I know that she is in danger, and I see you here. Surely, you are going to—"

But it was his turn to interrupt.

"In danger? Then you know where she is and what has happened to her? For God's sake, tell me quickly. I know nothing of her since she landed in Wilmington."

Mary Johnson had been trained by a strict taskmaster, and so she checked all superfluous expressions of surprise, and answered categorically.

"She is in New York, on a Confederate mission. It was madness sending so well-known a person there. There are hundreds who could recognise her. Her presence in the city was known, and unless she has already got away she can hardly do so. Any attempt to leave would probably lead to her arrest. I have some sure means of information, but that is the last I heard. It is more than probable that she is in prison now, and if so, things may go hard with her."

Something in these last words chilled Warwick's blood, but all he asked, was,

"What do you mean?"

Mary lowered her voice, and looked up and down the staircase before she whispered:

"It is said that she shot a Northern officer, who insulted her. The story has always been whispered but never exactly known. They will try to bring it home to her, if they get hold of her."

"She didn't do it?" was the breathless question.

"I don't know. She may have had to. But any way,

that won't make much difference now. And if they *should* give her a fair trial and fail to prove it, there are a hundred other reasons that they *can* give for imprisoning her. And she would not be the first if she died of heartbreak, so called fever in the prisons."

"Good God!" the man cried in intolerable pain. "What is the use of talking like that, if there is no way to help her? Tell me, can you think of nothing to be done?"

"Yes, I can," came her ready answer. "If you had not come to-day, I had meant to start to make my way through the lines to the North, and get to her. There are so many queer people and ways that I know, that perhaps I could do something. The only drawback is that I am rather well- known."

A new purpose was in Warwick's face. He scarcely seemed to heed her words as he said,

"You can tell me where to find her in New York?"

"Yes, unless something new has happened. In any case, I can send you to people who will know all that can be known."

"And you say that you could get through the lines? Can you put me in the way of doing the same?"

"Oh, yes," and then, clasping her hands in new excitement, "If you like, I will go to Richmond with you to-morrow to see about it."

"You are indeed the friend I needed," Warwick said, deeply touched. Then with a new idea, he asked:

"Do you suppose that Captain Arthur knew anything of what you have told me?"

She shook her head.

"He never cared to find out. He can think of nothing but that doll-faced girl." She paused, and then looked up thoughtfully at Warwick.

"I managed once or twice to listen to what you were saying. Do you mind telling me what he meant when he said that you could not marry Mrs. LeMoine?"

Warwick flushed deeply. It came hard to his reserve to discuss Antoinette with this woman, friend though she seemed.

"Because she has a husband living."

"Edward Castelle is dead."

How life seemed to surge around Warwick at the mere possibility that these words conveyed.

He hardly believed them, for had not Antoinette assured him to the contrary, not so very long ago.

"How do you know? How long is it since he died?"

"I know, as all the town knows, by seeing his sister wearing mourning for him. His name is over a grave in the cemetery. He was killed in one of the battles last April, and his body was brought home here and buried."

"And she never knew it!" There was a deep regret in his words, which his listener failed to fathom.

"Yes. She knew of it when she was a prisoner in the farmhouse. I am sure of that from some words I heard her say to Martin."

Warwick stood staring out into the deserted stretch of sun-baked street in a painful tumult of feeling.

How could she have so consummately deceived him, and to what purpose?

But he shook off the thought, as a dog might water. There was time enough for that afterwards. She was in danger now and needed his help, and nothing else mattered. He made some arrangements with the nurse for the next day, and then went his way. That way first took him to a cemetery where many a fresh grave told of the strain on the life of the nation.

The strong and the young were dying on the battle-fields, and the weak and the old were dying at home of heart-break and privations.

He found the simple tombstone of Edward Castelle, and turned away from the spot with fresh resolution.

He had carefully noted that the date was early in the past April. He was forced to realise that all that summer Antoinette had been free to marry him if she had chosen.

But she had not chosen, and "the queen can do no wrong," was his constant code.

Presently he stood and watched with a curious fascination a stately-looking, deserted old mansion. But when he caught a glimpse of its grief-bowed widowed mistress as she passed in, he lacked the heart to go and question her as to her brother's death.

After all did he not know enough? The dead was dead, with all his faults and failures; but he was alive in the light of the sun, free to plan and act.

And so, the next day he set forth for Richmond in the strange company of the little hospital nurse.

His cousin he had not tried to see again.

He could not but feel a strong suspicion that Arthur had all along known of Castelle's death, purposely leaving him in ignorance of it.

This aroused a hot resentment in him.

He sent him a few lines saying that he was starting for a sight of the Virginian battle-fields. More he would not add for fear of compromising Antoinette's safety.

CHAPTER XXXVII

THROUGH THE LINES

ARRIVED in Richmond, Warwick soon saw that Mary Johnson had spoken the truth when she had said that she knew strange people.

He was taken to confidential interviews in queer holes and corners, and with odd waifs of humanity.

When his purpose was announced one and all of these spoke discouragingly.

Running the land-blockade was no such joke as the English gentleman seemed to think. The Potomac was protected by gunboats, the fords were few, and carefully guarded.

The banks were constantly patrolled on both sides by pickets. A suspected spy might be hanged by either party before he had time to prove his innocence. The display of some English sovereigns raised a more sanguine spirit.

Before the first day was ended, a gloomy, cadaverous-looking man had undertaken the task of getting Major Warwick through to Washington, "All things permitten," as Mr. Nathaniel Butt cautiously stipulated.

He acknowledged to having one or two canoes stowed away in various woods, and to a thorough knowledge of the Potomac waters.

As preliminaries, a horse and light trap were bought in which to drive to the frontier.

Warwick packed a knapsack with one or two necessaries. With Mary Johnson's help he procured passes for the southern side of the frontier.

Then all was ready and before leaving he tried to thank her; but she waved his thanks aside.

"That is nothing. I do it for her. Have you a good memory? Then get these names and addresses in Washington by heart, for you must not let them fall into the enemy's hands if you should be searched. In Washington they will give you the New York names. That is safest. And what matters most of all, shall you have plenty of money in New York? Her life may hang on that."

"That is all right. I brought a letter of credit on a New York banker, in case of my search taking me North. Mr. Oliver it is addressed to."

"The Scotchman!" she said joyfully. "Why, that is the most important name that they would have given you in Washington. He is the centre of the Southern cause in New York. He can do for you what no one else can."

"That is good news, and now good-bye."

And the two so strangely thrown together grasped each other's hands warmly before separating.

It was in the darkness of the end of the night that Warwick drove out of Richmond, in a buggy with his new friend, Mr. Butt.

The dawn came, then the sunshine, and still they jogged along the heavy, red-clay roads. It was noon before they stopped to rest the horse at a darkey's solitary hut in the woods.

Here they had a meal of sorts, of yams and milk.

Warwick was impatient to be off, but the "pilot" refused to be hurried.

"I've got every hour arranged ahead, and there's no good to be got out of squeezing them on top of each other," he said.

However, after an hour or so, he consented to start.

Ever lonelier and more forest-hidden grew the road as they went on.

Sunset brought them to the house where they were to leave their horse and trap. Here they found a gaunt, ragged cavalry picket, resting their horses. From them they had the unwelcome news of their having that morning seen the northern patrols scouring the river bank where the newcomers were meaning to land. Mr. Butt took the tidings philosophically.

"Then they won't come back there to-morrow morning," he said, and did full justice to a supper of eggs and bacon, a rare treat in those days.

The night came with a clouded sky, and by nine o'clock there was an Egyptian darkness over the land. Then the silent guide put away his pipe and made a sign that the time had come.

As Warwick stumbled after him into the added blackness of the woods, he wished for some of the man's lithe dexterity instead of the clumsiness of his own bulk.

Branches and roots seemed to reach out to entrap him. Vines and briars twisted themselves around him. How did his companion avoid such snares in the darkness?

He was not cheered by the information that there

were still two miles between them and the banks of the Potomac.

On they went for half an hour in Indian file, the guide as stealthily as any woodland creature of the night. Warwick marking his course by stumbles, and cracking of branches.

At last the guide whispered, "See the stars? We're nearly out now. Go softly."

Softly he tried to go. Then came the voice again.

"Hear the water? Better lie down and keep quiet while I have a look for the canoe."

This was an easier followed order than the last. Warwick had a humiliating feeling of being wanting in some sense that this other man possessed, some closer tie with nature.

He was not sorry though to stretch himself out in the dry grass that grew high and thick. He could hear it rustling under the movements of his guide. The soft song of the river seemed to draw him on his quest. The night was very still, save for it and the high shrill notes of the frogs.

Presently the guide came creeping back with the announcement that the canoe was all right.

Then came another move through the darkness. Warwick did his best to emulate the serpentine fashion in which Mr. Butt made his way among the reeds and grasses, without ever rising to the sky line. Over the river the darkness seemed to brood in more velvety folds than ever. It was by sense of touch alone that Warwick found himself embarked in a rough dug-out.

He followed the orders to lie down flat while the

guide seated himself in the stern with his face to the bow.

They had hardly been more than five minutes out in the stream when the canoe struck against some floating object. A darker bulk in the darkness loomed before them.

A hoarse voice that sounded right overhead, shouted, "Boat ahoy!"

Then the flash and sound of a fired musket startled the night.

Warwick guessed at once that they had struck a small boat fastened to one of the Northern gunboats on guard.

As a light was flashed down upon the water he gave up all hopes of evasion, and his heart was hot with pain at thought of the delay in his quest. Anything worse than delay he refused to think of.

But the current was strong, and already the light craft had been swept out of the radius of light into the sheltering darkness. Perhaps the man on watch thought that the jar had come from some floating log, for quietness settled down again upon the gunboat, and soon the canoe had been carried to a safe distance.

"Near shave that," muttered Mr. Butt as he fell to paddling again.

Twenty minutes more brought them to land. The guide did not, however, seem satisfied.

He said that they must have drifted further down than he had thought, that he was not quite sure of his whereabouts, and that it would be madness to attempt any move before dawn.

There was nothing for it but patience.

The two men together hauled up the canoe and hid it in the grass.

The shores about here seemed more swampy, and their shelter under the herbage of a bank was not of the dryest. However, they each had a drink out of the flask, munched a biscuit, and tried to possess their souls in patience. By this time Mr. Butt's reserve had weakened, and he entertained Warwick in a low monotone with many strange tales of the borderland adventures of the last three years.

"Spies and such vermin I've done, my best to keep clear of, though only the Judgment Day will tell how far I've succeeded," he summed up.

When dawn came the guide was all business again. He soon recognised his neighbourhood, and said that it was a good-enough position from which to start for Washington.

One reconnaissance sent him back to say that the country was thick with patrols. They must not think of moving in the daytime.

Then ensued more long hours of an inactivity which, through all the force of his self-control, fretted Warwick's soul. They had to keep closer to cover than at night, and the swampy vegetation was not a pleasant hiding-place.

Noon brought a fresh alarm. A gunboat that lay about a mile distant sent off a boat that landed not far from them. At first they were relieved to see that the party was on pleasure bent.

This pleasure, however, took a different aspect when it came to setting fire to the grass about a hundred yards from their shelter.

Mr. Butt swore with great fluency as the first whiff of smoke came to them. But after various sniffings he decided that the wind was in a safe quarter for them.

It seemed as though the sailors would never be inspired to return to the gunboat.

They roamed about in little groups, several times coming so near that Warwick could plainly hear their words. At last they saw fit to embark and row away, and at last the friendly twilight ended the long day.

What a relief to come out from their cramped shelter, and stretch themselves, and turn their steps inland towards thick woods!

Here they tarried until night had fully come. Then the guide proceeded to find the route to Washington.

Another day and night were spent in much the same fashion, lying low by day, travelling by night, dodging behind trees at the first hint of a patrol's approach. At last, daylight of the third morning found them within half a mile of Washington. Then came one of the tight places of the expedition, the crossing a guarded bridge. There were numerous morning wayfarers to keep them in countenance.

All the same, the sentry stared hard at the weatherbeaten, big man, who under his tramplike guise had yet the unmistakable military bearing.

Fortunately for them, the sentry was fresh from Irish soil, and not yet inclined to meddle unduly in the affairs of the Republic.

He let them pass in silence, and footsore and hungry they went on their road.

The guide seemed to know his way as well in the city

as in the woods.

He led Warwick to a small inn in a dingy suburban street.

The landlord was rather superior to what might have been expected in such a place.

He asked no questions as to where they had come from or what they wanted, but apparently took it for granted that they sought rest and seclusion.

While Warwick was enjoying the delights of a long-deferred bath and shave, Mr. Butt and the landlord had evidently a confidential interview.

When Warwick next met the latter, he said in a non-committal fashion, "I understand that I am to furnish you with some New York addresses. You had better go first to this hotel. Then communicate with your banker, who can furnish you with any necessary papers.

"In case of his absence or illness, it would be as well to lose no time in seeking out one of the gentlemen on this list," he paused, and then added significantly:

"I regret that I have no later news for you of any friends."

Warwick looked him in the face, and saw at once that the man was other than the plain innkeeper that he seemed. He felt that he might be implicitly trusted.

"Is there no one in Washington who might be better informed?" he asked in the sickness of hope deferred.

"No one who could know more than I do," was the answer, with a slight smile.

The landlord never spoke more confidentially than this, and Warwick respected his reserve.

With Mr. Butt he had quite a cordial parting before

that worthy vanished into space, the richer for Warwick's English gold.

CHAPTER XXXVIII

"THE RED WOLF OF DESPAIR AT THE DOOR"

MR. OLIVER, the sturdy old Scotch banker, had spent more than thirty years of his life in New York without having in any degree assimilated himself to his surroundings. A bust of the Queen, with the British flag draped behind it, occupied a place of honour in his drawing-room.

His children were educated by English tutors and governesses until old enough to be sent "home" to school.

With all his insularity he was a successful business man, and occupied a respected position.

With the war, he had seemed to draw more into his family shell than ever. It is certain that he came in for some of the unpopularity of all things British. There were even occasional rumours of his Southern sympathies, but these were not generally credited, or, if credited, were ignored.

Heedless alike of good and evil report, he went on his stolid way and held his tongue.

It needed a case of genuine distress in one of his country people to reveal the warm heart that beat under the somewhat grim exterior.

His greeting to Warwick had been most cordial.

"It does one's heart good to meet a man fresh from the old country in this fractious land," he said heartily.

"Not quite fresh, eh? Stationed at Halifax and been to the South, and made your way up through the lines? Strange idea of a pleasure jaunt! Well, and now I suppose you want to see the sights of New York?"

"My errand is business, not pleasure."

"Then I am even more likely to be of use to you. I am at your service."

Warwick looked straight into the keen, grey eyes, under their heavy, white eyebrows.

"I have come to find a lady, Mrs. LeMoine, and I have been given to understand that you can help me."

Instantly Mr. Oliver's face hardened into impassivity.

"Mrs. LeMoine?" he repeated, as though the name were strange to him. "And what made you suppose that I would know Mrs. LeMoine?"

Although guessing the reason of this caution, Warwick felt strangely baffled by it.

"I was told in Richmond that you could help me," he said. "I know that she is in danger, and I have come to do what I can to help her."

"She is in danger, yes," the other gravely acknowledged. "In too great danger, perhaps, for me lightly to reveal her whereabouts. Excuse me, but you are asking confidence from me, and I think you should first give it."

Warwick saw the necessity of frankness, and rapidly gave a sketch of the events of the past summer.

He may have revealed more than he guessed, for by the time the tale was finished, the stony reserve in the banker's face had changed to a fine glow of approval.

"And, like a brave Englishman, you came to the rescue," he said, with a hearty hand on Warwick's shoulder.

Then his face fell, as he went on:

"And the rescuing will be no child's play, either! It cost me my last night's rest, pondering how I could get her away. She is in a boarding-house, a quiet, decent-enough place. But the police have got on her track, and the place is watched night and day to prevent her escape. I don't understand why they haven't arrested her before now. They know well enough who she is, and they want her badly, too.

"It was a wicked deed, sending her here at all. A reckless attempt at propping up a falling cause with money. That is what she was sent to me for."

Warwick agreed with every word, but he was at a stage when all words seemed superfluous.

"Can nothing be done to get her out of the house?" he demanded.

"I think I may manage that, but then how to get her out of the country? With an appearance so striking—"

"She could go safely enough as an English officer's wife," was Warwick's quiet interruption.

The other stared at him for a moment speechless before bursting out:

"God bless you for an honest-hearted gentleman! It can be done! It shall be done, I say! And I shall give away the bride, too."

For nearly an hour longer these two men debated and schemed, until they had evolved some plan that seemed practicable. Over one point they differed long.

Mr. Oliver wished Warwick not to meet Antoinette until he himself had persuaded her to act as they wished.

Warwick stuck out for one interview, and finally
gained his point, although Mr. Oliver declared that
any previous meeting between them added to the
risks of the scheme.

At last everything was decided, and they proceeded
to put their plans into action. Meantime, whilst they
schemed on her behalf, Antoinette was sitting alone
in her dingy bedroom in a gloomy boarding-house.

Her face was thinner and more worn, and showed in
its line the mental and physical strain through which
she had been passing.

It was two days since she had been out in the fresh
air, days in which she had sat there, momentarily
expecting her arrest.

The last time that she had gone out, she had been
tracked all the way, and she had decided not to venture again.

She felt a nervous horror of being arrested in the
street, with a gaping crowd gathering round, and she
preferred to await her fate indoors.

In these hours her isolation was pressing very heavily upon her.

Mr. Oliver, to whom her business had taken her, had
shown a very kindly interest in her. She had thought
of trying to let him know of her plight. But a remembrance of the peril that any intercepted
communication of hers might bring upon him had
checked her. She would bear her own burden.

"My lovers and my friends hast thou put away from
me and removed mine acquaintance out of my sight,"
she had murmured to herself with a fantastic smile.
She had already prepared for the end by destroying

all letters and paper, and by concentrating a few necessary belongings into a small hand-bag. There was nothing more to be done save wait.

Once she turned impetuously to her writing materials, and began a letter to Warwick. In these past two months the thought of him had grown nearer to her and the knowledge of his feeling for her had become the most steadfast part of herself.

Now, the courage failed her to pass out of his life and leave no sign.

He should know at least how fully she had learned to value the love that he had lavished upon her.

Sheet after sheet, she covered without a pause, but when once she hesitated, she wrote no more.

Glancing back over the pages she had covered, she sighed deeply, and then slowly tore them into little bits.

There were ten chances to one that they would never reach him. And even if they did, might it not be only to reopen a healing wound? Life had not taught her too great a faith in her fellow-beings.

No, let

> "Joy, and youth, and fame, and love and bliss,
> And all the good that ever passed her door"

go on their way, without any detaining supplication of voice or hand from her. She had given of the best that was in her for her country, let that be the only thing remembered of her.

As the fragments of paper fell in a white shower under her hand, a knock came at the door.

Was this, then, the end to her suspense, and were

the prison doors about to close on her? Instinctively she rose as the door opened. To her intense surprise only one figure stood there, and that was the black-cloaked, black-hooded form of a sister of charity. Antoinette gave a gasp that was almost a laugh. Then, feeling her strange visitor's silence to be intolerable, she began "I think you have made some mistake."

As the door closed, a soft little laugh broke out from under the black funnel bonnet. In the next moment this same bonnet was shoved back, revealing the rosy young face, and plentiful flaxen hair of Mr. Oliver's Scotch niece.

Maisie Oliver had made overtures of friendship to Mrs. LeMoine which the latter had skilfully eluded.

Her present work had no place in it for a young girl's friendship.

"Don't I make a fine sister of charity?" Maisie demanded gleefully. "But I mustn't waste time chattering. I am an emissary, Mrs. LeMoine!" Then with new gravity, "My uncle says that you are to do as you are told and act promptly now, if you would ever be a free woman again. You are not free now. The police are all around the house!"

"Yes, I know," was the quiet answer.

"Well, then, all the more reason you should be obedient. You are to put on this cloak and bonnet, and walk out of this house at once before they forget having seen me come in, or the twilight makes them pry closer.

"See, I have the black woollen gloves, and the bag that sisters always carry."

"But I cannot leave you here."

"You're not going to. I shall follow you in ten minutes or less."

"But they will arrest you!"

"Why should they arrest a white-haired, well-dressed
girl who comes out of a quiet boarding-house in
broad daylight, and who has her card-case and an invitation to dinner at the British Consul's in her pocket.
Pray, do I look like a disguised conspirator?" and
Maisie gave herself a triumphant twirl.

Under the covering of her big black cloak the girl's
dress had been of the most frivolously pronounced
fashion. Its colour was of a noticeably bright blue.
From under the cloak she had already produced and
pinned on an airy cockle-shell of a hat of the same colour. There was no possible scope for mystery in her
appearance. Her face was not even shadowed by a veil.

Antoinette recognised the careful shrewdness of her
details and a strange hope fluttered in her heart.

"You are to walk down the street to the church at the
corner," Maisie went on rapidly. "It's a Catholic
church, you know. Go in, and a woman, oldish,
dressed in black, my sister's maid, will join you near
the door. She will say 'May St. Anne lead you,' and you
will answer, 'She has led me to you.'

"You will go with her on foot to my sister's house.
She will take you at once to a room and dress you differently. Then you must wait for my uncle. I shouldn't
wonder if I were at the house as soon as you are.
There! you make a lovely sister."

While she talked, the girl had worked, and
Antoinette was already a slim, shrouded black figure.

What a friendly shelter that peaked bonnet seemed!

"But the risk to you all! I cannot—"

Antoinette began in a last bewildered protest, when Miss Oliver unceremoniously took her by the shoulders and shoved her to the door.

"You *must* be out of here before twilight!" she announced. "I'll follow you down. I'm going to find the landlady, and ask about a dressmaker whose name I invented five minutes ago, and I'm going to finish my talk on the steps, too! Off with you, now!"

Antoinette found herself going down the dark stairs and out into the street with somewhat shaky steps. It seemed like walking into inevitable destruction.

She could think of nothing but of how the French ladies had stepped forth from La Force into certain butchery.

The fresh sunshine and frosty air came to her as both mental and physical tonic, and she was ready to face the outside dangers.

Yes, there, across the street was the man at whom she had so often peered from her window. He was watching her now, but carelessly, she thought.

But her projecting bonnet hid him from view, and she must not turn her head. She might only listen for footsteps.

Up the long street she walked, not venturing to hurry. Twice she had the suspense of listening to following footsteps that overtook and passed her.

Both wayfarers, however, were of harmless aspect, and at last the church was reached.

Did ever the shelter of a church seem so welcome before? It was "sanctuary" indeed. From the steps she ventured to cast one backward glance down the street.

The man on watch was still lounging opposite the boardinghouse. Surely, she was safe! The friendly gloom of the church interior received her. Here, too, all went right. A plain, kind-looking woman came forward, and the formula was exchanged.

"Ye seem breathless. Sit down and rest for a moment. We can praise God even in the house of Rimmon," she said in a Scotch accent.

And so they tarried for awhile; and the peace of the place laid its soothing touch upon Antoinette's spirit.

"My soul doth magnify the Lord," came back to her from her early convent days.

Presently the woman touched her on the arm with a whispered inquiry if she felt ready for the walk.

As they left the church they saw the sky all golden with the sunset, and the joy of life rose again in Antoinette.

If only she might escape imprisonment and live and move in the light of the sun!

She walked easily and quickly beside her companion, who glanced at her stronger bearing with approval.

At last they came to a house that was evidently a comfortable home.

They passed swiftly in, and Antoinette found herself caught in the arms of a brilliant blue apparition.

"My own sister of charity! Captive of my bow and spear!" cried the shrill, girlish voice.

"Hush, Maisie! Get her in here before any of the servants see her dress!"

The last speaker was Mrs. Malcolm, whom Antoinette had already met.

Here was a bedroom where there was another disguise all ready for her to put on before any of the household should see her.

"I am famous at my stage get-ups," Mrs. Malcolm announced, cheerfully.

Antoinette looked with almost childish distaste at the dark wig and the heavy mourning dress laid out for her.

"Must I wear them?" she asked plaintively, and then laughed at her own folly.

"Fancy a just rescued creature like me objecting to anything!" she said gaily. Then, "How can I ever thank you both?" she went on with tremulous voice.

"Don't try," came quickly from Maisie. "Hurry with her get-up, Nan, and then bring her to have a comfortable meal, before they begin bothering her with interviews and with what comes next. She's had enough for the present."

CHAPTER XXXIX

WARWICK'S PLAN

ANTOINETTE lay resting on a sofa in a secluded little morning-room in Mrs. Malcolm's house.

With the removal of the pressure of immediate risk that strange, fatalistic calm that had weighed her down passed from her spirit. Her mind was now keenly alert in studying the dangers that lay around her, and in attempting to find some way to pierce them.

She knew that her present security, was only one of days, perhaps even of hours.

She knew as well as did Mr. Oliver that her disappearance would bring the full glare of public inspection upon him and his. She went over mentally all possible disguises, but they seemed but flimsy protections through the crucial test of leaving the city.

Her mission of raising money for the expiring Confederacy had been a failure. It had been foredoomed to failure, as Mr. Oliver had at first pointed out to her.

She had then nothing else to consider now but her own safety. That she now resolved to seek in a business-like fashion.

She would do her best to shake off this mood of listless fatalism that had crept over her. Hers was not a nature that ever yielded easily to despair.

The fire of logs crooned its low song of the woods.

The shaded lamp filled the room with cheerfulness. The morning seemed like an evil dream from which she had awakened. The door was softly opened, and she raised her head with the instant alertness of one who expects evil tidings.

The face of Maisie Oliver was, however, expanded in a broad smile of satisfaction.

"Uncle Oliver is downstairs settling all your affairs, like the dear old despot that he is," she announced. "Do you feel enough rested for visitors?"

Antoinette never noticed that the girl had not specified her uncle as the visitor.

"Dear child, I have had nothing to tire me."

The answer was cheerful, but it choked down a certain faintness of heart that the breathing space had been so short, that the time for action had come so soon.

She had risen and stood facing the door when the handle turned, and she saw Warwick standing in the doorway.

For a moment he contemplated her unfamiliar dress and dark hair with a perplexed aspect. Then the calm joy of attainment covered his face.

Was it a dream come in the midst of her loneliness, that those eyes rested upon with such tender scrutiny, that the voice deep with feeling said:

"At last! I have found you at last after such a weary search!"

" Did you come to look for *me?*"

A sob broke the words, and then she somehow found that his arms were around her, while her head sank to perfect rest on his breast.

Peace! Security! Had she ever known those words before.

Was there any earthly evil that could reach her through the barrier of those strong arms? For a short space there was a silence that spoke more than any words could have done. Then Warwick murmured low:

"And you really wanted me? Somehow I never dreamt of such good as that."

"Oh, I have wanted you every moment since I left you," the soft voice answered.

Then with a sudden start she tried to draw herself away from him.

"But, oh, how foolish and wicked I am to forget it all. You should never, *never* have come. I am a fugitive now. I had been run down by the police spies when these good kind people brought me here at great risk and put them off my tracks for a time. But I must not stay here to bring trouble upon them."

But Warwick's arm still held her, and there was no consternation in the face that looked down into hers.

"I know all about it," he said; "I planned the getting you here, with Mr. Oliver this morning."

"Oh, I might have known," she broke in; but he went on:

"And I fully realise that there is no time to be wasted here. Mr. Oliver says that they are sure to set a watch upon him as soon as your disappearance is known. I had hard work to get his permission to come here now. He thought it risky, but I could wait no longer for a sight of the dear face."

It was a pale, distressed one that tried to smile up at him.

"Ah, you must not stay long," she whispered, "you must not be mixed up in the—the last—"she drew sharp breath as she spoke the words.

He did not seem to heed them.

"No, I must not stay for I have work to do." Then seeming to concentrate his force into every word, he went on,—"You know the seeming impossibility of your getting safely out of New York. There is only one way in which it is feasible. Tell me, will you trust and obey me implicitly for the next few hours? It is the only chance."

"I *have* always trusted you—"

"And never obeyed me. Well, reverse matters now if you like. You needn't trust me, only obey me."

An involuntary laugh broke from Antoinette, but she persisted,—"I won't have you run any risks for me."

"What risks can come to a British subject?" he protested stoutly. Then more gravely,—"Obedience to our wishes is what you owe to those who are doing their best to save you."

The new sternness in his voice seemed to startle her.

"Does Mr. Oliver want me to do it?" she asked meekly.

"Yes, he does, if his wishes carry more weight than mine," Warwick answered huffily.

Lovers must have paused to squabble whilst Troy was burning.

"Ah, don't!" was her propitiating whisper, while one hand stole up towards his shoulder.

"Be good, and listen then. You are to get away from this house at once, at least in half an hour or so. There is a covered passage to their stable-yard. There

you will get into an open trap. They will give you a
boy's hat and coat, and young Oliver will drive you, so
that you will look like two boys. He will take you down
to the landing stage for the English mail boats—"

"But that is the place where there will be the
strictest watch—"

"Yes, I know. You could not possibly get on board an
outward bound steamer. But there is a Cunard boat
from England signalled coming in now. I shall go back
to my hotel and announce that I am going down to
meet my wife who is expected in her,—It's all right,
beloved, don't be startled—"

This tender soothing was in answer to a quick movement and murmur within his encircling arm.

"You are to be waiting for me, in an office on the
wharf, of which young Oliver has the key. There they
will have an ordinary travelling dress for you. And
there—if you will, my beloved, if you will—Mr. Oliver
brings a clergyman who shall marry us, before we
drive back to the hotel. You will be safe then, as an
English officer's wife, but to risk nothing, we shall
take the night train to Niagara, and soon be on British
soil."

There was a proud ring in these latter words that
stirred her heart, even as she started back in alarmed
protest.

"Ah, no, no!" she cried wildly. "Indeed, it cannot be!
God bless you for the noblest of men!" But I can never
commit such baseness as to let you save me at your
own sacrifice." Then with a new thought:—

"Oh, you mean that the marriage would be gone
through with as a blind, for, you remember what I told

you last summer—"

Her eyes fell before Warwick's smile. She was bewildered by this new attitude of possession on his part.

"I have forgotten all webs of deceit that you wove for me last summer! I only know that Edward Castelle died last April, and that you are free to marry me. That is all I need to know! Some day I shall tell you how I came to be so wise, and then I shall tell you what I think of the way you treated me. There is no time for it now!

"I am going to marry you to-night, and carry you off like Bluebeard. We shall have all the rest of our lives to quarrel in."

But Antoinette could only repeat wildly:

"Ah, no! It can never, *never* be! You *must* go away and leave me to my fate."

Then Warwick set his face as a flint, to the battle of their two wills.

"Do you know that it is not a mere matter of a certain time in imprisonment, but that there are threats against your life? I know this for a fact. They say that they have proof of your having shot a Northern officer."

The deep flush of shame at a recalled insult dyed Antoinette's face as she answered:

"It is true. I did shoot him. I—I was forced to, But he did not die. I only wounded him." Then, with a discordant laugh—"Doesn't even that show you how strange a wife I should make you! Believe me, it was because I felt the incongruity of it that I deceived you last summer. Indeed, I had no choice in the matter. Captain Arthur said that if I let you know I was free, he would take measures to make you give me up! You see by that what he thinks of me!"

The distress in her face wrung Warwick's heart.

"Damn Arthur and his opinions! I shall have it all out with him some day!" he said heartily. "But now, dearest, promise that you will do as I ask?"

"I must not," she sobbed, "indeed, I must not. I will not ruin your life."

"It seems to me that you are doing your best in that line at present," he commented grimly.

"Listen, then," he went on with the calm of despair. "If you drive me away from you to-night, I shall not leave New York. When you are arrested, as you must be, I shall know of it. Then I shall give myself up as a man who has just come through the lines with letters from Richmond. There are easily found proofs against me."

"No one would believe you."

"I shall make sure of that." Then, seeing her hesitate, he went on proudly: "If you object so much to marrying me, I will promise to leave you free as soon as we reach Canadian soil."

She looked up into the face hardened in pride and anger.

It was more than she could bear. Her two arms reached up to cling passionately to him, while she sobbed:

"You must know that you are all the world to me. Who else has ever cared for me and honoured me as you have done? It was you who awoke me again to life and love. And it is because of my love that I cannot do this thing."

Then a new note of security came into Warwick's voice.

"That acknowledged love gives me a right to save you. It gives me a right to your obedience. What a hound I should be if I could live on with you dead or imprisoned! Our lives are irretrievably bound together. It is too late now for any choice in the matter. You must yield to me."

The inevitableness of fate was in his words, and Antoinette was silent. Their lips met as in a sacramental seal. It was hard for Warwick in such a moment of attainment to loosen his arms and leave her in peril.

But there was much to be done in the next few hours that lay between them and safety.

CHAPTER XL

THE HOLY ESTATE OF MATRIMONY

HAVING once yielded, Antoinette cast aside all forebodings.

She would drink deep this wondrous unexpected joy that had come to her to-night, heedless that to-morrow might see the cup dashed from her hand.

If the next day she were to be a solitary prisoner, well, at any rate, she would have had to-day.

She was free, she was loved, and she would fight her best for her love and her freedom.

The two sisters could scarcely believe that this bright-eyed, flushed creature, who laughed so gaily, was the wan Sister of Charity who had come to their door a few hours previously.

The heavy mourning dress was flung aside, and a new English travelling suit of Maisie Oliver's substituted.

"I am so glad to get rid of that black dress, and of that horrible black hair," Antoinette announced.

Then, shaking down her own shining locks:

"But see! Will anyone please play barber, and clip it all away?"

"Good gracious! You are never going to cut your lovely hair off? Why should you?" screamed Maisie.

But Mrs. Malcolm was quicker.

"A good idea, though it *does* seem a pity! Can't you see, Maisie, how hard it would be to tuck up her hair under a boy's cap? It might loosen at a critical moment, and spoil everything. And it's rather the fashion just now to wear it clipped, they say. So, here goes, though I won't say much for my skill in barbering."

Antoinette shivered at the first ominous click of the scissors, and looked sadly at the fallen locks as she gathered them into her hand.

Then, with an attempt at a smile:

"A sacrifice to the fates," she said. "I suppose that I had better burn it?"

But Mrs. Malcolm stayed her hand.

"Give it to me. I shall save it, and send it to Major Warwick as a wedding present," and her words banished the momentary gloom.

"Poor you are never to see your own particular luggage again, I fancy," Mrs. Malcolm announced. "But we've put some things in one of our old sea trunks for you, and it will be on your carriage. It would never do for you to go to the hotel without any belongings. Everything in it is quite safe, if it should be searched."

"How good you are!" Antoinette murmured gratefully.

There was hearty laughter over the boyish outline of head and shoulders, as they clothed her in overcoat and cap.

But when they had crept silently out to the stable, there were warm womanly farewells before Antoinette climbed to the high, spidery vehicle.

As the soft, damp sea-wind smote her face, Antoinette rejoiced in the recovered sense of motion and activity.

"How I love the sea-fog! And how good it is to drive again!" she said, with youthful gaiety, and her friendly, boyish driver laughed with her. Through crowded streets, by the more open spaces of docks and wharves, they passed, until they drew up at a great black warehouse pile.

As a tall dark figure stepped out from the shadow of the doorway, they kept a wary silence.

But a low voice came—"It's Warwick."

Then Antoinette felt herself lifted down by arms as gentle as they were strong. Could any other arms in the world be like them? she wondered. Not another word was said, but she slipped her hand into his in the fashion of a child seeking familiar protection. "Be careful," he whispered. Only when they were well inside the building did he ask:

"Is all quite safe? You were not followed, nor alarmed?"

"No."

"That's right. They have a lot of their people about the steamer, taking stock of the arriving passengers. I forgot to count on that. But we'll soon be off again."

She laughed softly from the mere joy of his presence.

His arm encircled her, and for a moment he held her close. Then, securing the door behind them, he led her down the passages, and up stairs, and finally threw open the door of a lighted room.

She found herself in an ordinary, somewhat shabby, office, in the centre of which stood a little group of men.

There were Mr. Oliver and his son, with a somewhat grim-looking parson.

Mr. Oliver stepped forward, and took her hand in his hearty clasp.

"Mr. Dunn is an Englishman," he said, with an introductory wave of the hand, toward the clergyman, "and he will give Major Warwick his own prayer-book service. No Presbyterian could be trusted with such a job in a hurry. They're all too long-winded."

The parson stepped forward, and the two, brought together by such devious ways, stood before him.

As in a dream, Antoinette heard the words of the marriage service.

When Warwick's firm voice took up the words, "for better, for worse, in sickness and in health, to love and to cherish, till death do us part," she looked up steadily into his face. Had ever man given better proof of his right to use these words?

But ah, what if death, what if life were even now to part them!

Never before had she so cowered at the thought of a prison.

Warwick must have felt a shiver or a chill in the hand he held, for his eyes spoke courage to her, and her spirit answered his.

Her troth was spoken so sweetly and clearly that Mr. Oliver rubbed his hand over his eyes, and the lines of Warwick's mouth trembled.

To the spectators there was something very touching in this marriage under the shadow of deadly peril.

As the short ceremony ended, Warwick was the first to speak.

"You are safe now! You are an Englishwoman!" he said proudly.

He did not see the youthful Oliver shake his head dubiously. He had studied law and knew the slipperiness of the international marriage laws.

Antoinette, her hand on Warwick's arm, received the congratulations with a smiling face. In that moment, even in her quaint dress, she seemed rather the brilliant social queen, than the hunted-down political fugitive.

But the space for congratulations was short.

"You will find your bonnet and other things in here, Mrs. Warwick," the old banker said, opening the door into a side-room. "Take plenty of time with your get-up. It is of importance."

Antoinette was too practised a conspirator not to be well aware of this.

There was a looking-glass placed on the table, and she concentrated her thoughts on it. Not a precaution would she omit that tended safety.

Travelling hat, veil, gloves, all had been laid ready for her use.

With deliberate care she poised the smart little travelling-hat on her shorn locks and pinned a lace veil around it. She gave a strange smile of greeting to the face that looked back at her from the glass. "A bride!" she whispered to herself. Warwick's eyes were fixed expectantly on the door as she opened it. He did not even glance round as young Oliver came in.

The latter had been outside, and reported the coast apparently clear, and the carriage in waiting.

It was a hired cab, with luggage on the top, prepared for the arrival at the hotel.

They were off, together, alone in the darkness, and

Warwick drew his wife into his arms. Few words passed between them during that long drive. In silence they tasted the joy of each other's presence.

They were nearing their destination when Warwick came back to a consciousness of their surroundings.

"We'll need all our wits about us in a few minutes. We are sure to be closely inspected as we arrive at the hotel. Still, Mr. Oliver vouches for the people of the house. In any case we shall not be there long, for we take the midnight train for Niagara. You would rather get it through with at once, wouldn't you?"

"Oh, yes," she answered quickly.

"Would you mind it very *very* much if they were to take me away after all?"

"Don't, heart's dearest, don't!" he whispered hoarsely, while the hold of his arms tightened around her.

But she persisted: "But if they should, and you were never to see me again, you will always remember that it was for love's sake that I deceived you last summer, only for love's sake! Ah, if you knew how sorely I wanted to let you love me, but I felt that I had no right to, and"—her voice faltered—"and I had promised."

An ominous sound like the growl of a mastiff on guard came from Warwick.

"But, believe me"—the sweet low voice went on—"I *never* was what he thought me. Life was very hard on me when I was young, and I stood very solitary. I made mistakes, mad mistakes, but I never was bad. You do believe me, don't you?"

"Dearest, I would die for that belief! No human

power shall tear you from me now! Ah, take courage! In a few hours the danger will all lie behind, while ahead will stretch our happy life together."

"The promised land! I may be like Moses, and only see it from Mount Pisgah. But even then I shall have had my share, when I have had your belief."

"You shall have a lifetime of deepest devotion. Only, do not despond now, dearest."

Then she raised her face to his, while the wistfulness was gone from her voice.

"How could I despond *now?* Ah, you shall see presently that I can be brave."

And he *did* see, when with a tranquil face and assured manner, she leisurely followed him into the hotel.

Not a glance or movement showed that she was keenly conscious of the shabby little man who was furtively inspecting her trunk, or that she saw him lounge back to where another man of a slightly cleaner type was smoking and, after exchanging a few words with him, go out.

"I do not want any supper. I would rather rest for a bit," she said quietly when Warwick referred to her.

But she followed quite leisurely when he led the way, and did not even hasten to speak when the door had closed upon them.

She had not yet raised her veil, but as she seated herself, and began pulling off her gloves, she said:

"That was a police spy who was looking at my luggage. He spoke to another man and then went out of the house."

"Good God!" Warwick said, staring at her blankly,

his heart sinking with a sick dread. "Why did I ever
bring you here? I told Mr. Oliver that it was fearfully
rash, but he insisted that we must bluff them."

"He probably was right. That man being there may
have been only chance," she answered almost carelessly.

"Are you sure of his identity?"

"Yes. He had been pointed out to me—"

Then dropping her indifferent manner, she
laughed gaily.

"Who is it that is afraid now? Go down and get some
supper, and mention the fact that I am resting. I will
lock the door while you are gone."

"I will not leave you for a moment. They might carry
you off without my knowing."

She had risen and stood with her hand on his arm.

"Well, mightn't that be best? I wouldn't want to see
your eyes *then*, you know."

She had begun the words lightly, but as they ended
broke down and clung to him.

"My poor gay bridegroom! What a dower I bring
you!" she said with something between a sob and a
laugh.

"Antoinette! Don't!" he said with the sharpness of
intolerable pain.

"You know more of all this than I do! Try and think
what is best to be done, and I will do it."

The appeal in his voice again shook her composure;
but making a strong effort, she spoke calmly and
clearly, without, however, venturing to look up into
his eyes.

"I really believe that that man's presence here is

probably chance. They must hang about the hotels, you know. How could they possibly connect an English officer's wife arriving from England with the poor fugitive whom they had run to earth in a cheap boarding-house? They may not even know yet that I am safely away from there. But if you won't leave me— and perhaps I'd be as happy if you didn't—we can just stay here quietly. And you shall order some coffee and biscuits, or something of that kind, I shall keep my hat on, and when they bring it, I shall be stooping over my travelling bag in this dark corner. See?" and her smile had all its own charm.

They did as she had said.

Presently, with carefully secured door, they sat over their first little repast together.

It was as gay as a child's make-pretend tea-party. "Did you never see a woman pour out coffee before, that you stare so?" Antoinette protested. "You look like the ogre that ate up Red Riding Hood."

"That was a wolf," he corrected. "But I want you to take your hat off. I don't feel in secure possession of you while you look so ready to flit."

"It's safer with it on, if they should come to the door," she objected. Then seeing the pleading in his eyes, she yielded with a laugh and a blush. "You'll be dreadfully disappointed; in fact you may want a divorce," she began as she took off her hat.

But at sight of Warwick's horror-stricken face she asked gently, "Do you mind so much? It was for that drive in the boy's hat, you know."

But to her surprise a tender laugh broke from him.

"It makes you more adorable than ever," he

declared. "Only—what have you done with it all? It is my property, remember."

"Mrs. Malcolm is keeping it for you as a wedding present."

CHAPTER XLI

ON BRITISH SOIL

THAT bare little hotel room seemed like a friendly shelter when the time came to leave it and go forth again into the night and its perils.

It had been glorified by love even as the brightest home might have been.

Warwick could scarcely bring himself to leave his wife even to go down to pay his bill and order the carriage.

"I feel as though you might vanish if I were to let, you out of my sight," he said.

"I am not made of fairy gold," she jested back bravely. "But really, I think it is wiser for me to wait up here. And you know that the people of the house are friendly to us."

"Mr. Oliver says so," he said gloomily.

"Oh, of course they won't *say* anything. But go now."

He went. But it was with a pale, set face that Antoinette stood in the middle of the room and counted the minutes until his return.

Then came more of the scenes that passed like moving pictures across the hours of that eventful night.

The brightly lighted hotel corridors, free now from watchful loungers; the drive through the streets already quieting for the night; the stir and bustle of the large station;—they were all the setting to a possible peril.

Antoinette marked how lavishly Warwick was distributing money in his effort to shorten the ordeal.

He had just joined her where she stood beside the waiting train, when she felt a man brush against her in passing.

One glance told her that it was the face and figure that she had watched so despairingly from her window not twelve hours ago.

"Hast thou found me, oh, mine enemy?" was the cry that went up from the bitterness of her heart.

She never moved or looked round. She only stood with her head in its same steady poise, the heavily figured lace veil covering her face.

She saw the man just glance at Warwick and then turn away. But she saw, too, that he was in deep converse with an officer who stood by the steps at the other end of the car.

Was she to be followed and carried off just as safety seemed within her grasp?

"I think that we had better get in," she said in a low voice.

It was before the days of Pullmans, and the long, badly-lit car looked very uninviting on that winter night.

There were but few passengers, and these of the ordinary country type.

The very dulness and dreariness of the place seemed to have a certain sense of security.

With a quick glance Antoinette saw that the officer was standing over at the other door from where they had entered.

At this end there were several empty seats, and

touching Warwick on the arm, she pointed to the last one.

"Let us sit there," she said.

"You have a good eye for a strong position. You give the enemy no chance of a rear attack," he said, piling wraps into a corner to give her some comfort.

They were seated now, Warwick on the outside of the bench.

"I need a good eye. Tell me, are you a bit of an actor?"

He looked surprised, though some warning note in her tone made him repress it quickly.

"Not much of one," he acknowledged, "though my wooden type of countenance sometimes serves me as well. What's wanted now."

"Nothing much. Only don't look round or notice anyone while I speak. You see that officer by the door? Well, he was talking just now to the man who was on guard at my door all yesterday. And what is worse, I fear that this one is going in the train with us."

He was, and took a seat near where he had been standing, directly facing them.

"How can you ever bear it?" Warwick muttered.

"I can bear a good deal when I am beside you," she whispered back. "Only I wish that I might put up my veil."

"So do I. But you mustn't think of it. What a long strain it will be for you. Would it be easier if you sat with your back to him?"

She tried to suppress a little shudder.

"Ah, no. I would rather see the enemy. But shan't mind if you talk to me. Yes, hold my hand close in yours. It seems such a protection. Now, let us forget all about the danger, and talk about our two selves. Think, if they should come and take me away from you, how glad I should be to have it all to remember."

"*I will not* think of such a thing. They *cannot* take you away from me now. I shall kill someone before that happens."

Antoinette dared not make any outward sign of earnestness but her hand clung insistently to his.

"Indeed, *indeed*, that is what you must not do. That would only make my fate sure, and yours as well."

"For myself that is what I want."

"But if you were free you might always have power to help me. If the worst comes, always remember that. But I fear that in any case they would arrest you for the marriage."

"They would not dare to! The British Consul—"

"You hot-headed Englishman! Now be good, and talk to me as I ask. Tell me all about everything— yourself, I mean—ever since that night I left you."

"'Myself' was a very distraught being on that night. I thought the explosion had been on board the Nighthawk, and rushed off to the Point. I was standing there in the darkness when you went out to sea."

"And I was wanting so to come back to you," she whispered.

Breathlessly she listened while he told his tale of long waiting and search.

In that hour they forgot the watchful man on guard, the imminent peril, and thought only of each other.

"And in those dark days you could not but have thought that I had only made a tool of you?" she asked, with a timidness strange to her.

"Yes, that was the worst," he acknowledged, frankly. "But then that was only when every 'devil of the night' had power over me. At other times I could always catch glimpses of your real self—the truer, nobler self that is always there—through the tissue that the fates had woven. Then I thanked God, and took courage."

"They call love blind, but I think that real love always sees—like God, perhaps," came in the low voice that was as music to him.

"But I did mean to make use of you—at first, you know—before I knew—" she went on presently.

"Yes, I know. What does that matter now?"

When he went on to tell of his visit to Arthur in the hospital, she was very silent, and he left the subject, feeling that it pained her.

Then her own adventures by land and sea were to tell, and so the night hours wore on, while heart revealed itself to heart.

The morning sunlight was bright over the northern country, shining in its snow robe. The conductor had just passed through, telling them that the next stoppage would be Niagara.

"It's coming now," murmured Antoinette.

Warwick's jaw set like steel as they saw the officer gather himself together from his corner, and walk up the aisle of the car.

Antoinette leaned back with lazily half-closed eyelids, which she never even lifted as he paused beside their seat.

"Excuse me," he said in a civil enough voice. "But the conductor tells me that you are getting out at Niagara."

"Well, does the fact interest you?" Warwick asked, lounging back in his seat to look up at him. He had decided to enact the haughty British tourist.

"You will find that all facts interest me that have to do with the frontier traffic," came the sharp retort. "I am the officer in charge of the same in this train. Will you please inform me of your nationality."

There was something of the genuine soldier about the man, to which Warwick's heart warmed.

"I am an English artillery officer, now stationed in Halifax. I came to New York to meet my wife, who arrived from England yesterday, and we are returning through Canada, first visiting the Falls. I trust that is a satisfactory statement."

The official nodded with greater evidence of respect.

"Perfectly, if you have any papers to support it." Then seeing a movement of impatience on Warwick's part, he added almost apologetically, "We cannot take things on hearsay in war-times, you know."

Warwick had not thought it wise to show how thoroughly he was prepared for this emergency.

With a reluctant air he drew out his pocketbook.

"Here are my visiting cards with my London club on them, and here is a letter addressed to me at the Halifax barracks—a tailor's bill, you see. And here— yes, I thought I had it—is a passport from the British Consul in New York for Major Warwick and wife, British subjects. Is that sufficient?"

This latter document the officer was carefully perusing, ending with a long, keen glance of inspection of Antoinette.

"Yes," he said slowly, as he folded the paper. "I see

that it describes the lady, 'tall, slight, auburn hair.' Well, you see, we happen to be particularly on the lookout for a lady, 'tall, slight, auburn hair.' They were just about laying their hands on her in New York, when she gave them the slip last night and disappeared. It is supposed that she is making for the frontier. The Canadian Niagara is a regular hot-bed of rebels."

"Very interesting, I'm sure," yawned Warwick in his solemnest drawl. "But I scarcely see how it concerns us. What may the lady's name be?"

"She was calling herself Mrs. Drewitt, but her real name is Mrs. LeMoine, a notorious Rebel spy. A handsome woman, too, I believe."

"Then you have never seen her?" Warwick asked in a conversational tone, while the woman beside him wondered if her heavy heart beats could be heard.

She was wondering if there were room about that tightly fitting uniform for handcuffs to be stowed away, or had he them elsewhere?

"No," he answered slowly. "That's the trouble. If I had, I would ask your lady here to put up her veil and let me see her face," and he looked suggestively at Antoinette.

"I dare say that she will do that for you in any case," was the cheerful response.

Taking the hint, Antoinette raised her veil, and turned her face to the stranger with an amused smile. She was careful not to speak, for she knew how betraying is the languid southern accent to any ear trained to distinguish it. A quick flush on the man's face paid a passing tribute to her beauty.

"Thank you, madam, thank you," he said confusedly.

"You had better put it down. A draught might bring back your face-ache," Warwick warned her.

"Just then the train slackened speed and stopped with a clanking and jarring. "Niagara" came the call of salvation.

Was it really salvation or did the officer intend to detain them? For an instant that was the crucial question.

It was settled by his politely helping Antoinette down from the car, and turning away with a bow. The clear frosty air and noonday sunshine met her as bewilderingly as it might have done to some freed Bastille prisoner.

For a moment she clung to Warwick's arm helpless. Then came his whisper:

"*Try*, dearest, *try*. Just for a few more moments. He may be watching us still." Then they were safe in a carriage and driving towards the bridge. Around was a strange world of great fantastic forms of ice and snow, and glimpses down into whirling torrents of blue-green water, and shining clouds of mist. This bewildering new world was all of a piece with the bewildering new life dawning ahead.

They had passed the last ordeal of the customs guard, they were on the bridge, they were on British soil.

Their hands, clasped, while a deep "Thank God" broke from Warwick almost like a sob.

The old Clifton house was their destination, and there in the hall to Warwick's joy, he found a kindly, middle-aged English landlady.

Antoinette was by now drooping heavily upon his arm.

"My wife is tired out by travelling," he said, and the woman accepted his statement. She had during the last two years seen many a fugitive reach her door as the shipwrecked man gains dry land.

With speedy kindness she got her to a warm room, a comfortable sofa, and reviving bowl of soup.

The bright winter day was reddening to its close when they stood together at one of the windows looking out on the strange grand sight before them.

Could it be the vision of Nature in the might of her winter places that brought that wistful, exalted pallor into Antoinette's face?

Warwick had been watching her anxiously, awed by the evident intensity of her mood.

"What is it, dearest?" he said at last. "You have a remote spirit air about you. As though you might fade from my grasp even yet. Cannot you get free from the strain of the suspense?"

She smiled up at him in the same wistful fashion, though she grew even paler.

"Ah, yes. That troubles me no longer. It is already the past. But I am thinking of the future."

"The future! There can be nothing in that to trouble you."

He spoke sturdily, crushing down a growing misgiving.

"I don't know. When you have to leave me—"

"Leave you! I am not going to leave you!"

"But I cannot go to Halifax with you!"

"There is no need for us to go there at all. I can send

in my papers; in fact I fully intended to. I shall not let you tread American soil again in a hurry, so we can wait in Montreal until the spring navigation has opened, and then go to England. How would you like to come on a big game expedition into the Rockies? The world is all before us. But if you would rather be quiet we will settle down in Montreal. The general in command there is a cousin of mine, so that we should get plenty of amusement."

But she shook her head sadly.

"Your cousin! There you see, it is all the same thing over again. He will soon hear all sorts of stories about me, and he will be just like Captain Arthur! I shall bring you nothing but annoyances! And then you know, there is my promise to Captain Arthur that I would never take your name! No, listen—" as she saw him about to break in angrily.

"I know that I was wrong and weak to let you have your way about the marriage! I only did it because I knew that if harm came to me it would break your heart!

"But now you must go back to your work until you can end it in the proper way. And you must write and tell Captain Arthur how it all happened. Then perhaps he will give up his opposition, and not do you any harm with your people on my account." Here she paused, and Warwick spoke impetuously:

"I could be very wroth with you if it were not all so absurd! *Arthur's* disapproval! *Arthur's* opposition! What do they matter to me? Don't you know that he has never had anything to do with our family for years, has never even used the name since he left the navy?

That he is the son of the family black sheep?" But with a sob she persisted:

"But my promise! I must keep my pledged word to him!"

Warwick's face hardened, as he said:

"It strikes me that you made some rather more serious promises to me, last night."

"Oh, I will keep them, indeed I will!" she pleaded. "Let me only wait quietly until we can begin our new life far away from here in England. In Montreal there would be the Southerners who knew me, and your army friends, and it would all be the same thing over again. Let me wait quietly alone until you have left the army, and have perhaps seen Captain Arthur—"

"I will ask no man's leave to acknowledge my wife. I, too, can present an ultimatum. Either you promise now that as soon as you are rested you will come with me to Montreal and be introduced as my wife to my cousin and his friends, or we part definitely to-day. If I go, it will be in the belief that I have been twice duped, and made a tool of."

Each word fell heavy with its weight of sternness, and he had already drawn a few paces away from her.

"Oh, don't, don't!" Antoinette cried, raising her hands almost as though to ward off a blow.

Her eyes searched his face appealingly, but there was no trace of irresolution.

"Oh, I should kill myself if you were to leave me like that now," she wailed.

"That is the only way in which I shall leave you," was the quiet, determined answer.

"Then I suppose you will have to stay," and for the first time Warwick saw on her face the revelation of what she could be to the man she loved.

THE END